Susanna Gregory, a Cam[...] [...]thor of the acclaimed Matthew Bartholomew series of mediaeval mysteries as well as the Thomas Chaloner mysteries.

Visit the author's website at www.susannagregory.co.uk

Also by Susanna Gregory

The Matthew Bartholomew Series

A PLAGUE ON BOTH YOUR HOUSES
AN UNHOLY ALLIANCE
A BONE OF CONTENTION
A DEADLY BREW
A WICKED DEED
A MASTERLY MURDER
AN ORDER FOR DEATH
A SUMMER OF DISCONTENT
THE HAND OF JUSTICE
THE MARK OF A MURDERER
THE TARNISHED CHALICE

The Thomas Chaloner Series

CONSPIRACY OF VIOLENCE
BLOOD ON THE STRAND

A KILLER
IN WINTER

Susanna Gregory

sphere

SPHERE

First published in Great Britain in 2003 by Little, Brown

This edition published by Time Warner Paperbacks in 2004
Reprinted 2004
Reprinted by Time Warner Books in 2005
Reprinted by Sphere in 2006

A CIP catalogue record for this book
is available from the British Library.

ISBN-13: 978-0-7515-3341-5
ISBN-10: 0-7515-3341-6

Typeset in New Baskerville by
Palimpsest Book Production Limited,
Polmont, Stirlingshire
Printed and bound in Great Britain by
Clays Ltd, St Ives plc

Sphere
An imprint of
Little, Brown Book Group
Brettenham House
Lancaster Place
London WC2E 7EN

A Member of the Hachette Livre Group of Companies

www.littlebrown.co.uk

To Charles Moseley

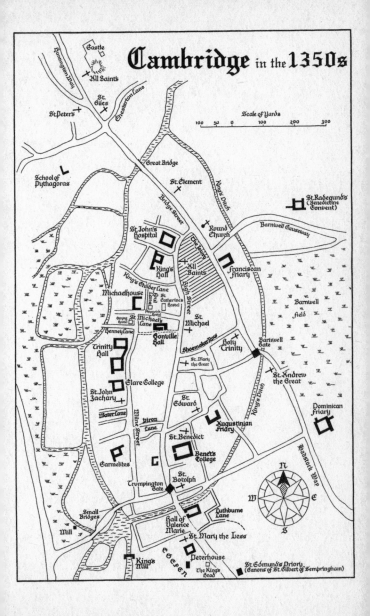

Cambridge in the **1350s**

Castle
All Saints
St. Giles
St. Peters
Huntingdon Way
Chesterton Lane

Scale of Yards
100 50 0   100   200   300

Great Bridge
School of Pythagoras
St. Clement
King's Ditch
St. Radegund's (Benedictine Convent)

Bridge Street
St. John's Hospital
Round Church
All Saints
Barnwell Causeway

King's Hall
Chapel Lane
High Street
Franciscan Friary

Michaelhouse
Cholar Lane
St. Catherine's Hostel
Barnwell Field
Barnwell

St. Michael
Gonville Hall
St. Michael's Lane
Physwick Hostel
St. Mary's Hostel
Henney Lane

Trinity Hall
Shoemaker Row
Holy Trinity
Barnwell Gate
St. Mary the Great

Clare College
King's Ditch
St. Andrew the Great

St. John Zachary
Water Lane
Milne Street
St. Edward
Dominican Friary

Augustinian Friary
Newnham Lane
St. Benedict

Carmelites
Benet's College
St. Botolph
Hadstock Way

Trumpington Gate
N
E
W
S

Small Bridges
Mill
Hall of Valence Marie
Luthburne Lane
St. Mary the Less

King's Mill
Peterhouse
The King's Head
St. Edmund's Priory (Canons of St. Gilbert of Sempringham)

PROLOGUE

Feast of Saint Josse (13 December), 1354, near Cambridge

THE WINTER THAT GRIPPED ENGLAND WAS THE WORST anyone could remember. It came early, brought by bitter north winds that were laden with snow and sleet. The River Cam and the King's Ditch – usually meandering, fetid cesspools that oozed around the little Fen-edge town like a vast misshapen halo – froze at the end of November, and children made ice skates from sheep bones. Both ditch and river thawed soon after, but not before claiming two lives: a pair of boys rashly ignored the ominous cracks and increasing slushiness, and plunged through the treacherous surface to their deaths.

At the beginning of December came the first heavy snows, smothering the countryside with an ivory blanket and transforming the brown desolation into a landscape of dazzling, pillowy white. As the snow continued unabated, buildings and trees disappeared beneath drifts. Because winter had come so early, people were unprepared. They had not cut enough firewood, stored enough vegetables, salted enough meat or ground enough grain. Ice choked the mills, and prevented them from satisfying the demand for flour. The price of food – already high after the plague that had ravaged the country five years before – began to spiral upwards again.

More than one family perished when the soft powder crusted over and sealed roofs or blocked chimneys, so that smoke from their fires suffocated them while they slept. Beggars, stray dogs and even folk tucked up in their beds froze to death during the night, and were found dusted silver by frost's brittle fingers. Others fell victim to shivering

1

agues, or hacking coughs that seared the lungs. Others still broke bones on the icy streets or were crushed by skidding carts or horses. Some refused to allow the weather to interfere with long-laid plans, and set out on journeys from which they never returned: they failed to take into account that icy blizzards could suck warmth and vigour from weary bodies, and make them long for rest among the downy-soft drifts at the sides of the roads – rest that turned into sleep of a more permanent nature.

Josse knew he was taking a risk by travelling from London to Cambridge when the weather was so foul, but he was young, strong and confident. He was a messenger by trade, a man who made his living by carrying written and spoken communications from one person to another. The early winter had been a boon for him, since his services had been in demand by people wanting to inform others about changes of plan brought about by the storms. Usually, Josse confined his business to London, where he lived, but he had been paid handsomely to deliver the letter from the Thames merchant to the Cambridge friar, and half a noble was not a sum to be lightly declined.

The journey of sixty miles would usually have taken a good walker like Josse two or three days. But the snows had slowed him down, and by the sixth day of travelling he had only reached the village of Trumpington, still two miles from Cambridge. He was frustrated by the time he had lost: buxom Bess at the Griffin Inn back at home had agreed to wait for him, but he knew it would not be long before she grew lonely and allowed another man to warm her bed. Bess would inherit the Griffin when its current owner died, so it was more than mere lust or affection that was driving Josse to complete his mission and return with all haste.

As he ploughed through the drifts, his feet felt like lumps of ice, and his legs ached from lifting them high enough to step forward. The lights of Trumpington's tavern gleamed enticingly through the sullen December day, golden rays of warmth in a world that was cold and white. He decided to rest, reasoning that an hour with a goblet of hot spiced ale in his hands would give him the strength needed to finish the journey before dusk. It was just after noon and, although the days were short, he still had about three hours of good daylight left – more than enough to allow him a brief respite from his journey. He pushed open the creaking door of the Laughing Pig, and entered.

Because ploughing and tilling were impossible as long as snow covered the ground, the tavern was filled with men. They were pleased to see a new face, and the taverner provided Josse with free ale in return for news from London. Josse was good at telling stories, and more time had passed than he had intended by the time he rose and said his farewells. The landlord tried to stop him, claiming that more snow was expected and that the road had been all but impassable earlier that day, but, with the arrogance of youth, Josse shook off the man's warnings, donned his cloak and set off down the Cambridge road. The landlord watched him go, then poured himself a cup of mulled ale, grateful that *he* was not obliged to undertake such an unpleasant journey.

Josse had second thoughts himself almost as soon as the landlord closed the door, shutting off the comfortable orange glow from the tavern and leaving him in the twilight world of black and white. However, he told himself that almost two weeks would have passed by the time he returned to London, and that Bess had a short memory. He hefted his pack over his shoulder and began to plough clumsily through the drifts.

The landlord had not been exaggerating when he said the stretch of road between Trumpington and Cambridge would be the worst part of the whole journey; it was not long before the effort of walking had the messenger drenched in sweat. Josse stopped for a moment to catch his breath, but the wind whipped around him, freezing the clammy wetness that trickled down his back. He started moving again, slowly and wearily. The day began to fade, dusk coming early because of the heavy-bellied clouds that slumped darkly overhead.

Fearfully, Josse began to wonder if he would ever reach Cambridge, and acknowledged that he should have listened to the landlord after all. His leg muscles were burning and his back aching, so he turned his mind to what celebrations might be held that evening to observe the feast of St Josse. He gave a thin smile and muttered a prayer. The saint for whom he was named would watch over him.

Soon, the darkness was complete. Clouds blotted out any light that might have come from the moon, and it began to snow, great stinging flakes that hurt his eyes and pricked his face like sharp needles. He sank to his knees, and felt the first hot tears of panic roll down his cheeks.

Then he saw a light. Eagerly, he staggered towards it, hope surging within him. St Josse was watching over him after all! The light came from a lamp swinging outside a priory chapel: the friars had evidently anticipated that there might be travellers on the road, and the torch was a beacon to guide them to warmth and safety. His chest heaving with the effort, Josse reached the priory, then plunged on to where other lights gleamed in the winter darkness.

He passed a noisy tavern with a crude drawing of a man wearing a crown swinging over the door. The King's Head, Josse surmised. Its occupants were singing lustily, yelling one of the bawdy songs that were always popular around Christmas time. Near the inn was a sombre building with a red tiled roof, which Josse supposed was one of the Colleges. Scholars were a rebellious, unruly crowd, and Josse was heartily glad there was no university developing in the area of London where *he* planned to live. A board pinned next to the sturdy gate told him that the College was called Peterhouse.

Next to Peterhouse was a church. A sharp new statue of the Virgin Mary stood on a plinth atop what was clearly a recently finished chancel, her blank stone eyes gazing across the road and her hand raised in benediction. An older, chipped statue stood forlornly down in the churchyard, and Josse recognised the characteristic square face and curly

4

beard of St Peter. Here was something that had happened frequently since the plague: an old church – in this case St Peter's – rededicated to St Mary, because many believed she was more likely to intercede on their behalf should the pestilence ever come again.

But it was no time for thinking about the Death and the changes it had brought, because Josse had at last reached the town gate. He started to make plans, his terror at almost being swallowed by the storm already receding. First, he would deliver his letter to the friar, then he would find a cosy inn, hire a pallet of straw near the fire and sleep until dawn the following day. And then he would set off towards home – to London, Bess and her tavern.

He hammered on the gate, hoping that the guards had not gone home early, secure in the knowledge that no sane person would want access to the town on an evening when a blizzard raged. He was in luck. The sergeant on duty was Orwelle, a reliable man who slept little because his dreams still teemed with memories of the Death – especially of the dear son he had lost. While his companions dozed, Orwelle usually stayed awake, idly rolling dice in games of chance against himself. He had finally managed to banish the chill from his feet, and was not pleased when a knocking meant that he was obliged to go outside.

Because it was bitterly cold, and Orwelle did not want to spend longer than was necessary away from the fire, his questioning of the messenger was brief. He asked to see the money that Josse carried and, satisfied that he could pay for his needs and would not beg, Orwelle opened the gate and allowed him inside.

Josse made his way up the High Street, drawing level with another of the town's Colleges, this one identified by a long and complex name that was carved into the lintel over the door. The title involved guilds and saints, and Josse could not make sense of the snow-filled letters. Someone, however, had taken a piece of chalk and had written a simple 'Bene't College' next to it. Josse rested there for a few moments, catching his breath and offering another prayer of gratitude to St Josse for a safe deliverance while he fingered the letter he was going to deliver.

As he stood, feeling his heartbeat slow and his breathing become more regular, he saw he was not the only man braving the elements that night. A scholar wearing a black tabard was struggling through the drifts towards him. The fellow glanced at Josse as he joined the messenger in the dim pool of light filtering through the College's glass windows. With a start, recognition passed between them, but before they could speak a peculiar hissing sound distracted them both.

At first, Josse did not know what had made the noise, but, suddenly, something of colossal heaviness landed on top of him, blotting out all light and wrapping him in an icy, wet coldness. He was too startled to do anything, but then he tried to move and found he could not. With a sharp stab of horror, he realised exactly what had happened: the snow from the roof of Bene't had fallen, probably loosened by the fire the scholars were burning in their hall. It had sloughed off like sand, and Josse had been standing in the wrong place at the wrong time.

He was held fast. He could wriggle one finger, but he could not move his arms or legs. He opened his mouth to shout to the fellow in the tabard to dig him out, but snow immediately poured into it, and he found he could not breathe, either. He became frantic, trying to draw air into his lungs. But he was helpless. His mind screamed in terror, even as a peculiar lethargy crept over him. His last thoughts were of bitter regret. He had almost delivered his message, and he could have spent Christmas with Bess, in London.

20 December 1354, Cambridge

Josse was not the only man to die as the small market town prepared to make the best of the miserable weather and celebrate Christmas. The icy winds had abated somewhat since he had reached Cambridge, and there had been no blizzards for several days. It was still cold, however, and the snow that had already fallen stood in large, odorous heaps, speckled brown, yellow and green with sewage, dirt and any other rubbish that could be caught in the wheels of carts or the hoofs of horses and flung up. Many of the drifts, including Josse's, had solidified into mounds of hard, unyielding ice, and the man who had recognised him was comfortable in the knowledge that it would be some time before the messenger was released from his icy tomb.

The parts of the river and the King's Ditch that had fast currents had broken free of the ice, and were once again ferrying their sinister olive-black contents around the town's edges. Offal, dead animals and discarded clothing bobbed past, turning this way and that, while shelves of ice jutted tantalisingly across the more sluggish sections, inviting the foolish or unwary to skate on them. The rutted surfaces of the town's roads froze nightly, creating a series of ankle-wrenching furrows that were then mashed into an icy sludge by the feet and wheels that ploughed along them during the daylight hours – a dismal cycle of freeze and thaw of which Cambridge's citizens had grown heartily weary.

Christmas was not the most important festival of the year, but it was one people enjoyed nonetheless. The celebrations began on Christmas Day and lasted twelve nights. Churches were decked with greenery – although some priests balked at pagan traditions being allowed in houses of God – and special foods were cooked by those who could afford them. However, Norbert Tulyet could not help but notice that the icy weather had made the town strangely subdued that year, and that the atmosphere of pleasurable anticipation was uncharacteristically lack-lustre.

Norbert had spent an agreeable evening in the company of a woman who had flattered him and made him feel important. Being told he was intelligent, handsome and worthy was not something that happened very often, and while he considered the woman right in every respect, it also engendered feelings of resentment that more people did not share her opinions. He felt particularly angry with his uncle, who claimed that Norbert was a disappointment to him, and constantly asked why he was not more like his own son, Richard. Richard Tulyet had been Sheriff for some years, but had recently been obliged to relinquish the post in order to help with the family business. Richard had not complained overtly, but he had made it clear that he would not have had to resign if his dissolute cousin had done what was expected of him.

Determined that Norbert should possess the means to support himself before he was turned loose on the world, his uncle had taken him to Ovyng Hostel, so that he might learn the skills necessary to become a clerk or a lawyer: the number of contested wills since the plague meant that there was no shortage of work for such men. But Norbert had not enjoyed his letters when he was a boy, and he did not like studying grammar, rhetoric and logic now that he was a man. He soon discovered that Ovyng was not a suitable place for a pleasure-loving fellow like himself.

Ovyng was a hostel for Franciscans who, not surprisingly, deplored Norbert and his excesses. In return, Norbert loathed everything about the Grey Friars – from their shabby habits and leaking boots, to their tedious lessons and preaching about morality. Fortunately for Norbert, Ovyng's principal was very grateful for the fees the Tulyets paid for their kinsman's education, and intended to keep their reluctant pupil for as long as possible. This meant that most of Norbert's bad behaviour went unreported, and the young man was free to do much as he wanted. His uncle continued to pay for the privilege of a University education, the friars made valiant but futile attempts to teach Norbert the law, and cousin Richard watched it all with thinly veiled contempt.

Earlier that evening, Norbert had informed Principal Ailred that he planned to celebrate the Feast of St Thomas with his uncle. Ailred had chosen to believe him, because he was not in the mood for an argument he knew he would not win anyway: Norbert would leave the hostel whether he had permission or not, but Ailred was sure it would not be to visit his family. Ailred was right: Norbert had other business in mind.

First, Norbert had been obliged to meet men who had lent him money. Their demands for repayment had become more aggressive over the last few days, and this was a problem, because Norbert had already spent the three pounds, eight shillings and fourpence they had lent him, and had none left to give back. Begging another day's grace, Norbert had escaped to the King's Head, where he had enjoyed a good meal – still to be paid for – and won a salted fish from another patron in a game of dice. The fish was tucked under his arm in a piece of sacking, and he planned to sell it to his ever-hungry Franciscan classmates. The evening had improved thereafter, and he had passed the next few hours with a woman whose company he enjoyed more each time they met.

By the time he left the tavern, he was drunk and it was late. Unfortunately for him, the clouds had thinned during the evening, leaving a full moon to illuminate Cambridge's dismal streets like a great white lantern. The snow reflected the moonlight, making it brighter than ever, and even the drunken Norbert knew it was not a good night for dodging proctors and beadles – the men who prowled the streets looking for scholars breaking the University's rules. Hoping to avoid such an encounter, he took the towpath along the river, weaving his way along it unsteadily. As he walked, icy water seeped through his shoes in a way that was far from pleasant, and his thoughts turned maudlin.

Much of his pique was directed against his cousin. It was Richard who had recommended the cut in Norbert's allowance, which had obliged him to borrow to pay for his pleasures. So, it was Richard's fault that he was now under pressure from the lenders to give it back. The latest demand had been intimidating, and he wondered whether he should break into his uncle's house in order to steal what he needed to pay them off. Since the town was full of travelling entertainers, all hoping to make money during the Christmas season, one of them would probably be blamed. Norbert's wine-soaked mind told him that burglary was a good idea, and he was about to wend his way to the Tulyet home on Bridge Street, when he spotted someone walking towards him.

He staggered quickly to one of the wall buttresses behind Trinity Hall and waited with a thudding heart. His first thought was that the figure was a beadle, who knew perfectly well that the back of Trinity Hall provided plentiful hiding places for undergraduates. Norbert did not want to be fined for drunkenness or to spend the rest of the night in a miserable cell with others who had enjoyed too much wine. But the man who hastened quickly through the snow was only Doctor Bartholomew from Michaelhouse, who was far too engrossed in thoughts of his patients to notice furtive shadows lurking at the backs of colleges.

The physician entered one of the hovels that lined that part of the river like a row of broken teeth. A candle burned dimly within, and, with wine-fuelled curiosity, Norbert tottered forward to peer through a gap in the woven willow-twig walls, all thoughts of stealing from his uncle temporarily forgotten. Inside, he saw Bartholomew kneeling on the ground to tend an old man whose painful, hacking cough fractured the silence of the night. The patient was Dunstan, and his equally ancient brother Athelbald hovered anxiously over them like a skeletal angel. Simultaneously fascinated and repelled by the treatment the physician was giving the sick man, Norbert edged around to the rear of the hut, where the twigs were more rotten and afforded a better view of the scene within.

He had not been watching for long when he became aware that he and Bartholomew were not the only men out at a time when most law-abiding folk were tucked up in their beds. Low voices drifted to him on the still night air, and Norbert stiffened, holding his breath and hoping the speakers would pass by without seeing him.

'I am growing weary of your demands,' one man hissed furiously, as he and a dark-cloaked companion drew level with the hut. 'You push me too far.'

Norbert heard Dark Cloak sneer his contempt. 'I have only just started.'

'You will be sorry for this,' warned the first man venomously, his beard wagging in the moonlight. 'I am not a man who easily forgives, and I have a long memory.'

'So do I,' claimed Dark Cloak in a furious whisper. 'You have done me a great wrong, and I do not let such matters pass unremarked. You *will* pay.'

Their voices faded as they moved along the towpath towards Small Bridges. Norbert rubbed his chin, trying to make sense of their conversation. He left his hiding place and set off after them; he was fortunate that all their attention was on their quarrel, or they would have heard his clumsy pursuit far sooner. They walked stiffly, as though being in such close proximity to each other was anathema, and Norbert was fairly sure the bearded one held a knife. He tried to walk closer, to hear more of their discussion. The disagreement reached a climax when the towpath met the Mill Pool, and the two men stopped dead in their tracks, facing each other like enraged fighting cocks.

'You committed a foul crime!' Dark Cloak was shouting, all attempt to keep his voice low forgotten. Norbert supposed it did not matter, since there were no houses nearby and no one was likely to overhear him anyway. 'You should think about that before you make those kind of threats.'

'I do not care what you—' Both men turned abruptly when Norbert trod on a rotten piece of wood and its sudden crack gave away his presence.

Norbert was not afraid. His drunken mind had been mulling over what he had heard, and it occurred to him that their argument could be turned to his advantage. What he had in mind was a tempting and easy alternative to burgling his uncle's house.

'Crimes,' he slurred with a dissolute leer, waving his fish at them. 'And blackmail. I heard you both, gentlemen. Crimes and blackmail are illegal, and unless you want me to repeat this conversation to the King's justices, you will make it worth my while to keep silent.'

The two men gazed at him in astonishment, before glancing at each other, then returning their mystified stares to the dishevelled, red-eyed spectre that swayed before them. Norbert became aware that the hostility that they had aimed at each other was now focused wholly on him. Suddenly he felt uneasy.

'It strikes me that *you* are attempting to blackmail *us*,' said the bearded man eventually, not bothering to hide his contempt at the ludicrous nature of Norbert's demand. 'You will also be fined or imprisoned if you take this tale to the Sheriff.'

This had not occurred to Norbert. He stood still for a moment, his mouth working like that of a landed fish as his alcohol-soaked mind thrashed about for an answer. But the bearded man was taking no chances. The knife was in his hand when he stepped forward. With horror, but far too late, Norbert realised that he had made a serious mistake in attempting to extort money from this pair. Gripping his fish like a talisman, he turned to flee, but he had taken no more than two or three steps before he felt something thump hard into his back. A searing pain drove all else from his mind. He felt his legs give way, and he slumped to the ground.

Dark Cloak eyed his companion uneasily. 'That was unnecessary.'

'What would you have me do? Pay him, as well as you? One of your kind is more than enough for me, thank you very much.'

Dark Cloak took a step away, not liking the expression

12

on his companion's face, and was glad he had thought to mention earlier that others knew his whereabouts and his business, or he suspected he might well have suffered the same fate as the unfortunate drunk. The bearded man made an annoyed sound when he saw that Norbert's blood had splattered up his sleeve. His weapon was stained, too, and he hurled it with all his might into the river, before scooping up a ball of snow to clean his hand.

Tossing away the knife had been premature, however. While Dark Cloak argued with the killer, Norbert struggled to his feet, trying to ignore the agonising ache in his back that made it difficult to breathe, and started to run. But his legs were heavy and unresponsive, as though he were moving through a vat of treacle. Terror drove him to put one foot in front of the other, forcing him along the towpath. He was aware that his attacker was coming up behind him, but pushed the knowledge from his mind, obeying some deep-rooted instinct that urged him to reach Ovyng Hostel. He passed the huts where he had watched Bartholomew tend the sick man just moments before, and felt the fish slip from his numb fingers. He glanced at it with regret as he staggered on, sorry to abandon it when it would have fetched a few pennies. But he no longer had the strength to carry it. He turned up Henney Lane, his breath coming in painful, laboured gasps, irrationally reasoning that his attacker would leave him alone now that he was no longer on the towpath.

He was wrong. The bearded man was behind him, watching dispassionately as Norbert's movements became increasingly erratic. Since he no longer had a dagger, he picked up a heavy stone. He hoped he would not have to use it: braining someone would be a messy business, and he did not want any more damage to his fine clothes.

Meanwhile, Dark Cloak had been startled by the speed and brutality with which his companion had reacted to Norbert. He was relieved that Norbert would not live to relate the incident to the Sheriff, but a murder was bound to spark off an investigation, and he had enough to worry about without being obliged to dodge one of those. He began to follow them. He watched his companion turn into Henney Lane after his victim, and supposed he should not have been surprised that the man had met the drunken challenge with instant and unhesitating violence. After all, he had done so before.

As Norbert's panicky gasps disrupted the silence of the night, the door to Athelbald's hut opened and the old fellow stepped out, pulling the physician with him. Cursing under his breath, Dark Cloak ducked quickly under cover and stood still and silent, while Bartholomew peered down the path in both directions, urged on by Athelbald, whose eyesight was poor.

'I heard breathing,' Athelbald insisted, shaking the physician's arm, as if that would give more credence to his claim. '*Heavy* breathing.'

'Well, there is no one here now,' Bartholomew replied, looking down the moon-shadowed path, from which Norbert and his assailant had already turned.

'What is that?' demanded Athelbald, poking at the sack-covered fish with his foot. The wrapping parted and the faint gleam of scales could be seen within.

'A fish,' said Bartholomew, sounding amused as he bent to inspect it. 'Tench, by the look of it. Salted.'

'For us?' asked Athelbald eagerly. 'Someone has left us a gift of salted fish?'

Bartholomew bent to inspect it. 'Not unless you like it rotten. It must have been thrown away, and a cat dragged it here. But there is nothing to see out here. Come back inside.'

The night was bitterly cold, and the old man willingly obliged, although Bartholomew continued to gaze around uncertainly, as if he sensed something was wrong. Dark Cloak held his breath, willing the physician to go back to his patient and mind his own business.

Eventually, Bartholomew turned to re-enter the hovel.

Plenty of rats inhabited the river bank; perhaps one of them had made the noises that had disturbed the old man. Suddenly, a high-pitched shriek cut through the air, and the physician took a step back outside. To Dark Cloak, the sound had been unmistakably human, but he hoped with all his heart that Bartholomew would assume it was just an owl hunting among the rubbish.

The physician listened hard, looking around him carefully. Then he gazed directly at Dark Cloak. Dark Cloak had no idea whether Bartholomew could see him, but decided he had better act while he still had the element of surprise. With a screech of his own, he exploded from the shadows and pushed Bartholomew with all his might, sending the physician crashing backward. With an easy, sinuous movement, he grabbed the fish before darting along the towpath in the opposite direction to the one Norbert had taken. He zigzagged through the cemetery surrounding the church of St John Zachary and made his escape, confident that Bartholomew would never recognise him, moonlight or not.

Bartholomew fell into the hut with such force that, for a moment, he was afraid the whole thing would come tumbling down, leaving the two old men homeless. Dunstan coughed in protest, while his brother made his way unsteadily through the door to see what was going on.

'Slipped on the ice, did you?' he asked with a cackle of amusement when he saw the physician sprawled on his back. 'I told you to watch your footing.'

'Someone pushed me,' said Bartholomew indignantly, scrambling to his feet. He knew there was no point in giving chase: his assailant could be hiding anywhere by now. It was cold and dark anyway, and the physician had no desire to be out longer than was absolutely necessary.

'He must have wanted his fish,' said Athelbald, a little resentfully when he saw the package had gone. 'You told me it was no good for eating.'

'It was not,' said Bartholomew. 'At least, I would not have eaten it.'

'Not everyone can afford fastidious tastes like yours,' grumbled Athelbald. 'It would probably have been all right with a few fish guts begged from the eel catchers and a good long boil in water from the river.'

Bartholomew felt faintly queasy.

'Come inside,' said Athelbald, taking the physician's arm to guide him back into the hut. 'Whoever it was meant you no harm, or he would have used a knife and not his fists. We would do well to mind our own affairs, and ignore whatever happened here tonight.'

Bartholomew conceded that he was right, and returned to his duties with the old man's ailing brother.

Meanwhile, Norbert had headed for Ovyng's door, hoping that once he reached it he would be safe. Already he had tried screaming for help, but few folk were rash enough to respond to howls in the night, and all that had happened was that he had wasted valuable energy. He gained the door and grasped the latch, praying that the officious friars had not locked it after he had been careful to leave it open. He never found out. No sooner had his fingers touched the metal than there was a crushing pain in his head that all but blinded him.

The bearded man watched Norbert crumple into the snow. Dispassionately, he saw his victim's eyes close, and a few moments later, heard his breathing stop. Norbert was dead. He dropped the stone and wiped his hand in the snow. It was too dark in the shadows of the lane to see whether the skull-shattering blow had stained his clothes, but he was fairly certain that it had not. He knew from experience that the first strike was relatively clean. He straightened his cloak, dried his wet hand on his jerkin, and made his way towards the High Street, thinking grimly about the unfinished business he still had to resolve with his dark-cloaked companion.

CHAPTER 1

22 December 1354, Cambridge

MATTHEW BARTHOLOMEW STUDIED THE MAN BROTHER Michael pointed out to him. The fellow's narrow face was framed by long grey hair that glistened with a generous coating of grease, and his unevenly bushy beard was dappled with white. He had moist hazel eyes and a set of enormous horse-like teeth, so large that his lips would never cover them without considerable effort and concentration from their owner. His clothes, however, were well-cut and elaborate, and he carried himself with a self-satisfied swagger, indicating that he considered himself to be the height of sartorial elegance and dashing good looks, even if the reality was somewhat different.

'So?' asked Bartholomew, bemused as he turned his attention to the dark-robed monk who knelt beside him. 'What do you want me to say?'

Michael sighed in exasperation. 'I have already told you. Were you not listening? I need you to give me your medical opinion of the man.'

Bartholomew regarded the burly Benedictine uneasily. 'You want me to examine him? On what pretext? I cannot just march up and foist my attentions on him out of the blue. He would complain to the Sheriff – and he would be quite right to do so.'

'Of course I do not want you to examine him,' snapped Michael impatiently. 'Well, not up close, at least. I want you to study him from a distance, and tell me what you think.'

Bartholomew laughed, amused by the bizarre nature of the request. They were crouching in the churchyard of St

17

Mary the Great, peering over a lichen-encrusted tomb to the Market Square, where the object of Michael's attentions was purchasing ink and parchment from one of the stall holders. The man was apparently unaware that he was being observed, although Bartholomew suspected it would not be long before he found out, given that the monk was far too large to be properly concealed by the ancient stone, nor was he making any effort to keep his voice low. Michael had already attracted curious glances from several passers-by, while a small dog cocked its head with pert interest as it watched his antics.

The Market Square was lively that morning, despite the bleak weather, as traders competed to sell their wares. Folk were more inclined to spend their money with the prospect of twelve nights of festivities looming ahead of them, so competition between vendors was fierce. The stalls' awnings snapped and hummed in the wind, people shouted, and animals neighed, bleated, crowed and honked. The air was rich with the odour of manure, fish and spices, and the market was a bright, cheerful rainbow in a town dominated by winter browns and greys. There was another splash of colour near Holy Trinity Church, where a troupe of entertainers dressed in red and gold juggled and tumbled for pennies, accompanied by a musician who played a pipe and tabor. The trill of the whistle and the thud of the drum were all but drowned out by the bustle and noise from the Market Square, and only the highest notes were audible.

Abruptly, Bartholomew stood up. It was a bitterly cold morning, with a frigid wind slicing in from the north-east and the threat of more snow in the air. Underfoot, the frozen ground crackled, and ice glazed the puddles in the High Street. It was no kind of weather to be hiding behind tombs in churchyards, and he decided it was time he returned to Michaelhouse, the College at the University where, as a Fellow and Master of Medicine, he lived, taught his students and saw his patients. Michaelhouse was not the warmest of places to be, either – there were fires in the kitchen and the communal halls, but not in the scholars' private rooms – but it was preferable to being outside.

'Agatha is making spiced oatcakes this morning,' he said, confidently anticipating that the mention of food would induce the fat Benedictine to abandon his peculiar fascination with the oily man in the Market Square.

He was wrong.

'Later,' said Michael, grabbing his friend's sleeve with a meaty hand. 'I need to know what you think about *him*. Can you see signs of incipient madness in his behaviour? Is there a hint of criminal intent in his movements?'

Bartholomew shook his head in exasperation before walking away across the graveyard, not deeming either question worthy of an answer. His feet were so cold that they felt as though they belonged to someone else, and he moved unsteadily across the spiky, crisp carpet of snow. Reluctantly, Michael abandoned his 'hiding' place and followed, tugging his thick woollen cloak around him. They reached St Mary's newly completed porch, and Bartholomew paused.

The University Church seemed to grow grander and more elegant each time the physician studied it. It had recently been renamed 'St Mary the Great', because the smaller church of St Peter Without had been rededicated as St Mary the Less. While Bartholomew examined its pleasing lines and handsome tracery, Michael glared back towards the Market Square. His quarry was still visible, the dark cloth of his hat bobbing among the stalls as he made his purchases.

'Well?' demanded Michael, determined to have an answer and aware that his friend had so far avoided giving one. 'What do you think? Can I instruct my beadles to arrest him on the grounds that his insanity makes him a danger to himself and to others, and have him evicted from the town?'

'I cannot tell such things from watching someone buy ink, Brother,' said Bartholomew, reluctant to be party to that kind of activity. 'We could stalk him all day and still not know the state of his health. I would need to talk to him, ask him specific questions – and even then insanity can be difficult

19

to diagnose. Why do you want to know, anyway?'

'He arrived in Cambridge a week ago,' replied Michael, his green-eyed glare still firmly fixed on the hapless figure in the Market Square. 'He *says* his name is John Harysone, but I am sure he is not telling the truth.'

'Why would he lie?' asked Bartholomew. 'And why does he warrant this kind of attention from you? Surely, you should let your beadles watch suspicious characters, not crawl around in cold cemeteries to spy for yourself.'

'I am not spying,' said Michael tartly. 'I am observing. You think that being Senior Proctor of the University of Cambridge means just counting fines and subduing rowdy undergraduates, but I can assure you I do a good deal more than that. It is my duty to ensure that the town is peaceful and trouble-free.'

'I thought that was the Sheriff's responsibility,' remarked Bartholomew. 'You are responsible for law and order only insofar as it affects the University.'

'If there is unrest in the town, then there *is* disorder in the University,' preached Michael. 'It has been a year since we have had any serious strife – and that is entirely due to me and the way I have organised my beadles. The Sheriff has nothing to do with it. *He* would not know how to avert a riot to save his life.'

Bartholomew agreed. 'Stephen Morice is not the Sheriff that Dick Tulyet was. It is a pity Dick was obliged to resign in order to help with his father's business.'

'Dick is a good man, and he and I worked well together,' said Michael gloomily. 'But Morice uses his office solely to make money for himself.' He grabbed Bartholomew's arm in a sudden, vicelike grip that made the physician wince. 'Harysone is heading towards St Michael's Church. He is going *inside*!'

The horror in Michael's voice as Harysone walked purposefully towards the small building that belonged to the scholars of Michaelhouse made Bartholomew smile. 'Visiting a church is not illegal, Brother. But I have lectures to prepare; I cannot spend all day stalking innocent men with you.'

'Harysone is not innocent,' said Michael with grim determination, watching with narrowed eyes as the man wrestled with the awkward latch on the church door. 'I can feel it in my bones.'

'That is the cold weather,' said Bartholomew practically. He broke away from Michael and headed for St Michael's Lane. 'I am going home. It is too chilly for this kind of thing.'

'Come with me to speak to him,' ordered Michael peremptorily. 'I shall only leave when we have assured ourselves that he has no sinister purpose in daring to set foot in St Michael's. For all you know, he may be planning to steal our silver.'

'He would be hard pressed to do that. We only use it on special occasions, and the rest of the time – like now – it is safely locked away. And anyway, he does not look like a man who needs to steal from churches. He is well dressed and appears to be wealthy.'

'I was at the Trumpington Gate when he arrived,' said Michael, watching Harysone give the door a vigorous shake in an attempt to open it. He was not successful. 'He had a cart with him, loaded down with what he claimed were philosophical texts written by himself. He said he was going to sell them here.' The monk turned to Bartholomew and raised a sceptical eyebrow. 'Have you ever heard a less convincing story?'

Bartholomew had heard a good many less convincing stories, and he told the monk so. It seemed to him that Harysone's reason for being in Cambridge was a perfectly valid one: if anyone wanted to sell academic texts, then Cambridge and Oxford were good places to be. They were full of scholars hungry for new knowledge and ideas, and Harysone could expect not only that copies would be purchased, but that they would be read and discussed by clever minds. Harysone might even learn ways to improve on his work.

21

'Well, I do not believe him,' declared Michael. 'I know his type. He is one of those men who makes his living by preying on the weak and the trusting. He will cheat widows, orphans and the weak-witted out of their inheritances, and will have every scrap of silver out of our churches before he melts away into the night.'

Bartholomew gave a startled laugh, astonished by the list of crimes Michael was blithely laying at the door of a man he did not know. 'Really, Brother! Do you have any evidence to suggest that he is a trickster?'

'Not yet,' admitted Michael. 'But I will. I have been watching him for the best part of a week now, and he will make a mistake before long. And then he can enjoy his Yuletide celebrations inside the proctors' prison!'

Bartholomew was nonplussed. 'I do not understand this at all. It is not like you to take a rabid dislike to visitors to our town without cause.'

'I have cause. Harysone disturbs me. I feel with every fibre in my body that there is something sinister about him.'

'That does not sound like you, either,' said Bartholomew doubtfully. 'You do not usually give credence to something as insubstantial as a "feeling". You usually demand solid evidence before judging a man.'

'I cannot explain it,' replied Michael impatiently. 'But I have been Senior Proctor for five years now, and I know a rotten apple when I see one. That man is a prince among villains, and I do not want him in my town.'

Bartholomew could think of nothing to say, but accepted that the Benedictine had gained enough experience to be able to identify potential troublemakers. Still, Michael was not immune to making mistakes, and the physician did not condone persecuting a man on the basis of a mere 'feeling'.

Harysone was still tussling with the sticky church door when Tom Meadowman, Michael's chief beadle, approached them, red faced and slightly breathless. The beadles were the proctors' private army, a stalwart band of men employed to keep hundreds of unruly and feisty scholars under control,

as well as patrolling the taverns to prevent explosive com-
binations of students, townsfolk and ale from occurring.

'Master Tulyet is looking for you, Brother,' said Meadowman, addressing Michael. 'His cousin Norbert has been
found dead – murdered, he says – and he wants you to look
into it.'

Richard Tulyet was a small man with a pale, fluffy beard that
made him look like an adolescent. He was intelligent and
well organised, and it had been a sad day for the town when
he had announced his resignation from the office of Sheriff.
His dissolute cousin Norbert was generally acknowledged to
be the major factor in this calamity, and it had not earned
the sullen youth any friends. It was widely believed that
Norbert had deprived Cambridge of the best, fairest and
most efficient Sheriff the town had ever had. Few believed
that his replacement, Stephen Morice, could emulate him,
and it had not been many weeks before people saw that
Morice was worse than inefficient: he was corrupt, too.

Michael, particularly, missed Tulyet. Relations between
town and University were invariably strained, and he had
enjoyed working with a man whose priority was to create a
city that was safe for everyone – scholars included. He had
also appreciated the fact that Tulyet had not competed with
him for authority, and was happy to let the University deal
with its own miscreants. He mourned Tulyet's resignation,
and seldom allowed an opportunity to pass without pointing
out that the town was less safe without Dick sitting in his
office at the Castle.

Tulyet was waiting for them in St Michael's Lane, where
snow lay in shoulder-high drifts in places. To the left was
the steeply gabled roof of Ovyng Hostel, while the tall stone
walls of Michaelhouse stood to the right. Although
Michaelhouse owned Ovyng, the hostel functioned as an
independent institution with its own rules and regulations.
It was not large, and its numbers had declined even further
since the plague, but it boasted eight scholars – a principal,

his assistant and six undergraduates – with two servants who cooked and cleaned. Five students, with Norbert being the exception, had taken vows with the Franciscan Order, and the hostel was reasonably well behaved by Cambridge standards – or at least Michael was not often obliged to visit it in his capacity of Senior Proctor.

'It is a pity Norbert is – was – not more like his cousin,' said Michael, as they made their way through the slush to where Tulyet and Nobert's classmates waited in a disconsolate huddle near Ovyng's main door.

'Everyone thinks that,' said Bartholomew. 'When he came to live here, after the plague took his own family, his uncle immediately assumed he would inherit the family business, since Dick was intent on remaining Sheriff. But I suspect Norbert was never asked what *he* wanted.'

'Norbert was a nuisance,' said Michael unsympathetically. 'He was on his final warning – one more night of drunken debauchery would have seen him banished from the University for ever. Still, it looks as though he will not be troubling us any more now.'

They reached the knot of people – Tulyet in his fine winter cloak, and the Franciscans shivering in their thin grey robes – and joined them in a wordless inspection of the body that lay, still partly buried, in a mound of snow near the door. Blood had flooded from an injury in the dead man's back and spread like wings into the snow around him. Bartholomew saw that Tulyet was right to assume his cousin had been murdered: there was no way the man could have inflicted such a wound on himself.

'Norbert might have remained covered until spring, if stray dogs had not sniffed him out,' said Ovyng's principal, Father Ailred, gesturing to several yellow mongrels that lurked hopefully nearby. As if the mangy beasts reminded him of his students, he turned and flapped large-knuckled hands at his flock, shooing them back inside the hostel. However, the death of a classmate was an interesting event, and Bartholomew noticed they did not go far. They hovered out of sight, but within earshot, on the other side of the door.

The physician turned his attention to Ailred. He had known the Franciscan for some years, and saw him almost daily, since Ovyng used St Michael's Church for its offices, although neither had sought to develop the acquaintance beyond a nod and a polite word when their paths crossed. Ailred was tall, with an ugly, blunt face and a lot of yellowish white showing at the bottom of his eyes. His head was bald, except for a frizzy grey crescent that hugged the back of his skull. He had a reputation for sober, painstaking scholarship that was precise and rarely in error. Bartholomew also knew that he was from Lincoln, and that he never tired of making comparisons between his grand city and the squalor of Cambridge.

'Norbert told me he was going to visit his uncle's house,' Ailred was saying, watching Tulyet nervously out of the corner of his eye as he addressed Michael. 'When he did not return, I assumed he had found somewhere warmer and more comfortable than our hostel.'

'When was this?' asked Michael. 'Last night?'

'It was not,' said Tulyet, shooting Ailred a cool glance of reproach. 'I have just learned that Norbert has not been seen since Tuesday – the day before yesterday. I was not even aware that he was missing.'

'Neither were we,' objected Ailred miserably. 'He often left and did not return for days. You know that. I used to report his absences, but you seemed as tired of hearing about them as I was of telling, and I thought we had reached a tacit agreement not to bother each other with his transgressions.'

'I suppose we did,' said Tulyet with a sigh. 'But it is unfortunate he was not missed sooner. Then he might have been saved.'

'It would have made no difference,' said Bartholomew, kneeling to inspect the body. 'Both injuries are fatal ones, and finding him sooner would not have changed the outcome.'

'Both injuries?' questioned Michael. 'I only see a wound to his back.'

Bartholomew parted Norbert's hair, frozen like old fur, to reveal an indentation in the skull. 'It looks as if he was stabbed and tried to run away – there is enough blood to suggest he did not die immediately and that he spent his last moments on the move. His assailant delivered the blow to the head when he reached the hostel door, although the knife wound would have killed him anyway.'

Tulyet closed his eyes. 'Horrible! It seems that whoever did this was determined that poor Norbert should die. But I suppose we should consider ourselves lucky to find the body today.' He cast a mournful glance at the leaden sky. 'More snow will fall this afternoon, and who knows when it will melt?'

'I have never known such weather,' agreed Ailred, obviously grateful to discuss something other than the awkward subject of the death of a student in his care. 'I am certain winters were not so hard when I was a boy in the fair city of Lincoln.'

'Who do you think did this?' asked Michael of the friar, indicating the corpse with a nod of his head. 'Norbert made a nuisance of himself with my beadles, and few regarded him as pleasant company – I am sorry, Dick, but it is true – but can you think of anyone who disliked him sufficiently to want him dead?'

Ailred was startled. 'Why are you asking me? It is obvious that Norbert visited some tavern, and his drunken tongue landed him in trouble with a townsman.'

'That is not obvious at all,' said Michael sharply. 'And I shall be obliged if you keep those kind of thoughts to yourself, Father. We do not want the University rioting because it believes one of its number has been killed by an apprentice – especially now.'

'Why especially now?' asked Ailred, puzzled.

Michael made no secret of his exasperation. 'Because it is only three days before Christmas, when students traditionally elect a Lord of Misrule to lead the festivities for the Twelve Days. Some of these might just as well be called "Lords of Incitement to Riot", since they urge their fellow students to engage in all sorts of michief against the town. I do not want to give them an excuse to justify violent behaviour.'

Ailred was disdainful. 'I had forgotten that unseemly custom. We do not indulge in pagan traditions at Ovyng; *we* are friars!'

Michael grimaced, knowing perfectly well that clerics were just as likely to misbehave as secular students, but he declined to argue. 'Regardless, keep your accusations to yourself until we understand what really happened. For all we know, one of his classmates may be the killer.'

'No!' exclaimed Ailred, appalled.

'My suggestion has as much evidence to support it as the solution you proposed,' said Michael crisply. 'So, I suggest we all refrain from jumping to conclusions before we have the facts. What can you tell me about Norbert?'

Ailred cleared his throat and glanced at Tulyet, clearly unhappy with the whole situation.

'It is all right, Father,' said Tulyet wearily. 'Norbert's failings were no secret, and we all know what kind of man he was. However, giving him virtues he never possessed will help no one, so you may be honest.'

'If you insist,' said Ailred reluctantly. He turned to Michael and spread his large hands, as though in apology. 'Norbert mocked our Order. He did not enjoy lessons, and he disrupted any he attended. He was lazy, disrespectful and selfish, and I do not think any of my students will claim him as a friend.'

'Then why was he tolerated here?' asked Bartholomew, who imagined that most masters would dismiss a student who was so badly behaved.

Ailred hesitated again.

'Money,' supplied Tulyet dryly. 'My father paid handsomely to have Norbert tutored here, and Ovyng is not a wealthy institution.' He turned to Michael. 'I want Norbert's killer caught, Brother. Since he was a student, his death is a University matter, and must be investigated by proctors rather than the Sheriff.' Bartholomew was certain he heard Tulyet add 'thank God' in an undertone. Tulyet was obviously as unimpressed by his replacement as was the rest of the town.

'I shall do my best,' said Michael. 'But this will not be an easy case to solve. Norbert was not popular, and I shall have to sift through all kinds of petty rivalries and dislikes in order to identify who took a fatal dislike to him.'

'I know,' said Tulyet tiredly. 'But I will help you in any way I can, and so will Ailred and the Ovyng students. I take it I am right to promise this, Father?'

'Of course,' said Ailred with a sickly, anxious smile. 'You can question them now, if you like, Brother. They are inside, waiting for lessons to begin.'

Bartholomew glimpsed a shadow flicker inside the door when the students were mentioned, and saw they were still eavesdropping on the discussion. He wondered whether Norbert's killer was among them.

'Who first saw the dogs uncovering the body?' asked Michael, who fully intended to interview Ailred's students, but in his own time.

'My assistant, Godric,' replied Ailred. 'We were returning from celebrating a mass when he spotted the dogs digging. When he went to drive them away, he saw they had unearthed a hand. He fetched a spade and we all watched while he completed what the mongrels had begun.'

'Did you observe any particular reactions among your charges?' asked Michael, without much hope. 'Any guilty glances or unease?'

'We were excavating a corpse, Brother,' replied Ailred acidly. 'Of course there was a degree of unease. We did not know whom we were about to discover. However, I can tell you for certain that I saw no "guilty glances". We were shocked, but none of us will prove to be your culprit.'

Michael watched while Bartholomew carefully pared away the rest of the snow that covered Norbert, hoping that the killer might have abandoned the weapon he had used, and that it might lead them to its owner. However, the culprit had done no such thing, and the physician had nothing to show for his painstaking excavation. The student had died face down, probably after a violent attack from behind. There was nothing to suggest he had known his assailant, but nothing to suggest he had not. The stab wound was wide and deep, indicating that it had been caused by a fairly large blade, but not one of abnormal size that would be easily identifiable.

Bartholomew sat on his heels and tucked his frozen hands under his arms in a vain attempt to warm them. He thought about the fear the young man must have felt, as he staggered towards the hostel already fatally wounded, and wondered why he had not shouted for help. The thought jarred something buried deep in his memory.

'You say he failed to come home on Tuesday night?' he asked. Ailred nodded.

'Why?' demanded Michael immediately. 'What have you found?'

'Nothing, but I was summoned to tend Dunstan the riverman then. He has an affliction of the lungs that produces an excess of phlegm, and—'

'We know,' interrupted Michael, forestalling what might prove to be a detailed description of some particularly unpleasant symptoms. 'You have been dragged from your bed for Dunstan several times since the weather turned sour. Did you see Norbert on Tuesday night?'

'I heard something: a screech. Then a man jumped out of the shadows and knocked me over. I told you about it the next day.'

'You did,' said Michael thoughtfully. 'But if you heard this scream, and an instant later someone knocked you head over heels, it was not the killer you encountered: he was murdering Norbert at that precise moment.'

'And there is no reason to assume the killer had an accomplice,' acknowledged Bartholomew. 'At least, not one that would be lurking so far away. It was just a thought; I was wrong.'

'It may be important,' said Tulyet, reluctant to abandon what might be a clue. 'Perhaps Norbert called for help, and you were the only one who heard him. Was it very late?'

'Past midnight,' replied Bartholomew. 'But the sound I heard may have been from an animal, not a person.'

'There is no reason to assume it was not Norbert,' pressed Tulyet doggedly. 'I know he left the King's Head at midnight on Tuesday, because the landlord hunted me down yesterday and insisted I pay the debts he had incurred. It *must* have been him you heard, and he was murdered as he walked home. Damn! Why did he have to die like this?'

Bartholomew was surprised to see the glitter of tears in Tulyet's blue eyes before he turned away to look towards the High Street – not surprised that Tulyet should show compassion, but that a man like Norbert should warrant it.

'Even if I had gone to his aid I could not have saved him from wounds like this,' he said gently. 'The man who pushed me was probably a beggar looking for somewhere to sleep, who had nothing to do with Norbert's murder.' He winced as he rubbed his frozen hands together. 'But I have done all I can here. The killer has left us no clues.'

Ailred dispatched a student to fetch a bier and offered to have Norbert delivered to Tulyet's house. Tulyet nodded his thanks, looked one last time at the place where his cousin had died, and then walked away with Michael and Bartholomew on either side of him.

'My father may feel obliged to ask Sheriff Morice to look into the matter, since Norbert was our kinsman – the nephew of a prominent town merchant,' he said as they walked. 'I shall do my best to dissuade him, but do not be surprised if you find a secular investigation in progress, as well as your own.'

'Thank you for the warning,' said Michael. 'But I am not worried by anything Morice might do. He is no Dick Tulyet.'

30

Tulyet smiled wanly. 'I trust you to find the truth, Brother. You will not fail me.'

'Lord, Matt!' said Michael uneasily, as Tulyet went to break the news of Norbert's death to his father. 'I shall do my best to oblige him, but Norbert had many enemies. I am not sure Dick's confidence in me is warranted this time.'

Bartholomew expected Michael to begin making enquiries immediately into Norbert's death, but the monk had different priorities. The physician was surprised to find himself being manoeuvred in the direction of St Michael's Church, away from Ovyng Hostel and the scholars who were anticipating being interviewed about their classmate's murder.

'He will not be there now, Brother,' said Bartholomew, astonished to think that Michael should even begin to imagine that Harysone had spent half the morning in that frigid little building. 'There is not much to do inside, so he will have looked around and left.'

'Nonsense,' said Michael firmly. 'There was real purpose in his movements as he fiddled with the lock. He was determined to enter, and I conclude that there was some specific task he wanted to perform. He will still be there and we shall catch him in the act.'

'You sound deranged,' said Bartholomew accusingly. 'You follow him all over the town because you do not like the look of him, and now you assign him some dark and sinister purpose for entering a church. He may have gone inside to pray. People do, you know.'

'Not him,' said Michael with conviction. 'He is not the type for prayers.'

'Enough, Brother!' said Bartholomew irritably. 'I have been up much of the last two nights with Dunstan, and I am too tired for this. It is also freezing out here. I have humoured you long enough today: it is time to go home.'

'Just a few more moments,' said Michael, not to be diverted from his purpose just because his companion was weary and cold. He smiled when a familiar figure emerged from the north porch as they approached. It was Beadle Meadowman, huddled deep inside his cloak. 'I left a guard here when we went to see Norbert, to make sure Harysone did not escape.'

'He has not come out,' said Meadowman, flapping his arms vigorously in a futile attempt to drive the chill from his body. His usual good temper was gone, and he clearly did not appreciate being ordered to lurk in north-facing porches when there was a bitter wind blowing. 'But then, I did not see him enter, either.'

'What do you mean?' demanded Michael peevishly. 'You must have done. We all saw him battling with the latch.'

'I took my eyes off him for a moment – just a moment – but when I looked again, he had gone,' said Meadowman. He was not at all intimidated by Michael's irritation, and was not going to apologise for his lapse, either. He was obviously as frustrated and bemused by Michael's obsession with Harysone as was Bartholomew, and had had enough of orders to stalk the man when there were better and more productive ways to pass a morning. He gave a careless shrug. 'So, maybe he entered, and maybe he did not.'

'Did you look inside?' asked Michael testily. 'To see whether he was there?'

Meadowman pursed his lips disapprovingly. 'You told me to watch the door. You did not say I should search for him.'

Bartholomew grinned at Michael's exasperation, while Meadowman looked defiant. Michael glowered at both of them, then turned to the church.

The latch on the porch of St Michael's was notorious for being temperamental. Michaelhouse scholars, who came at least once a day for prayers, were used to its peculiarities, and most were able to open it with a minimum of jiggling. The scholars of Ovyng, Garrett, St Catherine's and Physwick hostels, who paid Michaelhouse a fee to use the building on a regular basis, were also familiar with it. But to anyone unaware of its idiosyncratic nature, the latch presented a formidable barrier, and more than one would-be visitor had been thwarted by it in the past. Michael gave it one or two expert shakes, and the door sprung open.

The two scholars walked through the timber porch and entered the short nave, while Meadowman seized the opportunity to slip away to his other duties. It was even colder inside the church than it was out, which was probably the real reason why the beadle had declined to search it for Harysone. The air was still and damp, and ice-glazed puddles showed where water had leaked through the roof during the last sleety downpour and had collected in depressions on the floor. Most of the window shutters were open, but the glass was thick and opaque, the building shadowy, and the winter day dull and grey, so it was difficult to see anything at all.

The church smelled of cheap incense and damp plaster, with an underlying musty odour emanating from an array of ancient vestments that were hanging on a row of hooks near the porch. Michaelhouse's scholars believed that these grimy robes, which were liberally spotted with mould, should be either cleaned or thrown away, but the Master always demurred, claiming that they might 'come in useful one day'. Bartholomew supposed they would remain festering on their rusty hooks until they turned to dust, since he could not imagine anyone willingly donning the things when there were newer and less odorous ones available.

Harysone was not in the nave, so Bartholomew and Michael walked towards the chancel, their feet on the flagstones making the only sound. The church comprised the nave and chancel, two aisles and two chapels. The south chapel was usually called the Stanton Chapel, named for Michaelhouse's founder who was buried there. It was one of the finest examples of modern architecture in Cambridge, but the chancel was the building's crowning glory. It was larger than the nave, and boasted simple, but elegant, tracery in its arched windows, while its walls were painted with scenes from the Bible in brilliant reds, blues, yellows and greens.

When the sun shone, light pooled in delicate patterns on the creamy-white of the floor, although that day the whole building was gloomy, and no lights pooled anywhere.

Bartholomew noticed that one of the candles on the high altar had wilted, and that wax was dripping on the floor. He went to straighten it and scrape away the mess with a knife, while Michael gazed around in agitation.

'Harysone is not here!' he muttered angrily.

Bartholomew shrugged as he worked. 'We were at least an hour – probably longer – with Norbert. I am not surprised that your quarry has left.'

Michael was disgusted. 'Now we shall never know what he was doing.'

'Meadowman said he may not have come in at all. Perhaps he gave up on the latch and went away. Or perhaps he exited through the south door.'

'Why would he do that?' called Michael testily, prowling around the lovely Stanton Chapel, as though anticipating that Harysone might be hiding behind the founder's tomb.

'Because the latch jammed and he found himself unable to leave through the north one?' suggested Bartholomew, giving the pewter candle-holder a quick polish on his sleeve.

'You are right!' exclaimed Michael triumphantly, when he went to inspect the exit in the south aisle. It was larger than the north door, but using the smaller entrance tended to keep the building warmer. The south aisle was occasionally employed as a mortuary chapel for parishioners, but most of the time it stood empty and its door was permanently barred. 'Someone has been out this way.'

The door had been left ajar, and the monk opened it fully to peer out, before shutting it again. A stout plank of wood prevented anyone from entering from the outside, and he studied it thoughtfully before replacing it in its two metal clasps. Bartholomew pointed out that anyone might have opened it, and that its use did not necessarily imply wrongdoing on Harysone's part. Michael listened patiently, but did not agree. Seeing neither was going to accept the other's point of view, they abandoned the discussion and headed to the north door. As Bartholomew jiggled the latch, the monk forgot his tirade against Harysone, wrinkling his nose and indicating the row of robes that hung nearby.

'The stench of those things is growing stronger by the day. They are too rotten ever to wear again, and I cannot imagine why Master Langelee does not throw them away.'

'Langelee never throws anything away if he thinks it may be useful. Michaelhouse is not wealthy, and he is just being prudent, I suppose. Shoes.'

'What are you talking about?' asked Michael, confused.

'Shoes,' repeated Bartholomew, pointing at the robes. 'I think someone is hiding from you.'

Michael followed the line of the physician's outstretched finger and his lips compressed in grim satisfaction. Poking from under the untidy, bulky folds of material was a pair of scruffy leather shoes. Someone had evidently slipped in among the albs and chasubles in the hope that he would be hidden – as he would have been, had he not left his feet in full view. Michael marched across to the line of hooks, and ripped the gowns aside.

The face that looked back at him was not Harysone's. Nor was it the face of any living man. It was a corpse, with a pallid blue tinge about its mouth and lips, and unseeing eyes that were half open, half closed.

Michael leapt back with a yell of alarm, bouncing into Bartholomew and almost knocking the physician from his feet. The sound was loud in the otherwise silent church, and it startled some pigeons that had been roosting in the rafters. They flapped in agitation, showering the floor below with dried droppings and floating feathers.

It was odd to see a corpse standing as though it were alive, and even Bartholomew – no stranger to sudden and unusual death, thanks to his association with the University's Senior Proctor – found it disconcerting. Carefully, he pushed a fold of cloth away, and saw that several of the robes were wrapped around the man's arms and upper body, holding it upright. The hood of an alb lay in a tangled chain across the corpse's chin so that its head was raised, as though looking forward.

'Who is it?' demanded Michael, as if Bartholomew should know.

'He looks like a beggar,' said Bartholomew, pointing at the man's threadbare clothes. 'He must have come here to escape from the cold.'

'He should have chosen another church, then,' remarked Michael, placing a flabby white hand across his chest to indicate that the presence of a corpse among the decaying ceremonial robes had given him a serious shock. 'Everyone knows St Michael's is the chilliest building in Christendom. Is that what killed him? Cold? Not Harysone?'

'Harysone?' echoed Bartholomew, startled by the question. 'Why should he kill a beggar?'

'To prevent him from revealing Harysone's intention to steal from our church. You saw for yourself that one of the candles had been tampered with.'

'Harysone is well-dressed and has been spending money on inks and parchment in the Market Square,' said Bartholomew impatiently. 'If he is a thief – and there is nothing to suggest that he is, other than an irrational suspicion on your part – he would not be interested in our paltry pewter. He would go to St Mary the Great and help himself to gold crosses and silver patens.'

'Those are guarded,' countered Michael. 'One of my beadles is always on duty there, and it would be impossible to steal anything.'

Bartholomew made a dismissive gesture. 'You are quibbling, Brother. My point is that a well-heeled thief would not choose St Michael's when other places offer better potential. And you certainly cannot accuse Harysone of killing this man. He might have been here for hours before Harysone arrived – assuming Harysone entered at all, that is.'

'Then you have some work to do,' said Michael, indicating the body with a peremptory wave of his hand. 'This fellow

died on University property, and his death must be investigated by me.'

'You will have to find someone else to help,' said
Bartholomew wearily. 'As I told you, I was up most of the
last two nights with Dunstan, and I have already examined
one corpse for you today.'

'This cannot wait,' said Michael sternly. 'I need to know
how this man died and whether someone – such as Harysone
– gave him a helping hand to Paradise. You would not want
a killer to evade justice just because you are chilly and had
an interrupted night of sleep, would you?'

With a long-suffering sigh, Bartholomew moved the robes
away from the slight figure that nestled inside them. It would
have been simple for the beggar to escape the enveloping
folds had he wanted to do so, and Bartholomew supposed
that he had wrapped them around himself in an attempt to
be invisible and keep warm at the same time. It was a clever
ploy, and would probably have ensured that he would not
be evicted to spend the day – or night – outside.

Bartholomew shivered and wondered whether he should
experiment to see whether the particular angles of the cloth
would reveal whether the man had wrapped them himself,
or whether someone else had done it for him. But he was
so cold that he could barely think, and he did not feel like
inserting himself among the damp, smelly robes to assess
the varying ways in which they might end up around him.
Instead, he unravelled the folds and forced them to release
their grisly burden. It did not take long, and he soon had
the body resting on the floor.

Trying not to rush, just because he wanted to return to
Michaelhouse and huddle near the fire, he sat back on his
heels and studied what lay in front of him. He realised that
thicker clouds must have massed outside, because the
church was so dark he could barely see the body, let alone
examine it. Michael fetched the candle from the altar, but
its cheap tallow did little to help, and its main contribution
to the task was to release an oily, pungent odour that

competed valiantly with the stench of rotting cloth.

Bartholomew leaned close to the corpse in a vain attempt to inspect it. The man had not been wealthy: his clothes were frayed, patched and woefully inadequate for the rigours of a Fenland winter. His hands were soft, however, and notably uncalloused, suggesting that his ill fortunes had not forced him into manual labour to earn his bread. One thumb was missing, but the wound had healed long ago, and Bartholomew supposed some ancient accident had robbed him of it.

Satisfied he had learned all he could by looking, he began his physical examination, suspecting this would reveal little more and that he was lingering in the church for nothing. The corpse felt icy cold, but Bartholomew's own hands were not much warmer, and he decided the temperature of the body would tell him little about when the man had died. Struggling to see, he checked quickly for wounds, then inspected the neck to see whether the man had been strangled. His brief examination revealed nothing. He stood, trying to rub the ache from his knees, and shrugged helplessly at Michael.

'I do not know what killed him, Brother, but I am guessing it was the cold. I cannot tell you when, though. It is so chilly that the usual methods for estimating time of death – body coolness, stiffness, decay and so on – are useless. He might have crept in here this morning, but could equally as easily have been here for a couple of days.'

Michael grimaced. 'That is an unpleasant notion, Matt. I do not like the thought of saying my prayers while corpses peer at me from decaying albs.'

'I imagine there are few who would. But all I can tell you is that this man was poor and that he probably suffered miserably from the weather. There is no injury that I can detect, so I doubt that your friend Harysone had anything to do with his demise.'

'What about poison?' suggested Michael hopefully.

'There are no lesions or bleeding in the mouth. He did

38

not scratch or claw at his throat. I suppose he might have been given something soporific, but I really do not see why anyone would kill a beggar using potions that are usually expensive.'

'And there is nothing on his body to tell us who he is?'

'As you see,' said Bartholomew, indicating the sad remains that lay in front of them. 'He owned no purse – or none that is with him now.'

'I will ask my beadles to make some enquiries,' said Michael. He cocked his head. 'But the bells are ringing to announce the midday meal. Meadowman can deal with this poor fellow's remains, and this afternoon I shall set about trying to discover what happened to Norbert.'

'And what about Harysone?' asked Bartholomew archly. 'Has he been granted a reprieve now that you have Norbert's murder and identifying the beggar to take up your time?'

'Certainly not,' said Michael haughtily. 'Master Harysone has not heard the last of me yet.'

After the midday meal, Bartholomew went to prepare the lecture he was to give that afternoon, while Michael delegated a student to read part of Duns Scotus's *Ordinatio* to his small group of sombre, erudite Benedictines. The monk rubbed his chin as he left Michaelhouse, wondering whether to concentrate his attention on the violent murder of Norbert or on discovering the identity of the beggar who had died in the church. Duty told him he should go to Ovyng and speak to Norbert's classmates, but the unsettled, albeit irrational, feeling he had experienced ever since he had first set eyes on Harysone made him more inclined to look into the death of the beggar, since a nagging suspicion told him that Harysone was involved.

Michael was not normally a man given to wild and unfounded prejudices against people he barely knew, but he liked to think he had developed an ability to single out at least some folk whose intentions were not entirely honourable. And all his instincts screamed at him that

Harysone's presence in the town was one he could do without. Bartholomew might have been unable to prove that the beggar had come to harm at Harysone's hands, but Michael knew there were ways to kill that defied detection, and some deep, feral instinct convinced him that Harysone had not been tussling with the sticky door merely to admire St Michael's dented pewter.

He pondered for a moment more before turning left and striding up St Michael's Lane towards the High Street. Norbert's murder would be difficult to solve, given that the fellow had so many enemies in the town, and the investigation did not appeal to Michael in the slightest. He decided to leave Norbert until the following day and interview Harysone instead: Norbert was dead and nothing could change that, but Harysone represented crimes to be committed in the future – and they might be prevented.

Harysone, however, was not at his lodgings in the King's Head, nor was he browsing among the stalls in the Market Square. Michael scratched his head thoughtfully, then began a systematic trawl of the town's taverns, becoming more determined to find the man with each unsuccessful enquiry. When he met Meadowman near the Brazen George, the beadle informed him that Harysone had been in the Hall of Valence Marie, selling copies of his manuscript.

'He is doing what?' spluttered Michael, outraged. 'Peddling his inferior scholarship to some of the greatest minds in the country?'

'I do not know about that,' said Meadowman stoically. 'But he sold Valence Marie two copies of his treatise, and then went to Bene't College.'

'And what would this "treatise" be about?' demanded Michael archly. 'Harysone was never a student here, and I doubt even Oxford would accept the likes of *him* into their midst.'

'Valence Marie's porter told me it was about fish,' said Meadowman. 'And suchlike.'

'Fish?' echoed Michael in astonishment. 'Harysone told

40

me it was a philosophical tract. And what do you mean by "and suchlike"?'

Meadowman shrugged, glancing up the High Street to where he could see two undergraduates emerging nonchalantly from the Brazen George. If he caught them, he could fine them fourpence, and he itched to be away after them.

'You will have to read it yourself,' he said. 'You know I am not a man for words.'

'I shall never read it,' vowed Michael, abandoning his beadle and heading purposefully towards Bene't, which was all but hidden behind a vast bank of snow. A great mass of icy slush had sloughed from its roof ten days before, and the mound had grown even more when snow shovelled from the street had been added to it by students who were too lazy to haul the stuff away.

But by the time Michael reached Bene't, Harysone had already left, taking with him four marks from scholars interested in reading the treatise and leaving two copies of his work behind. No one knew where the man intended to go next, and Michael was forced to admit defeat. Midwinter Day was looming, and the few hours between dawn at eight and dusk at four passed far too quickly. Michael was running out of daylight. He decided to return to Michaelhouse for the evening, to sit by the fire and allow a cup of mulled wine to banish the chill from his limbs.

The following morning, Ralph de Langelee, Master of Michaelhouse, made a decision that was very popular with most of his students. Because there were only two days left before Christmas, he declared that lectures would be limited to mornings only, while afternoons were to be spent in preparations for the festivities to come. Some undergraduates were dispatched to gather firewood, so that the scholars could relax in rooms that had at least had the chill taken out of them, while others were sent to barter for special foods in the Market Square. Most were delighted by the unexpected reprieve, and Langelee was generally declared

41

to be the best Master since Michaelhouse's foundation.

Bartholomew was both pleased and frustrated by the enforced break. The two free afternoons would allow him to work on his treatise on fevers and visit his family, but there was a huge amount that his students needed to know if they wanted to be decent physicians, and he hated wasting time. Ever since the plague, there had been a chronic shortage of trained medical men, and Bartholomew was working hard to redress the balance. Teaching was suspended altogether during the Twelve Days, and he fretted that his students were being deprived of too much valuable learning time.

He attended morning mass in the church, although his mind bounced between worrying about his students' poor grasp of Maimonides and considering the beggar he had found the previous day. He wondered who the man could be, and why he had chosen frigid St Michael's in which to die. Michael said that Meadowman's enquiries among the town's other beggars had so far revealed nothing, so it seemed that the fellow would be buried in a pauper's grave and be forgotten for ever if no one came forward to claim him as kin.

Bartholomew glanced across to the south aisle, where the body lay under a sheet, and then started to think about whether there would be enough ready-dug graves to last the winter. Digging frozen ground was almost impossible, and he had taken it upon himself to arrange for each church to prepare a few holes before the weather turned bad that year. If there were many more cases like the beggar's, then they would soon run out.

After breakfast, he had planned to lecture his students on the part of Roger Bacon's *Antidotarium* that dealt with mint, but Michael had other ideas. The monk had reluctantly conceded that he needed to forget Harysone for a while and begin his investigation into Norbert's murder, but he wanted Bartholomew with him when he interviewed the students at Ovyng. Although he was a skilled investigator, it always helped when the physician was there to gauge reactions and observe suspicious behaviour. Michael believed Ovyng represented his best chance of catching Norbert's killer, and hoped to discover that one of Norbert's classmates had tired of his cruel tongue and dissolute behaviour, and done away with him. With luck, the case would be resolved quickly and without the need for a complex investigation that would give rise to rumours and speculation about whether a townsman was responsible. Michael did not want Norbert's murder to spark fights or ill feeling between the University and the town during a volatile period like the Twelve Days.

It had snowed again during the night, but the fall had been light, and many feet had already trodden a groove between the ice-cliffs along St Michael's Lane. The wind sucked dried pellets of ice from the ground and hurled them in the scholars' faces as they walked, causing Michael to claim that a more severe winter had not been experienced since the Creation. Bartholomew argued that there was no way to tell, and they were still debating the issue when they arrived at the hostel.

Ovyng was a large house that had been bought for Michaelhouse in 1329, using funds left over from the founder's will. Michaelhouse could have used the building as accommodation for its own members, but numbers had been low since the plague, and instead Langelee leased it to Ailred for a modest fee. Ovyng was a pleasant place, with a large chamber on the ground floor that served as lecture hall and dining room, and two attic rooms that were used as dormitories.

When Bartholomew and Michael arrived, they found the five students sitting on wooden benches, listening to a lecture given by Ailred himself. It was on Thomas Aquinas's *Sermones*, and was a careful exegesis of one of the more difficult sections. It was solid scholarship, but not exciting, and the students looked bored. Three gazed out of the window at the lumpy white blanket that smothered the vegetable patch, while the other two sat bolt upright in an effort to stop themselves from falling asleep. Ailred's assistant slouched at the back of the class, checking logic exercises that had been scratched into wax-covered tablets.

'You know why I am here,' said Michael, as Ailred faltered into silence and the students regarded the monk expectantly. 'Norbert.'

'We did not kill him,' said Ailred's assistant immediately. He was a large, raw-boned fellow with a ruddy face and teeth that had been chipped into irregular points. He was not much older than his charges, and Bartholomew supposed he had been hired because his youth and inexperience meant that he was cheap. 'We did not like him, but we did not touch him.'

'I am accusing no one,' said Michael, although the cool green gaze that rested on the face of each Franciscan in turn suggested otherwise. 'I merely want the truth. Does anyone know anything that may help us find the perpetrator of this dreadful crime?'

'Not really,' said the assistant. 'He was not one of us, you see.'

'Godric means that he was not a Franciscan,' elaborated Ailred, when the monk's face indicated that there were several ways this comment could be interpreted, all of them incriminating.

'It was not just that,' persisted Godric. 'He never even tried to be friendly, and he slept more nights away than here.'

'Godric!' whispered Ailred in exasperation, closing his eyes and giving them a hearty massage. He looked exhausted, as though the murder of his student had deprived him of sleep. Bartholomew wondered whether the friar's tiredness derived from the fact that Norbert's death represented a sizeable loss of income, or whether there were deeper, more sinister reasons for it. 'When I said we should answer the Senior Proctor's questions truthfully, I did not mean that you had to betray every one of Norbert's misdemeanours.'

'Betray away,' said Michael, beaming at Godric. 'A

catalogue of Norbert's indiscretions may prove very useful.'

'I do not see how,' said Ailred. 'But Godric is right about Norbert's sleeping habits: he was not often found in his own bed. In fact, his repeated absences were one of the reasons why he was not missed for two days. He often stayed away – sometimes with whores, sometimes in taverns and sometimes at his uncle's house.'

'I knew he flouted the rules,' said Michael. 'But I did not realise he did so on such a regular basis. Why did you not tell me this before?'

Ailred shot him a pained glance. 'The fees paid by his family were important to us. We did not want him dismissed, although God knows he had no business here. As long as we kept him, the Tulyets would continue paying for his tuition.'

The other Franciscans had been talking among themselves while the exchange between Ailred and Michael took place; now they seemed to have reached a consensus. They nodded encouragingly at Godric, who was evidently their spokesman.

'Unfortunately, we have little to tell that will help you catch your culprit,' he began apologetically. 'Norbert was unfriendly, lazy and refused to comply with our rules. He made offensive remarks about our Order and he stole our ink and parchment. We think he took them in order to write to Dympna.'

'Dympna?' asked Michael, puzzled. 'Who is he?'

'She,' corrected Godric. He glanced at his colleagues, suddenly unsure. 'Well, we assume it was a she. She sent him notes, which we sometimes saw. She always asked him to meet her in the same place.'

'I do not see how this is relevant,' said Ailred impatiently. 'Norbert liked women – ask any of the town's whores – but I do not see how investigating a particular one will lead you to his killer.'

'I am not so sure,' said Michael thoughtfully. He turned to Godric. 'When did this woman last write to Norbert?'

Godric ignored the pained expression on his principal's face. 'He had a letter from her the evening he disappeared.'

Ailred sighed. 'This kind of speculation is dangerous, Godric. It may lead the good brother along the wrong road entirely, and cause him to waste time and effort.'

Godric turned apologetically to Michael. 'I am only trying to help. Dympna *did* send him a message that afternoon, and he *did* go out soon after he read it, but perhaps I should not have assumed the two were connected.'

'Do you still have this letter?' asked Michael. 'It might help if we were to see it.'

Godric shook his head. 'He either took it with him or threw it away. We have searched his belongings, but it is not there – not that note or any of the others.'

'Was this relationship with Dympna a recent affair?' asked Michael. 'Or one that had been going on for some time?'

'I think recent,' replied Godric. 'We first saw a note about a week ago, but there could have been others before that.' He smiled suddenly, so that his loutish face softened and became almost attractive. 'You are wondering why we pried so unashamedly into Norbert's personal life, Brother. Being friars, none of *us* receive notes from young ladies, and we were naturally curious about a man who does.'

'Naturally,' said Michael expressionlessly. 'Did you meet this woman, or see Norbert with her?'

'We saw him with women,' replied Godric precisely. 'But since we do not know what Dympna looks like, we do not know which one of them was her. However, I doubt whether any of the rough ladies he courted openly was Dympna. I think he only ever met her in secret.'

'Why?' asked Michael curiously. 'You have just said you do not know what she looks like, so she could be any of the prostitutes Norbert enjoyed. God knows, he was fined enough times for that.'

Godric's expression was earnest. 'I think she is better than the others. She *wrote* to him – on *parchment*, using a *pen*!'

Parchment was expensive, and while some people could

read, far fewer extended their education to the more skilled process of writing. The very act of putting pen to parchment suggested a woman who was a cut above the average.

'Did you read these personal notes?' asked Bartholomew of Godric. 'You know what was in them and who they were from, so you must have done.'

'Really, Godric!' exclaimed Ailred in horror. 'I thought you had more honour. Did no one ever teach you that it is wrong to pry into the personal missives of others?'

'I am sorry, Father,' muttered Godric, red-faced with embarrassment. 'We meant no harm. We were just curious.'

'Being nosy is not an excuse,' said Ailred sternly. 'But since you have already broken faith with a colleague by reading letters not intended for your eyes, then I suppose there is no further harm in telling us what was in them. What did they say?'

'Nothing much,' said Godric, still shamefaced. 'They were rather curt, actually, and not at all like the kind of love-letters we have heard sung about in ballads. They just mentioned her name, and a time and a place for a meeting, followed by a series of numbers.' He brightened. 'They were probably astrological observations, to do with the best time for practising love.'

'You seem to have a very rosy view of Norbert's love affairs,' said Bartholomew, trying not to laugh at the notion of the lazy, hedonistic Norbert engaging in anything as orderly as running his life according to the alignments of the celestial bodies. Godric, like many men who entered the priesthood young, had some very odd ideas about courtship.

'You said these notes specified a meeting place,' said Michael, ignoring the friar's embarrassed reaction to Bartholomew's observation. 'Where was it?'

'St Michael's Church,' replied Godric.

'Our church?' asked Michael, startled. 'Are you sure?'

Godric nodded. 'I know Norbert spent his last night at the King's Head, but it was Dympna's call for love that sent him out in the first place. He went to meet her!'

47

Godric and the others could tell them no more about the mysterious Dympna, nor could they identify anyone in particular who wanted to harm Norbert, so Bartholomew and Michael made their farewells and walked back to Michaelhouse. As soon as they opened the gate they saw Bartholomew's slight, dark-featured book-bearer picking his way across the yard towards them. The yard's rutted, potholed surface was a danger at the best of times, but it was worse when snow camouflaged its hazards. Cynric gave a nervous grin as he approached, and Bartholomew felt a wave of apprehension that the normally nonchalant Welshman was so clearly uneasy.

'It is cold today,' said Cynric, glancing up at the heavy-bellied clouds above. 'It will snow again tonight.'

'What is wrong?' demanded Bartholomew. Cynric never wasted time with idle chatter about the weather. 'Is my sister unwell?'

'No, but I have a message from her,' replied Cynric. 'Well, not her. From her husband, Oswald Stanmore. You know that I am married to his seamstress, and that my wife and I have a room at his business premises on Milne Street. He asked me to come here to see you.'

'You are gabbling, Cynric,' said Bartholomew, becoming alarmed. His book-bearer was never garrulous, and certainly did not normally waste breath telling people things they already knew, such as the names of their own brothers-in-law and their servants' domestic arrangements.

'Sir Oswald has an unexpected guest,' said Cynric. 'A woman. Well, a woman and two men, actually. They arrived in Cambridge more than a week ago, but Mistress Stanmore only met them yesterday. They asked her to recommend a decent tavern, because they had been staying at the King's Head, but one of the gentlemen found it was not to his taste.'

'I am not surprised,' said Michael, wryly. 'The King's Head is no place for decent folk.'

'Mistress Stanmore felt obliged to invite them to stay with

her,' Cynric continued nervously. 'She said it would have been rude not to, because the best inns are full at this time of year.'

'Who are these folk?' asked Michael, amused by Cynric's rambling. 'Joseph and Mary?'

'I do not think the lady is pregnant,' replied Cynric, quite seriously. 'I could not tell under her cloak, but her husband is not a man who would turn a lady's head.' He scratched his nose. 'Although I suppose he must have turned hers at one point, or they would not have wed.'

'Who is he?' asked Bartholomew, wondering whether Cynric had started his Christmas celebrations early, and had been at the ale. 'Do I know him?'

'Sir Walter Turke,' said Cynric. 'I do not believe that you have met.'

The name meant nothing to Bartholomew. 'Why are you telling me all this?' he asked.

'You knew Turke's wife during the pestilence,' replied Cynric uneasily. 'She had the disease, but survived.'

'There were not many of those,' said Michael, unnecessarily unkind. 'This woman should come leaping to your mind.'

But she did not, and Bartholomew gazed blankly at Cynric, searching the half-forgotten faces in his memory for a woman who had married a fellow called Turke. He tended to suppress thoughts of those black, dismal days, when his painstakingly acquired skills and experience were useless in the face of the wave of sickness that swamped most of the civilised world, and nothing came to him.

'Actually,' said Cynric, speaking reluctantly when he saw Bartholomew was not going to guess who he meant. 'You were betrothed to her yourself. But after the Death, she went to London and wed Sir Walter Turke instead. Her name was Philippa Abigny.'

His message delivered, Cynric escaped to his other duties with obvious relief. A private man himself, he disliked witnessing the rawer emotions of others, and he had had no idea how the physician might react to the news. He need not have worried. Bartholomew did not react at all, too startled by the sudden incursion of his past into the present to know what he thought about the prospect of the beautiful Philippa Abigny touching his life again.

'Philippa Abigny,' echoed Michael in astonishment, watching Cynric all but run in the direction of the kitchen before Bartholomew or Michael could question him further. 'I did not think she would ever show her face here again. What she did to you was not right.'

'You mean because she broke our betrothal to marry someone richer?' asked Bartholomew. 'Perhaps it was for the best. Who knows whether we could have been happy with each other?'

'You can probably say that about most things,' said Michael philosophically. 'But she was wrong to abandon you so abruptly. You could have applied to the Pope to have her marriage annulled, you know. You would have been within your rights, given that your betrothal had been of several years' duration.'

'But then I would have had to marry her,' Bartholomew pointed out. 'And I am not sure that is what I wanted.'

Michael chuckled. 'You prefer the lovely Matilde these days, I suppose. Well, whatever you think, it will be interesting to see Philippa again and to assess what you have missed by allowing her to slip through your fingers.'

Bartholomew nodded absently. He stood in the middle of Michaelhouse's yard, with Michael sniggering lustfully beside him, and wondered how the sudden and unexpected arrival of someone who had played such an important part in his past would affect his future.

CHAPTER 2

BARTHOLOMEW WOKE IN AN UNEASY MOOD THE NEXT morning, with Philippa Abigny at the forefront of his thoughts. It was the last day of Advent – the period of fasting and prayer before Christmas – and the time when people readied themselves for Christmas. Long before dawn, Michaelhouse buzzed with activity. Servants scurried here and there, carrying pots, pans and supplies of various kinds, watched over by the critical, all-seeing eyes of that most illustrious and feared of College servants, Agatha the laundress.

Women were rarely employed by the University, because it was a domain inhabited by men, many of whom had taken priestly vows of celibacy. In order to avoid unnecessary temptation, the University ensured that contact between scholars and ladies was minimal, and its beadles patrolled assiduously, aiming to prevent long-deprived students from straying to taverns or other town venues where they might encounter members of the opposite sex.

Laundresses, however, were a necessity, and to surmount the problem, the University stipulated that any ladies hired should be so physically unattractive that they would repel even the most desperate of scholars. Ugly, but competent, washer-women were highly prized commodities, and Colleges and hostels guarded them jealously. Michaelhouse had Agatha, a mountain of a lady with a bristly chin, powerful arms, mighty hips and an unshakeable conviction that she had survived the plague because she was a favourite of God's. She took her College duties seriously, and, as the Twelve Days approached, no member of Michaelhouse could expect to find himself exempt from running her errands or from becoming embroiled in her frenzied arrangements.

51

The scholars left the early-morning chaos and attended mass. On the way back Michael fretted that the fuss was likely to mean a delayed breakfast, but he had underestimated Agatha, who was quite capable of producing meals and overseeing festive preparations at the same time. The undercook rang the bell to announce the beginning of breakfast at precisely seven o'clock, just as Master Langelee was leading his scholars through the gate into Michaelhouse's yard.

When the College had been founded in 1324, no expense had been spared by Hervey de Stanton in establishing the institution that he hoped would pray for his soul in perpetuity. It comprised a pair of accommodation wings, each two storeys high, linked by a central hall. Below the hall were kitchens and a selection of storerooms and pantries. The servants' wing stood behind these, along with outbuildings that included a barn, a brewery, a bakery and a series of sheds that were used for storage. Thirty years had taken their toll, however, and some of the once fine buildings were in dire need of repair. The north wing, where Bartholomew lived, had a leaking roof and faulty guttering, so that students and their masters were regularly doused with icy water in wet weather, and the walls were so slick with damp that mould marched up them in thick green columns.

While Bartholomew studied some loose tiles on the stable roof, Michael headed for the hall, his eyes fixed unblinkingly on the door beyond which his breakfast was waiting. He was not happy to find his progress interrupted by the appearance of Beadle Meadowman. Meadowman was looking flustered. In one hand he held the arm of a student, while the other gripped a smirking woman. The woman was called Una, and she was one of the town's prostitutes, while the student was one of Bartholomew's aspiring physicians. Bartholomew regarded the lad with weary resignation. Martyn de Quenhyth was always in some kind of trouble,' although the physician thought that even dealing with Quenhyth's silly scrapes was preferable to dwelling on his impending encounter with Philippa.

Quenhyth had arrived in Cambridge the previous September, determined to become a physician. Langelee had accepted him at Michaelhouse because he was able to pay the requisite fees, but Bartholomew had been less than impressed, and found Quenhyth arrogant, intense and joyless. The lad was no more popular with his fellow students, and was constantly the butt of their practical jokes. Bartholomew suspected that the teasing would stop if Quenhyth made an effort to be pleasant, but Quenhyth was just not the pleasant type.

He was tall and gangly, with long, ink-stained fingers that were tipped with gnawed nails. A thatch of brown curls had been hacked with a knife to reduce it to the length required of scholars, and his uniform was worn exactly according to the College's prescription. He possessed a mean, thin nose and a pair of pallid eyes that he turned accusingly on a group of his classmates, who just happened to have gathered nearby to study a psalter – something that immediately aroused Bartholomew's suspicions. He guessed they had adroitly manoeuvred themselves into a position where they would be able to hear what was happening. Among them were Sam Gray, a bright student with a cruel sense of humour, and Rob Deynman, a dull-witted lad who was tolerated at Michaelhouse because his wealthy father paid double fees.

'What have you done this time?' Bartholomew asked of Quenhyth, glancing at Una and hoping it was nothing too indecent. She giggled and winked at him.

'I have done nothing wrong,' declared Quenhyth primly. 'I am sure you know who is to blame, and it is not me!' He cast another venomous glower in the direction of the sniggering lads who vied for positions around the psalter. 'Your other students do not appreciate that I am here to learn, not to take part in their pranks. They are always trying to get me into trouble.'

'And what have they done now?' enquired Michael, giving Gray and Deynman a glare of his own to indicate what he thought about behaviour that kept him from his breakfast.

'They put a whore in my bed while I was asleep,' replied Quenhyth resentfully, giving Una a look that was every bit as black as the ones he had given the students. 'She was there when I awoke this morning.'

'I am not a whore,' objected Una hotly. The amused smirk was gone, replaced by an expression of righteous indignation. 'We call ourselves "Frail Sisters" these days. That means I have a trade, and am every bit as good as any other craftsmen. Lady Matilde – you know her, Doctor.' Here she gave Bartholomew a lascivious leer. 'She organised us into a proper guild, and said we should not let people look down at us when we are only earning an honest crust.'

'Frail Sisters?' asked Bartholomew, regarding Una uncertainly. 'I have not heard that expression before.'

'It is nicer than "whore".' She glowered at Quenhyth.

'The Honourable Fraternity of Frail Sisters should have told you that scholars are off limits for your many charms,' said Michael drolly. 'And so are the insides of Colleges and hostels.'

Una waved a dismissive hand. 'We are in and out of those all the time, Brother. Why should Michaelhouse be any different?'

'Because it is the place where both the Senior and the Junior Proctor reside,' replied Michael mildly. 'And unless you want to lose your night's earnings in fines, you would do well to remember that.' He snapped his fingers at the sniggering Gray. 'See the Frail Sister off the premises, Sam. And if I catch her here again, I shall hold *you* personally responsible.'

Quenhyth shot Gray a triumphant sneer when he saw that Michael had correctly identified the author of his troubles. Una blew Michael a salacious kiss before flouncing away on Gray's arm, accompanied by whistles and cat-calls from the psalter-reading students.

'I went to bed after compline – as Master Langelee said we should – and when I awoke *she* was there,' explained Quenhyth unpleasantly as Una left. 'She told me she had been there all night, and that we had had all manner of fun. She is lying, of course: I would remember doing the things *she* described.' He gave a fastidious shudder, and Bartholomew struggled not to laugh.

'I caught him trying to usher her out through the back gate,' said Meadowman disapprovingly. 'He spun me this tale about finding her when he awoke, but that does not sound very likely to me. A red-blooded man does not sleep when there is a handsome whore in his bed, especially a fine, strong lass like Una. Do you not agree, Brother?'

Wisely, Michael declined to enter that sort of debate while there were students listening with unconcealed delight. He fixed the hapless Quenhyth with a glare. 'You shall spend the day in the proctors' prison, while we shall give this matter some thought. Take him away, Meadowman.'

Quenhyth's indignant wails could be heard all across the yard as he protested his innocence to anyone who would listen, and a good many others besides.

'I do not know how you tolerate that self-righteous youngster in your classes without boxing his ears,' said Michael to Bartholomew as he resumed his walk to the hall. 'And I do not blame Gray and Deynman for trying to cut him down to size.'

Bartholomew wholly agreed with him.

The bell had finished chiming by the time the scholars had ascended the spiral staircase to the hall. A huge fire roared in the hearth, so that the room felt airless and stuffy after the chill of the morning. Fresh rushes were scattered across the floor in readiness for Christmas, and the sweet scent of them mingled pleasantly with the aroma of burning wood and the baked oatmeal that was being readied behind the servants' screen. Bartholomew and Michael walked to the dais and took their places at the high table, facing the ranks of assembled students in the body of the hall.

Presiding over the meal was the Master, Ralph de Langelee. He was a powerfully built man, who looked more like a mercenary than a scholar, and many who knew him believed he should have remained a soldier and left the business of education to those capable of independent thought. But despite his intellectual failings, Langelee was proving to be a fair and capable Master, which surprised many people. The College had been infamous for its mediocre food and chilly, fireless rooms before Langelee had arranged for himself to be elected. Two years on, Michaelhouse had wood and peat aplenty for the common rooms, and the quality of the food had improved. This was due at least in part to the fact that he had delegated the College finances to Michaelhouse's newest Fellow, John Wynewyk, who was good at driving hard bargains with the town's tradesmen.

To Langelee's left was Thomas Kenyngham, an elderly Gilbertine friar with fluffy white hair, a dreamy smile and a mistaken belief that all men were as good and kindly as him. The cadaverous theologian Thomas Suttone perched on Kenyngham's left, turning his unsmiling face towards the students, like Death selecting a victim. At the end of the table sat the Dominican music and astronomy master, John Clippesby. It was common knowledge that Clippesby was insane, although Langelee maintained there was no reason why this minor inconvenience should interfere with his teaching duties.

Bartholomew and Michael sat on Langelee's right, with Father William, who was also Michael's Junior Proctor. William was a stern, uncompromising Franciscan, whose inflexible beliefs and bigoted interpretation of the rules he was paid to enforce were swelling the University's coffers to the point of embarrassment. Michael confided to Bartholomew that William had fined more students in his first month of office than most other junior proctors caught in a year. However, Bartholomew also noticed that neither Michael nor the Chancellor had made any serious attempts to curtail the Franciscan's fiscal enthusiasm.

On Bartholomew's right was the last of the Fellows, Wynewyk. Wynewyk had been elected at the beginning of the Michaelmas Term, and was still clearly bewildered by some of the customs and practices of his new College. That day, he seemed puzzled by the fact that Clippesby had a fish under his arm. The other Fellows were used to Clippesby's idiosyncrasies, and Bartholomew found that he only noticed them if someone else pointed them out.

'Put it away, Clippesby, there's a good fellow,' said Langelee, following Wynewyk's gaze to where glazed eyes and a gaping mouth leered from beneath the music master's tabard. 'You know we do not allow animals to join us for meals.'

'This is not an animal,' said Clippesby, placing the thing carefully on the table. Bartholomew saw Wynewyk glance uneasily towards the door, as if wondering whether he would be able to reach it unimpeded, should it become necessary. The other scholars were merely impatient, giving the impression they wanted Clippesby to have done with his antics so they could get on with their meal.

'Is *is* an animal,' argued Father William immediately. He detested Clippesby, partly because William was not a man to waste his meagre supplies of compassion on lunatics, but mostly because Clippesby was a Dominican, and William did not like Dominicans. 'It is a fish, so of course it is an animal. It is not a stone or a vegetable, is it?' He leaned back and folded his arms, pleased with this incisive piece of logic.

Clippesby did not concur. 'This is an interesting philosophical question,' he said, turning his mad-eyed stare from the fish to the friar. 'Is a *dead* fish an animal? Or, since it no longer possesses life, is it something else?'

'Just because it is dead does not mean that it has changed,' argued William, determined not to be bested.

'But it *has* changed,' pressed Clippesby, waving the fish in the air, oblivious to the rotten scales that fell from it. 'A dead fish cannot be the same as a live one.'

'I agree with Clippesby,' said Bartholomew, earning himself a hostile glare from Michael for prolonging the debate, and an equally irate one from William for supporting his opponent. 'If you accept Aristotle's philosophy, you would argue that the fish has undergone what he termed "substantial change". This can occur in all substances that are composed of matter and form in the terrestrial region and, of course, all these forms and qualities are potentially replaceable by the other forms and qualities that are their contraries. That is what has occurred in Clippesby's fish.'

'It is?' asked Langelee doubtfully, clearly having forgotten his Aristotelian natural philosophy.

Bartholomew was surprised by the question. 'Of course! While one form is actualised in matter, its contrary is said to be in privation but is capable of replacing it. Obviously, each potential form or quality must become whatever it is capable of becoming, otherwise it would remain unactualised and that would be a contradiction.'

'Well, that shut everyone up,' said Michael gleefully, in the bemused silence that followed. 'Well done, Matt. Now let us say grace and eat.'

'*Oremus,*' began Langelee hastily, before someone could ask his opinion of the physician's postulations. He professed to be a philosopher, but was invariably confounded even by that discipline's most basic theoretical tenets. '*Spiritum nobis Domine, tuae caritatis infunde: ut, quos sacramentis paschalibus satiasti, tua facias pietate concordes.* And so on. *Dominus vobiscum.*'

'About time,' grumbled Michael, as he sat. 'I am starving, and I am tired of all this Advent fasting and abstaining from meat. It is not natural.'

Bartholomew shot him a sidelong glance, wondering whether the monk had genuinely forgotten the meaty meals he had devoured over the past few weeks or whether his intention was merely to deceive his colleagues into believing he had been following the season's dietary prohibitions – similar to those of Lent, although not quite so long.

'There is only one more day for you to endure,' said Kenyngham kindly. 'And then it will be time for feasting, as we celebrate the birth of our Lord.'

'Cynric told me that Philippa Abigny's brother, Giles, is here, too,' remarked William, somewhat out of the blue. He beamed at Bartholomew in a friendly fashion, as though he imagined the physician would be pleased to chat about the presence of his old fiancée in the town.

Bartholomew's heart sank, and he realised that even if he managed to put Philippa from his mind, his colleagues' interest was such that they would be constantly raising the subject. Giles Abigny, after all, had known them, too.

'Do you remember Giles, Michael?' the friar went on airily. 'He was Matthew's room-mate during the Death.' He wrinkled his nose in disapproval. 'I recall him very well. He was a flighty fellow with long yellow hair. I would have fined him, if I had been Junior Proctor then.'

'I am sure you would,' muttered Bartholomew. He did not know how the Franciscan dared to be so strict with others, given his own appearance. William's habit was so stiff with filth that it was virtually rigid, while there were circles of ancient dirt under his cracked, yellow fingernails. He was too mean to pay a barber to shave his tonsure and opted to do it himself, which resulted in an irregular oval that sprouted hairs in varying stages of growth. The spiky curls that surrounded the tonsure were brown and thick with grease.

'Short of stature,' added Michael, recollecting Giles Abigny, as he reached for the ale jug. 'But with the same fair complexion and blue eyes as his beautiful sister. You were a fool to let her go, Matt. You should have married her while you had the chance.'

'She married someone else,' said Bartholomew tartly. 'I had little say in the matter.'

Michael scratched his head as memories floated back to him, most more than slightly distorted by time. 'Philippa went to London after the Death, because she was restless in Cambridge and Giles was no longer here to look after her.'

'He did not look after her, anyway,' said William pedantically. 'She was at St Radegund's Convent, under the watchful eye of the abbess. I recall that there was some pressure on her to take holy vows and become a nun, so that the convent could keep her dowry.'

'That was not going to happen as long as Matt was courting her,' Michael pointed out. 'But, fortunately for Philippa, parents and abbess died during the plague, and Giles left her free to choose her own destiny. She followed him to London, doubtless anticipating that Matt would not be long in joining her. What happened to Giles, Matt? He was never a very committed scholar.'

'I have no idea,' said Bartholomew stiffly. He had tried to put his entire association with the Abigny family behind him. He had liked the flighty and unreliable Giles, but Philippa's defection to another man had not encouraged him to maintain a correspondence with her brother.

'He became a law clerk,' said Michael, snapping his fingers as fragments of memory drifted back to him. 'Although the post was not an especially prestigious one.'

'Why did you not marry Philippa, Matthew?' asked William bluntly. 'I was under the impression it was a sound match.'

'The problem arose with Philippa herself,' said Michael, carelessly dispensing the details of Bartholomew's failed love affair as he might give a public lecture. 'Once she had sampled the delights of London, she realised she could not bear to spend her life as the wife of an impoverished physician, so she married a wealthy merchant instead. And that was the end of Matt's hopes for wedded bliss – with her, at least.'

'You are better off here, with us,' said William, in what was meant to be a consoling tone, but served to make Bartholomew wonder where he had gone wrong.

He pictured Philippa's merry eyes and grace. He could have been celebrating Christmas with her that year, surrounded by their children. But even as the cosy image entered his mind, he knew the reality would have been different. Michael was right: Philippa had set certain standards for her life, and Bartholomew's haphazard way of collecting fees from his patients would never have met them. He would have made her miserable with poverty, while she would have nagged him to spend time with wealthy clients who needed an astrologer rather than a physician. Abruptly, the image faded to a chamber with a meagre fire, occupied by a discontented wife and dissatisfied children. He supposed he should be happy with what he had: his teaching, Michaelhouse, his poor patients with their interesting diseases, and Matilde. The thought of Matilde coaxed a smile to his face.

He tried to analyse his thoughts rationally, to determine why Philippa's presence in the town should matter to him. Logically, he knew he should not care, but illogically, the prospect of encountering her filled him with dread, and he seriously considered visiting a friend in some nearby village until she had gone. But he enjoyed Christmas, with its feasts, games and entertainment. And he liked the chaos that ensued when the students elected their Lord of Misrule, who would dictate what happened in Michaelhouse over the Twelve Days. It would be a pity to miss that, just because a woman he had once loved happened to be passing through.

Or would it? Michael would drag him into Norbert's murder investigation, while Gray was almost certain to be elected Lord of Misrule. Because Gray was Bartholomew's student, he suspected that he might be held responsible for some of the lad's wilder schemes – and Gray could be very wild indeed. Perhaps it would be a good time to renew friendships with folk who lived somewhere other than Cambridge. But then hard pellets of snow pattered against the hall's glass windows, and he was reminded that it was no time to be considering journeys into the country.

'We should not be discussing this lady here,' said Kenyngham sympathetically, breaking into his thoughts. 'It is never wise to dwell on matters that were once painful.'

'True,' agreed Michael, as though he had many jilted fiancées of his own to consider. 'Now, what were you saying earlier about unactualised forms and qualities, Matt?'

'I do not hold with talking at the table,' said William, who did not want to resume a debate that he would probably lose. 'The season for chatter at mealtimes is not yet upon us, so summon the Bible Scholar, Master, and let us consider some religious text.'

Langelee snapped his fingers, and the student who received a free education in return for reading from the scriptures during meals stepped up to the lectern. The lad opened the book and rested his elbows on the edge of the stand, then gave a howl of alarm as the whole thing toppled to the ground with a resounding crash. After the initial shock, the other students started to laugh.

'God's blood!' swore Langelee. 'What happened?'

'Someone has taken a saw to it,' said Bartholomew, who could see the tell-tale striations in the wood from where he sat. He found himself looking at Gray, whose face revealed nothing, and Deynman, whose expression bespoke abject guilt. 'I suppose this was one of the tricks planned for the Season of Misrule.'

'William will have to do without his Bible today,' said Langelee. 'And if the lectern is mended, I may be prepared to overlook this sorry incident.'

Deynman puffed out his cheeks in a sigh of relief, although, predictably, there was still no reaction from Gray. Bartholomew thought Gray should choose his accomplices with more care; Deynman had given them away almost at once. But it would not matter for much longer, because Gray planned to leave Michaelhouse soon, to take up a prestigious post in Suffolk. Bartholomew was certain he would be successful – the lad was too sly and manipulative to do otherwise.

'What have you been doing to produce such a healthy appetite?' said Langelee of Michael, watching the monk peel three hard-boiled eggs and eat them whole, one after the other. 'Another murder? You have not had one of those for a year now – although I suppose you solved some in Ely last summer.'

'Tulyet's cousin,' replied Michael, selecting the largest

piece of bread in the basket. 'He was found murdered in St Michael's Lane.'

'I heard,' said Langelee. 'That is too close to Michaelhouse for my liking. I hope you catch this killer quickly.'

'Then there is the puzzling case of the body in the church,' Michael continued. He leaned back to allow a servant to ladle a quantity of oatmeal into the bowl in front of him. 'Go on, man! Fill it! A dribble is no good for a man of my stature.'

The butler's face was expressionless as he spooned the thick porridge into Michael's bowl until there was a glutinous meniscus across the top. Only then did the monk incline his head to acknowledge that it was sufficient.

'Eat slowly, Brother,' admonished Bartholomew automatically, as the monk fell on the food like a starving peasant. 'There is enough for everyone, and this is not a race.'

'Huh!' muttered Michael, not bothering to hide his contempt for the physician's advice, since he knew perfectly well that Michaelhouse occasionally ran out of food before everyone had been served. And the fastest eaters were invariably the ones who secured seconds.

'Norbert's case will not be difficult to solve,' declared William, giving his horn spoon – still stained from his previous meal – a cursory wipe on the sleeve of his filthy habit. 'He was a vile lad, and Ovyng is well rid of him, although Ailred will miss the fees. But what about this other case – the body in the church? I have not heard about that. Is this another murder? You have not mentioned it to me – your Junior Proctor.'

'Matt said it was natural,' replied Michael, ignoring the reproachful tone of William's voice.

'I did not,' objected Bartholomew. 'I said he probably died from the cold. That is not the same thing.'

'So, he could have been frozen deliberately,' mused William with relish. 'That would be murder in my book. I shall set about making enquiries immediately.'

'Lord!' muttered Michael, alarmed by the prospect of

the Franciscan on the loose, accusing all and sundry of a murder that had never happened. 'We must find out who he was first. Will you do that? He was a beggar, who perhaps sought sanctuary from the weather in our church, and—'

'In *our* church?' interrupted Langelee in horror. 'You mean St Michael's?'

'No, the other one,' mumbled Michael facetiously. He spoke more loudly. 'He was hidden among the rotten albs, Master, although Matt thinks he had wrapped himself up for warmth. I was going to tell you about it yesterday, but it slipped my mind.'

'You must discover the identity of this man immediately,' said Langelee, alarmed. 'I cannot have unnamed corpses appearing in my church. And just before Christmas, too. I shall have to have it resanctified.'

'I shall do that – after I discover the killer,' offered William generously. 'Do not worry, Master. I shall have the whole matter resolved by nightfall. I shall begin by asking the Dominicans what they know about the matter.'

'You will spend your time discovering this beggar's name,' ordered Michael sternly. It would not be the first time the Franciscan used a crime to indulge his hatred of Dominicans, and Michael could not afford wild and unfounded accusations to damage the fragile truce between the Orders.

'We cannot sit here and chatter all day,' said Langelee abruptly, standing to say the final grace. He was a fast eater, and disliked sitting for longer than necessary when a busy day lay ahead of him. 'We all have work to do. *Pax vobiscum.*'

Several students looked at their full bowls in dismay, realising too late that they should have eaten instead of eavesdropped on the lively conversation at the high table. Michael's spoon made a harsh scraping sound as he reached the bottom of his dish – he was not a man to fall victim to Langelee's disconcerting habit of cutting mealtimes short – while Bartholomew and the others hastily drained theirs. Langelee dismissed the assembled scholars, marching purposefully from the hall in order to begin the many tasks that fell daily to the Master of a Cambridge College. Wynewyk hurried after him, muttering officiously about documents that needed to be signed if the scholars wanted food, drink and fuel for the Christmas season.

Michael reached for another piece of bread before the servants cleared the tables. 'I am glad I did not listen to your advice about how to eat, or I would be facing a morning without breakfast.'

'Gobbling is not good for you,' said Bartholomew stubbornly. 'It unbalances the humours and gives rise to pains in the stomach.'

'Christmas is a wonderful time for men with healthy appetites,' said Michael, thinking fondly of the gobbling that was to come. 'Twelve days with no teaching and plentiful food and wine.'

'But then come January and February,' said Bartholomew gloomily. 'I dislike those months, They are dark and cold, and it is painful to lose patients from afflictions of the lungs – like Dunstan the riverman. He will not see Easter.'

Michael was silent. Dunstan had been a loyal, if toneless, member of his choir for many years, and he was fond of the old man. It was hard for him to see Dunstan's suffering and be powerless to help.

'These are strange times,' announced Suttone, walking out of the hall with them. 'The Devil stalks the land, and God and His angels weep at what they see. Sinful men fornicate in holy places and debauchery, lust and greed are all around us. The river freezing in November is a testament to the fact that the end of the world is nigh. Things were different when I was a boy.'

'People always think the past was better than the present,' said Bartholomew, who had grown used to the Carmelite's grim predictions. 'But I do not think they are very different now – except for the Death, of course.'

'The Death,' pronounced the Carmelite in a booming voice that was sufficiently sepulchral to send a shiver of unease down Bartholomew's spine. 'It will come again. You mark my words.'

'But not before Christmas,' said Michael comfortably. 'We shall at least have a good feast before we die.'

Bartholomew found he could not dismiss Philippa from his thoughts, and barely heard Suttone regaling Michael with details of the plague's return as he walked across the yard to his room. He recalled how she had admired the fine oriel window in the hall, but had thought Bartholomew's chamber cold and gloomy. He remembered walking with her through the herb garden, when the summer sun warmed the plants and sweetened the air with their fragrance. And he was reminded of the times he had climbed over the College walls like an undergraduate after the gates had been locked, because assignations with her had made him late.

'I thought you might like this,' said the insane Clippesby shyly, breaking into his thoughts by sidling up and offering him a stained and lumpy bundle. Bartholomew could see a glistening tail protruding from one end of it. He was being offered the fish that Clippesby had taken to breakfast.

'He has just eaten,' said Michael. 'He does not need to consume a squashed pike just yet, thank you. And anyway, it has been dead far too long already. It stinks.'

'It is a tench,' said Bartholomew. 'Where did you find it, Clippesby?'

Clippesby was pleased by the physician's curiosity. 'On Milne Street, near Piron Lane. It had been tossed there, probably by someone walking past.' He turned a resentful gaze on Michael. 'Matt knows perfectly well that I am not bringing this for him to eat. It is common knowledge that tench have healing powers.'

'Do they?' asked Michael of Bartholomew doubtfully.

Bartholomew nodded. 'Pliny says that tench applied to the hands or feet can cure fevers, jaundice, head pains and toothache. But, more importantly, I am sure this was the fish I saw the night Norbert died. Whoever pushed me over grabbed it before he escaped.'

'Then how did it end up abandoned on Milne Street?' asked Michael. 'It is a wretched thing – already rotten, despite its salting. Why would your attacker risk capture for it?'

'Perhaps he did not know its state when he acted,' suggested Bartholomew. 'He only learned it was bad when he took off the wrappings – at which point he discarded it.'

'It was thrown into some bushes,' added Clippesby helpfully. 'I would not have noticed it, but one of the cats mentioned it was there, so I went to look.'

'A cat told you to ferret about behind some shrubs?' asked Michael dubiously. 'You should choose your friends more carefully, man. You do not know what you might unearth, foraging around in places like that.'

Bartholomew surmised that Clippesby had observed a cat expressing an unusual interest in the spot where the fish had been thrown and had gone to investigate. The mad musician's claims about talking to animals nearly always had some rational explanation behind them.

'We have already deduced that Norbert's killer and the man who pushed me were not the same,' the physician mused. 'So, I suppose this means that the tench is also irrelevant.'

'Probably,' said Michael. 'But I do not want to dispense with evidence prematurely. Will you store it in the basement, Clippesby? Hide it well, or we may find it served up for dinner in a week. You know how Michaelhouse's nasty policy of "waste not, want not" works these days.'

Smiling amiably, Clippesby wandered away with his fishy prize, stopping to exchange pleasantries with the porter's cockerel as he went.

'Do you really think the tench might be significant to Norbert's case, or was that just a ruse to remove Clippesby and the rank odour of fish?' Bartholomew was laughing.

Michael remained sombre. 'Both. William thinks it will be simple to solve Norbert's murder, because it will be easy to identify people who did not like him. But he is wrong: I think it will be very difficult to isolate the real culprit. Perhaps your assailant had nothing to do with Norbert, but I will keep him in mind until I am absolutely certain. And since he considered the fish sufficiently important to grab before he ran away, we shall keep that, too.'

'Look,' said Bartholomew, pointing to the front gate as it was suddenly flung open and an important visitor was ushered inside. 'There is Sheriff Morice, waving to catch your attention. He is all yours, Brother. I have work to do, and I should probably pay my respects to Phillippa . . .' He faltered. Meeting the woman he had almost married was not something he wanted to do at all.

'Wait,' said Michael, shooting out a fat, white hand to prevent Bartholomew from escaping. The physician did not bother to shake him off. He had decided that an interview with the corrupt Sheriff was infinitely preferable to an encounter with Phillippa Abigny. 'I do not trust him,' Michael continued, 'and it would be good to have a witness to anything he says.'

'Brother Michael!' said Morice, advancing on the monk with a smile that reminded Bartholomew of a leering demon he had once seen on a wall painting. Morice was a dark-haired, swarthy man with curiously blue eyes and a beard and moustache that went some way, but not all, to disguising a mean-lipped mouth. His shoulders were slightly rounded, and he might have been a scholar, were it not for his extravagant robes and handsome water-resistant boots.

'Sheriff,' said Michael politely. 'What brings you to our humble abode?'

Morice looked around him, noting the rotting timber and the loose tiles on the roof, and seemed to concur with Michael's description. 'I have come about Norbert. The boy was a wastrel and the Tulyets are well rid of him, but murder is murder, and I do not want the relatives of wealthy merchants slain on my streets. Have you done anything or shall I look into it?'

'I have been investigating,' said Michael coolly. 'Norbert was a student, and therefore his death comes under University jurisdiction.'

'But he was the kinsman of a burgess,' said Morice, not at all disconcerted by Michael's unfriendly tone. 'So his death comes under my jurisdiction, as far as I am concerned. Will you hand the culprit to me now, or shall I hunt out the guilty scholar myself?'

'What makes you think the killer is a scholar?' asked Bartholomew, feeling his hackles rise at the man's presumption. 'Since Norbert spent his last few hours in a tavern, it is likely the murderer was a patron of the King's Head – a tavern frequented by townsfolk.'

Morice's dark features broke into a sneer. 'I guessed this would happen. You know the identity of Norbert's killer, but you are protecting him by having a townsman convicted of the crime instead. Very well, then. I shall initiate my own enquiries. *I* will expose the culprit – be he one of the beggars in tabards who claim to be students or the Chancellor himself.' He turned on his heel and stalked across the yard.

'No wonder Tulyet was so keen for you to investigate,' said Bartholomew, watching the Sheriff shove the porter out of the way when the man fumbled with the door. 'He knows any enquiries Morice makes will not reveal the true killer.'

'But they may result in a scapegoat,' said Michael worriedly. 'And you can be sure that Morice will demand full punishment according to the law. If I do not want to see innocent scholars hang, there is no time to waste.'

'Do you need help?' asked Bartholomew reluctantly. He was loath to leave the College now he knew that Philippa was in the town.

Michael smiled. 'I plan to spend the day learning exactly what Norbert did on his last night, which will mean time in the King's Head, and I do not need you for that. But I may need you tomorrow, if my enquiries lead me nowhere.'

Bartholomew had a bad feeling that Michael would be unsuccessful and that the Twelve Days of Christmas were going to be spent tracking down a killer.

'Philippa Abigny,' mused Michael, as he lounged comfortably in a chair in the conclave that evening. The conclave was a small chamber that adjoined the hall, used by the Fellows as somewhere to sit and talk until it was time to go to bed. It was a pleasant room, with wall hangings that lent it a cosy atmosphere, and rugs scattered here and there. Although there was glass in the windows – fine new glass, made using the latest technology – the shutters were closed, and rattled occasionally as the wind got up outside. The wooden floor was well buffed and smelled of beeswax, so that the conclave's overwhelming and familiar odour comprised polished wood, smoke from the fire and faint overtones of the evening meal that had been served in the hall.

It was already well past eight o'clock, and Bartholomew, William and Michael were the only ones who had not gone to their rooms. William was there because there was still wine to drink and, despite his outward advocacy of abstinence and self-denial, the friar was a man who liked his creature comforts, particularly the liquid kind. Michael was there because he was obliged to be at the church at midnight to perform Angel Mass, and did not want to go to bed for only a few hours. Bartholomew had remained because he was unsettled by Philippa's presence in the town.

'Philippa Abigny,' echoed William, walking to the table, where the wine stood in a large pewter jug. He stumbled near the door, where the floorboards had worked loose within the last three weeks and needed to be fastened down. Reluctant to hire a carpenter to solve the problem so near the expensive season of Christmas, Langelee had placed a rug over the offending section, but it tended to 'walk' and was not always where it needed to be. William refilled his goblet, then carried the jug to Michael, who had been hastily draining his cup to ensure he did not miss out. Bartholomew followed suit, feeling that plenty of wine was the only way he would sleep that night.

'Philippa Abigny,' said Michael again, setting his cup near the hearth so that the flames would warm it, then leaning back in his chair.

'Are you two going to spend all night just saying her name over and over?' snapped Bartholomew testily. 'I have said I would rather talk about something else – like Norbert's murder. What did you learn today, Brother?'

Michael's expression became sombre. 'After Norbert left Ovyng the night he died there is an hour unaccounted for until he arrived at the King's Head. He met a woman there, but of course no one will tell me who she was.'

'Was he drunk and free with his insults?' asked William. 'If so, then the case is solved: one of the patrons in the King's Head is the guilty party.'

'He was drunk, but apparently no more insulting than normal. I understand some kind of gambling was in progress, but, again, no one will tell me who Norbert played. However, the innkeeper hinted that Norbert lost more than he won, so there is no reason to think he was killed by a disenfranchised gaming partner. He apparently left in reasonable humour.'

'That can change fast,' warned Bartholomew. 'Even a small insult is sometimes enough to turn tipsy bonhomie into enraged fury. Men soaked in wine are not rational people.'

'True, but there is nothing to suggest that happened to Norbert. He left the King's Head at midnight, and no one who lives between the tavern and Ovyng admits to hearing any affray.'

'So, now what?' asked Bartholomew. 'Where will you go from here?'

Michael sighed. 'I do not know. Morice's men followed me today, so I decided to concentrate on the taverns. I was afraid they would conclude that the killer was at Ovyng if I spent too much time there. Damn Morice! He will make my work much more difficult.'

'Not necessarily,' said William meaningfully.

Michael frowned. 'What do you mean? I want no help from him or his men – I could not trust anything they told me.'

'But his soldiers would be more than happy to spend an afternoon in a tavern with free beer,' said William. 'And Morice would agree that his mother killed Norbert, if the price were right.'

'You mean Michael should bribe the Sheriff?' asked Bartholomew uneasily.

William shrugged. 'It would not be the first time, and the fines I have imposed on rule-breakers means that the proctors' chest is nicely full at the moment. We can afford it, and I would like to see Norbert's death properly investigated by men like me, who know what they are doing, without the "help" of Morice and his men.'

Bartholomew turned to Michael, horrified. 'You have bribed Morice before? You should be careful, Brother! Corrupting a King's official is a criminal offence, and you may find that Morice is the kind of man to accept money, then make a complaint about you.'

'Believe me, I know,' said Michael dryly. 'But the man is impossible to reason with, so we may have to resort to desperate measures if no answer to this crime is forthcoming. He is making no serious effort to investigate himself, but is concentrating on thwarting me. He does not care about avenging Norbert, only about seeing whether he can turn the situation to his advantage. We have not had a corrupt Sheriff for so long that I barely recall how to deal with them.'

They were silent for a while, each thinking his own thoughts. Michael and William considered the problem of an awkward Sheriff and a difficult murder, while Bartholomew found his mind returning to Philippa's pretty face, flowing golden curls and slender figure. He was disconcerted to find he could not remember certain details – what her hands looked like, for example – although other things were etched deeply in his memory. He knew how she laughed, that there was a freckle on the lobe of her left ear, that she liked cats but not dogs, and that she hated the smell of lavender.

The hour candle dipped lower. A little less than three hours remained before Angel Mass marked the beginning of Christmas Day, and there was an air of expectation and excitement in the College. Bartholomew opened a shutter and gazed through the window. Lights burned in almost every room, as scholars elected to remain awake, rather than rise early. Snow was in the air again, and came down in spiteful little flurries that did not settle. It had snowed when the Death had come, too, he recalled, and the bitter weather had added to the miseries of both patients and the physicians who tended them. Philippa had disliked the cold. She preferred summer, when the crops grew golden and the land baked slowly under a silver-white sun.

'Did you discover the identity of the man we found dead among the albs?' he asked of William, pulling his mind away from his reverie.

'No one knows him. Not even Bosel the beggar, who works on the High Street.'

'You have spoken to Bosel?' Michael was disappointed. 'Damn! He was my best hope.'

'I even asked the Dominicans whether they had killed him,' William went on airily.

Bartholomew regarded him in disbelief. 'But there was nothing on the body to suggest he was murdered. I told you I thought he had died of the cold.'

'How did the Dominicans respond to this subtle probing?' asked Michael curiously. 'Did they confess?'

William grimaced. 'They did not. However, unlikely though it may seem, I believe they were telling the truth.'

'And why is that, pray?' asked Michael, amused.

'Because most have not been outside their friary since this sudden cold spell began,' replied William. 'Dominicans are soft and weak, and need to crouch in their lairs with roaring fires and plenty of wine.' He took a deep draught of his claret and stretched his feet closer to the flames with a sigh of contentment.

'I can cross the Dominicans off my list of suspects, then,' said Michael wryly. His expression hardened. 'However, there is one man I cannot dismiss: Harysone.'

'Not this again,' groaned Bartholomew. 'There is no reason to think that Harysone had anything to do with this death, either.'

'Only the fact that we saw him go into the church, and then moments later we discover a corpse in it. What more do you want?'

'We did *not* see him go into the church,' Bartholomew pointed out. 'We saw him fiddle with the lock, but then we went to see Norbert's body and we do not know if he entered or not. The latch sticks, and Harysone would not be the first would-be visitor to be thwarted. He may have given up and gone elsewhere.'

'Well, it was not to another church,' said William authoritatively. Bartholomew and Michael stared at him questioningly, and the Franciscan looked pleased with himself. 'I made a few enquiries about that, too. I asked in all the churches whether a man matching Harysone's description had visited on Thursday, and was told he had not.'

Bartholomew was doubtful. 'But most would have been empty,' he pointed out. 'It was daytime, and people were working.'

'Not so,' said William, bristling with pride at his cleverness. 'It is Christmas, and the time when peasants deck out the churches with greenery. All of them were busy, except ours: in a scholars' church like St Michael's such pagan practices are not permitted.'

'I heard Langelee giving my choir – which comprises mostly townfolk – permission to deck it out this evening,' said Michael wickedly. 'It will be as green with yew and holly as any other, come tomorrow.'

William shot out of his chair and looked set to stalk to the hapless building and strip it bare there and then. He faltered when Michael pointed out that there was a frost outside, but a fire and wine inside. It did not take much to persuade the Franciscan to sit and resume their discussion.

'So,' concluded Michael. 'We do not know why Harysone wanted to enter St Michael's, but we do know that he did not visit another church. Therefore, I suspect that he *did* enter St Michael's, and that his business there was successful.'

'You cannot be sure about that,' said Bartholomew, thinking that the monk was allowing his dislike of the man to interfere with his powers of reason. 'And anyway, if folk were merrily pinning holly to rafters, who knows what they did and did not see? Harysone is not particularly noticeable; he could easily slip past people unobserved.'

'We will know tomorrow, Brother, because you have *me* to help with the enquiry,' said William confidently. He stood and stretched, unsteady from the amount of wine he had drunk. 'But we should go to bed, and snatch an hour of sleep before Angel Mass. Tomorrow you and I will catch a killer, and Matthew can face the woman who should have been his wife.'

Bartholomew winced and went to fill his cup again, feeling that he needed yet more wine to dull the peculiar sensation of unease and dissatisfaction that gnawed at him. He heard a sudden yell, and whipped around just in time to see William shoot across the floor in a blur of flapping habit and windmilling arms. The Franciscan collided with the door and went down hard. For a moment, no one said anything, then William released a litany of curses that would have impressed the most foul-mouthed of stable-lads. Bartholomew exchanged a startled glance with Michael, wondering how the friar had acquired such an extensive vocabulary of secular oaths.

'My leg,' shouted William, more angry than in pain. 'It is broken!'

'It is not,' said Bartholomew, inspecting it. 'It is bruised.'

'But you do not know the agony it is giving,' bellowed

William, outraged. 'It is growing more painful by the moment.'

'Bruises are painful,' agreed Bartholomew. 'But it will feel better in a day or two.'

'It *is* broken,' said Michael with a wicked smile. 'You will be confined to College for the next two months while it heals, William. What a pity! It will be hard to lose my Junior Proctor for so long and the fines chest will suffer. Shall I fetch wood and bandages for a splint?'

'It is *not* broken,' declared Bartholomew, wondering what the monk thought he was trying to achieve by contradicting his diagnosis. 'So it does not need a splint.'

'It is and it does,' said William firmly. 'And I shall want crutches, too, although I cannot venture out of the College as long as there is ice on the ground. I might slip and do myself an even greater mischief.'

'Just splint it, Matt,' advised Michael, preparing to fetch the equipment the physician would need. He lowered his voice, so that William could not hear. 'You will be doing us all a favour. I do not want his "help" to solve Norbert's murder, and this is a perfect chance for me to be rid of him without embarrassing tantrums.'

Reluctantly, Bartholomew set about immobilising the damaged limb, becoming even more certain as he worked that William was exaggerating the seriousness of his injury. William made a terrible fuss, however, and his unfriarly shrieks soon had scholars hurrying to the conclave to see what was happening. The other Fellows formed a silent circle around the stricken friar, while the students jostled each other at the door in an attempt to see what was going on.

'Langelee will pay for this!' William howled, snatching with ill grace the goblet of wine Suttone offered him. 'I told him he should pay a carpenter to mend the floor, and not just hide the damage with a rug.'

'I will hire one tomorrow,' said Langelee tiredly. 'We can probably raise the funds somehow.'

'We cannot,' said Wynewyk immediately. 'We have spent

every last penny on supplies for the Twelve Days, and our coffers will be empty until Ovyng pays us rent for next term.'

'Hiring a carpenter will not be necessary,' said Kenyngham. 'I had some training with wood before I became a friar. I shall mend the floor – but not until the Twelve Days are over.'

'Very well,' said Langelee, although he did not seem happy with the notion of entrusting saws, hammers and nails to the other-worldly Gilbertine, even if it would save the College some money. He turned to William. 'Your leg will confine you to your room for some days, but we shall have the floor mended by the time you have convalesced.'

'Convalesced,' mused William with a gleam in his eye. 'I shall certainly convalesce – with good food and wine! But I cannot abandon Michael completely. He can bring suspects for interrogation here, to Michaelhouse.'

'I do not think so,' said Michael hastily. 'We do not want criminals and miscreants in the College, thank you very much!'

'We do not,' agreed Langelee firmly. 'I am sure we can find some administrative duties to occupy your time, Father. There is always teaching. That will not require you to walk.'

'It will,' cried William, seeing that he was about to exchange duties he enjoyed, for ones he did not. 'I cannot teach unless I pace. However, I am sure I can do something to help Michael.'

'Yes, you can, actually,' said Michael. 'You can deal with the beadles' claim for more pay that we have been avoiding all year. Thank you for your kind offer. I accept most gratefully.'

William's face was a mask of unhappiness as he was carried from the conclave.

After William had been settled in his room with a jug of wine, Bartholomew retired to his own chamber to nap until Angel Mass. He slept well, despite his fears that he would not manage a wink, and wondered whether he owed that to the wine or to the fact that William's leg had allowed his pre-sleep thoughts to concentrate on medicine.

Just before midnight he woke, when the sky was at its darkest. He hopped across the icy flagstones in his bare feet, aiming for the water Cynric left for him each day. The temperature had plummeted since he had retired, and the water had started to freeze so he was obliged to smash a crust of ice with the heel of his boot. He lit a candle, then began to shave, jumping from foot to foot in a futile attempt to stave off the painful, aching sensation in his legs that always accompanied standing on Michaelhouse's stone floors in the winter.

Shaving completed, he donned shirt and hose, then tugged on a pair of shoes – new ones in the latest fashion that were fastened with an ankle strap and had stylish pointed toes. Over the shirt, he drew on a laced gipon – a garment with long sleeves and a padded body that was thigh length and very warm. His scholar's tabard went over that.

Quietly, so as not to wake the scholars who were still sleeping, he headed across the courtyard to see William. The friar's snores were loud enough to have made sleep impossible for the two students who had been instructed to stay with him that night. One was Quenhyth, who sat self-ishly close to the lamp as he read some medical tract; the other, a Franciscan novice called Ulfrid, was rolling gambling bones on the windowsill to pass the time. Both looked up when Bartholomew arrived, and Quenhyth went through an elaborate pantomime designed to ensure that his master knew he had been working.

'William will fine you if he catches you playing with those,' said Bartholomew in a low voice, addressing Ulfrid and trying to ignore Quenhyth.

Ulfrid slipped the bones inside his scrip, although he did not appear to be disconcerted to be caught breaking the College's rules about games of chance. He was a pleasant lad, with a scarred face resulting from some childhood pox.

'Sorry,' he whispered. 'But I won these bones in a bet with a man in a tavern, and it is hard to resist playing with things that are new.'

Bartholomew struggled not to smile, thinking about the various Franciscan and University rules the student had just blithely admitted to breaking – frequenting taverns, gambling and enjoying possessions. 'What kind of bet?' he asked conversationally.

Ulfrid was dismissive. 'The fellow had written an essay – he called it a book – about fish, and claimed that Galen's cure for infected wounds was to allow a living crab to eat out the rotten parts. I told him that Galen recommended an oyster, not a crab, and that it was but one of many remedies for that particular condition.'

Bartholomew was impressed. 'You are not a student of medicine, yet you know Galen?'

Ulfrid grinned. 'Your description of cures for infections last week was so vivid and horrible that you claimed the attention of every student in the room, even though most were supposed to be listening to different lessons. You will not find a scholar in the College who does not know Galen's solutions for festering wounds. It served me well, though: it won me a pair of dice.'

'I am glad to hear it was of some use,' said Bartholomew, not sure what he should deduce about his teaching skills from Ulfrid's careless confidences. 'The man who wrote this essay – was his name Harysone?'

Ulfrid nodded. 'He is staying at the King's Head while he persuades people to buy his book. However, if his knowledge of Galen is anything to go by, I think folk should save their money.'

Bartholomew was inclined to agree. 'Why was he making bets?'

'He wants to make lots of people aware of his book,' said Ulfrid disapprovingly. 'You know how it is: if people know about a thing they are more likely to buy it, regardless of whether it is good or bad. The same thing happened last

79

year with gum mastic – it was said to remove the scent of wine from the breath and was an excellent glue. People's obsession with it faded after a while, but not before enough had been sold to float the ark.'

'So, Harysone is selling his wares,' mused Bartholomew. 'It seems he was telling Michael the truth. He said he was here to dispense copies of his work.'

'He dances,' said Ulfrid, more disapprovingly than ever. 'In a way I have never seen before. I did not know whether to laugh or be offended. It reminded me of a Turkish whore I once saw in Bath. His display certainly seized everyone's attention – which I imagine was what he intended.'

Bartholomew took his leave of Ulfrid, and wandered into the yard. There were three masses planned for Christmas Day, a pattern that would be repeated at churches, friaries and abbeys all over the country. At midnight there was Angel Mass, a pretty occasion, with candles filling the church with golden light, and the building rich with the scent of freshly cut branches. Bartholomew went to his room to don his ceremonial gown and hat, then waited in line with his colleagues until Langelee led the procession to St Michael's.

Wynewyk went first, struggling under the weight of an immense cross that was part of the College's treasury and that had been a gift from a wealthy benefactor. Bartholomew hoped he would not drop the thing – at least, not while the townsfolk were looking – and was grateful it only made an appearance on special occasions.

Behind Wynewyk walked Langelee, resplendent in his best robes. He cut a fine figure, his broad shoulders and barrel-shaped body made even more impressive by the addition of ample gold braiding and tassels. Bartholomew thought he looked like a wall hanging, and preferred the simpler style of the Fellows' ceremonial gowns. These were ankle-length, and tied with a belt at the waist. They were made of scarlet worsted cloth, and the hem and neck were trimmed with fur – ermine for most, although Bartholomew's was squirrel. The hats matched, and formed a 'hood turban' once they had been twisted around the head and the folds arranged properly.

The students followed the Fellows, also dressed in their finery, and bringing up the rear were the servants. Agatha the laundress was at the very end, doubtless believing that the best had been saved for last. She wore a sleeved surcoat that was designed to hold the contours of the body. In Agatha's case this was unfortunate, given that those contours should have been reserved for her eyes only. She had persuaded the barber to arrange her hair in the latest fashion, which comprised vertical plaits running from the temples to the jaw and held in place by a net. It made her face appear even larger and more square, and Bartholomew saw several onlookers gape at the spectacle as she strode majestically past them.

'Langelee has hired jugglers for the Twelve Days,' said Clippesby to no one in particular as they walked. Talking while processing to mass was frowned upon, but without William's disapproving presence, the scholars were more inclined to break the rules. 'They are due to arrive tomorrow.'

'Are you sure?' asked Kenyngham, surprised. 'We have never had jugglers before.'

'Jugglers, singers *and* dancers,' elaborated Suttone disapprovingly. Since arriving at Michaelhouse, he had adopted some of William's more austere habits and had become increasingly humourless and dismal. 'It is wrong, in my humble opinion. The Twelve Days should be a time for prayer and contemplation, not for heathen rites.'

'We have been praying and contemplating all through Advent,' commented Michael bitterly. 'I think it is an excellent idea to hire a few entertainers. After all, King's Hall does it.'

'King's Hall is a secular institution,' argued Suttone. 'It is a training ground for men who will eventually work as clerks for the King. Michaelhouse, however, is a College noted for the religious vocations of its Fellows and masters.'

'Not all of them,' said Clippesby brightly. 'Matt has

81

not taken major orders, and neither have Langelee and Wynewyk.'

'Nonetheless, I feel it is inappropriate to demean our celebrations by adding a secular element to them,' insisted Suttone primly. 'I want no jugglers, dancers or singers at any feast *I* attend.'

'The jugglers are not very talented,' Clippesby went on, ignoring him. 'I saw them performing in the Market Square, before Langelee secured their services for Michaelhouse.'

'Heaven help us!' breathed Wynewyk uneasily. 'If you find fault with them, they must be dire indeed. You are not a critical man.'

'Do you mean the troupe who wear red and gold?' asked Bartholomew of Clippesby, recalling that he had watched them from behind a tombstone when Michael had been stalking Harysone. 'You are right: they are not very good.'

'There are four of them,' Clippesby went on. 'Two men and two women.'

'Women?' gasped Suttone in a horrified screech. '*Women?*'

'Excellent,' said Michael, rubbing his hands together in gleeful delight. 'That should liven the place up a little.'

'You will be disappointed with their work,' warned Clippesby, as if he imagined that the monk's pleasure derived solely from anticipation of the troupe's artistic talents. 'However, the election of the Lord of Misrule will provide us with a good deal of enjoyment.'

'Do not tell me Michaelhouse permits *that* dreadful custom, too!' groaned Suttone, holding one bony hand to his head in despair. 'I thought we were above that kind of thing.'

'We are not, thank God,' said Michael vehemently. 'Who will the students elect? Do you know, Matt?'

'I hope it is not Gray again,' replied Bartholomew uneasily. 'He is too clever, and knows exactly how to create the most havoc. We would be better with someone more sober – like Ulfrid – who would temper his excesses with common sense.'

'You sound like William,' said Michael disapprovingly. 'Where is your sense of fun, man? This is the season when conventions are abandoned and regulations are relaxed. It has its purpose: the easing of rules makes people understand why they are there in the first place, and actually serves to enforce the proper order of things when the celebrations are over. And anyway, it does not hurt for convention to be flouted for a few days each year.'

'It depends on what exactly is being flouted,' Suttone pointed out. 'But we shall see. How are your enquiries proceeding over the death of Norbert?'

'They are not,' said Michael gloomily. 'I spent yesterday trawling the taverns in search of anyone who might be able to tell us about Norbert and his woman – Dympna. But I discovered nothing I did not already know.'

'Dympna?' asked Kenyngham, startled. 'But she is a saint.'

'You know her?' asked Michael eagerly. 'Who is she? Why do you imagine her to be saintly? She cannot be that virtuous if she was dallying with Norbert.'

'No, I mean she is a *saint*,' repeated Kenyngham. 'She was a princess in ancient times, who allowed herself to be slain rather than succumb to the unwanted attentions of her incestuous father. She was kind to the poor and especially understanding of the insane.'

'Clippesby should petition her, then,' said Suttone matter-of-factly.

'I doubt a long-dead princess has been sending Norbert notes,' said Michael, disappointed. 'I need to know about a real, living Dympna, not someone who died centuries ago.' He turned back to Bartholomew. 'I have nothing to pass to Dick Tulyet – at least, nothing I feel I can tell him. Norbert had huge debts, and I have learned that if women were not available to satiate his needs, then men would do. This means that I cannot even be sure that Dympna is a lady. She could be anything, even an animal.'

'Animals do not arrange to meet their lovers by writing notes, any more than do dead saints,' Bartholomew pointed out. 'So, I think you can safely confine your enquiries to living humans.'

Angel Mass passed without incident, and Bartholomew forgot Philippa as he admired what the parishioners had done to the church. Every window boasted a woven wreath of yew and rosemary, and someone had managed to climb up to the rafters to hang bunches of herbs from them, so that the church was sweetly fragrant with their scent. It even masked the stale odour of the old albs. Mistletoe, being a pagan plant, was, of course, banned from churches, although Bartholomew saw white berries hidden among one or two of the wreaths, as the townsfolk staged a discreet rebellion. As he watched Michael and Kenyngham celebrate mass at the high altar, the latter's aesthetic face rapt as he performed his sacred duties, the physician wondered what Christmas would bring to Michaelhouse and its scholars that year.

CHAPTER 3

AFTER ANGEL MASS, THE SCHOLARS RETURNED TO Michaelhouse, where they slept until dawn heralded the second service of Christmas Day – Shepherd's Mass. Bartholomew dozed fitfully, partly because the mellowing effects of the wine had worn off, but also because he was not unaffected by the excited anticipation that pervaded the town. There was an atmosphere of celebration and eagerness, especially among children, whose eyes shone bright in the candlelight, and the air was thick with the smoke of early fires as people began their culinary preparations. Stews and specially hoarded foods were being readied, while cakes and fruit were brought out from storage.

As they walked, Bartholomew felt something brush his face, and looked up to see flecks of white sailing through the air, swirling around the scholars' robes and settling on cloth-clad shoulders. They darkened the charcoal-grey sky further still, but brightened the streets where they began to settle, whitening the dull brown muck of previous falls.

'Damn!' muttered Michael, glowering at the sky as though the flakes were a personal insult. 'It is not supposed to snow until January at the earliest. We have suffered calamity after calamity since the Death – hot summers, where the grain baked to dust in the fields, wet autumns that brought floods, and now early snows.'

'I remember snow at Christmas when I was young,' said Bartholomew. 'It is not as unusual as everyone claims.'

'It *is* unusual,' declared Suttone, who had been listening to the discussion, and who never allowed an opportunity to pass without mentioning his ever-increasing obsession

85

with impending death and destruction. 'The weather has grown more fierce because of the plague.'

'It has not,' said Bartholomew, becoming weary of explaining that while diseases might well be affected by the climate, the reverse was impossible. 'The weather is determined by winds and tides, not by sickness.'

'The weather is determined by God,' corrected Suttone severely. 'Is that not so, Kenyngham?'

'You just said it was caused by the plague,' countered Bartholomew immediately.

'Gentlemen, gentlemen,' said Langelee mildly. 'You can save this sort of thing for the debating halls. And you are all wrong, anyway. In the words of Aristotle, both the plague and the bad weather are things that just happen, and no amount of reasoning and philosophising will help us understand why.'

'Those do not sound like Aristotle's sentiments to me,' said Bartholomew, feeling that Langelee was seriously mistaken. 'He was a philosopher, and his life was spent speculating about things that have no obvious explanation. He never claimed that because there was no immediate answer we should not try to think of some.'

'He did other things, too,' said Langelee, enigmatically vague. 'But I do not have time to teach you about them now. Here we are at the church. Silence, if you please.'

Having had the last word, he led his scholars inside St Michael's, where the temperature was even lower than the frigid chill of outside. As the first glimmers of sunlight filtered through the windows, dulling the gleam of gold from the candles, the ceremony began.

Shepherd's Mass was an important event, and the church was full. The scholars from Ovyng, Physwick, St Catherine's and Garrett hostels were there, along with the folk who lived in the parish of St Michael. These were a mixed bag, ranging from the families who occupied the seedy shacks that lined the river, to some of the wealthiest merchants in the town. Since benches were provided only for the old or sick, the rest of the parishioners were obliged to stand together in the nave.

Obvious barriers were apparent. The rich were at the front, where they could see what was happening; their servants stood behind them, forming a human wall to prevent them from coming into contact with the rabble who massed at the back of the church. With some trepidation, Bartholomew looked for Philippa, but she was not there. He did not know whether to be disappointed or relieved.

Sheriff Morice stood near the rood screen. He looked smug and affluent, and a redness in his cheeks suggested that he had not bothered to wait for the end of mass before imbibing a little breakfast ale to drive away the chill of early morning. By contrast, the folk from the riverbank huts were pinched and white, some with a cadaverous look that indicated starvation might well claim them before winter relinquished its hold.

Although the men, women and children at the rear of the building were jammed elbow to elbow and scarcely had room to stand, one member of the congregation had plenty of space. This was Robin of Grantchester, the town's surgeon. He was short and slightly hunched, with dark, greasy hair and a mournful expression that did little to inspire confidence in those unfortunate enough to fall prey to his dubious skills. His clothes were caked in old blood, none of it his own, while the knife bag he carried at his side clanked ominously with his every movement.

Halfway through a psalm, Bartholomew became aware that Michael had stopped chanting, and was glowering towards the nave with an expression that caused more than one person to shift uneasily. However, the real object of his glare was blissfully unaware that if looks could kill then his soul would already be well on its way to the next life. Harysone was present, holding a wide-brimmed hat in his hands and looking very imposing in his black cloak and matching gipon. Bartholomew could see the pale gleam of his long teeth from the chancel, and was reminded of one of the mean-eyed rats that lived near the river.

'What does *he* want?' hissed Michael venomously. 'He has no right to be here.'

'He has every right to be here,' whispered Bartholomew. 'He is doing nothing wrong.'

'He has come to see whether we have discovered the man he killed,' determined Michael. 'Look! He keeps glancing across at the albs.'

'Actually,' said Bartholomew, for the first time fully appreciating why the monk detested Harysone so, 'he is looking at Matilde.'

Matilde, unofficial leader of the town's prostitutes, was the most attractive woman in Cambridge, as far as Bartholomew was concerned. Possessing a natural beauty that needed no potions or pastes to enhance it, her hair always shone with health and her face was pure and unblemished, like an alabaster saint's. Men had been complaining for years now that they had been unable to secure her personal services, and it appeared that she had abandoned her life of merry pleasure among those wealthy enough to afford her, to devote her time to the town's women – prostitutes or downtrodden, homeless or afraid.

That morning, she wore her best blue cloak, which caught the mysterious colours in her eyes and made them even more arresting than usual. Her dress was cut close in the latest fashion, revealing her slender, lithe body, and the way Harysone was ogling her with his moist, glittering eyes made the physician want to march down the aisle and punch him.

But Bartholomew was not Matilde's only friend present that morning. The physician saw Harysone crane backward, then forward, then fold his arms with a sullen expression. Several of Matilde's 'Frail Sisters' had clustered around, shielding her from Harysone's lascivious gaze. Moments later a couple of their menfolk began to jostle the unwelcome visitor. Finding himself crowded between a rough bargeman and a burly carpenter, Harysone took a step towards the porch. Carpenter and bargeman followed, until Harysone had been neatly herded to the door. Yolande de Blaston, the carpenter's wife, just happened to open it and, with a nudge from one of her sturdy elbows, Harysone was gone.

'Good,' said Michael with satisfaction. 'Now I can concentrate on my prayers.'

Bartholomew said nothing, although he felt enormous relief that Matilde had been rescued from the man's open lust. He glanced at her, and saw that she was wholly unaware of the service that had just been performed on her behalf; her attention was fixed devoutly on the altar.

Eventually, it was time for Michael's choir to make its appearance. Bartholomew knew that the monk had been practising with his motley collection of singers for weeks, and that improvement had occurred with frustrating slowness. Most enrolled only because Michaelhouse provided free ale and bread after services, and the applicants' musical ability was never considered. Despite his bluster and sharp tongue, Michael was a compassionate man, who declined to refuse membership to the desperate souls for whom choir was the only way of ensuring a regular meal. Consequently, it was the largest body of singers in Cambridge, and had a reputation for volume.

It comprised men and boys from the poorest houses in the town, with a smattering of scholars to justify its name of the Michaelhouse Choir. The tenors included Dunstan and Athelbald, Bartholomew's riverside patients, although Dunstan was too ill to be present that day. Among the basses were Isnard the bargeman and Robert de Blaston the carpenter, who had removed Harysone from the church.

While Kenyngham and Suttone muttered sacred words and moved sacred vessels, Michael's choir took deep breaths to provide a little entertainment for the watching scholars and townsfolk. As they girded themselves up for music, a murmur of nervous apprehension rippled through the congregation.

Before people could think of leaving, Michael raised his arms and the sound began. A boy's voice broke the silence, singing the *vox principalis* high and clear, so that the notes soaring around the rafters seemed to come from the throat of an angel. The boy was joined by a *vox organalis*, and the voices fluted and wrapped around each other, producing a harmony that was exquisite. The congregation exchanged glances of startled pleasure, and Bartholomew saw Michael look pleased with himself. The two singers were Clippesby and the Franciscan novice Ulfrid, and Bartholomew felt a surge of pride that Michaelhouse should possess such talent.

But then the solos ended, and it was time for the chorus. It began with the basses, a grumbling mass of indistinguishable words, which comprised several notes produced simultaneously, although Bartholomew was fairly certain there was only supposed to be one. The tenors joined in, although they stopped after a few moments when frantic signalling from Michael indicated they were early. Conversely, the children did not start singing at all, and he was obliged to sing their part himself until they realised they had missed their cue. To make up for their tardiness, they sang more quickly, and had soon outstripped the basses and were surging ahead.

The piece moved into a crescendo when the voices suddenly and unexpectedly came together, and the singers felt they were on familiar ground. Michael waved his arms furiously in an attempt to make them sing more softly, but the choir were having none of that. They knew their words and their notes, and they were determined that everyone should hear them. The sound was deafening, and the friars celebrating the mass grew distracted and flustered. Kenyngham poured wine into the wrong vessel, and Suttone knocked a paten off the altar, sending it clattering across the flagstones – except, of course, that the choir drowned any sound it might have made.

Langelee swung a censor rather more vigorously than was necessary, directing clouds of throat-searing incense in the choir's direction in an attempt to silence at least some of them. It did not work, although Bartholomew noticed that the scholars from Ovyng, who were standing uncomfortably close to the choir and were in the line of Langelee's fire, were tugging at hoods and coughing. Father Ailred's face was almost purple as he struggled not to choke, while Godric had the folds of his cowl pressed to his face.

But it was over at last – and rather abruptly, as though the singers had suddenly run out of energy – and the church was flooded with a blessed silence. There were sighs of relief all around, and the mass continued. Bartholomew saw tears running down Ailred's face, but suspected that these were caused by incense-induced coughing, rather than emotion. Godric gazed up at the rafters with his mouth open, although whether he was inspecting the greenery or was dazed from the singing, Bartholomew could not tell. Meanwhile, their students, neatly tonsured and clean for the occasion, stood in a line. All appeared to be healthy and well rested, and it did not seem as if any harboured a guilty conscience over the violent death of Norbert.

When Kenyngham and Suttone had completed the mass, the scholars formed their processions again and made their way back to their colleges and hostels. Michaelhouse went first, followed by Physwick, Ovyng, Garrett and St Catherine's hostels. It was an impressive sight, with black-, blue- and red-robed scholars walking through the falling snow, led by acolytes and crucifers.

The choir had been promised food and a penny for their labours, and Langelee was gracious as he handed out coins, congratulating various members on their performances. Many of the town children were there, too, since it was a tradition that Michaelhouse provided them with bread on Christmas morning. Bartholomew leaned against the servants' screen at the back of the hall and watched with satisfaction the sight of the needy eating their fill at the College's expense.

Once the choir had dined and been sent on their way with Langelee's diplomatic praise still ringing in their ears, the scholars attended the Mass of the Divine Word, which was the longest of the three Christmas Day offices, and the most peaceful. When it was over, and the scholars were once again marching through the snow, Langelee broke ranks and dropped back to walk with Bartholomew.

'I keep forgetting something I must tell you.'

'What?' asked Bartholomew, not liking the tone of the Master's voice. He was sure whatever Langelee had to say was not something he would want to hear.

'The feast this afternoon,' said Langelee. 'You know it is our custom to invite guests from the parish to help us celebrate?'

'You have invited my sister and her husband,' said Bartholomew. 'You hope they will donate some of their money to the College.'

'Obviously,' said Langelee. 'Oswald Stanmore is a rich man, and it does no harm to remind him that Michaelhouse has deep but empty coffers. But I was not thinking about him.'

'Sheriff Morice,' suggested Bartholomew. 'You told us a week ago that he was coming. None of us relish the prospect of his company, but we have all agreed to behave and not tell him that he is a corrupt manipulator who took office only to further his own ambition.'

'Ambition is why most men become sheriffs,' said Langelee, puzzled that Bartholomew should imagine otherwise. 'But I am not referring to Morice, either. I have invited Walter Turke. He is a wealthy merchant, and I thought I might persuade him to become a Michaelhouse benefactor. I can assure you I had no idea you were once betrothed to the woman who is now his wife. All that happened a long time before I came here.'

'I see,' said Bartholomew, his thoughts whirling. He wondered whether he might still be able to hire a horse, so that he could ride away into the snow and avoid what would doubtless be a wretchedly awkward experience. A noisy public feast was certainly not the venue he had envisaged for his impending reunion with Philippa.

'I am sorry,' said Langelee, sounding genuinely contrite. 'I would not have invited him had I known your predicament. When Stanmore told me he had a rich fishmonger staying with him, it just seemed natural to invite him to our feast.'

'Philippa married a fishmonger?' asked Bartholomew, startled.

'I thought you knew,' said Langelee, embarrassed.

'I knew Turke was a merchant, but I assumed he was something more . . .' Bartholomew cast around for the right word '. . . more distinguished than a peddler of fish.'

'Distinguished be damned! The Fraternity of Fishmongers is a powerful force in London, and Turke is its Prime Warden. But just because he made his fortune in fish does not mean to say that he deals with it directly. He will have apprentices for beheading and gutting, and that sort of thing.'

'I suppose so,' said Bartholomew, knowing that merchants at the top of their professions concentrated on the commerical, rather than the more menial, aspects of their work. It was likely Turke had not touched a scaly body in years, and the image of Philippa living in a house that reeked of haddock and sprats, which had sprung unbidden into his mind, was almost certainly wrong.

'Never mind Turke,' said Michael, entering into their conversation. 'What about Philippa? She is the one Matt is itching to see. Did you invite her?'

'I hardly think that—' began Bartholomew indignantly.

'She accepted the invitation,' interrupted Langelee. 'I have not met her yet, and it will be interesting to see the woman who captured Bartholomew's heart.' He clapped a sympathetic hand on the physician's shoulder. 'But I appreciate this might be difficult for you – unrequited love and all that. If you would rather absent yourself, then I shall grant you dispensation to do so. It is only fair, since it is my fault that you are faced with this awkward situation.'

'I would like to absent myself,' said Suttone in a gloomy voice behind them. 'I do not want to spend all day watching the antics of acrobats.' The last word was spoken with such distaste that Michael started to laugh. It was as though the Carmelite regarded entertainers in the same light as the town's Frail Sisters.

'All Fellows are obliged to attend College feasts, and malingering is not permitted,' reprimanded Langelee sharply. He turned to Bartholomew. 'But I can tell her *you* are indisposed – that you ate something that set a fire in your bowels, and that you cannot stray far from the latrines.'

'That image should reawaken her romantic feelings for you,' said Michael gleefully.

'No,' said Bartholomew, although Langelee's offer was tempting. 'I have to meet her sooner or later, and today is as good a time as any. You can keep the fiery bowel excuse for another occasion. Who knows when I may need it?'

Michaelhouse was a whirlwind of activity for the rest of the morning, and Bartholomew offered his services to Agatha, hopeful that keeping himself occupied would take his mind off the impending meeting with Philippa. He carried tables and benches from the storerooms, rolled casks of wine from the cellar to the hall, and even lent his skilful hands and eye for detail to repairing a marchpane castle that had suffered a mishap in the kitchens. But he was wrong: the chores Agatha set him occupied his body, but left his mind free to ponder all it liked. Meanwhile, Michael went to pursue his enquiries into the death of Norbert, although his glum expression when he returned indicated that he had not met with success.

'Well?' asked Bartholomew, as he joined the monk in the middle of the freshly swept yard. 'Is Norbert's killer in your cells?'

Michael gave a disheartened sigh. 'My beadles have been unable to trace anyone who will admit to dicing with Norbert in the King's Head and, although Meadowman dug through all that snow outside Ovyng, he has not found the weapon that killed Norbert.'

'I imagine not,' said Bartholomew. 'Knives are not only expensive, but can often be traced back to their owners. I doubt the killer would just have dropped one near his victim. It would be tantamount to leaving a note with his name on it.'

'That is not always true,' said Michael. 'But it would have given me a starting point. I spent much of the morning searching the room where Norbert slept, hoping that one of these notes from Dympna might be there.'

'I take it you found nothing?'

Michael grimaced in disgust. 'Godric insists that Dympna sent Norbert several messages over the last few days, but not one was among his possessions. Meanwhile, Ailred confided that Godric is a romantic soul, who probably made a mistake when he took vows of celibacy, and that Dympna might be a figment of a lustful imagination.'

'I thought all Ovyng's students had seen these letters. They must have been real.'

Michael's expression was weary. 'Ovyng's friars are relatively well mannered, and tended not pry into Norbert's affairs. They knew he had missives, and one or two – like Godric – glimpsed the name Dympna and a few numbers scrawled on to a parchment. But no one ever took the opportunity to study the things properly.'

Bartholomew was thoughtful. 'If Norbert received several messages, you would think that at least one would still exist. Do you think the killer destroyed them?'

Michael frowned. 'I imagine Dympna would have been noticed if she had entered Ovyng and started to rifle through Norbert's belongings.'

'Dympna might have nothing to do with his death,' warned Bartholomew. 'Just because Norbert went to meet her that night does not mean *she* killed him.'

'The lost hour might be more significant than I first believed,' mused Michael thoughtfully. He saw Bartholomew's puzzled look, and reminded him, 'There was an hour unaccounted for between the time Norbert left Ovyng and when he arrived at the King's Head. Since he received one of these mysterious notes before he went, I am inclined to accept Godric's suggestion that Norbert had a tryst with Dympna.'

'And then went to the King's Head and spent a good part of the night gambling in company with another woman?' asked Bartholomew doubtfully.

'I now know – Meadowman told me after Shepherd's Mass – that the woman in the tavern was a Frail Sister. Una, to be precise. So, I deduce that Dympna met Norbert earlier, at a more respectable time in the evening. Can we conclude that Dympna went home after the tryst, and was asleep when Norbert reeled from the King's Head? Or was she lying in wait, and stabbed him for having a dalliance with Una? Is that why none of these letters survive? She demanded them back before she killed him, so that we would be unable to trace her?'

'If Dympna was Norbert's lover, then the fact that she sent obtuse messages indicates she was not a sweetheart who could be openly acknowledged. He might have been protecting her by destroying her notes.'

'Perhaps,' acknowledged Michael reluctantly. 'Although, in the absence of any other clues I am loath to dismiss this woman's role too quickly.'

'Matilde will tell you if there is a Frail Sister called Dympna.'

'She says there is not,' said Michael. He gave a huge, dispirited sigh. 'Dick Tulyet asked me how the investigation was progressing, and I could see from the expression in his eyes that he was wondering whether to put his faith in Sheriff Morice instead.'

'He was not,' said Bartholomew firmly. 'He knows these things take time. What about your unidentified corpse? Have you learned who he is yet?'

'You have a way of making me feel most incompetent,' grumbled Michael. 'I have been so busy with Norbert that I have not had the chance to follow up where William left off.'

He looked up as Langelee sauntered across the yard with the wild-eyed Clippesby and the sombre Suttone at his heels. The College was ready, and the Fellows had nothing more to do until their guests arrived. Wynewyk joined them, brushing snow from his tabard and polishing his shoes on the backs of his hose, while even the spiritual Kenyngham was fluffing up his hair and arranging the folds of his habit. All the Fellows were freshly shaved, and their hair was trimmed and brushed. Their ceremonial robes had been shaken free of dead moths for the occasion, and together they made for an impressive display.

'You had better change, Matthew,' said Suttone, evidently deciding that the physician was letting the side down with his threadbare gown and patched tabard. 'Philippa will be here in a moment, and you do not want to greet her looking like Bosel the beggar.'

Clippesby agreed. 'You will not impress her in those clothes.'

'It is not my intention to seduce her, you know,' said Bartholomew irritably, knowing he was less splendid than his colleagues, but also aware that there was not much he could do about it at short notice. He decided he would invest in a new set of ceremonial robes later that year – as long as there was not a book or a scroll he would rather purchase first, of course.

'You must make sure she knows what she has lost,' said Langelee. 'You do not want her thinking she has had a narrow escape while she frolics with Turke in bed tonight. You should aspire to her not frolicking at all, because she is pining for you.'

'I shall aspire to no such thing!' said Bartholomew, laughing. 'Our betrothal ended a long time ago, and there have been other women since Philippa.'

'Oh, plenty,' said Michael, as if he had kept a list on his friend's behalf. 'But none of them have been able to compete seriously for your affections – with the exception of Matilde.'

'You cannot mean Lady Matilde the courtesan,' said Kenyngham, a bewildered expression creasing his saintly face. 'So, I assume you refer to another Matilde. There are so many people in our little town these days that it is difficult to pray for them all.'

'Right,' replied Langelee, shooting the Gilbertine a bewildered look for his innocence. 'But you cannot have Matilde, Matt, so you had better make do with this Philippa instead.'

'I do not want to "make do" with Philippa,' said Bartholomew. He noticed that his colleagues were exchanging meaningful glances and was suddenly exasperated with them. 'What is wrong with you all today?'

'We are only trying to help,' said Langelee, offended. 'If you wed a respectable lady, like Philippa, we can make sure that you still do a little teaching for us. Unfortunately for you, Matilde is not the marrying type, you see. She came to Cambridge to escape constant matrimonial offers, and it is common knowledge that she likes her freedom. So, we have decided to find you another woman.'

'But I do not want another woman,' objected Bartholomew. He saw the Fellows interpret this to mean he had set his heart on Matilde and hastened to put them right. 'I do not want anyone.'

'So, you will be taking major orders, then?' asked Clippesby, wide eyed. 'Will you become a monk or a friar?'

'Neither,' said Bartholomew firmly. 'And I can find my own women, thank you.'

'You have not done very well so far,' said Langelee bluntly. 'Women who pass through your hands like ships in the night offer no satisfaction. You need a wife. Or are you intending to keep Matilde as a lover and retain your Fellowship at the same time? I suppose that would work, as long as you are discreet.'

'It is no one's business what—' began Bartholomew angrily.

'I will fetch mint from the herb garden for you to chew,' interrupted Clippesby helpfully. 'She will notice that when you kiss her.'

'Kiss her?' echoed Kenyngham, aghast. 'But she is a married woman!'

'It is not unknown for marriages to be annulled, Father,' said Langelee meaningfully, having dissolved an awkward liaison himself not long ago. 'Do not look so shocked. I am sure you lusted over married matrons in your youth.'

'I can assure you I did not!' exclaimed Kenyngham, simultaneously appalled and indignant. 'I am—'

'Here she comes,' said Clippesby, in what amounted to a bellow as there was a polite knock on the door. 'Ready yourself, Matt. Try to look alluring.'

Bartholomew shot him an agonised glance as the porter opened the gates to admit the first guest. Fortunately, it was only Robin of Grantchester. The dirty surgeon had been to some pains to make himself presentable: he had washed his hands. He wore lilac-coloured hose, a dirty orange tunic and a green, old-fashioned cloak that had probably not been new when King Edward II had been murdered in 1327. Bartholomew was surprised that the surgeon had been invited to Michaelhouse, since it was highly unlikely the College would persuade *him* to part with any of his meagre fortune. Michael evidently felt the same. He turned to Langelee as student 'cup-bearers' hastened forward to greet Robin with a goblet of wine.

'What is he doing here? He will never help Michaelhouse. He is not wealthy – you must have seen the state of his house on the High Street.'

'But rumour has it that he arranged a substantial interest-free loan for the Franciscans,' said Langelee. 'And he was involved in lending money to Valence Marie to develop their library.'

'Robin?' asked Michael, eyeing the dirty surgeon in disbelief. 'You jest, man!'

'I do not,' said Langelee. 'He did not donate the money personally, but he certainly had a hand in the organisation. Ask Pechem of the Franciscans.'

'Our Master has misunderstood something,' said Michael,

as Langelee went to do his duty as host. 'Robin as a phil-anthropist, indeed! I have never heard such an unlikely tale!'

The second person to arrive was Sheriff Morice, dressed in finery fit for a king. He had evidently been spending some of the money he had accrued from his corrupt practices, because all his clothes were new. The predominant colour was blue, with silver thread glittering in the frail afternoon light. His plump and dowdy wife hung on his arm like a large brown leech. Morice spotted Michael and sauntered across the yard to speak to him.

'My investigation into Norbert's death is going well,' he remarked, his eyes cold and calculating. 'I have several culprits in my prison awaiting interrogation.'

'I am pleased to hear it,' said Michael smoothly. He nodded in the direction of the gate as more guests arrived. 'But here comes Dick Tulyet. I am sure he will be delighted to know that you are close to a solution. Dick! Welcome! Morice here has just informed me that he has all but solved Norbert's murder.'

Tulyet grimaced. 'I hear your cells are full, Morice, but the patrons of the King's Head are not the culprits. They were all drunk the night Norbert was killed, and I doubt any could even draw their daggers, let alone kill with them.'

Morice sneered. 'But they hear rumours. One will tell me what I want to know. *I* will find your killer, Tulyet, and the Senior Proctor will not.' He strutted towards Suttone, who fluttered about him like an obsequious crow.

Michael took Tulyet's arm and pulled him aside. 'Tell me about Dympna – Norbert's secret lover who wrote him notes. Did you know her? Who is she?'

Tulyet gazed at him. 'I thought he had many lovers, not just a single person. And how do you know she was called Dympna?'

'Does this mean that you do not know her?' said Michael, disappointed.

'I do not know any woman called Dympna,' said Tulyet. 'But you will waste your time if you follow that line of enquiry.

Norbert would never have indulged in a relationship with a woman who could write: that would have made him feel inferior, which was something he hated. Dympna will lead you nowhere, Brother.'

While the exchange between Tulyet and Michael took place, Bartholomew was experiencing grave misgivings about the wisdom of meeting Philippa in such a public place. Gradually, Langelee's suggestion that he spend the afternoon in hiding became increasingly attractive, and he took two or three steps away. But he had dallied too long, and the last guests arrived with a sudden flurry. First, came his sister with her husband at her side. Edith's black curls contrasted starkly with Oswald Stanmore's iron-grey hair and beard, and both wore tunics of a warm russet colour. Edith's cloak was blue, while Stanmore's was Lincoln green, and together they were a handsome couple. Edith smiled sympathetically at her brother.

'I tried to prevent Langelee from extending his invitation to our guests, but you know what he is like. He thought Walter Turke might give funds to Michaelhouse, and was oblivious to my hints that he should keep his hospitality to himself. I was hoping she would be gone before you knew she had even been here.'

'How long has she been with you?'

'Four nights – since Wednesday,' replied Edith, 'although she arrived in Cambridge ten days ago, and was enduring the dubious delights of the King's Head. In all fairness to her, she was reluctant to stay with us out of deference to your feelings: her husband accepted my offer immediately, however, and that was that. Meanwhile, Cynric has been steering you away from places he thought she might be, while I told her that you are too busy to visit. I am sorry, Matt. I did not want you to find out like this.'

Bartholomew smiled, thinking that the cold weather and his determination to do as much teaching as he could before term ended meant that he had been out very little, and Edith might well have succeeded in preventing a meeting of the two parties had Langelee not interfered.

'You need not have gone to such efforts on my behalf. I do not mind seeing Philippa again.'

Stanmore finished greeting Langelee, and turned to take his wife's arm. It was cold in the yard and he wanted to go inside, where there would be a fire in the hearth and hot spiced ale warming over the flames. As Edith moved away, Bartholomew saw the three people who had been behind her, and found himself at a loss for words.

The older of the two men was much as Bartholomew imagined a wealthy fishmonger would look. He had an oiled beard, sharp grey eyes, and every available scrap of his garments was adorned with jewels or gold thread. The buckles on his shoes were silver and his buttons were semi-precious stones. Each time Walter Turke moved, some shiny object caught the light and sparkled.

The second man was Giles Abigny, who had once been Bartholomew's room-mate. Gone were the flowing yellow locks and the mischievous smile of the student in his twenties. Abigny in his thirties was crop-haired, sombre and wore the drab garments of a law-court clerk – a blue over-tunic, called a cote-hardie, with buttoned sleeves, and a dark mantle with a metal clasp on the right shoulder. His brown hat was high crowned, and was decorated with a feather that had seen better days. He was heavier, too, indicating that he spent rather more time at the dinner table now than when he had been younger. He clasped Bartholomew's hand warmly, and promised that they would talk later, once they were settled and comfortable.

The woman who accompanied Turke, however, was not Philippa. She was Turke's wife; it was evident in the proprietorial way in which he handled her. She was as tall as Philippa had been, but much larger. Her expensive clothes could not hide the fact that she was both pear shaped and the owner of several chins. Her hair was completely concealed under a matronly wimple, and her skin was blemished and tired, although some attempt had been made to

102

disguise the fact with chalk paste. She was, in short, middle aged, overweight and unattractive.

Bartholomew recalled Edith's words – that she had not wanted him to 'find out like this'. The truth became painfully clear: Philippa was no longer Turke's wife, and the man had remarried. Edith had not wanted Bartholomew to learn that Philippa was dead by meeting the next Mistress Turke. The physician felt a surge of sadness for the young woman with the golden hair and blue eyes, who had gone to London in search of a better life than he could offer her. He hoped she had found happiness before she had died.

'Hello, Matt,' said the woman, approaching him with a smile. 'Do you not remember me? I am Philippa.'

Langelee was about to lead his guests across the yard and into the hall, when Agatha strode up to him and announced in a loud whisper that the boar was 'still bloody' and that the meal would not be ready for some time. Rather than wait indefinitely in the hall until the beast rotating over the kitchen fire was cooked to Agatha's exacting standards, Langelee decided to take the guests to his own quarters. Gray and Quenhyth were dispatched to stoke up the fire and remove any soiled linen that might be lying around, while Langelee procrastinated in the yard until Gray's hand appeared in the window to let him know that the chambers were presentable.

It was a colourful group that crowded into the two rooms, with the merchants and Sheriff adding yellows, greens and blues (and Robin's lilac and orange) to the scholars' cere-monial reds. The atmosphere was tense, however. Morice seemed uneasy with his predecessor in such close proximity, while Tulyet barely acknowledged that Morice was there, giving the impression he felt little but contempt for the man.

Robin of Grantchester looked hopelessly out of place. He stood near the hearth drinking steadily and eyeing the wine goblet as though he might take it with him when he left. Bartholomew tried exchanging pleasantries, but abandoned his efforts when Robin accused him of attempting to steal his professional secrets. Refraining from retorting that Robin had no secrets of any kind that Bartholomew would want to know, the physician backed away, gesturing to Suttone that he should entertain the man. Suttone obliged, and Bartholomew heard him informing the surgeon that the Death would soon return to Cambridge, and that he had better be prepared for it. This grim news was met with some pleasure by Robin, who had made a lot of money the last time the plague had raged.

Meanwhile, it was painfully obvious that Oswald Stanmore did not like the merchant to whom he had opened his house that Christmas. Edith tried hard to keep the peace, interrupting with a change of topic whenever one man looked set to offend the other and keeping the discussions light-hearted and uncontroversial. Abigny sat on a stool in a corner and watched them with cynical amusement, while Philippa was offered Langelee's best chair, which faced the fire and effectively absolved her from the general conversation. Clippesby crouched at her feet, like a lap-dog, and told her about the final confession the boar had made before it was dispatched to become the centrepiece for the feast. Bartholomew was grateful to Clippesby, because the musician's deranged chatter meant that he was not yet obliged to talk to Philippa himself. Instead he went to speak to Abigny.

'Giles,' he said warmly. 'We have not had news from you for years. What have you been doing since the plague?'

'The plague years were good times,' said Abigny fondly. 'I was carefree then – with only myself to worry about.'

'Are you married, then?' asked Bartholomew politely.

Abigny shook his head. 'But I am betrothed, and will be wed this summer.'

'Then you should not stay away from her too long,' said Bartholomew, not without rancour. 'Or you may find that she has grown tired of waiting and has abandoned you for a fishmonger.'

Abigny shot the physician a rueful smile. 'I was sorry when

Philippa told me she had broken her trust with you. Believe me, I would rather have a scholar for a brother than a fish merchant. At least my home would not smell of eels.'

'You live with them?' asked Bartholomew, surprised.

Abigny's smile was bitter. 'You should have warned me to pay more attention to my studies, Matt. When I came to seek employment in London, I found my knowledge lacking. I had no choice but to throw myself on the mercy of my brother-in-law.'

'I thought your parents left you a fortune.'

'A fortune does not last long in the hands of a man with fickle friends and a fondness for women. I squandered my inheritance, and when I was eventually obliged to find work I discovered I had forgotten – or had never learned – my lessons here. Walter bought me a post, as part of his wooing of Philippa, but it is not a very good one.'

'I see,' said Bartholomew, a little disconcerted by Abigny's blunt confidences.

'I doubt it,' said Abigny. 'I go to the law courts every day and file records no one will ever want again. Then I go home to Turke's house for my bed and my meat, and spend my evenings watching him turn my sister into a bore.'

'Is she happy?' asked Bartholomew, glancing to where Philippa was listening to Clippesby's ramblings with an expression that combined disbelief and unease. He supposed someone should rescue her, for he knew that conversations with Clippesby could be daunting to those unused to them.

'In general. Walter is not a dashing physician with black curls and a merry laugh, but he is enormously wealthy, and well placed to wrangle token employment for indolent brothers.'

Bartholomew felt Abigny should either earn himself the kind of high-paying post that he obviously thought he needed or marry his fiancée before she saw what she was letting herself in for. Seeing a man wallow in such self-pity was not pleasant, and he was half inclined to suggest Abigny should pull himself together.

'Why are you here?' he asked instead, good manners prevailing. 'If you dislike being with Walter and Philippa in their home, their absence should have given you some freedom.'

'It was tempting, believe me. But Philippa represents much that is good in my life, and if she wants to make a pilgrimage to Walsingham in the depths of winter, then it is my duty to travel with her and ensure she comes to no harm.' He gave a sudden grin, and for a moment Bartholomew glimpsed the rakish scholar he had once known. 'Remember my skill with the sword, Matt? I was in the thick of many a brawl with the town's apprentices.'

Bartholomew smiled back. 'Do not chance your arm now. Since Michael has become Senior Proctor fines for fighting are quickly imposed and zealously enforced.'

'I can imagine,' said Abigny, laughing softly. 'Who would have thought that fat, sly monk would have inveigled himself into such a position of power? He has done well for himself.'

'I give up!' Edith came up to them, her face dark with anger. 'I have been trying to keep the peace between them since the first evening they met, when Walter was condescending about Oswald's trade. But if they want to squabble in front of Master Langelee, then I can do no more to keep them apart.'

Abigny vacated the stool, and gave her hand a squeeze as he helped her to sit on it. 'You have managed admirably so far. Walter is an argumentative man, and that you have kept him and Oswald from each other's throats for four days is nothing short of a miracle.'

'If Oswald does not like Walter, why did you invite him to stay in the first place?' asked Bartholomew practically.

Edith sighed impatiently at her brother's inability to see that there were complex social waters to be navigated when invitations were issued. 'Because we knew Philippa – and Giles – from your betrothal. When we met by chance on the High Street and Walter asked us to recommend a decent tavern, I had no choice but to offer him the use of my own home.'

'I tried to save you,' said Abigny. 'I suggested you would have no room because of various relatives who were staying. It would have been easy to agree, and to direct us to the Brazen George.'

Edith smiled. 'It was good of you to try to get us off the hook. But manners dictate that Walter, Philippa and you should stay with us. However, I wish I had known then that Oswald and Walter would argue constantly. Walter is a difficult man.'

'We will be on our way tomorrow,' said Abigny comfortingly. 'And I will make sure it is at first light – before Walter is awake enough for squabbling.'

'Thank you,' said Edith sincerely. She looked up, as more people began to force their way into the already crowded room.

'Jugglers,' said Abigny in surprise, as he saw the newcomers. He began to back away. 'You must excuse me. I dislike this kind of thing.' He left the chamber with an abruptness that verged on the rude.

Edith watched him go with raised eyebrows. 'How odd! I thought he enjoyed professional entertainers. He was always a young man ready for singing and dancing.'

'He is no longer a young man,' Bartholomew pointed out, leaning against the wall as he watched the entertainers Langelee had hired elbow their way through the throng. Agatha apparently needed more time for the boar to cook, and was searching for ways to keep minds off growling stomachs. The jugglers' progress towards the Master was unmannerly, and Turke's face turned an angry red when one jostled him hard enough to make him spill his wine. The juggler regarded Turke challengingly, as though daring him to make a scene, then sneered disdainfully when the fishmonger looked away and began mopping at the stain on his gipon.

Langelee nodded to them to begin their performance, and

a hush fell over the room as they lined up. They were a shabby pack of individuals, whose costumes had seen better days and whose faces were heavily painted. There were two men and two women, all wearing red tunics, grubby yellow leggings and scarlet and gold chequered hats. Clippesby's assessment had been accurate: the two men and one woman could juggle after a fashion, but the performance of the other female, who stood apart and played the whistle with one hand and a drum with the other, was jerky and irregular, as though she could concentrate on a rhythm or on producing the correct notes, but not on both at the same time.

Her eccentric tunes did nothing to help her colleagues. They missed their cues, and the floor was soon littered with fallen missiles. Abandoning juggling, they turned to tumbling, which consisted of cartwheels that threatened to do serious injury to their spectators, and the kind of forward rolls that even Michael could have managed. Everyone was relieved when Agatha arrived, flour dusting her powerful forearms and boar fat splattered across her apron.

'Tell the Master the meat is done, and that folk should come and get it while it is hot,' she whispered to Bartholomew.

'Good,' said Bartholomew. 'It is not safe here with all these flailing legs and arms. I do not want to be setting broken limbs for the rest of the day.'

'I do not like them,' said Agatha, gazing belligerently at the hapless jugglers. 'I have never seen such a paltry display of tumbling.'

'They do leave a bit to be desired,' agreed Edith. 'I am surprised Master Langelee hired them. They are called the Chepe Waits, and were the very last troupe to be offered employment in the town this year. Michaelhouse has done a great kindness by taking them in; the weather is so foul at the moment that anyone without a roof will surely perish before dawn.'

'Let us hope we have a roof to wake up to,' said Agatha grimly. 'And that this uncivilised brood has not stolen it from over our heads. I told the Master that I did not want them in my College, but he said it was too late, because he has already paid them. I suppose he chose them because they are inexpensive.'

'Perhaps that is why they are called the Chepe Waits,' suggested Bartholomew, unable to resist the obvious.

Agatha gazed at him blankly for a moment before understanding dawned and she released a raucous screech of laughter that silenced conversation in the rest of the room as though a bucket of water had been dashed over its occupants. If Agatha was surprised to find herself the sudden centre of attention, she did not show it. She glanced around imperiously.

'Boar's done,' she announced. 'And the burnt bits have been scraped off the pies.'

'You heard the lady,' said Langelee, beaming around at his guests. 'Dinner is served.'

Bartholomew was not at all amused to discover that his colleagues had contrived to seat Philippa next to him during the feast, and soon became exasperated by their tactless nods, winks and jabs to the ribs. Having Giles Abigny on the other side was not much of a consolation, either, since his old friend made little attempt to converse and seemed intent on imbibing as much of Michaelhouse's wine as Cynric would pour him. Bartholomew remembered Abigny as an amiable and amusing drunk, who had been the instigator of many a wild celebration of nothing. But the years had turned him morose, and he sank even lower into the pit of self-pity when he was inebriated. Bartholomew braced himself for a trying afternoon.

The boar made its appearance, complete with rosemary twined about its feet and an apple in its mouth. It was 'sung in' by a reduced version of Michael's choir, which could nevertheless muster sufficient volume to drown all but the most boisterous conversation. Agatha had prepared other seasonal foods, too – mutton, veal, cheese, apples and souse.

Bartholomew disliked the pickled pig feet and ears that comprised 'souse', and was surprised when Philippa offered to eat his share.

She ate his share of Christmas frumenty – hulled wheat with spices that had been boiled in milk – and cakes, too, and devoured even more sugar comfits than Michael. Bartholomew wondered whether her healthy appetite derived from unhappiness, and tried to imagine what life would be like with the stout, aggressive fishmonger who sat on her other side. He found he could not, and was mystified – and a little hurt – that Philippa should have abandoned him in favour of such an unattractive specimen. He supposed the lure of wealth held more appeal than he had appreciated.

Once memories of the slender lady he had known were expunged from his mind, Bartholomew began to see some of the old Philippa in the woman who sat gorging herself at his side. Her voice had not changed and her facial expressions were familiar, and he found himself recalling things about her that he had forgotten. He remembered walking in the water meadows by the river, and eating hot chestnuts on another Christmas Day, laughing when they scalded their fingers and burned their tongues.

'You have changed,' he said. 'I barely recognised you.' He stopped short of total honesty by confessing that he had not recognised her at all.

'I was slimmer,' she said, leaning back to allow Cynric to fill a bowl with rich beef stew. 'But I was unhappy then, locked away in that convent.'

'Were you?' asked Bartholomew, surprised. He had always believed their courtship had been a whirlwind of delight for both of them.

'Not with you,' she added hastily, sensing that she might have offended him. 'But under the eagle eyes of that abbess. Then there was the Death hanging over us. We knew it was coming, but all we could do was wait to see who would live and who would die. It was not pleasant.'

'I suppose not,' said Bartholomew, thinking his first years

at Michaelhouse – until the plague arrived and Philippa left – had been among the happiest of his life. He had just completed his medical training, and was finally free to put all he had learned into practice. It had been an exhilarating and fascinating time, and his dalliance with Philippa had only added to the pleasure.

'I hope you are not angry with me,' she said, digging into the stew with a large horn spoon that she produced from the pouch she carried at her side. 'I know it must have been a shock, to learn I had decided to bestow my affections on another man.'

'It was,' said Bartholomew vaguely, thinking it would be rude to say otherwise. In truth, he barely recalled what he had felt when her terse missive informing him of her marriage had arrived. By that time, she had been gone for more than a year, and he had been busy with his teaching and patients. He remembered thinking he had not missed her as much as he should have done, and that he should have visited her in London. He had been upset when the letter came, but could not recollect whether it was because he had lost a woman he had loved or because it was rather insulting to be treated in so cavalier a manner. He decided to change the subject.

'Do you have children?'

'Walter has three sons from a previous marriage – his first wife, Isabella, died during the Death. Our physician has been calculating horoscopes to tell us when to try for babies, but I think his arithmetic is lacking.' She gave him a side-long glance. 'I do not suppose . . .?'

'Do you live near the fish markets?' asked Bartholomew, hastily seizing on another topic before she demanded that he spend the rest of the day deciding when Walter should avoid apples or eat fiery spices to turn him into a rampant and potent lover. He disliked producing horoscopes, and there was something about their randomness that made him certain they were worthless anyway.

'Friday Street,' she said, reaching for a dish of lemon

butter. 'It is a very pleasant road, and our house is the best one. It is old – dating back to the Conqueror – but I like it. It was the house that made me choose Walter over John Fiscurtune, who owned a smaller home nearby. Fiscurtune had also asked me to marry him.'

'Old houses are often better than new ones,' said Bartholomew diplomatically, watching her eat the flavoured fat with her spoon. 'Since the plague, craftsmen have been in such high demand that many do not care whether their work is good or bad.'

'Pass the butter,' came Michael's aggrieved voice from further along the table, indicating that he was unimpressed by the fact that Philippa had not seen fit to share it.

'I see you have not changed, Brother,' retorted Philippa icily, relinquishing the bowl. She turned to Bartholomew. 'He is still a fat, greedy man.'

Bartholomew decided that the subject of appetites and weight was one he would be wise to avoid with both Philippa and Michael. 'You were telling me about your house,' he prompted.

'Walter made some additions to it, which means we can *say* it is new,' she replied. 'It has pretty columns around the main door and large arched windows, like those of the Temple Church on the River Thames. There are two sleeping chambers on the upper floor, a separate kitchen block, and it has a latrine with a roof.'

Bartholomew was genuinely impressed. Most latrines were open to the elements, which allowed for the dispersal of poisonous miasmas, but made for chilly and unpleasant experiences in inclement weather. 'How deep is the pit?' he asked curiously, wondering whether Turke had gone with the recent fashion for a shallower trench that could be emptied regularly, or had opted for a deep one that would be used until full and then sealed.

'Matthew wants to know how deep is our latrine pit,' said Philippa to her husband in a voice loud enough to silence the buzz of conversation around her.

'Could you not think of anything more pleasant to discuss?' hissed Clippesby disapprovingly behind her back. 'Why can you not talk about music or art?'

'The depth is about the height of a man,' said Turke proudly. 'And we have it cleaned *once a month*! I will not have it said that Walter Turke has smelly latrines. I always say that a man who does not pay attention to his latrines is a man who cannot be trusted.'

He shot Stanmore a look that indicated he thought his host's sanitary arrangements left something to be desired. Stanmore bristled angrily, and was only stopped from making a rude retort by Edith's warning hand on his arm. Turke ignored the furious cloth merchant and turned to Langelee.

'How often do you have Michaelhouse's emptied?'

'Fairly regularly,' said Langelee vaguely, not meeting Bartholomew's eye. He had recently elected to go from twice a year to once, overriding the physician's objections that it was unhygienic. 'But I would not recommend lingering in them.'

'Edith tells me you are on a pilgrimage,' said Bartholomew to Philippa, deciding that he had better prove Michaelhouse men were capable of discussing subjects nobler than sewage disposal.

'It is Walter's pilgrimage,' said Giles Abigny in a low, angry voice, speaking for the first time since the meal had started.

The physician saw that this topic would be no less contentious than latrines, and sensed that the winter journey was a source of dissent among the three travellers. Fortunately, Langelee was regaling Turke, Edith and Stanmore with a tedious account of how many hazelnuts the orchard had produced that year, and Bartholomew had only Abigny and Philippa to worry about. Nevertheless, he decided that yet another subject was probably necessary in the interests of harmony.

'It is cold for the time of year,' he ventured hopefully.

'It *is* cold,' agreed Abigny bitterly. 'And no time to go traipsing across the country. But Philippa wanted to be the dutiful wife, and I insisted on accompanying her. So, here we all are.'

'Could Walter's journey not have waited until spring?' asked Bartholomew, giving up on diplomacy and deciding to yield to whatever topics his guests wanted to discuss.

'He needs to atone for a sin,' said Philippa, clearly reluctant to elaborate. 'Since it is a serious sin, it was decided he should leave immediately. The saints are more likely to grant him forgiveness if we travel in terrible weather, anyway, and then perhaps they will bless us with a baby.'

'The fact that Walter has failed you in that area has nothing to do with sin,' said Abigny nastily. 'Fiscurtune was murdered in November, and Walter was limp long before that.'

'Walter's sin is murder?' asked Bartholomew uneasily, looking over at the merchant, who was helping himself to blancmange, apparently engrossed in Langelee's hazelnut discourse.

'It was self-defence,' said Philippa, casting an uneasy glance at her husband. She seemed relieved that he was listening to Langelee.

'His victim was a fishmonger called John Fiscurtune,' said Abigny. 'Fiscurtune was a loathsome man, but even loathsome men are entitled to keep possession of their lives, and not have them snatched away during gatherings of the Worshipful Fraternity of Fishmongers.'

Bartholomew tried to make sense of Abigny's claims. 'Turke killed a colleague at a guild meeting?'

Abigny drained his cup, waving it at Cynric to indicate he wanted it refilled. 'Fiscurtune was caught engaging in dishonest practices, which brought the Fraternity into disrepute. Well, perhaps "dishonest" is unfair: what happened is that he decided to ignore the Fraternity's regulations when it came to salting. He made several folk ill by experimenting with new – cheaper – techniques of preservation, and the Fraternity wanted him expelled.'

'Walter argued against the expulsion,' said Philippa in a

114

low voice, so that she would not be overheard, 'despite the fact that he and Fiscurtune had hated each other since Isabella died – Walter's first wife was Fiscurtune's sister, you see – but he was outvoted. Fiscurtune blamed Walter, which was unfair.'

'This happened in November,' Abigny went on. 'Furious that his former brother-in-law had failed to help him, Fiscurtune stormed into a meeting of the guild and levelled all sorts of charges against Walter. Walter grabbed a knife, they fought and Fiscurtune was stabbed. Walter told the coroner that Fiscurtune armed himself first, and since the coroner is a friend of the Fishmongers' Fraternity, it is no surprise that Walter was deemed innocent.' His tone of voice suggested that he strongly disagreed with the outcome.

'Giles,' whispered Philippa, glancing at her husband again. 'You should not drink wine, if you cannot hold your tongue. Do you want to lose your post at the law courts over this?'

'You are right,' said Abigny resentfully. 'I should not criticise my brother-in-law when I owe him so much. After all, Fiscurtune dared to do just that, and look what happened to him.'

'You mentioned earlier that Fiscurtune asked you to marry him,' said Bartholomew to Philippa, fascinated by her brother's drunken revelations. 'You said you selected Walter because he had a better house.'

'She should not have chosen either,' stated Abigny harshly.

'No?' demanded Philippa, angry now. 'You were lucky I picked Walter, Giles, because Fiscurtune would not have bought you your post.'

'I sense you are bitter about Fiscurtune's death,' said Bartholomew to Abigny. 'Was he a friend?'

'Certainly not,' said Abigny indignantly. 'He was greedy, corrupt and sly: I would never have allowed Philippa to marry him. Comfort and riches have their price, but there is a limit to what one should pay – and Fiscurtune was well beyond it. However, if I sound bitter, it is not because Fiscurtune was murdered, but because Walter used his money and influence to evade justice.'

'It is the way things are,' said Philippa tiredly, although Bartholomew sensed she was not entirely comfortable with the situation, either. 'The fraternities are powerful in London and no Crown official wants to make enemies of them. I hear Cambridge is no different: Sheriff Morice will also find in a man's favour if his purse is sufficiently deep.'

Abigny looked around him with a shudder of distaste. 'You should have accepted Philippa's offer all those years ago, Matt, and come to live with us in London. It is better than Cambridge in all respects.'

'She never asked me to London,' said Bartholomew.

'I did,' said Philippa indignantly. 'But you never bothered to answer that particular message. Are you telling me it never arrived?'

'It did not,' said Bartholomew. He wondered what might have happened if it had. Would he have left Cambridge and gone to her? Or would he have elected to remain at Michaelhouse? He realised that he did not know, and was surprised to feel relief that the letter in question had apparently been lost in transit.

Philippa regarded him with sombre eyes. 'Pity. I assumed your silence meant you no longer cared for me. My life – and yours – might have turned out very differently had you replied.'

Bartholomew was not sure whether that was good or bad. 'This pilgrimage,' he said, wanting to return to the subject that set questions clamouring in his mind – which were easier to address than the complex gamut of emotions that raged when he thought about his courtship of Philippa. 'Whose idea was it to go?'

'Fiscurtune's kinsmen suggested it,' said Philippa shortly. 'But the details are Walter's business and no one else's. We should not be discussing it – especially here, in this public place. Anyway, the whole affair will be forgotten as soon as we return from Walsingham.'

Abigny laughed unpleasantly. 'There are rumours that Fiscurtune's murder could prevent Walter from being elected Lord Mayor next year. Walter wants the matter dead and buried as soon as possible – which is why he embarked on this ridiculous pilgrimage. However, I feel it takes more than riding a few miles through the snow to atone for cold-blooded slaughter.'

Bartholomew glanced at Turke and saw he was wearing a dagger, attached to a belt at his waist. He hoped Michael, Stanmore or Langelee would not say anything that might prove fatally offensive. He appraised Turke anew, seeing that the man possessed considerable physical strength under all his glitter, and that his hands were strong and calloused, not soft and unused to work, like those of many wealthy men. He sensed that Turke would be a formidable enemy to anyone rash enough to cross him – as the unfortunate Fiscurtune had evidently discovered.

CHAPTER 4

IT WAS NOT LONG BEFORE BARTHOLOMEW RAN OUT OF conversation with Philippa, while Abigny grew even more morose. The physician pondered the death of Fiscurtune, and tried to imagine what it would be like to be in Abigny's position. He decided that living in poverty was preferable, and thought Abigny should leave the Turke household, as it was obviously making him unhappy. But Abigny seemed devoted to Philippa, even to the extent of accompanying her on the pilgrimage, and Bartholomew supposed the situation was more complex than he understood.

With no one to talk to, he was obliged to watch the antics of the Chepe Waits in order to pass the time. After a while, they finished their act and approached the high table. Abigny immediately excused himself and left, promising to return later, while Philippa devoted her entire attention to eating wet suckets – dried fruits soaked in a sugary syrup. Turke was deep in conversation with Wynewyk, who was regaling him with a complex analysis of the College accounts, and Bartholomew supposed the merchant had decided that even a dull subject like institutional finances was preferable to watching the Waits. Langelee tossed the jugglers some silver pennies and told them to go behind the servants' screen, where food had been set aside.

'It is not there,' replied the larger of the two women, whose head of golden plaits formed a tight, artificial-looking helmet around her head.

Her voice was deep, and Bartholomew was startled to note that she needed a shave. With amusement, he realised she was a man. He glanced quickly at the others, and saw that the other woman was also male, with a shadowy chin and a

118

pair of hirsute legs. He could now see that the two 'boys' were women, and the moustaches and beards that clung to their perspiring faces were made from horse hair. He recalled thinking there was something odd about them when they had appeared in Langelee's chamber earlier, and was surprised he had not guessed then. Cross-dressing was a common practice in Christmas entertainment, and he should have expected it.

'What do you mean?' demanded Langelee impatiently. He had been talking to Stanmore, and was clearly annoyed to interrupt what might prove to be a lucrative discussion to speak to jugglers. 'I asked Agatha to leave bean stew, bread and a platter of meat for you.'

Agatha, who was serving the wet suckets, overheard him. 'Michaelhouse does not provide vagabonds with two meals when the rest of us make do with one,' she said sternly. 'They have already eaten their fill of the food intended for you and your guests, Master.'

Langelee turned enquiring eyes on the Wait. 'Well, madam?'

Langelee was not an observant man, and was infamous for his undiscerning taste in women, so Bartholomew supposed he should not be surprised by the fact that the Master failed to notice anything amiss in hairy legs and an advanced beard in the 'lady' he addressed.

'It is a lie!' said the Wait angrily. 'We have taken nothing we were not owed.'

Agatha drew herself up to her full height, clearly intending to tell the Waits exactly what she thought of them. Fearing the exchange would offend his guests, Langelee placated her quickly by launching into an effusive monologue that praised her efforts with the feast. Suitably flattered, she moved away to ensure the wet suckets were properly shared out, and that the servants did not leave trails of sticky droplets across the guests' shoulders.

'What is your name?' Langelee asked, turning back to the Wait.

'Frith of Lincoln.' The man indicated his associates. 'These are Jestyn, Makejoy and Yna.'

Langelee raised puzzled eyebrows. 'Frith is a strange name for a lady, but I suppose it is none of my affair. You have been hired for the Twelve Days, but you can consider our contract broken if you steal again. Do I make myself clear?'

Frith nodded sullenly. Bartholomew was unsettled by the expression of dislike that darkened his face, and hoped the man would not drop dead animals down the well or set the College alight as the scholars slept. His comrades seemed more amenable, however, and led him away before he could say anything else. Agatha leaned over Bartholomew's shoulder.

'I saw them steal most of a suckling pig and some comfits. They have no right to be sullen and resentful when Michaelhouse has given them employment. They would have been sleeping in the streets if the Master had not offered them beds, food and a few pennies.'

'I do not like such people,' said Philippa, gazing distrustfully at the Waits when Agatha had gone. 'I would never employ them myself, because I would not want them in my house.'

'Nor I,' declared Turke, finally losing interest in Wynewyk's monologue. 'Never let it be said that Walter Turke hires inferior jugglers.'

Abigny had had much the same reaction earlier, Bartholomew recalled, although at least he had not been rude enough to imply that his hosts were lacking in taste. They all watched Frith arguing with Cynric at the other end of the hall, until the book-bearer shoved him behind the servants' screen, presumably to prevent anyone from witnessing the squabble any further. Meanwhile, Bartholomew saw Deynman leering adoringly at the man called Jestyn, and realised the students were already well on the way to becoming drunk. He sincerely hoped the lad would pass out before he discovered the hard way that Jestyn's tempting bosom was nothing more than artfully packed straw.

The noise in the hall gradually rose, partly because it was necessary to shout over the choir, and partly because the freely flowing wine loosened tongues and vocal cords. Bartholomew's senses were reeling, and he felt the need to step outside for some fresh air. It was stuffy. The fire was blasting out heat like a furnace and people were crammed into a room that usually accommodated only half that number. He started to stand, but Turke reached out and grabbed his arm. The physician was startled by the strength of the grip that held him.

'I hope you are not thinking of taking my wife with you,' said the fishmonger with unmistakable menace.

Bartholomew removed the offending hand politely but firmly. 'I am going alone,' he replied, although a number of more colourful responses came into his mind.

'She is no longer yours,' said Turke. 'So do not expect to take up where you left off.'

'I would not dream of it,' said Bartholomew icily, thinking Turke need have no worries on that score. As far as Bartholomew was concerned, *his* Philippa had gone to London and never returned. He did not know the woman who had chosen a husband because he had a roofed latrine.

'My sister is an honourable woman, Walter,' said Abigny sharply. He had returned from his sojourn outside and had resumed his efforts to drink himself insensible. 'And Matt is a man of integrity – unlike most merchants I know.'

Abigny's words were obviously intended to be insulting, and Turke's face obligingly flushed with anger as his hand dropped to the hilt of his knife. Bartholomew backed away, seeing the Turke household had some serious problems and he would do well not to be caught in the middle of them.

'I am leaving now,' he said. 'The noise is making my head buzz. If Mistress Turke wants some air, I am sure her husband will escort her.'

'Normally, I would ask my manservant Gosslinge to do it,' said Turke. He removed his hand from his dagger and rested it on the table, a wide, strong fist that looked capable of killing. 'But he disappeared on business of his own five days ago. I know it has been impossible to hire decent servants since the plague, but I expected more of Gosslinge. He has been with me for many years.'

'I see,' said Bartholomew, thinking Gosslinge was probably justified in fleeing from a man like Turke. There were kinder, more considerate men in Cambridge, who would pay a fair wage for a loyal retainer.

'We have been in this miserable town for ten days now,' Turke grumbled on. 'Philippa's horse went lame, so we have been obliged to rest it. I could hunt the alehouses for Gosslinge, I suppose, but I have better things to do. Perhaps I should pay some of these good-for-nothing students to look for him. I want him back tonight, because I intend to leave tomorrow.'

'You will be going nowhere, if this snow continues,' said Langelee, politely ignoring the insult to his scholars. 'I hear the London road is already impassable, and the route north is likely to be the same. You may have to remain in Cambridge until milder weather brings about a thaw.'

'We shall see,' said Turke importantly, as though snow would not dare fall if it inconvenienced him. 'But I shall be angry with Gosslinge when he deigns to show his face. I want to complete my business at Walsingham and go home. I do not want to be away longer than necessary.'

'What does Gosslinge look like?' asked Michael helpfully. 'I can ask my beadles to look for him.'

'That would be acceptable,' said Turke ungraciously. 'He is a beggarly-looking man, with thin hair and a mean, pinched face. And he is missing a thumb.'

The following day, just after dawn, a number of people gathered in St Michael's Church. Walter Turke and Philippa were there to make an official identification of their servant's corpse. Giles Abigny, nursing a fragile head and looking distinctly unwell, had apparently been pressed into service as Turke's clerk, lest the procedure require official certification. Langelee was also present, still aiming to secure a benefaction for his College, and keen to let Turke know that Gosslinge's mortal remains had been respectfully treated at Michaelhouse's expense.

Langelee was not the only one hopeful of reward: Sheriff Morice had arrived in a flurry of flapping sleeves, clanking spurs and crafty eyes, determined to make Turke aware that Cambridge's secular authority also took an interest in the corpses of visiting merchants' servants, and that his men were available to provide coffins, dig graves and erect head-stones – for a price, of course. Michael led them to the south aisle and drew back the sheet that covered the corpse.

'That is Gosslinge,' announced Turke grimly. 'Damn the man! Now what am I supposed to do? Where can I hire another good servant?'

'Poor Gosslinge,' said Philippa softly, reaching out a gloved hand to touch the body. 'I am sorry he came to this.'

'It is his own fault,' said Turke harshly. 'I told him to stay close, and he disobeyed. Look where it has led him.'

'Servants always think they know best,' agreed Morice with a grimace of sycophantic sympathy. 'And their deaths are nothing but an inconvenience.'

'Gosslinge's clothes are very shabby for a retainer,' said Bartholomew, puzzled by the man's rags. Even if Turke was mean with his wages – which seemed likely – he would not want his retinue dressed poorly, because that would reflect badly on him. The servants of wealthy merchants tended to be a good deal better dressed than Bartholomew was ever likely to be.

'He sold his livery, I imagine,' said Turke with tight-lipped anger. 'Was a purse found on his body? If so, then its contents belong to me. I did not give him permission to dispense with clothes that were purchased at my expense.'

Philippa was obviously embarrassed by her husband's outburst. 'Gosslinge wore a black tunic and hose, with a yellow belt,' she said, addressing Bartholomew as though Turke had not spoken. 'I suppose someone must have found his corpse and stripped it. These rags certainly did not belong to him.'

'Were his clothes worth stealing?' asked Bartholomew, aware, even as he spoke, that it was a stupid question. After the plague, when everyday goods were expensive, virtually anything was worth stealing by those who owned nothing.

Philippa nodded. 'They were of good quality and very warm. Walter says it is better to buy one good garment than several cheap ones.'

'I am right,' asserted Turke. 'Never let it be said that Walter Turke's servants are badly dressed.'

'How many people did you bring with you?' asked Bartholomew.

'Just Gosslinge,' replied Philippa. 'It would not be right to go on a pilgrimage with a large retinue, though we did hire a pair of soldiers before we left London – to repel robbers.'

'Where are they?' demanded Michael. 'Did they argue with Gosslinge at all?'

'They barely acknowledged each other,' said Abigny. 'The soldiers are rough mercenaries, and Gosslinge was a man who could barely slice his meat without fainting at the sight of the blade.'

'Blade,' mused Bartholomew thoughtfully. 'Did Gosslinge own a knife? Could it have been stolen with the rest of his clothes?'

'He had a dagger,' replied Abigny. 'It was too large for a man of his size, and he was clumsy with it.'

'*I* do not recall,' said Turke carelessly. 'But I doubt it is worth retrieving. I am more interested in his clothes. *They* were expensive.'

'We shall look for everything,' promised Michael. 'Now, where are these soldiers? It is possible that they stole Gosslinge's belongings and hid his body. Mercenaries are experienced corpse looters, after all.'

'I can answer that,' interjected Morice smoothly. 'They are in the Castle prison, where they have been residing for

124

the last eleven days. Within hours of Master Turke's arrival here, they visited a tavern and were involved in a brawl. I shall release them when he leaves, so they can accompany him, but until then they can stay where they are.'

'I do not want them back, thank you very much,' said Turke stiffly. 'I shall hire new ones – ones that can behave themselves. Your prisoners can find their own way back to London.'

'Pay them what they are owed first,' advised Abigny practically. 'We do not want a pair of cheated killers on our trail as we make our way into the wilds of Norfolk.'

'I suppose not,' admitted Turke reluctantly. 'Very well. See they are paid, then dismiss them. Perhaps Morice will keep them locked up until we are safely away.'

'I might,' said Morice, a predatory gleam in his eye. 'We can negotiate the cost of their stay later, when we have a little privacy.'

'Why do you want to know about the soldiers, Brother?' said Philippa curiously. 'You said last night that Gosslinge died of the cold. Are you now suggesting he did not, and they might have harmed him in order to snatch his possessions?'

Michael shook his head. 'There is nothing to suggest that happened. Matt believes he froze to death, then someone found his body and took the opportunity to strip it.'

Turke sniffed. 'The thief will be easy to catch, Brother. All you need to do is look for Gosslinge's clothes.'

'A thief will not be stupid enough to wear stolen apparel in a small town like Cambridge,' said Michael. 'And given that he hid the body among the albs to cover his tracks, I predict he is not totally witless.'

'I am sorry Gosslinge was treated so disrespectfully,' said Philippa, staring down at the corpse. 'But desperate folk are driven to desperate measures, and it would be wrong to judge a man with hungry children by our own principles. I, for one, do not want to persecute such a person. We shall bury Gosslinge, and there will be an end to the matter.'

'I want my livery back,' said Turke. A cunning expression crossed his face. 'Or, better yet, Michaelhouse can keep the clothes when they are found as payment for Gosslinge's burial.'

'I do not know about that,' said Langelee indignantly. 'Suppose they never appear?'

Turke scowled. 'I am offering you a good bargain. The cost of the clothes will more than pay for a mass and a grave. But if you would rather return the livery to me when I pass through Cambridge on my return journey, then I shall pay you in another way.'

'Coins are best,' said Langelee hopefully.

'I have something better,' said Turke. 'He handed Langelee a small leather pouch. 'That will cover the expense – and more besides.'

Langelee investigated the pouch's contents gingerly. 'I am not sure this is sufficient – there is not much of a market for dried slugs in our town.'

Turke gave a gusty sigh that echoed all around the church. 'It is a relic. It may not look like much, but used properly will bring you great wealth. Never let it be said that Walter Turke is niggardly with his payments.'

Abigny swallowed a snort of disgust.

Langelee tried to hand it back. 'Coins are better, if it is all the same to you, Master Turke. And if you add a little extra, we will say prayers for your soul, too.'

'I shall expect those regardless,' countered Turke. He nodded at the pouch. 'And that is all the payment I am prepared to give, so you had better make the most of it. It is St Zeno's finger.'

'St Zeno?' asked Langelee resentfully. 'I have never heard of him.'

'Then your education is lacking,' retorted Turke rudely. 'Zeno is a friend to fishermen, and his finger will allow any who touch it to be successful anglers. It could bring you a fortune.'

'Not at the moment,' said Abigny wryly. 'The river is

frozen solid. I tossed a rock on to it this morning, and it skidded clear across the surface like a toy.'

Turke raised his eyebrows, and turned to his brother-in-law. 'I had not noticed. But I dislike ice, as you know, and I have better things to do than throw stones on frozen rivers.'

'St Zeno *is* associated with fishermen,' said Michael, addressing Langelee. 'He was an Italian bishop.'

'He did not like loud wailing during his masses for the dead,' added Bartholomew, irrelevantly repeating the only scrap of information *he* could remember about the obscure cleric.

'It seems this is a valuable relic,' said Morice with interest, reaching out to take it. 'It might be a suitable payment for keeping two dangerous mercenaries out of action while you continue your journey.'

'No,' snapped Turke, snatching it from him and thrusting it back into Langelee's reluctant hands. 'It should stay here, in a church, where it belongs. I have something else in mind for you – a snail from the Holy Land. It, too, has magical powers.'

'So do I,' muttered Michael facetiously to Bartholomew. 'And they are telling me that Langelee and Morice have just been most brazenly cheated. Incidentally, did you notice that Harysone was decked out in a set of black clothes the day we found Gosslinge dead? He might have been revisiting the scene of his crime, to ensure the corpse was still hidden.'

'Too risky,' said Bartholomew. 'Especially this week, when the churches are full of people with their holly wreaths and armfuls of greenery.'

'You are wrong, Matt. Harysone was up to no good when we watched him. I *shall* find out if he stole Gosslinge's clothes.'

It had snowed heavily during the night, and all the roads that led to and from Cambridge were closed by deep drifts. Oswald and Edith Stanmore could not return to their estates in Trumpington, and were obliged to remain in Cambridge at their business premises on Milne Street. This pleased Turke, who claimed he did not want to go to some rustic hall, preferring the pleasures of a town to those of the country. Bartholomew saw Stanmore struggling not to make some rude retort, while Edith smiled politely. Philippa closed her eyes, mortified by her husband's manners, and Abigny stepped forward to give her hand an encouraging squeeze when Turke was not looking. They began to walk to Milne Street together, Turke strutting ahead, and the others following behind.

It was still early. Only a few people had trodden in the snow, and it was still white and powdery as Bartholomew and Michael made their way to the King's Head to interview Harysone about Gosslinge and the stolen livery. It hid the filth and muck of the Cambridge streets, clung to roofs in thick white blankets, and piled itself in dense clots in the branches of trees. When the wind blew, they fell, scattering on the ground below. The frozen river formed a thin seal across the water, and prevented its unsavoury aromas from permeating the town. For the first time in years, the town air smelled fresh and clean.

'Look!' said Michael, gripping Bartholomew's arm, as he pointed across the street. 'It is Harysone! He has saved us a walk.'

'So it is,' said Bartholomew, recognising the man's black cloak and broad-brimmed hat. 'He seems to be emerging from morning mass at St Botolph's. How very suspicious.'

'There is no need to be facetious, Matt,' said Michael stiffly. 'You may be reluctant to acknowledge there is something nasty about him, but I shall not be happy until he is either away from the town or in prison. I am sure if he has not already done something criminal then he will do so soon.'

'If you say so,' said Bartholomew. He did not want to admit he had experienced similar feelings when Harysone had leered at Matilde in the church the day before.

Michael intercepted Harysone, while Bartholomew sat on

the low wall that surrounded St Botolph's churchyard and waited, listening to the conversation with half an ear as he watched people struggle through the High Street snow.

'Gosslinge,' Michael announced without preamble. 'How do you know him, and why were you meeting him in St Michael's Church four days ago?'

'I know no Gosslinge,' replied Harysone startled, 'and I can assure you I have met no one in St Michael's Church. It is always locked, and I have never managed to gain access.'

'You gained access yesterday,' pounced Michael. 'I saw you there at Shepherd's Mass.'

'True,' admitted Harysone. 'But that is the only time I have been inside it, and I was disappointed. I expected a collegiate church to be pretty, but that one is plain and stinks of mould.'

'What did you want when you tried to enter it last Thursday?' pressed Michael coolly. 'I watched you myself, fiddling with the latch.'

Harysone regarded him with raised eyebrows. 'What is this about, Brother? Has something been stolen? If so, I can assure you that I had nothing to do with it.'

'A student called Norbert was murdered near Ovyng Hostel a few nights ago,' said Michael, abruptly switching subjects in an attempt to keep his suspect off balance. 'I do not suppose you know anything about that?'

Harysone's eyebrows almost disappeared under his hair as he registered his surprise. 'Why should I? I do not even know where Ovyng Hostel is. I am a stranger, here only to sell copies of a modest treatise—'

'Norbert was in the King's Head before he died,' interrupted Michael. 'I understand you are staying there.'

'But I have not murdered anyone. You must look elsewhere for your culprit, Brother.'

'Have you been dicing?' asked Michael. 'I have it on good authority that Norbert was dicing the evening he died.'

'Dicing is not illegal. At least, not if goods, rather than coins, are the currency. That is the law, as I understand it.'

'Is that a yes or a no?' demanded Michael impatiently, declining to quibble with the man over ambiguities in the statutes that governed the land.

'I keep telling you: I am a stranger here. I would not know your Norbert if he spat in my face or gave me a gold noble. I speak to many folk in the tavern – I am a friendly sort of man. But I have committed no crime, and I advise you to leave me alone, or I shall make a complaint to your Chancellor. Now, excuse me. I am busy.'

With dismay, Bartholomew saw Matilde walk through the Trumpington Gate and turn down Small Bridges Street at that precise moment. Harysone was after her in a trice, almost running in his haste to reach her. Bartholomew abandoned Michael and hared after them, catching up just as Harysone was about to offer her a steadying hand. Bartholomew shot between them and took her arm himself, just – but only just – managing to make the whole thing appear natural.

'Matthew!' Matilde exclaimed, amused by his sudden appearance. 'What is wrong?'

'Nothing,' he muttered, hauling her away, while Harysone stood forlornly in the middle of the road with disappointment written clear across his rodent-like features.

'Oh, it is him,' said Matilde, glancing discreetly behind her. 'He seems to be everywhere I look these days. I am told he has penned some kind of treatise on tench and is here to sell it to the unwary.'

'Do not allow him near you,' advised Bartholomew. 'Michael thinks he will commit a crime.'

'Not with me, he won't,' she said playfully. 'Do not worry, Matt; the man makes me uneasy with his huge teeth and glittering eyes. I have no intention of forging a friendship with him. But this is where you and I must part ways: I am going along the towpath to visit poor Dunstan the riverman and you have business back the way you came, I believe. I know you only walked this way to save me from Master Harysone.'

Bartholomew watched until he was sure Harysone would not try to pounce on her again, then retraced his steps back to the High Street. Michael was chuckling to himself.

'That was quite a manoeuvre, Matt, and it showed Harysone he is no match for a Cambridge man. Your only mistake was that you did not send him bowling into the snow when you shoved him out of the way.'

'I have just thought of something,' said Bartholomew, walking with the monk back along the High Street. 'Matilde gave me the clue: tench.'

'The fish you saw the night Norbert was killed, and that later reappeared in Clippesby's loving hands at our breakfast table? What about it?'

'Matilde said Harysone was writing a treatise on tench; you told me it was about fish. The point is that Norbert was dicing the night he died, and Harysone just intimated he was also gambling, but not for coins. What if he was gaming with salted fish? What if Norbert won one from him?'

'But your tench was not found with Norbert's body,' said Michael. 'It belonged to whoever pushed you – and *he* was not the killer, because the scream you heard suggests that Norbert was being killed by someone else at the time.'

'Perhaps Norbert dropped the thing when he was fleeing for his life, and some beggar pushed me in order to get it. I know from the way his wound bled that Norbert went some distance before he died, so he could have been attacked on the riverbank near Dunstan's house.'

'Yes,' said Michael, pleased with the logic. 'That makes sense. But even better, it tells me I was right from the beginning: there *is* a link between Harysone and a serious crime. At the very least, he and Norbert gambled together and Harysone lost a fish to him on the night of the murder.'

'We need evidence, though,' warned Bartholomew. 'It is a good theory, but it is based on conjecture, not on facts.'

'It will do for now.' Michael pointed down the High Street. 'But there are Ailred, Godric and their novices, just about to celebrate mass. Let us see whether they have anything new to tell us – although I do not hold much hope. I have interviewed them almost every day since Norbert's body was discovered, and no one has betrayed himself yet.'

They met the Franciscans outside St Michael's Church, where the students shivered in their thin habits and stamped their feet to try to keep warm in the biting wind. Ailred told Michael they planned to bury Norbert that afternoon, and asked whether the murderer had been found.

'No,' said Michael shortly.

'Sheriff Morice made yet another arrest this morning,' said Ailred uncomfortably. 'Robin of Grantchester. But I do not think he is responsible. Why would the town surgeon kill Norbert?'

'Because Norbert once called him a bloody-handed lunatic?' suggested Godric, taking the question literally. 'No man likes to be insulted or called incompetent.'

'But it is not a motive for murder,' said Michael. 'You are right, Ailred: Robin should not be in prison – not because I do not think he is capable of murder, since he risks that every time he sees a patient, but because he is too cowardly to attack someone with a knife.'

'He does own knives, though,' Godric pointed out. 'Bags of them. And they are always covered in blood, so no one would know whether it belonged to Norbert or a patient.'

'Robin has been associated with certain acts of generosity,' said Ailred. 'He arranged for Bosel the beggar to borrow a cloak for the winter, and he was involved in lending the Carmelites funds to replace habits lost in a fire. It seems to me that Morice has assumed Robin possesses money to buy his freedom, and *that* is the real reason for his arrest. This could never happen in Lincoln. There are no dishonest officials in *that* lovely city.'

'I am sure there are,' said Bartholomew immediately.

'Neither Morice nor his men have been investigating Norbert's death properly, so they cannot have discovered anything I have not,' said Michael, interrupting what was likely to be a futile debate. 'I have worked hard on this case – I owe that to Dick Tulyet.'

'But you have learned nothing, for all that,' said Ailred, disappointed. 'Robin's arrest is just another of Morice's ventures for making himself richer, and Norbert's killer still walks free.'

'I know,' said Michael grimly. 'However, I assure you that Norbert may be dead, but he is not forgotten. I shall—'

'There is Cynric,' interrupted Bartholomew, watching his book-bearer make his way through the snow at a rapid pace. 'Something is wrong.'

'I have some bad news,' said Cynric without preamble when he arrived. 'Walter Turke tried to skate on the frozen river, just after he identified Gosslinge's body. The ice was not strong enough, and he fell through.'

'He should not sit too near the fire to begin with,' said Bartholomew, knowing that rapid warming could cause the heart to fail. He started to move towards Milne Street, thinking Philippa would want him to tend her husband. 'And there should be plenty of dry blankets to wrap around him. Warmed milk will help, but not wine.'

'No,' said Cynric, catching up with the physician and gripping his arm so that he was forced to stop. 'They could not save him. He is dead.'

Philippa was distraught. She sat in Oswald Stanmore's comfortable solar and wept inconsolably. Stanmore hovered behind her, a helpless expression on his face as he tried to hand her some wine. Edith hugged her and let her cry, and Abigny stood near the wall looking sombre. Bartholomew studied him, attempting to gauge the emotions there. Grief? Sadness? Bartholomew did not think so. Guilt or relief? They seemed more likely.

'I do not believe he went skating,' Philippa wailed. 'He could not swim.'

'You do not need to be able to swim to skate,' Michael pointed out gently. 'Most people do not anticipate that they will fall through the ice, or they would not do it in the first place. Walter must have imagined it was sufficiently strong to bear his weight.'

'But he never skates,' wept Philippa. She gazed at each one in turn with reddened eyes. 'You met him. Did he seem to you like the kind of man who would go skating?'

'She has a point,' muttered Michael to Bartholomew. 'He seemed a cheerless, pompous sort of fellow, and I cannot imagine what would induce him to don a set of bones and chance his luck on the river.'

'A few of my apprentices were out there this morning,' said Stanmore soberly. 'But they are small and light, and it was obvious the ice was not strong enough to support an adult. I do not understand what Turke was thinking of.'

'But he would not do it!' Philippa shouted. 'Why will none of you listen to me? He was not a skating man! He was a fishmonger – a respectable and honoured Prime Warden in the city of London. He would *never* have gone to play on a river!'

'Where is he?' asked Bartholomew, wondering whether the corpse might yield clues that would explain Turke's aberrant behaviour. 'Perhaps he was not skating, but walking along the river bank when he fell.'

'I do not want you touching him,' cried Philippa, standing to confront her former fiancé. 'I have seen how you treat corpses, and it is not respectful. I will not have you mauling Walter!'

Bartholomew stepped away from her, his hands raised in apology. 'I am sorry; I did not mean to cause you distress. Of course I will not touch him, if you do not want me to.'

'Good,' said Abigny, speaking for the first time. 'Walter's corpse has been through enough indignities. We shall take him back to London and have him buried in St James's Church on Garlicke Hythe. That is where all the important fishmongers are interred. Perhaps you can suggest someone who will embalm him for us?'

Philippa gave a shriek of grief, and Edith glowered at

Abigny, warning him to watch what he said. Abigny grimaced, and his expression became unreadable again. Bartholomew frowned. Why had Abigny seemed pleased Turke's body was not to be examined? Was it because he knew an examination might reveal some clue as to why the pompous fishmonger had decided to skate on dangerous ice – perhaps something concealed in his clothing or in his scrip? Or was he afraid the evidence might suggest Turke had not skated at all – that someone had coaxed him on to unsafe ice to bring about his death?

'Turke died at the Mill Pool, near the Small Bridges,' said Stanmore in the silence that followed Abigny's remarks. 'The current is more slack there than in the rest of the river, so it is usually the first part to freeze.'

'Was he wearing skates?' asked Bartholomew.

Stanmore gazed at his brother-in-law as though he were insane. 'Of course he was wearing skates, Matt! How do you think we know he went skating? They were tied to his feet with thongs.'

'I would like to see,' said Michael. 'I might recognise who made them, and then perhaps whoever sold them to Turke might tell us more about—'

'Hateful things!' sobbed Philippa bitterly. 'Take them from his poor body before I see it. Will you do that, Giles?'

'Walter's death does not come under your jurisdiction, Brother,' said Abigny, ignoring her as he fixed the monk with a steady gaze. 'Walter was not a member of the University, and he did not die on University property. This matter belongs to the Sheriff, and he is sure to want to make his own enquiries.'

'Summon him, then,' said Michael impatiently. 'I am not questioning anyone's authority; I am merely trying to help.'

'I have already sent Morice a message,' said Stanmore, disapproval thick in his voice. 'But he says he cannot come until later, so we shall have to wait before we remove Turke to St Botolph's.'

'St Michael's, not St Botolph's,' said Philippa in a low

voice. 'The Michaelhouse priests I met yesterday – Kenyngham, Clippesby and Suttone – will give me their prayers. They are decent men, and I would rather have them than people I do not know.'

'Kenyngham will arrange a vigil,' said Bartholomew, thinking the officious, selfish fishmonger would need the prayers of a saintly friar like Kenyngham, if he was ever to escape Purgatory. He was surprised Turke's body was still at the Mill Pool, but understood that Stanmore would not want to remove it before the Sheriff had given his permission. However, Michael pointed out that bodies should not be left lying around until the secular courts deigned to find time to examine them, and suggested they remove him to the church themselves.

'Morice is a curious fellow,' said Stanmore, marching down Milne Street towards the Small Bridges with Bartholomew and Michael at his heels. Abigny and Edith had been left to comfort Philippa. 'He has been after Turke like a lovesick duck ever since he arrived in the town, but now the man is dead, Morice cannot even be bothered to inspect the body.'

'Not so curious,' said Bartholomew, who thought the Sheriff's behaviour was painfully transparent. 'Turke alive was able to dispense monetary favours; Turke dead is not a source of income, and so not worth the effort. Morice is interested only in events and people that might result in financial rewards for himself.'

'There is always Philippa,' said Stanmore. 'A wealthy widow is easier prey than a miserly fishmonger who was used to sycophants and corrupt officials.'

'Philippa will not be wealthy until the courts grant her Turke's fortune,' Bartholomew pointed out. 'You know what lawyers are like. It could take months, by which time Philippa will be back in London and Morice will not be in a position to benefit. And how do you know Turke left Philippa his wealth, anyway? She said he had sons from a previous marriage; they may inherit everything, and she may be destitute.'

'You could be right,' admitted Stanmore. 'But I am unsettled by her claim that Turke was not a man for skating. What is she saying, do you think? That she believes someone killed him?'

'I thought at first that grief was speaking,' said Michael. 'You know how people sometimes deny something terrible has happened by snatching at straws. But now I am not sure. She is right: Turke did not seem the kind of man to grab a pair of skates and go dancing on the river.'

'And there is Gosslinge's death,' added Bartholomew.

Michael's eyes narrowed. 'You said he died of the cold.'

'I believe he did. But do you not think it odd that a servant and his master should die so soon after each other?'

'It is a pity Philippa ordered you to stay away from Turke's body,' said Michael soberly. 'I would like to know what you think of it.'

'Giles would not,' said Bartholomew, recalling the reaction of his old room-mate when the physician had agreed to comply with Philippa's wishes. He had been pleased, almost relieved, and had immediately initiated a discussion about how to transport the body away from Cambridge.

They reached the Mill Pool, where people had gathered to stare at the body. It was covered with a sheet, and a group of boys wearing the livery of Stanmore's household formed a knot on one side of it, while two of Morice's soldiers stood on the other. A row of heads peered from the bridge above, braving the cold winds to have a tale to tell over the fire that night. Christmas was a time for stories, after all.

When the boys saw Stanmore, one of them darted up to him. Bartholomew recalled that his name was Harold, a lad of about fourteen years with a freckled face and wide, guileless eyes. He looked angelic. Bartholomew knew he was not.

'We thought we should wait here until you came back, sir,' said the boy in a breathlessly childish voice. 'The soldiers had a poke at him, but no one else has been near.'

'Thank you, Harold,' said Stanmore. 'But go home now and take the others with you. This is no weather to be out

137

loitering. Tell Cynric to hurry up with the stretcher, and we shall remove Turke to the church ourselves.'

'But—' began Harold, glancing around at his fellows.

'Now,' said Stanmore firmly.

'I saw—' .

'Go!' said Stanmore, giving the boy a gentle shove. 'Your hands are blue, and you are not wearing your cloak. An apprentice with frost-eaten fingers will be no good to me, so home you go. That goes for all of you.'

Reluctantly, the boy walked away, casting resentful glances over his shoulder as he went. Bartholomew did not blame him for wanting to stay. It was not every day that a guest of his master's died in odd circumstances, and Harold, like most lads of his age, had a ghoulish curiosity.

'Poor Turke,' said Stanmore. 'He died without atoning for his sin – although he never seemed particularly sorry to have taken a knife to one of his colleagues, as far as I could tell.'

'Dead as a nail,' said one of the soldiers, approaching Stanmore with a confident swagger and indicating the body with a jerk of a grubby thumb. 'It is a pity, since the Sheriff had hopes that he might donate a little something for the town. But these things happen. He should not have been skating anyway. The ice is thin, like parchment.'

Bartholomew looked to where he pointed and saw the jagged hole in the centre of the Mill Pool, made by Turke crashing through it. The surrounding ice was cracked and scratched, as though Turke had fought hard to escape, while the snow on the river bank was scuffed and churned where his would-be rescuers had milled around, unable to help him in time. A piece of rope lay nearby, and parallel lines on the ice indicated where Turke had finally been pulled free. The soldier was right: the ice in the middle of the pond was far too thin for safe skating.

'What do you think, Matt?' asked Michael, pulling the cloth away to reveal the blue features of the fishmonger underneath.

'I think he is still alive,' said Bartholomew in horror, noting the slight puff of the lips as the man breathed.

'I was told he was dead!' said Stanmore indignantly, struggling to lift one end of Turke's stretcher, while Michael grabbed the other. Sheepishly, trying to make amends for their mistake, Sheriff Morice's henchmen stepped forward to seize a corner each, leaving Bartholomew to take the middle. 'He certainly looked dead – blue and chilled.'

'That is because he was in cold water,' said Bartholomew, noting that crystals of ice were forming in Turke's sodden clothes. He wondered whether he would be able to snatch the man back from the brink of death or whether it was already too late. 'Hurry!'

He did not want to jostle Turke by ferrying him up the narrow stairs that led to Stanmore's solar, so they took him to the ground-floor room that Cynric and his wife shared, where the physician knew there would be a fire and space to work. Rachel was startled by the sudden and unannounced appearance of a 'corpse' in her home, but fetched blankets and bowls of hot water quickly and without needless questions. Everyone – Philippa, Abigny, Stanmore, Edith, Michael, the two soldiers, Cynric and Rachel – crammed into the chamber to watch, advise or help.

Bartholomew knew it was important to warm his victim as soon as possible, so that vital organs could begin their normal functions again. He also knew that heating a frozen person too quickly would place excessive strain on the heart, which would then stop beating. It was a fine line between one and the other, and he was not entirely sure of the limits of either. It was not uncommon for people to fall through rotten ice in the winter, and so it was an operation he had been called upon to perform on several occasions in the past. Sometimes he was successful, and sometimes he was not.

Watched intently by a distraught Philippa, he removed wet clothes and replaced them with heated strips of linen. He concentrated on the torso first; the limbs were less urgent. When he came to remove the unconscious man's knee-high hose, Philippa stopped him, and, with an odd sense of decorum, she whisked them off under a sheet. It seemed a peculiar thing to do when the rest of him had been so brutally exposed to view, but the physician supposed she imagined she was doing her bit to preserve her husband's dignity.

Some of the blueness faded from Turke's face, and Bartholomew began to hope there might be a chance. Philippa insisted on touching her husband, stroking his brow and murmuring to him. She was often in the way, but Bartholomew hoped her voice might work its own magic and pull the man back from the brink of death. Meanwhile, Abigny watched from the door, an anxious expression on his face, although who the anxiety was for – Philippa, Turke or himself – was impossible to say.

After a while, Turke's eyelids fluttered and he muttered something incomprehensible. Philippa seized his hand and her soft calls rose to a crescendo as she pleaded with him to speak to her. Turke's eyes opened a second time, and he stared at the ceiling.

'I am here, Walter,' Philippa shouted. 'Come back to me!'

Turke turned his head very slightly in her direction, and his eyes appeared to focus on her face. He swallowed, then spoke. He uttered two words in a low, hoarse voice that had everyone straining to hear him. And then he died.

Bartholomew spent a long time frantically pushing on Turke's chest in a futile effort to make the heart beat again, but he knew the situation was hopeless. Eventually, he stopped, rubbing a hand across his face as he did so. It was hot in the room, and his attempts to revive his patient had been vigorous. Sweat stung his eyes and he could feel rivulets running down his back under his clothes.

'Just like the Death,' said Philippa softly. 'Medicine could not help people then, either.'

Bartholomew spread his hands helplessly. 'I am sorry, Philippa. I did all I could.'

She touched him on the cheek as tears began to spill from her eyes. 'It is not your fault. You did your best.'

'We will have to tell Sheriff Morice what has happened,' said one of the soldiers nervously. 'But it should make no difference, should it, whether Turke died now or earlier?' There was an almost desperate appeal in his eyes.

'Are you asking whether Morice will be angry with you for sending him word that Turke was dead when he was still alive?' asked Michael archly. 'I would not want to be so grossly misled by any of my beadles, but then my approach to these matters is infinitely more professional.'

'But Turke died anyway,' insisted the soldier. 'There was nothing Morice could have done had he been here himself. Was there?'

'No,' said Stanmore, evidently wanting the men gone from his house and deciding that telling them what they wanted to hear was the best way to do it. 'You saw for yourselves he was barely conscious.'

'We did,' said the soldier, relieved. 'We should go and make our report, then.'

'Will you or Morice be investigating further?' Edith asked, catching the soldier's arm as he prepared to escape.

He was puzzled by her question. 'We have investigated, lady. He was skating and the ice was thin. What else is there to say? It was an accident.'

'I agree,' agreed Abigny, a little too keenly for Bartholomew's comfort. 'All we can do now is take him home and give him a decent burial.'

'Very well,' said Stanmore, nodding to the soldiers to indicate they should be on their way. 'But tell Morice I expect him to pay his respects to Mistress Turke today. I do not want her to return to London claiming Cambridge men have no manners.'

'What did Turke's dying words mean?' asked Michael curiously after the soldiers had gone. 'They made no sense to me.'

'Nor to me,' said Philippa, straightening her head-dress.

This time her grief was controlled. She was the dignified fish-monger's widow, bearing her lot with grace and stoicism. By contrast, Bartholomew felt drained physically and mentally, and all he wanted was to return to Michaelhouse and lie down. 'I must buy some black cloth for mourning clothes,' Philippa added as the physician moved towards the door.

'I have plenty,' offered Stanmore. 'I always keep a good supply of black, because so many scholars and clerics need it and, combined with this new fashion for black clothes to symbolise grief, there is always a demand for it.'

'I will arrange to have your husband taken to St Michael's Church,' said Michael. 'That is what we agreed before . . .' He trailed off, not liking to dwell on the fact that they had discussed Turke's funeral arrangements while he had still lived.

Philippa nodded. 'And Matt will ask his friends to say masses for Walter's soul. I think I will bury him here. I should continue the pilgrimage at the soonest opportunity, and Walter's corpse will slow us down.'

'But you must return to London, so that we can inter him at Garlicke Hythe,' said Abigny, horrified by her plans. 'You know that is what he would have wanted.'

'He would have wanted me to complete the pilgrimage for him,' insisted Philippa stubbornly. 'His immortal soul is more important than his mortal remains. We cannot go all the way to Walsingham and back to London with him. It would not be practical.'

'Then we should settle for taking him home,' argued Abigny.

'I want to go to Walsingham,' said Philippa, becoming tearful again. 'I made promises to saints that I would go, and I do not want to break them, or I may never have a child.'

'Would you like me to do anything?' offered Michael kindly, not pointing out that with Turke dead she was free to take a man who might not need divine intervention to produce a baby. 'It seems Morice's men regard the matter as closed, but I could make some enquiries, since you had questions earlier about his death. Perhaps I can learn why he was near the river, or discover his state of mind. Sometimes having answers makes a loss easier to bear.'

'No, thank you,' said Philippa flatly. 'Walter is dead, and that is the end of the matter. I do not want you or the Sheriff to look into his personal affairs. I want his memory respected.'

'Michael would be respectful,' said Bartholomew, surprised by her sudden change of attitude. 'But it was you who told us that Walter would not have gone skating. Are you not curious to learn more about that?'

'No,' said Philippa firmly. She pointed to two sheep bones that had been tied to Turke's expensive shoes with pieces of leather. Now they lay on the floor in a sodden heap with the rest of his clothes. 'I can see he was wearing skates, and so my initial claim was obviously wrong. Please respect my wishes and leave him alone.'

'She is right,' agreed Abigny. 'No amount of questioning will bring him back, and there is no point in causing distress by prolonging the incident. I shall arrange for him to be prepared for his journey to London.'

Philippa stared angrily at her brother for a moment, then took Edith's arm and strode from the room. Abigny scurried after her, and Bartholomew could hear them arguing as they crossed the yard and climbed the stairs that led to Stanmore's solar.

'How strange,' said Stanmore, watching them in puzzlement. 'It was not many moments ago that she was so distraught with grief she could barely speak. Now she seems almost cold.'

'Poor choice of words,' said Michael, indicating the corpse. 'But I know what you mean. What can you tell from the body, Matt?'

'Philippa asked me not to examine it. She made her feelings quite clear about that.'

'That was before he died. You have just spent an hour

poking and prodding at him, so how can she object to a little more now?'

'Go and ask her,' suggested Bartholomew. He nodded wryly when Michael hesitated. 'You see? You do not really believe she will give us her permission.'

'Michael is right to suggest an examination, Matt,' said Stanmore. 'There is something odd about this incident. She was convinced that Walter would never skate on the river, and was obsessed by that point earlier. And yet she did not once mention it when we were trying to revive him here.'

'That is because she saw for herself that he was wearing skates,' said Bartholomew.

'But was he actually skating?' asked Michael, leaning down to inspect them. 'I doubt he was. If you look here, you can see that one of the leather thongs crosses the blade. Not only would such an arrangement reduce friction and slow the skater, but it would quickly wear through and break.'

Bartholomew stared at the monk in astonishment. 'What makes you such an expert on icy pastimes all of a sudden? I did not know you could skate.'

'Of course I can skate,' said Michael testily. 'How could I not, growing up in East Anglia, where the land is flat, the water plentiful, and the winters long and cold? And I can tell you that Turke did not travel far on these particular skates.'

'He travelled far enough to break the ice,' said Bartholomew soberly.

'Unfortunately, I cannot tell much about these,' Michael went on, taking one skate and examining it minutely. 'They are cheap, sold by every butcher in the Market Square in winter. In fact, they are so common that Turke may even have found them abandoned by a previous skater.'

'They break,' added Stanmore, to explain the extravagance of disposing of something that could be reused. He, too, was a Fenman and knew about skating in cold winters. 'They eventually crack when weight is put on them, especially by an adult. You often see them discarded.'

'Inspect Turke, Matt,' instructed Michael impatiently. 'I will lift the covers, if it salves your conscience, so all you have to do is look. But I want to know the exact cause of his death. Oswald is right: there is something odd about this incident.'

As it transpired, there was nothing to see. There was no wound or mark on the body, with the exception of some scratches that had probably been inflicted as Turke was rescued. There was no abrasion or bump on the head, no bleeding and no signs that he had been strangled or suffocated. A hard push on Turke's chest revealed water in his lungs, although not enough to drown him. As far as Bartholomew was concerned, Turke's death was exactly as it appeared: he had fallen in the river, and had frozen.

'Does anyone know what Turke meant by "Templar"?' asked Michael. 'No Knights Templar exist these days, so I cannot imagine what he was talking about.'

'I did not hear him say "Templar",' said Stanmore, surprised. 'I heard him say "temper" and "you". His meaning was quite clear: he was telling Philippa to mind her temper, as a husband's final piece of advice to his wife.'

'That would be an odd thing to say to her,' said Michael warily. 'She has never struck me as a woman given to sudden rages.'

'I did not hear "Templar" or "temper",' said Bartholomew. 'I heard "you" though, and I thought the other word was "Dympna".'

'It was not,' said Michael with determination. 'That would mean there is a link between Turke and Norbert, and that is not possible.'

'Why not?' asked Bartholomew. 'Norbert was murdered after Turke arrived in Cambridge.'

Michael rubbed a hand over his eyes. 'A connection between a wealthy fishmonger and a debauched and worthless idler? I do not think so!'

'Do not be too hasty to dismiss it,' warned Bartholomew. 'Consider two things. First, Turke was a merchant and

Norbert was a merchant's nephew – both well-connected men with access to wealth and power, even if Norbert did have to go through his uncle for his. And second, Turke was a fishmonger. There was a fish on the ground the night Norbert was murdered.'

'A fish?' asked Stanmore, bewildered. 'What kind?'

'A tench,' said Bartholomew. 'Although I do not think the type is relevant.'

'Nothing about it is relevant,' said Michael. 'You used the fish to connect Norbert to Harysone. Now you are using the same clue to connect Norbert to Turke.'

'You said yourself there is something strange about Turke's death, and I think it odd that Turke and his servant should die in such rapid succession,' argued Bartholomew. 'Perhaps the three deaths are related. There is nothing to say they are not.'

'But you said Norbert won the tench from Harysone by dicing, and dropped it as he fled for his life,' said Michael. 'How can that possibly have anything to do with Turke? And you told me earlier there was nothing odd about Gosslinge's death. Have you changed your mind?'

'I think there is something odd about the *timing* of Gosslinge's and Turke's deaths, not the deaths themselves – they both appear to be accidental and caused by the cold. And I think Turke muttering "Dympna", the fact that he and Gosslinge were in the fishmongering trade, and that Norbert won a fish indicates all three deaths may be related. Perhaps Harysone is the factor that connects them.'

'I would like you to be right,' said Michael. 'You know how dearly I would like to catch that man doing something wrong. But even I cannot see how he can have anything to do with Turke and his servant, just because Norbert happened to win a tench before he died.'

'You are wrong about Turke's last words, too,' added Stanmore. 'He did not say "Dympna".'

'Temper, Templar, Dympna,' mused Michael thoughtfully. 'We all heard different things, and there is no way to prove

146

which of us is right. However, there is one other thing we should consider.'

'I know,' said Bartholomew, anticipating what the monk was going to say. 'We might not know what Turke meant, but Philippa certainly did. Her behaviour changed from grief-stricken to coolly contained almost the instant he spoke to her.'

When Bartholomew and Michael arrived back at Michaelhouse, an afternoon meal was ready, and the students were in a state of excitement; they were going to elect their Lord of Misrule, who would run the College for the Twelve Days. This was an ancient tradition and, although some of the Fellows were keen to have it abolished, the students were equally determined to see it continue. The Lord of Misrule had absolute power over all College members, and everyone was obliged to do what he ordered. Usually, this was confined to ordering the Fellows to serve the students at the dinner table, or obliging them to listen to lectures written and delivered by students for their edification. Sometimes the pranks could be amusing, but sometimes they were a nuisance, and other times they were a genuine menace.

Bartholomew felt guilty about joining a room full of celebrating scholars while the woman he had loved was so fresh in her grief, but there was nothing he could do to help her, and it seemed a pity to curb his enjoyment because of the death of a man he had barely known. Resolutely, he pushed the fishmonger from his mind, and tried to give his full attention to the events unfolding in the hall. With some trepidation the Fellows took their places. The students were already there, and there was an atmosphere of tense anticipation among them. Rather unwisely, considering his unpopularity with the undergraduates, Father William had ordered two of his students to help him up the stairs, keen not to miss anything.

'I do not approve of this ceremony,' he boomed, sitting

on a bench with his damaged leg propped in front of him as he ate stewed turnips and cold meat left over from the feast. 'Why can we not elect a Boy Bishop, instead? That would be much more in line with the teachings of the Church, and is what the scholars at Valence Marie do.'

'There is no difference, as far as I can see,' said Kenyngham. 'A Boy Bishop is just as likely to cause mischief as is a Lord of Misrule. It is only the name that is different, not the activity.'

'But a Boy Bishop is obliged to give a sermon in the church,' argued William. 'And a church is the best place for these lads at this time of year.'

'You would not say that if you heard some of the sermons,' said Suttone, picking up the remains of an eel and gnawing along its backbone with his large teeth. 'Believe me, William, it is best to keep this sort of thing well away from the sacred confines of God's houses.'

'Let us proceed,' said Langelee, addressing the waiting students. 'Who are your candidates?'

'Gray and Quenhyth,' called the Franciscan Ulfrid, a mischievous grin creasing his face.

Quenhyth was immediately on his feet, his face flushed with outrage. 'I will not be party to such a disgraceful spectacle! I have no time for stupid pranks and only want to study. You can leave me out of this!'

'Silly boy,' muttered Michael, shaking his head in reproof. 'He should have accepted the nomination, and taken the opportunity to avenge himself on those who have plagued him since September.'

'Quenhyth is a dull boy,' said Suttone, spitting eel bones on to the table, where they landed with a light pattering sound. 'He talks about his lectures and his reading, but nothing else.'

'He is unwise,' said Bartholomew. 'By standing down, he has effectively ensured that Gray is elected. And Gray will make his life a misery over the next twelve days.'

'Gray had better not try to make *my* life a misery,' said

148

William threateningly. 'I will not be harassed by a group of boys.'

'You have no choice,' said Langelee sternly. 'You must bide by any decisions the Lord makes, while at the same time promising no retribution in the future. You know this; we have been through it before.'

William growled something incomprehensible, and snapped his fingers for Cynric to fetch him some wine. The gesture did not go unnoticed by Gray, and neither did Cynric's long-suffering grimace. Bartholomew was certain William would soon pay for his abrupt treatment of the servants.

'I nominate me,' said Deynman, loudly and rather unexpectedly. For a moment, no one spoke, and everyone in the hall stared at the lad whose limited intelligence would never see him pass his disputations.

'You cannot nominate yourself,' said Gray eventually. 'It is not done.'

'Who says?' demanded Deynman, uncharacteristically pugilistic. 'Just because it has not been done before does not mean that it cannot be done now. And anyway, you were Lord of Misrule last year, and I do not want you again. This year it should be me.'

Several of the students began to cheer his audacity, while Gray looked as black as thunder. 'But I have made arrangements,' he said in a low, angry voice. 'I will ensure that no one will ever forget my last Christmas at Michaelhouse: my reign will be remembered for decades to come.'

'Lord!' breathed Michael in alarm. 'I do not like the sound of that. It does not bode well for us Fellows, of that you can be sure.'

'I do not care about the Fellows, only that we still have a College at the end of it,' said Langelee worriedly. 'Gray's idea of a memorable time might be to set the place alight and dance in the flames.'

'It is not,' said Bartholomew, defensive of the student who had been with him since the plague. 'He knows there are

149

limits. I cannot say the same for Deynman, however, so you had better hope Gray wins the election.'

But Gray did not win the election. The students were amused by the fact that Deynman had issued a direct challenge to Gray, who was a bully, and the vote for Deynman was almost unanimous. Gray was furious, and slouched on his bench with a face that could curdle milk.

'Good,' said Deynman, rubbing his hands together. 'Give me your tabard, Master Langelee. I shall wear it until Twelfth Night, so that everyone will know that *I* am in charge.'

'Very well, but you had better not spill anything on it,' said Langelee, reluctantly handing over the garment. 'I want it back clean.'

'Do not worry,' said Deynman carelessly, indicating that Langelee would be unlikely to be able to wear the item again. He turned to address his new 'subjects'. 'There are some things I should make clear. First, you have to do anything I say . . .'

'Within reason,' cautioned Ulfrid warily. 'You cannot ask us to do anything dangerous or too nasty. For example, I refuse to be the one to remove Father William's habit and wash it.' The chorus of cat-calls and laughter made William gape in astonishment. Ulfrid hastened to explain to the bemused Fellows. 'That was on Gray's list of things to do during the Twelve Days. It is something that should happen, but none of us wants the task.'

'Brother Michael can do it,' said Deynman. 'He is big, strong and used to unpleasant sights.'

'I am sure we can come to some arrangement,' said Bartholomew hastily, anticipating that Michael would refuse to undertake such a gruesome task, which might result in all manner of chaos. 'If William will relinquish it willingly, then Michael can take it to Agatha—'

'I will not have that filthy thing in my laundry,' came Agatha's voice from behind the servants' screen, where she had been listening and probably enjoying herself – at least, until she had been mentioned in connection with William's infamous robe. 'The bonfire is the best place for that.'

'I will buy a new one,' said Deynman generously. 'And then no one need touch it. That is my second command: William's vile habit shall never again make an appearance in Michaelhouse.'

'Now just a moment,' began William indignantly. 'This is a perfectly serviceable garment. I admit it is marred by one or two stains—'

Whatever he had planned to say was drowned by laughter. The students hefted their new leader on to their shoulders and carried him to the conclave, which they evidently intended to wrest from the Fellows for the next few days. Gray followed them, a thoughtful expression on his face. His train of thought was obvious to anyone who knew him: Deynman was fond of Gray, and would listen to anything he suggested. So, while Gray might not be Lord of Misrule himself, being the friend of one was the next best thing. Gray would have his power after all.

'You cannot take the conclave!' exclaimed Kenyngham, his usually benign face filled with dismay. 'It is where the Fellows go in the evenings.'

Bartholomew regarded him uncertainly. The Gilbertine was not a man who usually cared much about personal comforts. Indeed, Bartholomew would not have been surprised if Kenyngham had failed to notice that the conclave was unavailable, so immersed was he in spiritual matters.

'The Fellows can use the hall instead,' said Deynman carelessly, struggling out of his friends' grasp and walking towards the friar. If he was annoyed to have his authority contested quite so soon after his election, he did not show it. 'That is what this season is all about – changing things and breaking customs.'

'But I might want to go into the conclave,' protested Kenyngham, becoming distressed.

'Do not worry, Father,' said Deynman kindly, after glancing questioningly at his friends to ensure he had their support. Everyone liked the Gilbertine, and there were nods and smiles all around. '*You* can come in any time you like. The other Fellows are banned, though.'

Kenyngham raised a blue-veined hand as he muttered a blessing. Deynman gave him a conspiratorial wink, then followed his colleagues. Several stumbled over the loose board as they went, unused to the conclave floor's irregularities.

'What was that about?' Bartholomew asked Kenyngham, as they walked together across the hall to the spiral staircase that led to the yard. 'You do not usually care about such things.'

'I find the conclave more peaceful than the hall.'

'You will not if it is full of celebrating students,' said Bartholomew, wondering why he felt the friar was not being entirely honest with him.

He watched Kenyngham head towards his room, then went to his own chamber, intending to leave Michaelhouse before Deynman had time to flex his new muscles of power and ask him to do something inconvenient or silly. The other Fellows had the same idea, and there was a concerted dash for the gate. Bartholomew decided to visit Dunstan, partly because he wanted to see whether there was anything he could do to help the old man, but partly because he hoped Matilde might be there. As he walked along the river bank towards the crumbling huts, he thought about Turke, and wondered what the death of her husband would mean for Philippa and her comfortable life on London's Friday Street.

CHAPTER 5

THERE WERE MORE CELEBRATIONS IN MICHAELHOUSE THAT night, with the Lord of Misrule sitting in Langelee's seat for the St Stephen's Day supper. Predictably, the Fellows had been instructed to serve, while Deynman was surrounded by his friends at the high table. Agatha, of course, was considered far too venerable to sit with the rabble, so she was placed at Deynman's right hand, looking pleased with herself as she swilled back plentiful quantities of wine.

The atmosphere was light-hearted and jovial, and everyone seemed to be enjoying himself – although one or two Fellows were grim faced. This merely increased the students' amusement. Warned by Langelee that the College wine supplies were low and would not support a season of continuous drinking, Deynman had solved the problem with large sums of money. The cellars had been restocked, and the kitchens received a welcome boost of new and interesting victuals.

'Now we shall have the Chepe Waits,' decreed Deynman, standing and waving a slopping cup to give emphasis to his instruction. 'And everyone has to talk while he is eating – English or French, not Latin. We will have no silence or Bible-reading at any meal for the next two weeks.'

'Twelve days,' corrected Suttone grimly, struggling with a bowl of leeks. 'Let us not lose count, please. William knew what he was doing when he broke his leg – at least he is not being submitted to this kind of indignity.'

'He is also unable to protect himself,' said Michael, striding past him bearing a platter loaded with meat. His hands and mouth were greasy, and it was clear that he had been working on the 'one-for-you-and-one-for-me' principle. 'Because he could not move, those students were able to rip that habit off him and replace it with a new one. As you can imagine, he complained bitterly.'

Bartholomew could imagine. 'His leg is not broken, you know,' he said in a low voice to the monk. 'If I were to remove the splint, he would be able to walk perfectly well.'

'Leave the splint where it is, if you please,' said Michael firmly. 'I want William incapacitated while I am investigating Norbert's death. I do not want him "helping". And anyway, you know he hates the Misrule season. It is better for everyone if he stays in his room.'

'I am surprised the Chepe Waits are still here,' said Clippesby, arriving with a bowl of nuts. 'Frith had a fight with Agatha, and they have all been questioned by the Sheriff about a theft from the King's Head. I thought they would have been dismissed.'

'Apparently, the King's Head victim declined to take the matter further,' said Michael, helping himself to a thick slice of pork before flinging a considerably smaller one on to Cynric's trencher. 'Did you want that, Cynric? If not, throw it across to Quenhyth; he needs a bit of flesh on his bones. So, the Waits were released without being charged. I cannot help but wonder whether they bribed Morice to drop the investigation.'

'Frith outwitted Deynman shamelessly this morning,' said Suttone, doling out leeks into the bowls that were shared by two people on the high table, and four people in the body of the hall. 'He threatened to leave Michaelhouse immediately unless Deynman signed a statement promising to hire the troupe for the entire Misrule season. The boy was dismayed at the prospect of being unable to supply entertainment for his "court", and quickly agreed to Frith's terms.'

'That was a low trick,' said Bartholomew, angered partly by Deynman's gullibility, but mostly because the Wait had used Deynman's dull mind to get what he wanted. He had not been impressed by the entertainers' talents or their manners, and he had intended to advise Deynman to dismiss them. Now it seemed he was too late.

The Waits, assured of employment for the foreseeable future, were complacent. Their tumbling was less energetic, and they dropped their balls and sticks with greater frequency than before. They looked dirty, too, and neither of the 'women' had shaved. One had dispensed with the annoyance of his yellow wig, and the resulting combination of large bosom, balding head and bewhiskered face was not attractive. They did not bother with a lengthy performance, either, and it was not long before Frith announced they were going to rest. They retreated behind the servants' screen, and Bartholomew arrived in time to catch Jestyn drinking from one of the wine jugs.

'That is not for you,' he said coolly, taking the receptacle from the entertainer's hands. 'And it is rude to drink from the jug, anyway.'

'I was thirsty,' said Jestyn, unrepentant. 'I am I hungry, too. What is there to eat?'

'They have already had their meal,' said Michael, coming to refill his meat tray. 'They cannot be hungry again already.'

'How would you know what we feel?' demanded Frith insolently.

'You had better keep a civil tongue, or I shall see you throw no more balls and coloured sticks in Michaelhouse,' said Michael sharply.

'We have been hired for the whole festive period,' said Frith gloatingly. 'We have an agreement with Deynman, and we will only leave if *he* dismisses us. What you think is irrelevant.'

'Do not be so sure about that,' said Michael with cold menace. Frith regarded him silently for a moment, and apparently realised it would not be wise to antagonise a man like Michael. He recanted, forcing a grin on to his unwholesome face.

'Take no notice of us, Brother. We have been in rough

155

company for so long that we have forgotten our manners. I am sorry if I offended you. We mean no harm.'

'We do not,' agreed one of the women. She had dispensed with false beard and moustache in the interests of comfort, although her hair was still gathered under her cap in the manner of a young man. She was a robust lady, with a prominent nose and a pair of shrewd green eyes. She wiggled her hips and effected a mischievous grin 'My name is Matilda, but my friends call me Makejoy. Would you like me to show you why, Brother?'

'He is busy,' said Bartholomew, reluctant to do all the work while Michael frolicked behind the screens with the likes of Makejoy. He could tell from the expression on the monk's face that he was interested. 'Come on, Brother. There are people waiting for their food.'

'In a moment,' said Michael, perching a large rump on one of the trestle tables and folding his arms. He was clearly in no hurry to resume his labours. 'I have questions for these good people.'

'What kind of questions?' demanded Frith, instantly wary. 'If you are referring to that theft at the King's Head, then yes, we were in the tavern that night, and no, we did not take the gold. The Sheriff agreed there was not enough evidence to make a case against us, so do not think you will succeed where he failed.'

'Gold?' asked Michael innocently. 'Would this be the gold Cynric saw you counting?'

The Waits exchanged uneasy glances. 'No one saw us count anything,' said Jestyn unconvincingly.

'Really?' asked Michael sweetly. 'You sleep in the room above the stables. Were you aware that it adjoins the servants' quarters, and that a previous master drilled a series of spyholes in the walls to allow a watchful eye to be kept on visiting strangers such as yourselves?'

'We must have been counting the coins Deynman gave us,' said Jestyn quickly. 'He threw us a handful after our performance last night.'

'He gave you silver, not gold, and I can assure you Cynric knows the difference. Now, I shall say nothing of this to Morice, but there is a price: I want some information.'

Bartholomew was amused by Michael's tactics. He suspected that Morice knew perfectly well the Waits were guilty of theft, and, since even a hint of criminal behaviour was normally sufficient for the wrongdoer to be expelled from the town – or worse – it was obvious that Morice had been persuaded to overlook the matter. The physician wondered how much of the stolen gold had been left in the Waits' possession once Morice had taken his share.

However, it also stood to reason that the corrupt Sheriff would be keen for the incident to be buried and forgotten. He would not be pleased if Michael presented him with irrefutable evidence of the Waits' guilt. Morice would never allow Frith to reveal Morice's own role in the affair, and it was not unknown for people to be stabbed in dark alleys or to disappear completely. Morice was a dangerous man as far as the Waits were concerned, and Michael had them in a nasty corner by threatening to go to him.

'When you first arrived in the town, you stayed at the King's Head,' said Michael, fixing Frith with the unwavering stare he usually reserved for unruly students. 'Now, there was another guest present at the time called John Harysone. What can you tell me about him?'

'Who?' asked Makejoy nervously.

'Come, come,' said Michael impatiently. 'I know the tavern was busy, but you must have noticed Harysone. He is a bearded fellow with teeth like a horse and an oily, mal-evolent character.'

'The one who dresses in black?' said Frith sulkily. 'I know nothing about him – only that he hired a private room. We, on the other hand, slept in the hayloft with other less wealthy patrons.'

'Did you speak to him?' pressed Michael. 'Or see him talking to anyone else?'

'No,' said Makejoy. 'And we would tell you if we had; we

owe nothing to the man, so it does not matter whether we say anything that would land him in trouble. He arrived here the same time as us – eleven days ago now, because we came on the fifteenth day of December. I noticed him immediately. His long teeth make eating difficult, you see, so his noonday meal was a curious thing to watch – and I have seen him in the tavern since.'

'But you have not exchanged words?' asked Michael.

Jestyn shook his head. 'I nodded at him, as fellow travellers do, but he did not acknowledge me. He stared straight through me, then turned his attention to his duck pie. In fact, he spoke to no one. He declined all company, even that fishmonger's wife.'

'Do you mean Philippa Turke?' asked Michael. 'I heard she and her family took a room in the King's Head before they went to stay with Stanmore.'

'We wondered why they had left,' said Frith. 'But while they were there, your black-cloaked fellow failed to show them any of the courtesies usually exchanged between fellow travellers. Perhaps that is why they abandoned the King's Head – to seek more pleasant company elsewhere.'

Makejoy frowned thoughtfully. 'Their servant sat with Harysone, though. Remember?'

'They shared a table, but did not speak,' said Frith. 'It was busy that night, and all the other seats were taken. Harysone was displeased that he was forced to share, and cut short his meal. He took his wine with him. I remember that, because I was hoping he would leave it behind.'

'That would be Gosslinge,' said Michael in satisfaction. 'In company with Harysone. You were right, Matt: there is a connection between them.'

'They shared a table, but not words,' Bartholomew pointed out. 'It does not sound like a meaningful encounter to me.'

'We shall see,' said Michael, pleased with the discovery nonetheless. He addressed the Waits again. 'Did you know that Gosslinge is dead? He died in our church, where

158

someone relieved him of his clothes. I would not find them if I looked among your travelling packs, would I?'

'You would not,' said Makejoy huffily. 'And I resent the implication that we are thieves.'

'But you *are* thieves,' Michael pointed out. 'We have already established that – it is why you are answering my questions, remember?' He heaved his bulk off the table and picked up his tray. 'However, while I am prepared to over-look a theft from the King's Head, I will not be so lenient if anything disappears from Michaelhouse. Do I make myself clear?'

The Waits nodded resentfully and Michael left, taking his meat with him. Bartholomew filled his jug with wine from the barrel.

'So,' he said conversationally. 'You never met Gosslinge or Harysone before you arrived in Cambridge?'

'We told you: we have never set eyes on Harysone before,' replied Frith.

Bartholomew straightened. 'And Gosslinge?'

'Tell him, Frith,' said Makejoy, after more uncomfortable glances had been exchanged. 'If you do not and he finds out, he will assume we have done something wrong. And we have not.'

'We knew Gosslinge,' admitted Frith reluctantly. 'But when we heard he was dead, we were afraid to tell anyone about it. You can see why: that monk immediately accused us of stealing his clothes, even though we are innocent.'

'How do you know him?'

'We were hired to perform for Walter Turke in London,' said Makejoy. 'We juggled and sang at a feast he held for his fellow fishmongers. It was Gosslinge who told us where we could change and provided our food.'

Bartholomew stared at her, his mind whirling. 'When was this?'

Frith blew out his cheeks in a sigh. 'June or July, I suppose.'

'Who hired you?' asked Bartholomew. 'Turke himself?'

'His wife,' replied Frith. 'She sat next to you at the Christmas feast.'

Bartholomew frowned in puzzlement, recalling that when he had discussed the Waits with Philippa she had announced, quite categorically, that she did not like such people and never employed them. As the two of them had been struggling to find things to talk about, her recognition of folk she had met before surely would have been a godsend as a conversational gambit. Yet she had not mentioned her previous encounter with them. Why? Had she forgotten them? Was their performance an unpleasant memory that she had suppressed?

Her brother's reaction had been equally odd: Abigny had claimed he disliked jugglers, and had left Langelee's chambers as soon as they had arrived, then had excused himself when they had approached the high table later in the hall. And Turke? They had jostled him and spilled his wine, but he had declined to make a fuss. What did that say about his relationship with the Waits? That he knew them but was loath to admit it to people he wanted to impress? That he declined to indulge in an undignified squabble with menials? Bartholomew supposed the Waits could be lying about being hired by the Turke household, but he saw no reason why they should.

'Did you speak to Gosslinge, here in Cambridge?' he asked.

'Oh, yes,' said Frith bitterly. 'I asked him if he would recommend us to potential employers, since it was proving difficult to find a situation for the Twelve Days. We had offered ourselves to virtually every merchant in the town, you see, but they had already made other arrangements and had no need for us. But Gosslinge refused to help.'

'Now we shall have marchpanes,' declared Deynman, standing again and deluging Suttone with wine as he waved his goblet around. There was a chorus of laughter, while the morose Carmelite surveyed the red stains on his robes with weary resignation.

'That pale wool is an impractical colour for a habit,' said Deynman defensively, blushing with embarrassment. He was not a naturally rebellious lad, and his antics so far had been tame compared to the stunts that Gray had arranged the previous year. However, Gray was sitting near to his friend at the high table, and Bartholomew saw it would not be long before matters took a turn for the worse. Gray was clearly plotting something. He leaned towards Deynman and was constantly muttering in his ear.

Wynewyk and Clippesby emerged from behind the servants' screen carrying a huge tray on which sat a huge marchpane image, dressed in blue and white cloth. It was the Virgin Mary. It was fairly large, reaching mid-thigh height, and its face was swathed in a veil. It was not uncommon for Michaelhouse to buy carved marchpanes for the Christmas season, but none had been so finely wrought as this one. Students, Fellows and servants alike watched its progress through the hall in awed silence, and even the Waits were impressed – Frith began a stately march on pipes and tabor to accompany it. Clippesby and Wynewyk set the image on the high table and stepped away.

'Good,' said Deynman approvingly. 'But we cannot see the detail on her with all these clothes and veils. Let us take them off.'

'For the love of God, no!' cried Suttone, leaping forward to prevent such a sacrilege. 'What are you thinking of, boy? You go too far!'

Deynman faltered, unsettled by the vehemence of Suttone's protest, while the silence in the hall was so thick that Bartholomew could hear an insect buzzing in one of the windows. Gray gave Deynman a none too gentle prod in the ribs to prompt him.

'But we must,' said Deynman, agitated. 'It is part of the performance.'

'I will not stand by and see you haul the vestments from our Blessed Virgin,' declared Suttone, drawing himself up to his full cadaverous height. 'Lord of Misrule you may be, but I will not permit heresy to take place in my College. What would the Bishop and Head of my Order say when they learn what sort of revelries Michaelhouse condones?'

Gray came slowly to his feet. '*You* will not permit it, Father? How will you stop us?'

Suttone was taller and probably stronger than Gray, but it did not take much to intimidate the friar from his pedestal of self-righteousness; he was a coward at heart. He appealed to his colleagues. 'Come to my aid,' he pleaded. 'You know I am right and this cannot be allowed. And tell Gray to sit down, Matthew. I do not like him glowering at me like a tavern brawler.'

'The Lord of Misrule can do what he likes,' declared Gray. He snatched up his goblet and gave his friends a grin that was full of mischief. 'We will not allow the Fellows to renege on their agreement to allow us free rein, will we?' There was a chorus of nervous agreement, and Gray jumped on to the table, hands on hips as he gazed around him with naked disdain. 'This is the Twelve Days,' he declared, glaring at his cronies until they met his eyes. 'You have been looking forward to it for months. It is *our* time, when we are free to amuse ourselves and have fun. We will not allow a Carmelite to stand in the way of the best Christmas celebrations Michaelhouse has ever known, will we? Well? What do you say?'

This time the chorus of voices was stronger, and several students came to their feet, raising their goblets in a sloppy salute to Gray.

'But this is different,' objected Suttone feebly. 'Stripping the Virgin!'

'We shall play "Strip the Virgin" later,' promised Gray, referring to a well-known game that was popular in venues like the King's Head. The students cheered in delight. 'But now we shall strip the marchpane.'

'Matthew!' cried Suttone, turning beseechingly to the physician. 'Gray and Deynman are your students. You must prevent them from doing this.'

But the high table was some distance away, and Bartholomew's path was blocked by Gray's friends. The physician knew they would stop him if he walked in their direction, and he did not want to start a fight he could not win. He glanced around for Langelee, but the Master was not in the hall, and Bartholomew supposed he had gone to the cellars for more wine. Michael was as hesitant as Bartholomew to interfere with Gray's plans, and merely stood near the servants' screen, drinking the wine he should have been serving.

Meanwhile, Gray started to sing a tavern song, and the words were immediately picked up by the other students and the servants. Bartholomew noticed that even Clippesby was joining in, although the lyrics were obscene, and should not have been in the repertoire of a Dominican friar. The song involved a good deal of cup banging, and the hall was soon awash with noise. Gray leaned towards Deynman and muttered something in his ear. Deynman shook his head, but Gray was insistent, and Deynman's hand started to move towards the marchpane Madonna.

Suttone's frantic protests were inaudible through the singing, as Gray had doubtless intended. Deynman's fingers tightened around the veil and cloak and, with a flourish, he whipped them off. Underneath, the figure was no Madonna. It was a model of Father William, complete with filthy habit, grimy hands and a tonsure that was irregular, bristly and made from real hair. The sculptor had captured the fanatical gleam of the friar's eyes and the pugilistic pout of his lips. A miniature wineskin dangled at his side, and one foot was resting on a copy of the Rules of St Dominic, the laws and ordinances by which the Dominican Order was governed. In one of his hands was a vast purse with the word 'fines' written on it, while the other grasped a book that had ribald songs inscribed on its tiny pages.

There was an appreciative roar of delight from the students, and Bartholomew and Michael exchanged a grin of relief. Suttone rubbed a hand over his face and left the hall, while

Clippesby laughed long and hard. Langelee was suddenly among them, holding a casket of wine in his powerful arms. He gaped at the figure, set down his barrel and traced a forefinger down the line of its habit, clearly impressed.

'Good God!' he muttered in amazement. 'It looks real!'

'It is William in every respect!' cried Clippesby, perching on the high table to inspect the figure in greater detail. William did not like Dominicans, and Clippesby had been on the receiving end of a good many unprovoked insults. He was obviously delighted that the dour friar had been the butt of the students' joke. 'I wish he could see it. Shall we take it to him?'

'I do not think so,' said Gray wisely. 'He will not see the amusing side and will fine us all for worshipping graven images or some such thing.'

'I can assure you we will not be praying to it,' said Langelee, standing back to admire the statue and its clever details. There was even a broken sandal strap, just like William's. 'But you are right. He will not see the humour. Who made it?'

'It was—' began Deynman.

'That we shall never reveal,' said Gray, interrupting firmly. 'William is vengeful, and I do not want to see someone mercilessly persecuted for what is only a little fun. But shall we just stand here and look at it, or shall we eat him?'

'Eat him!' yelled the students as one.

Deynman grabbed a knife and began paring away sections of the model, enjoying himself enormously. The students cheered as he worked, particularly when he attacked the head.

'Who will eat this?' he cried, waving his trophy in the air.

'Not me,' said Michael in distaste, although he was not normally a man to refuse something edible. 'It has hairs in it. Real ones.'

'Of course it has hairs,' said Deynman. 'It is a head. Will you eat it if I remove them?'

'Well . . .' said Michael, clearly tempted. William's head

represented a sizeable chunk of marchpane, and the monk would have a larger share if he accepted it. He adored the expensive almond-flavoured paste, and such a generous portion was not an offer to be lightly dismissed.

'Give it to me,' said Clippesby, snatching the head from Deynman. He broke it in half, and gave part to Michael. Then he began to pull away smaller pieces, handing them to the students. 'We shall all partake of William's head.'

'You have given me the bit with the hair in it,' said Michael, aggrieved, but making no move to share. 'They are not *his* hairs, are they? If so, then none of us should be eating it.'

'They are from a horse,' said Deynman. 'We wanted William's own, but I could not bring myself to gather them, even when he lay in a drunken slumber after he had broken his leg.'

It was not long before everyone had been given a piece of William – with the notable exception of Gray. The Waits had also been left out, although all four stuck out their hands hopefully when the tray came past. Deynman held up his portion, and a respectful silence fell over the assembly.

'To William,' he announced, and thrust the treat into his mouth. The students, Fellows and servants repeated his words and followed suit. Bartholomew did not, suspecting that there was a good reason why Gray had declined his share.

There was. Within moments, the hall was full of gagging and spitting sounds.

'Horrible!' cried Michael, flinging away his piece so hard that it disappeared from view near the conclave door. He stuck out his tongue and began to wipe it with a piece of linen, pulling the most disagreeable of faces as he did so. Others were not so genteel. A good many mouthfuls ended up on the floor, and Bartholomew saw Quenhyth being sick.

'Salt,' said the physician, taking a careful lick of his own piece, 'instead of sugar.'

Gray sat in his chair and laughed until he wept, and Bartholomew saw he had had his revenge on the College that had declined to elect him its Lord of Misrule. Gray was not the only one to indulge in spiteful laughter. Bartholomew looked towards the servants' screen and saw the Waits were equally amused.

Quenhyth was waiting for Bartholomew the following morning when the physician emerged from the kitchens, where he had been helping the other Fellows to clean up after breakfast. Deynman had decreed that the servants should spend the day in the conclave, while the Fellows scrubbed the trays and pans used at the feast the night before. No one was happy with this arrangement: the servants complained that the Fellows would make more work by not cleaning their utensils properly, and the Fellows had not performed such base chores for years and did not want to start now. But Deynman's orders were law, and they were all obliged to obey them.

'Are you better today?' asked Bartholomew, recalling that it was Quenhyth who had vomited after eating the salty marchpane.

Quenhyth grimaced. 'No thanks to Gray. He might have made someone seriously ill with that prank. I hope Master Langelee sees he pays for his irresponsible behaviour.'

'What did you want?' asked Bartholomew, knowing that Langelee would do nothing of the kind. The Master had thoroughly enjoyed the joke, and considered a mouthful of salt a small price to pay for such rich entertainment.

'I am consigned to gate duty,' said Quenhyth resentfully. 'Deynman says Walter the porter is to deliver a lecture on creation theology, while I am to guard the door.' He pouted angrily. 'I have a disputation in a few weeks and I must study. I cannot afford to waste time on foolery like this.'

'Just do it, Quenhyth,' advised Bartholomew. 'If you rebel, you will only find yourself in trouble. Your fanatical attitude to your studies has not endeared you to your fellow students, and you would be wise to do as they ask until the Twelve Days are safely over.'

'I will not permit them to dictate the pace of my studies,' declared Quenhyth hotly. 'Education is a sacred thing, and it is not for the likes of Deynman to tell me when I can and cannot read.'

'Right,' said Bartholomew, seeing that his advice was wasted. 'But why are you telling me all this? There is nothing I can do to relieve you of your gate duties.'

'I did not imagine there would be,' said Quenhyth unpleasantly. 'No man can control that pair of louts – not even their teacher. But I came because you have been summoned by a patient. He wants you to attend him at the King's Head.'

'The King's Head?' asked Bartholomew, surprised. He was not usually called to tend the patrons of that particular tavern. The landlord tended to recommend the cheaper services of Robin of Grantchester, who was a townsman and not a member of the University. 'Who is it?'

Quenhyth shrugged. 'The messenger was vague about the name: it was something like Harpoon or Hairspoon.'

'Harysone?'

Quenhyth shrugged again. 'It could have been. But I must get back to my post. Gray may let robbers into the College, just to blame their presence on me. Of course, Deynman has given four thieves permission to stay here, anyway. I know the Chepe Waits from of old, and they are not honest folk.'

'How do you know them?' asked Bartholomew, walking with him across the yard to fetch his cloak and bag. The morning was icy again, and winter lay cold and heavy on the town. A rich, metallic scent in the air indicated they were in for yet more snow soon.

'My father hired them once. They spend most of their time in London, hawking their skills to merchants, and my father asked them to perform at my sister's marriage last year. I sensed it was a mistake, given they are so obviously vagabonds, but he persisted anyway. I was proved right, of course.'

'How?'

'They stole a silver chalice. Well, they claimed they did not, and the thing was not among their possessions when

167

they were searched, but they were the culprits, nevertheless.'

'How do you know those Waits and ours are the same people?'

Quenhyth gave him a weary look. 'I remember their names: Frith, Makejoy, Yna and Jestyn. They wear each other's clothes, so the men are women and the women men. They say it is to make people laugh, but I think it is because they encourage men to seduce the "ladies", then demand payment for their silence. You know how severely lewd acts are punished these days.'

'How do you know they stole your father's chalice?' asked Bartholomew, thinking it would have to be a desperate man who would try to seduce one of the stubble-chinned 'ladies' of the Chepe Waits. Still, he recalled, Langelee had been fooled, and there was no accounting for taste.

'The Waits were the only strangers to enter the house that day, and the chalice was found to be missing after they left. I tried to tell Langelee about it, but he would not listen. I confess I am surprised to see them in Cambridge – I thought they confined their activities to London.'

'If they steal from every household they visit, they will not stay in business for long,' said Bartholomew, thinking Quenhyth was mistaken. 'Even in a large city.'

'I followed them for a while, hoping to reclaim our property. They do a lot of business in Chepe, with fishmongers, cordwainers and other wealthy merchants. Later, they went to Kent, presumably to help with the harvest.'

'Fishmongers,' mused Bartholomew, thinking about the Waits' claim that they had been hired by Turke. Philippa had mentioned that she lived on Friday Street, and he wondered whether her house was anywhere near the Waits' territory. 'Is Friday Street close to Chepe?'

'Yes,' said Quenhyth, looking disdainfully down his long nose at Bartholomew. 'Friday Street is part of Chepe. Do you know nothing about London?'

'Not much,' said Bartholomew, who had found it dirty, dangerous, noisy and crowded on his few brief visits.

'Friday Street is dominated by the fishmongers' homes. It is near Fishmonger Row and Thames Street. Chepe, obviously, is on the river and convenient for bringing supplies of fish to the city. It is near Quenhyth, where my family live. My father is a fishmonger, too, although he is not as rich and powerful as Master Turke was. Turke did not remember me when we met at the feast, but his wife did, and she asked after my family. She is a good woman.'

Bartholomew regarded his student thoughtfully. Did the fact that Philippa lived in Chepe mean the Waits had indeed been telling the truth when they claimed they had performed for her? Or were they lying, because they were dishonest folk who regularly stole from the people who hired them? Impatiently, he pushed the questions from his mind. All of this was irrelevant. Philippa's choice of entertainers – and her willingness, or otherwise, to acknowledge them – was none of his affair. But he had a patient to attend, and that was his business.

'Chepe is a place of contrasts,' Quenhyth chattered, while the physician collected his bag. 'The merchants' houses – like the ones on Friday Street – are among the finest in the city, while some of the alleys are a foretaste of Hell in their filth and debauchery. Of course, violence is not always confined to alleys. Only a few weeks ago, Walter Turke himself stabbed a man in Fishmongers' Hall.'

'So I heard. But how do you know about it?'

'My father was there and he saw it all. The victim was called John Fiscurtune. Incidentally, he was the same fellow who recommended the Chepe Waits to my father. I later informed Fiscurtune that they were not the sort of people he should be advising honest folk to hire, but he told me to mind my own affairs. He was not a pleasant person, and I am not surprised Turke took a knife to him. No one liked him, not even his own family. It was rumoured that his son found him so vile he tossed himself in the Thames to avoid future encounters with him.'

'So, Fiscurtune knew the Waits, too?' asked Bartholomew,

baffled by the complex social connections that were emerging as Quenhyth gossiped.

'I do not know if he knew them personally, but he certainly told my father to hire them. Perhaps he liked bad juggling and hairy women. By the way, I saw Frith talking to Norbert in the King's Head the night he died, so you should tell Brother Michael to question *him* about that particular murder.' His eyes gleamed with spite.

'You tell him,' suggested Bartholomew.

'I have,' replied Quenhyth resentfully. 'But he said the Waits talked to lots of folk the night Norbert was murdered, because they were looking for someone to hire them. He is a fool to dismiss them from his enquiries so readily, though. He will find them responsible, you mark my words.'

Bartholomew sensed Quenhyth felt the same about the Waits as Michael did about Harysone. Quenhyth believed the jugglers had wronged him, and he was not a lad to forgive and forget: he was determined to make life uncomfortable for them. Bartholomew listened with half an ear as Quenhyth described what had happened when he had made himself known to the Waits in Cambridge. He claimed they had been appalled to learn of his presence, although Bartholomew suspected that they had merely warned the boy to mind his own business. Frith did not look the kind of man to be cowed by someone like Quenhyth.

'I also saw them at the King's Head with Giles Abigny,' added Quenhyth, still talking, even though Bartholomew was already out of the gate and starting to walk up the lane. 'Since they "entertained" his sister in Friday Street, I suppose they were hopeful he might buy their services a second time. That was before Master Langelee hired them for Michaelhouse, of course.'

The physician turned. 'How do you know the Waits played for Philippa?'

'I told you,' said Quenhyth impatiently. 'I watched them very carefully after they stole from my father, and one of their engagements was in the Turke household. But I could tell Abigny had not hired them this time. They made rude gestures as he walked away. I saw them with another fellow in the King's Head, too – a man with huge teeth and a habit of showing off his dancing skills. Perhaps they were trying to recruit him.' He sniggered nastily.

'Harysone?'

'The man who has summoned you? I did not know they were one and the same.'

'What were you doing in the King's Head?' asked Bartholomew archly, wondering how the student came to be in possession of so much information. If Quenhyth had been in the tavern long enough to see the Waits with Abigny, Gosslinge and Harysone, then he must have been there for some time.

Quenhyth's face puckered into a scowl. 'Gray told me there was a messenger waiting with a letter from my father. I should have known better than to believe him, because he had played exactly the same trick on me the week before. And, sure enough, Father William appeared as I waited for the "messenger" to arrive. It cost me fourpence. But before I left, I saw Harysone sitting with Frith. However, the tavern was busy, so I could not hear what they were saying.'

'Are you sure they were speaking, not just using the same table?' asked Bartholomew, recalling that the Waits had denied exchanging words with Harysone.

Quenhyth's expression became uncertain. 'I think they were talking. Why? Is Harysone a criminal? He looks like one.'

Bartholomew rubbed his chin, wondering what was truth and what was malicious gossip intended to harm the Waits. 'Why did you notice all these things?'

'If you had been the victim of a vile theft, then been made to look foolish when you could not prove your accusation, you would notice every move the Waits made, too,' said Quenhyth bitterly. 'I hate them.'

* * *

As always, when there was a deviation from the expected in terms of weather, those in authority at the little Fen-edge town were wholly unprepared for the consequences. In the summer, they were taken aback when there was a drought; they were stunned by the floods that regularly occurred in the spring; and they were aghast when rains interfered with the harvest. Snow was no different. Even though some fell most years, the town officials never thought about it until it arrived. Spades and shovels for digging were always in short supply, while no one stocked firewood so that ice could be melted in sufficient quantities to meet the demand for water.

This year was the same. Morice's soldiers had been pressed into service to clear pathways through the larger drifts, but, in the absence of proper equipment, their progress was slow. There was a particularly vast bank outside Bene't College, but the soldiers had decided this was simply too daunting to tackle, and so dug their path around it. Carts stood where they had been abandoned by their owners, some buried so deeply that only the very tops were visible. In one, a horse had been left, frozen where it had died between the shafts.

People also seemed bemused by the fact that the river had iced over, and that some traders were experiencing difficulties in transporting their goods along the waterways that wound through the Fens. It was as if it had never happened before, and people discussed the weather at every street corner, remarking that it was the most severe winter they had ever known, and that times were changing for the worse. Friars and lay-preachers were out in force, exhorting all who would listen that the climate was a sign from God that evil ways had not been sufficiently mended after the warning of the plague. The world would end in ice and fire, they claimed, if folk did not repent, wear sober clothing, give away all their possessions to the poor, cut their hair and wear sackcloth, be kind to animals and avoid the town's prostitutes.

Cynric met Bartholomew on the High Street, and when

he heard that the physician intended to visit the King's Head to tend Harysone, he insisted on accompanying him. Bartholomew did not object, glad to have Cynric and his ready blade behind him when he entered the notorious tavern. They passed through the Trumpington Gate, and walked the short distance to the inn, which stood opposite St Edmund's Priory. The priory doors were firmly closed, suggesting the Gilbertines wanted no part in the noisy Christmas revelry that was taking place in the rest of the town. The King's Head, on the other hand, was bursting at the seams. As Bartholomew and Cynric approached, two men hurtled through the door and rolled across the trodden snow of the road, where they climbed groggily to their feet. The door slammed behind them.

'Now look what you have done,' said one. 'You got us thrown out.'

They walked away arm in arm, although their progress was unsteady. Bartholomew drew his cloak more tightly around his shoulders to disguise the fact that he wore a scholar's tabard underneath, and opened the door with some trepidation.

He need not have worried. The inn was full of people he knew, all of whom raised their goblets to him in festive salutation. Some were patients, who came to mutter weepy-eyed gratitude for past treatments, while others worked at Michaelhouse. Although taverns were not places where women were found with much regularity, Agatha was different. She sat in a large seat near the fire, and held forth to a group of townsfolk who nursed ale in calloused hands and prudently nodded agreement from time to time.

'You know you cannot come in here,' said the taverner to Bartholomew with a sanctimonious expression on his face. 'The University forbids me to sell ale to scholars.'

'So I understand,' said Bartholomew, looking hard at a group of young men who were attempting to make themselves invisible by huddling into their cloaks. They were the Franciscan friars from Ovyng, and the burly Godric was at the head of their table. Godric flushed deep red when he saw he had been recognised, and buried his face in his jug. 'I was summoned by Master Harysone. Is he here?'

'Oh,' said the taverner, relieved. 'I thought Brother Michael had sent you to see whether I would sell you a drink. It is Harysone you want, is it? He is in his chamber, unwell. It is not because of my cooking, though – and you can tell him that.'

Bartholomew climbed the stairs and knocked at Harysone's door. A weak voice told him to come in. He flipped open the latch and entered one of the tavern's more pleasant rooms. Fresh rushes were strewn on the floor, and the walls had been painted with hunting scenes. A huge pile of books near the window caught the physician's attention. They were crudely made, with heavy wooden covers sandwiching a thin layer of parchment. There were at least thirty copies, and he wondered how many of the things Harysone intended to sell in Cambridge.

Harysone lay on the bed, fully dressed, even though there was a fire blazing in the hearth and the room was stuffy. For the first time, Bartholomew was able to study him at close quarters. Harysone's teeth were his most arresting feature: they were long and yellow, and it did not seem possible that they could be real. His next outstanding characteristic was his eyes, which glittered like a rodent's, and Bartholomew sensed something highly unpleasant about the man. Even the thought of those moist orbs settling on Matilde made him nauseous.

'Are you the physician?' Harysone asked. 'Close the door; you are letting the cold air in.'

Bartholomew complied. 'What can I do for you?'

'In a moment, in a moment,' said Harysone testily. 'First, I must establish whether you are sufficiently well qualified to treat me. Where did you train, and what books have you read?'

'I studied at the universities in Oxford and Paris,' replied Bartholomew. 'And I cannot possibly provide you with a list of all the books I have read. However, if you would like someone who can, I can suggest one or two names. Robin of Grantchester will not overwhelm you with medical knowledge.'

'Not a surgeon, thank you very much,' said Harysone with a shudder. 'I do not like men who poke about inside men's bodies with sharp knives. It is not natural. Are you a local man?'

'I suppose so,' said Bartholomew. 'Why?'

'Just conversing. I want to know something about you before I reveal any intimate secrets.'

'There is no need for you to divulge anything personal,' said Bartholomew, alarmed by the nature of the consultation Harysone seemed to have in mind. 'I am a physician, not a confessor.'

'Nevertheless, you will want to know details about my birth and suchlike, so you can construct a horoscope to determine my course of treatment. That kind of information is very personal, and might be dangerous in the wrong hands.'

'I see,' said Bartholomew, declining to mention that the date of a man's birth was hardly sensitive knowledge. He stepped forward, wanting to examine the man, identify the cause of his illness, recommend treatment and leave. He found, again, that he appreciated exactly why Michael had taken such a dislike to Harysone, and why Matilde found him unsettling. 'Shall I . . .?'

'In a moment!' repeated Harysone aggressively. 'You are as bad as that landlord, all business and no time for a chat.'

'Have you had chats with many other people here?' asked Bartholomew, reluctantly taking the opportunity to question Harysone, since he seemed willing to talk about any subject other than his malady. He decided he would try to learn whether Harysone would admit to speaking with the Waits, as Quenhyth had seen him do, or sitting with Gosslinge, as the Waits had claimed.

Harysone pulled a face of disgust. 'The patrons of this

tavern are an uncivilised crowd. I wish I had arrived early enough to secure lodgings at the Brazen George, where the clientele is more genteel. Here, I have been obliged to pass time with blacksmiths, grave-diggers and even jugglers!'

'Jugglers?' asked Bartholomew innocently.

As Harysone regarded him with his wet eyes, Bartholomew had the feeling that the man knew he was Michael's colleague and that his mention of the Waits was deliberate. Harysone had told Bartholomew he had met the entertainers, because he knew that he had been seen with them. He was covering his tracks. Bartholomew wondered why he should feel the need to take such precautions, and whether that in itself was significant.

'Terrible folk,' Harysone went on, eyes fixed unblinkingly on Bartholomew. 'A number of us arrived in the town on the same day – the Chepe Waits, a fishmonger and his household, and me – so I suppose the jugglers imagined a bond between us. I put them right with one or two steely glances.'

'What about Walter Turke? Did you talk to him?'

'The fishmonger?' asked Harysone disapprovingly. 'I did not. The man is a lout, for all his fine clothes, and I wanted nothing to do with him, his fat wife or his snivelling retainers.'

'Retainers?' asked Bartholomew, interest quickening at the plural. 'I thought there was only Gosslinge.'

'There were two,' corrected Harysone. 'A fair-headed clerk and a rascally servant. The servant and I were obliged to share a table one night. I ate my food, then excused myself as soon as was polite. Nasty little fellow. He was missing a thumb and smelled of mould.'

Bartholomew smiled to himself, wondering what Abigny would say if he thought Harysone believed him to be a servant, then thought about the smell of mould on Gosslinge. Did that mean Gosslinge had hidden himself among the rotting albs on more than one occasion? Had he made it a habit to linger there, perhaps hoping to overhear private conversations? But why St Michael's? Surely the man would have fared better in a church with a larger secular congregation. Bartholomew rubbed his chin. Or was it a scholar whom Gosslinge had wanted to watch?

'I find it odd that the inn's two most wealthy patrons – you and Turke – did not find solace in each other's company,' said Bartholomew, aware that Harysone was preparing to change the subject. 'And Philippa Turke is a pretty woman.'

'Fat,' said Harysone dismissively. 'And married. I do not waste my time on wedded matrons – they are more trouble than they are worth. But I am a gentleman, and the fishmonger is not the kind of fellow with whom I like to associate. He is rude, loud and overbearing.'

'He is dead,' said Bartholomew bluntly. 'He fell through some ice while skating.'

Harysone gazed at him. 'That was him? I heard about the accident, but I did not know Turke was the victim.' His expression became predatory, and he licked his lips with a moist red tongue. 'Perhaps I should visit his woman, and offer her the help of a gentleman. You are right – she is pretty after a fashion, and a widow is so much more attractive than a wife.'

'My sister is looking after her,' said Bartholomew quickly, not liking the notion of Harysone lurking around Philippa any more than he had Matilde. 'She does not need any gentlemanly help.'

'Pity,' said Harysone. 'But never mind. She was no more friendly to me than was her arrogant husband, so I would doubtless be wasting my time anyway. But enough of me. Have you heard about my book?'

'Book?' asked Bartholomew keenly. 'You own one?' Books were expensive and rare, and no scholar ever passed up an opportunity to inspect a new volume.

'I have written one,' said Harysone proudly. 'It is a devotional treatise concerning fish.'

'Oh, that,' said Bartholomew, unable to stop himself from sounding disappointed as he glanced at the pile of tomes near the window. 'I thought you meant a real one.'

Harysone glared at him. 'It is a real one. It has covers, a

spine and erudite contents. What more do you want?'

'Forgive me,' said Bartholomew, realising he had been rude. 'You say it is about fish?'

'We can learn a great deal from fish,' said Harysone preachily. 'I use them allegorically, to shed light on the human condition. I have been told by eminent theologians that my work is a remarkable piece of scholarship. Would you like to buy a copy? I happen to have a spare.'

He gestured to the stack near the window, so Bartholomew went to fetch one. He sat on the bed again and opened the boards to reach the parchment inside. Harysone had evidently hunted down the cheapest scribe he could find to make copies of his treatise; its few pages were full of eccentric spelling and peculiarities of grammar.

'*Troute is Best Servd with Vinnegar, but Sturgeon May bee Ate with Grene Sauwse, if you have It.*' He glanced up at Harysone. 'That does not sound devotional or allegorical to me.'

'You have started in the wrong place,' said Harysone testily. 'I included other information, too, since I wanted my work to be comprehensive. Try reading the part where I recommend specific fish for particular ailments. You will learn a great deal from that, I can promise you.'

'Later,' said Bartholomew, laying the tome down. 'I have other patients, and cannot stay here all morning, pleasant though that might be. How can I help you?'

'I have injured my back. I was dancing an estampie last night and it just went.'

'"Went"?' asked Bartholomew warily. 'What do you mean?'

'You know. Went. It started to hurt. It took all my strength to return to my room, and I have been lying here in pain ever since.'

'Has it happened before?' asked Bartholomew, wondering what kind of dancing the man had been engaged in to reduce him to such a state.

'Never. Now, I know there are sense-dulling potions you can give me, so I shall have some of those. And then you can calculate my horoscope.'

'First, I think we should see what the problem is. Lie on your stomach, please.'

'Are you asking to *look* at it?' asked Harysone uneasily. 'My own physician does not embarrass me by wanting to inspect my person, so why should you? And anyway, the problem lies with the bones and, unless you can see through skin and muscle or intend to pare away my flesh to see what is underneath – which I will not permit – looking will do us no good.'

'There may be tell-tale bulges or dents,' persisted Bartholomew.

'Very well,' said Harysone with a long-suffering sigh. 'But be careful.' He winced when the physician's hands came in contact with his skin. 'And please keep those cold hands to yourself. You can adjust my shirt, but only as long as your fingers do not touch me. What have you been doing? Throwing snowballs?'

Bartholomew pulled up Harysone's fine linen shirt to reveal a bony back that was none too clean. There was no obvious indication that anything was wrong, but Harysone claimed the pain was lower, near the base of his spine. A fluttering hand indicated where, so Bartholomew eased the undergarments away, then stared in surprise.

There was a small round bruise in the place Harysone had indicated, and in the centre of it was something dark. Bartholomew fingered it gently, ignoring Harysone's protestations of pain. It was the tip of a knife, which had been driven into the hard bones and broken off in the wound it had caused.

'How did you say you came by this?' he asked again.

'Dancing,' said Harysone impatiently. 'We have been through this. I was dancing an estampie, and there was a sudden pain. I came here, thinking rest might help, but it is still sore.'

'I am not surprised,' said Bartholomew. 'So, you do not know you have been stabbed?'

Harysone twisted around to regard him in astonishment.

179

'Stabbed? I have not been stabbed, man! I damaged my back while twirling with a pretty tavern wench.'

'There is a knife tip here. If you lie still, I will remove it.'

Harysone howled in agony while the metal was extracted, although the operation did not take more than a moment. Bartholomew moved quickly when potentially painful procedures were required; he had learned that fear and anticipation only served to make things worse. When he had the small metal triangle in the palm of his hand, he showed it to Harysone.

'That was in me?' the man asked, taking Bartholomew's hand so that he could inspect the object without touching the pool of gore in which it lay. 'How did it come to be there?'

'I have no idea,' said Bartholomew. 'But it seems extraordinary that you do not.'

Harysone's mouth hardened into a thin line. 'It was those students,' he said. 'Friars from Michaelhouse. They were behind me when I was dancing. *They* stabbed me.'

'The attack on Harysone has provided me with just the excuse I need to investigate him,' said Michael, rubbing his hands together gleefully when Bartholomew told him about the incident later that morning. 'I am delighted he summoned you, Matt. If he had asked for Robin of Grantchester or Master Lynton of Peterhouse, I might never have learned of it.'

'Neither might Harysone,' said Bartholomew dryly, not impressed by the skills of the other two men who practised medicine in Cambridge. 'Lynton prefers writing horoscopes to examining patients, while Robin would not know a stab wound if he had watched one inflicted.'

'And the wound was definitely caused by a knife?' asked Michael.

Bartholomew passed Michael the triangle of metal he had prised from Harysone. 'You can see from its shape that this is the tip of a blade. According to Ulfrid – the novice who

180

saw him in action at the King's Head – Harysone's dancing is sinuous, so the weapon may have been aimed elsewhere, but missed its target in all the movement.'

'You make him sound like a bumble-bee,' said Michael disparagingly. 'Yet he claims the pain occurred during an estampie. An estampie is a slow dance compared to many.'

'Ulfrid said the man dances like a Turkish whore, whatever that means. I suspect Harysone's attacker not only missed what he was aiming for, but damaged his blade into the bargain.'

'We shall have to buy him a new one, then,' said Michael nastily, 'and see whether he is more successful a second time.'

'I doubt Michaelhouse students did it, though. I imagine they just happened to be there at the time.'

'I agree. But he has made an accusation against members of the University – against members of my own College – so it is the Senior Proctor's duty to investigate. But first I shall retrieve Clippesby's tench, and then we shall see what Harysone has to say when we present it to him.'

Michael's timing was fortunate. Agatha had located the smelly object in the depths of the cellar, and was turning it this way and that as she considered whether some of it might still be good enough to add to a stew. Bartholomew was appalled, suspecting that it was sufficiently rotten to poison anyone who ate it, although Agatha claimed that putrefaction was nothing a few herbs and plenty of onions could not overcome.

'It went bad because someone skimped on the salt,' she declared, examining it with expert eyes. 'It would have been perfectly serviceable if the preserving had been done right.'

'An apprentice must have practised on it,' said Michael, not particularly interested. He wrinkled his nose. 'But Norbert must have been drunk indeed to imagine he did well by winning this from Harysone. I have seldom smelled anything so rank.'

He wrapped it in a cloth and left, heading for the King's

Head with Bartholomew in tow. They had just turned into the High Street when their attention was caught by a sudden rumble near St John's Hospital. Opposite was a line of decrepit houses, which the Sheriff and the town burgesses had recently declared unfit for human habitation. However, these homes had occupants, who were not about to move just because some wealthy businessmen decided their homes were an eyesore and wanted the land they were built on. The hovels remained, becoming shabbier and more derelict with each passing season, and one of them had met its end that morning. It had a thatched roof, and the weight of water from a wet autumn, combined with recent snowfalls, had been too much for the ageing structure. With a groan, it had collapsed inward, taking the walls with it and leaving nothing but a heap of snow-impregnated rubble.

'Robert de Blaston the carpenter lives there,' whispered Bartholomew, aghast. 'With his wife Yolande and their ten children.' He joined the throng running towards the house, some wanting to help and others just to watch the unfolding of a tragedy.

The rubble was still settling when he arrived, and powdery snow that had been hurled into the air was drifting downward like fine dust. Bartholomew scanned the wreckage in horror, trying to spot anything human. All he could see were smashed beams, piles of mouldy thatch and a broken door on which a child had painted a bright flower. Bartholomew felt sick. He started to move toward the mess, but someone caught his hand and stopped him.

'It is not safe, Matthew,' came a woman's low, pleasant voice.

Michael seized the physician's other arm when he tried to shake her off. 'Matilde is right, Matt. Wait until it has settled, then we can go in with ropes and planks.'

Bartholomew stared at Matilde. 'But Yolande is a friend of yours.' Yolande de Blaston was one of the town's more energetic Frail Sisters, with a list of regulars that included the Mayor, a number of burgesses and several high-ranking

University men. Her occupation doubtless explained why most of her children looked nothing like her carpenter husband.

'She is safe,' said Matilde. 'She and her family are staying with me, because Robert knew the snow would weaken his roof.'

'No one was in?' asked Bartholomew, slow to understand.

She smiled at him. 'You are a good man to be concerned for a tradesman and his family. But Yolande and her brood are well, and filling my little home with their noise and laughter. I do not know what they will do now, though. They cannot stay with me for ever, nor can they pay the high rents charged in the town.'

'Yolande should make use of her contacts,' said Bartholomew, jumping as a beam snapped and the rubble settled further. Dust flew out in a choking cloud. 'Perhaps the Mayor can help.'

'You mean she should pressure her regulars into doing something for her?' asked Matilde, her eyes twinkling in amusement. 'I am surprised at you for making such a suggestion, Matthew! But it is a good idea. I shall recommend that she acts on it.'

'There is nothing to do here, Matt,' said Michael. 'We should go to the King's Head, before Harysone decides to go dancing somewhere we cannot find him.'

'Harysone?' asked Matilde distastefully. 'I do not like him. His teeth are too long.'

'You are a woman of discerning taste,' said Michael cheerfully. 'I do not like him, either.'

'I will walk with you,' said Matilde, handing Bartholomew her basket to carry. It was heavy, and he looked under the coverings to see why. There was a slab of ham, a pudding made with currants and spices, and bread. There were apples, too, albeit wrinkled and shrunken, and a bottle containing figs soaked in what was probably honey. That would cost a small fortune, he thought.

'I admire a woman with an appetite,' said Michael, one

hand snaking towards some fruit. 'You are right to carry victuals with you: you never know when hunger might strike.'

'They are not for me,' said Matilde, laughing as she pushed the monk away. 'They are for the old men who live on the river bank – Dunstan and Athelbald. If I ate this kind of fare every day, I would be the size of Philippa Turke.'

Bartholomew glanced sharply at her. 'Why do you mention her?'

She gave him an innocent smile. 'Only because Edith tells me you and Philippa were once sweethearts – betrothed, no less. I had no idea you liked large women, Matthew.'

'I like any women,' said Michael comfortably, as though the comment had been directed at him. 'Fat, thin, tall, short. They are all God's creatures, and I treat them accordingly.'

'Philippa was different when we were courting,' said Bartholomew defensively, before Michael could delve too deeply into his personal preferences in Matilde's presence. Although he could not explain why, he always felt uncomfortable when Michael made lewd comments in front of the woman he admired, and something made him want to protect her from them, despite the fact that her former profession had probably left her more than adequately equipped to deal with the likes of Michael. 'She has changed in more ways than just her size.'

'It must be odd to see her again after so many years,' said Matilde expressionlessly. 'I imagine you were delighted to learn she was here.'

'Not exactly. I did not know what to think. She came with her husband, who was undertaking a pilgrimage.'

'But he is now dead and she is a widow,' said Matilde. 'That means that she is free to pursue any potential partner she pleases. Perhaps she will pursue you.'

'She has grown too large to pursue anyone, I would imagine,' said Michael, blithely ignoring the fact that he cut no mean figure himself. 'Still, I suppose she may hanker for the handsome physician who captured her heart when she was in the flower of her youth.'

'Her husband was very wealthy,' said Matilde, addressing Bartholomew. 'So, your Philippa is probably anticipating a rosy future for herself.'

'She is not "my" Philippa,' said Bartholomew, a little nettled. 'And I am sure Turke's sons will inherit most of his wealth, if not all of it. Indeed, she may be even poorer than me.'

'We shall see,' said Matilde, retrieving the basket from him when they reached St Michael's Lane. Without a backward glance, she walked away, heading for the sorry hovels that lined the river bank. Bartholomew gazed after her, resentful of her insinuations, while Michael chuckled softly.

'She is jealous, Matt. That is a good sign. Now you have two women who would like you to be their husband – a fat, greedy widow or a retired courtesan. It is quite a choice!'

'There is Giles Abigny,' said Bartholomew, recognising the short, neat figure hurrying through the Trumpington Gate before a heavy dray cart pulled by four large horses blocked it. Abigny wore his travelling cloak and his brown hat with the drab plume. Michael headed towards him, the rotten fish still clamped under his arm, and Bartholomew began to wonder whether they might be destined to spend the whole day in company with the thing.

'Nasty weather,' said Abigny amiably, rubbing his gloved hands together in an effort to warm them. 'I do not recall another winter like it. Did you know that the London road is now totally blocked? And the Ely causeway has been impassable since before Christmas, or Philippa and I would have left by now. We are marooned, unless we want to go to Huntingdon.' He shuddered fastidiously.

'Where have you been?' asked Michael, glancing through the gate at the snow that was piled high on each side of the road to Trumpington. 'It is no day for a stroll, and you are limping.'

Abigny grimaced, and raised one foot to show where the leather on his boot had been slit. 'Chilblains. You have no idea how painful they can be. I always thought they were an old man's complaint, so what does that tell you about me, Matt?'

'That you should wear thicker hose and larger shoes,' said Bartholomew. 'And that you should wash your feet each night to ensure the wounds do not fester. Do you want a potion to ease the discomfort?'

Abigny shot him a surprised smile. 'My old room-mate is a physician, and yet I did not think to ask him for a remedy! I would be eternally grateful if you could provide me with anything that would make walking less of an ordeal. When can I have it?'

'I will bring it this afternoon.'

'If walking is so painful, then why are you out?' asked Michael nosily.

'I had business to attend,' said Abigny. He gave the monk a faint smile. 'You do not want the details. Suffice to say that arranging the transport of a fishmonger's body to a distant burial site is not an easy matter. There are many factors that need to be taken into account.'

'Out there?' asked Michael, indicating the Trumpington Road, where there stood two Colleges, the King's Head, a church, two chapels, the Gilbertine Friary, a windmill and a smattering of houses, but nothing that would help solve the problems associated with taking a corpse to London.

'Out there,' agreed Abigny with an enigmatic smile. 'But it is too chilly to talk here and my feet pain me. I am sure you two have much to occupy your time, so I shall be on my way. Do not forget that potion, Matt. If you deliver it today, I shall leave you my worldly goods when I die.'

'Your fiancée might have something to say about that,' said Bartholomew. He watched Abigny hobble away, then turned to Michael. 'What did you make of that?'

They started walking again, but had the misfortune to meet a cart coming the other way, spraying up dirty snow with its great wooden wheels as it went. Bartholomew ducked behind a stack of barrels, but Michael did not, and swore furiously at the grinning carter while he brushed the filth from his cloak.

'What do you mean?' demanded the monk testily, looking in both directions for more carts before making his way to the tavern. 'Make of what?'

'Make of the fact that Giles is in pain, yet is willing to walk outside the town. You know as well as I do that no embalmers or coffin-makers live out here. So, what was he doing?'

'He has behaved oddly ever since he arrived,' said Michael. 'Like Philippa's, his reaction to Turke's death is curious. I told you yesterday there was something unsavoury about the whole incident, and Giles's secretive manner has done nothing to make me think any differently.'

'Turke's death *and* the fact that Philippa did not mention she had hired the Chepe Waits in London,' added Bartholomew. 'Frith and Makejoy told me about that, and so did Quenhyth.'

Michael shrugged. 'I do not think the Waits are important – not like her strange reaction to her husband's death. Perhaps she had simply forgotten about the jugglers. Even you must see that a band of travelling entertainers is not something that is likely to occupy the mind of a woman with a household to run for very long.'

'I disagree. Entertainers are hired for important occasions – events that stick in people's memories. And the Waits are memorable, because their act is so poor.'

'Perhaps there were more talented members in the troupe at that time,' suggested Michael. 'Or they wore different costumes.'

'Not according to Quenhyth. He recalls them just as they are – the same people and the same clothes.'

'So, what are you saying? That Philippa has a sinister motive for not telling you she hired a troupe of vagrants? Perhaps she wants to woo you – as Matilde believes – and thinks admitting to an association with the Chepe Waits will put you off. Or perhaps she guessed – correctly, I imagine – that you would not be interested in the details of her

187

household affairs. Talking about how to hire vagrants is not recommended as a topic to impress potential suitors with.'

'I am not a potential suitor,' objected Bartholomew. 'And even if she regards me as fair game now – which I am sure she does not, given that she decided against me when I was younger, fitter and less grey – she certainly did not do so while her husband ate his dinner next to her.'

Michael raised his eyebrows, his expression mischievous. 'She may have realised Turke ranked a poor second to your charms, and so decided to move him into the next world.'

Bartholomew sighed impatiently. 'Do not be flippant, Brother! I am uneasy about this link between her and the Waits. There is also the fact that her dead manservant – Gosslinge – was in the King's Head with Frith. I am sure it is significant.'

'Do not forget we have been told that Harysone was in the King's Head with the Waits, too,' said Michael. 'So, what shall we do? Shall we arrest Philippa and take her to my prison, where I can question her about the men she hired last summer? Or shall I arrest the Waits, and demand to know why Philippa denied knowing them?'

Bartholomew gave him a rueful smile. 'You are right, there is nothing to be gained from these speculations. Philippa will be gone as soon as the snow clears, and I will probably never see her again.'

CHAPTER 6

WHEN BARTHOLOMEW AND MICHAEL REACHED THE KING'S Head with the fish it was past noon, and they discovered Harysone had ignored the physician's advice to rest, and was in the tavern's main room, holding forth to a group of pardoners. The pardoners wore black cloaks and wide-brimmed hats, and Michael became aware that there was a similarity in their clothes and the ones favoured by Harysone. His eyes narrowed with dislike: Michael detested pardoners, and was as rabid in his loathing of them as William was in his hatred of heretics and Dominicans.

'So that is why I detected a spirit of evil in the man,' the monk said, nodding with grim satisfaction when he saw his suspicions had some basis. 'He is a pardoner. You know how I feel about pardoners.'

'I do,' said Bartholomew hastily, hoping that a prompt reply would deliver him from the diatribe he sensed was going to follow. It did not.

'Pardoners are an evil brood,' Michael hissed, beginning to work himself into a state of righteous indignation. 'They travel the country and make their fortunes by preying on the sick, the weak and the gullible. They peddle false relics, and the promises of salvation they offer in their pardons are nothing but lies.'

'Speaking of false relics. I wonder whether that thing Turke gave Langelee is really a saint's finger,' said Bartholomew, attempting to change the subject. He did not think Harysone's occupation was relevant to the enquiry, especially since he was not practising his trade in the town, but was only selling his books.

189

'Not if it originated with a pardoner,' said Michael, refusing to take the hint. 'It is probably not even a finger. Did you inspect it?'

'I did not,' said Bartholomew vehemently. 'I do not interfere with potentially sacred objects to satisfy my idle curiosity. It is not unknown for men to be struck down for mistreating holy relics.'

'Their pardons are the most wicked thing of all,' said Michael. 'They spend their evenings writing them on old pieces of parchment, to make them appear ancient, and then they sell them to the desperate for high prices. The last pardoner I had the pleasure to drive from my town had a box that contained pardons for every sin from gluttony to lust.'

'Did you buy any?'

Michael ignored him. 'They allow criminals to salve their consciences by purchasing pardons, instead of giving themselves up to the law. And, of course, they encourage vice.'

'How do they do that?' asked Bartholomew, seeing Michael was in full stride and would not be stopped until he had had his say. For a man normally so sanguine, it was remarkable how the mere mention of pardoners could reduce the monk to paroxysms of bigotry.

'By dispensing pardons for future use,' Michael replied angrily. 'I saw Mayor Horwood making a bulk purchase of five pardons for adultery just before All Souls Day – one for the sin he had just committed with Yolande de Blaston, and another four for their assignations over the coming month. It is not right! Do you know why there are so many pardoners in Cambridge now? Because it is Christmas, and they know the lords of misrule will be encouraging behaviour that normally sends folk rushing for a confessor. I shall have to ensure their stay is so uncomfortable that they all leave at the earliest opportunity.'

'They are doing nothing wrong,' Bartholomew pointed out. 'Pardoning is not against the law.'

'It should be,' declared Michael. His eyes narrowed as he

watched the object of his dislike begin a curious sequence of motions. 'What is he doing over there? I thought you said he was in such pain that he was barely able to stand.'

'That is what he told me.' Bartholomew was surprised to see Harysone out of bed, let alone moving with such vigour. 'I gave him a dose of poppy juice and laudanum, but it seems he exaggerated his agonies – either that or my medicine is more potent than I thought.' He strongly suspected the former, and supposed the removal of the metal, combined with an effective pain reliever, had all but banished any discomfort Harysone might have suffered.

'Yes, but what is he *doing*? Is it a contortion that will ease his pain?'

'Not one he learned from me,' said Bartholomew, watching the peculiar movements of the pardoner with open curiosity.

'Now I shall show you an estampie with music,' Harysone announced to his companions, blithely unaware that he was the object of Michael's hostile attentions. 'Landlord?'

The landlord clapped his hands and one of his patrons stepped forward. The man began to sing a well-known song called 'Kalenda Maya,' the words of which had been written by the famous troubadour Raimbault de Vaquieras a century and a half earlier. It was a love lament, telling of how the singer would fret until he received news that his lady still loved him. The King's Head rendition made it sound as though the singer was giving his woman an ultimatum, and was more threatening than pining. Although Bartholomew did not much care for the 'carol-dancing' that was currently popular, nor for the new vigorous jumping dance called the 'saltarello', he liked estampies. Harysone's idea of an estampie, however, was unique, and Bartholomew could see why he had believed the pain in his back had originated with it.

The pardoner began by standing with his hands at his side. Then, as the dance began, he produced an elaborate walk that was part strut and part slink, and reminded Bartholomew of a chicken he had once watched after it had been fed large quantities of wine. Then followed a series of leaps, each one involving a lot of leg flexing and windmilling arms. Harysone's hips ground and rotated like those of Ulfrid's Turkish whore, and his entire body seemed to undulate and quiver, partly in time with the music, but mostly not.

'That is disgusting,' said Michael, turning away. 'I cannot watch.'

Neither could Harysone's fellow pardoners. After a few moments of appalled astonishment, they drained their cups and left, obviously unwilling to be associated with the figure that gyrated so obscenely in the middle of the tavern. They cast apologetic grins at the landlord and muttered that they were going to St Botolph's, where a strong brew called church ale was being sold by the scholars of Valence Marie. Church ale was a popular Christmas tradition, and was usually dispensed in graveyards or – if the rector gave his permission – inside the church itself, hence its name. Bartholomew had always assumed it was sold on holy ground so that the services of a priest could be easily secured for those who drank too much of what was often a very poisonous tipple.

There were a number of women present in the tavern, and Harysone had their undivided attention. Agatha was among them, and she watched Harysone with her jaw open so wide it was almost in her lap. The fierce and sturdy matrons who served ale to the tavern's fierce and sturdy patrons had been brought to a standstill, thirsty customers forgotten, while several of the Frail Sisters were spellbound. One of them trotted forward and joined the pardoner, trying to match her movements to his. The men in the tavern had much the same reaction as Michael, and turned to their drinks so that they would not have to see.

'Enough, Master Harysone,' cried the landlord in agitation, as more of his regulars headed for the door. 'Thank you for the demonstration. It has been most enlightening. Now, sit down and rest, and I shall bring you some ale.'

'Thank you, landlord,' said Michael, assuming that he was included in the offer as he settled himself opposite Harysone.

'Watching that particular performance has induced in me the need for strong drink. You had better make it some of that lambswool you brew at this time of year, not just common ale.' Lambswool was hot ale mulled with apples, and the King's Head Yuletide variety was known to be mightily powerful.

The landlord was too relieved to see Harysone stop dancing to take exception to Michael's cheeky demands. He nodded to a pot-boy, who went to ladle the hot liquid into three jugs, then stood over the monk's table, wiping his hands on a stained apron. 'Pig,' he stated bluntly.

Michael glared at him. 'I beg your pardon?'

'Pig,' repeated the landlord. 'It is what we are serving today. Roasted pig, cooked with some old pears I found at the back of the shed and a few onion skins for flavour. Do you want some?'

'I do,' said Michael, oblivious to the fact that the landlord had made his midday offering sound distinctly unappealing. Bartholomew supposed it was the man's way of informing Michael that the presence of the Senior Proctor in his inn was an unwelcome one, and he hoped to shorten the visit by making the monk believe there were no victuals that he would want to linger over. 'And I shall have some bread, too.'

'Bread?' asked the landlord, as though it was some exotic treat. 'We do not have that.'

Michael gazed at him. 'No bread? What kind of tavern does not keep bread? How do you expect me to eat the juice and the fat from the pig? Lick the platter?'

'Flour is expensive these days,' said the landlord. 'The price of a loaf has trebled since the snows came, and most of my patrons cannot afford such luxuries.'

'That is true,' said Bartholomew to Michael. 'The cost of grain has risen hugely since the mills were forced to stop working by frozen water. You will have to make do with pig.'

'Brother Michael,' said Harysone, baring his huge teeth in a strained grin of welcome as the landlord went to the kitchen. 'How nice to see you again.'

His eyes glittered moistly as they moved up and down Michael's person. Instinctively, the monk hauled his cloak up around his neck, like a virgin protecting her maidenly virtues. Bartholomew sat next to Michael, and resisted the urge to draw up his hood when he was treated to the same disconcerting appraisal. Harysone reached under the table and produced a copy of the text he had shown the physician earlier, thumping it in front of Michael with a loud crack that made several people jump.

'Here is my little BOOK,' he said loudly, apparently determined that everyone in the tavern should hear him. 'You have not seen it yet, Brother. Perhaps you have come to purchase a copy, so that you, like other folk with a thirst for answers to the greatest of philosophical mysteries on Earth, can improve your knowledge – especially relating to fish.'

'Fish?' queried Michael, unable to help himself. 'What do they have to do with philosophy?'

Harysone pretended to be surprised. 'How can you ask such a thing? Fish were fashioned by God on the second day of creation, before trees and after cattle.'

'Fish did not make an appearance until day four,' argued Michael immediately. He was a theologian, after all, even if his duties as Senior Proctor meant he did not spend as much time studying as he should. '*After* trees and *before* cattle.'

'Details,' said Harysone dismissively. 'But a learned man, such as yourself, would find a great deal to interest him in my small contribution. You can have it for virtually nothing – three marks.'

'You charged the scholars of Valence Marie two marks,' said Michael with narrowed eyes. 'Do you imagine me to be a fool, easily parted from his money?'

'The price has risen since I visited Valence Marie,' said Harysone blandly. 'You know how it is. A week ago, bread cost a penny, now it is three. The more people clamour for a thing, the more valuable it becomes.'

Michael reached out to examine the book, tugging the heavy wooden cover open, then turning the pages. 'It is not very long,' he remarked critically. 'And the writing is enormous. Did you scribe it for those with failing eyesight?'

'Yes,' said Harysone, unoffended. 'Scholars have trouble with their eyes, because they spend their time reading ancient manuscripts in bad light. So I ordered my clerk to make the writing large.'

Michael snapped the book closed. 'Unfortunately, I have no time to debate with you the statement: "Bonéd Fishe, not Womin, were phormed from Addam's Ribb", which is a pity, because I am sure I would enjoy myself. But while we are on the subject of fish, do you recognise this?' He slapped the tench on to the table, so hard that the head broke off to career across the surface and drop to the floor on the other side. An unpleasant odour emanated from it.

'Tench,' said Harysone, with a fond smile. 'The queen of fish.'

'This particular queen of fish was in the possession of Norbert when he was murdered,' said Michael uncompromisingly, even though there was scant evidence to prove such a statement, and the monk himself had not even been entirely convinced about the tench's relationship with the dead man. 'I have been told he won it from you in a game of chance.'

'Yes,' said Harysone, frowning thoughtfully. 'I did lose a tench to a man, now that you mention it. But I do not know his name, nor do I see how my fish could have had him murdered.'

'So, you did not kill him to take it back again?' asked Michael bluntly.

Harysone's expression hardened. 'I did not. It is not an especially good specimen, as you can no doubt see, and was already past its best when this man – Norbert you say he was called – won it from me. He was welcome to it. But I do not have to sit here and listen to your accusations.' He started to stand. 'So, if there is nothing else . . .'

'Just the matter of your wound,' said Michael, indicating that the pardoner was to sit again. 'You claim you were stabbed by a student.'

'It pains me dreadfully,' said Harysone, adopting a pitiful expression as he lowered his rump on to the bench. 'I shall have to claim compensation from your University, because the injury inflicted on me by a scholar means that I am unable to work. Indeed, I can barely walk.'

'I am not surprised you are in pain if you prance around so vigorously,' said Bartholomew pointedly. 'The wound is not deep, but I told you to rest, not writhe about like a speared maggot.'

'I was dancing,' said Harysone stiffly. 'Although I am a pardoner by trade, I am famed for the rare quality of my jigs. I practise most days, and my body is used to the movement. Dancing will not hurt my back – unlike knives.'

'I did not realise you were a pardoner.' Michael pronounced 'pardoner' with as much disgust as was possible to inject into a word without actually spitting. 'You told me you were here to sell copies of your . . .' He gestured at the tome on the table, declining to call it a book.

'Pardoners can write devotional philosophy as well as anyone else,' said Harysone sharply. 'In fact, I imagine we do better than most, given the religious nature of our vocation.' He attempted to look pious, but merely succeeded in looking more sinister. 'But you will want to know what happened last night when I was grievously injured. I was giving a demonstration of my dancing when I became aware of an intense pain in my back. I staggered towards a table, where I thought to support myself until the agony eased, and it was then that I noticed the scholars.'

'How do you know they were scholars?' demanded Michael. 'Students are not permitted in taverns; it is against the University's laws.' He failed to add that students frequently disobeyed that rule, especially around Christmas, when lectures were suspended and there was an atmosphere of celebration. He also declined to mention that he knew Michaelhouse students sometimes patronised the King's Head – Ulfrid had been open about the fact that he had won a pair of dicing bones from Harysone in that very tavern.

'So is frolicking with whores in alleyways, I imagine,' replied Harysone tartly. 'But it still happens. And I knew they were students because I could see Franciscan habits under their cloaks – and the landlord told me those lads were from Michaelhouse.'

'Why did he tell you that?' asked Michael sceptically.

Harysone gave an elegant shrug. 'Because I asked why his inn was so attractive to men of the cloth. There were Dominicans and Carmelites here, too, if you are interested. He told me they are able to sample the Christmas spirit in a tavern, but not in their friaries.'

'He is right,' muttered Bartholomew to Michael. 'Father William told me the Franciscans intend to ignore the whole festive season. They even had lectures between Shepherd's Mass and the Mass of the Divine Word on Christmas morning, and there was no kind of feast at all.'

'I heard the same of the Carmelites,' replied Michael in an undertone. 'That is what happens when you join a mendicant Order, Matt: but note that only friars cancelled Christmas, not monks. My Order did no such thing. I am not surprised mendicant students seek solace elsewhere.'

'Why do you think it was the Franciscans from Michaelhouse who stabbed you?' asked Bartholomew of Harysone. 'Why not someone else?'

Harysone sighed. 'Because the Michaelhouse men were *behind* me. If someone I was *facing* had wielded the weapon, then the knife would have been lodged in my front.'

'Pity,' said Michael ambiguously. He glanced sharply at Harysone, as though he had just thought of something. 'The Chepe Waits – whom you have already said you do not know – were accused of stealing from someone at the King's Head. I do not suppose their victim was you?'

'Why do you ask?' countered Harysone, fixing Michael with his glistening eyes.

Michael sighed irritably. 'I am not interested in playing games, Master Pardoner. Did one of the Chepe Waits remove a quantity of gold from you or not?'

'It was returned,' admitted Harysone reluctantly. 'And the Sheriff informed me that there was no need to press charges. I decided he was right.'

'Why?' asked Bartholomew curiously. Harysone did not seem the kind of person to overlook a theft. The pardoner was in Cambridge to make money by selling his book, and Bartholomew imagined he would want anyone punished who came between him and his gold.

Harysone gave an elegant shrug. 'The money was returned – with a little extra as interest. It is Christmas, and so I decided to be generous.'

Bartholomew wondered what Sheriff Morice had discovered about the pardoner to induce him to forget the incident. He also speculated about how much the ill-fated venture had cost the Waits: now it seemed they had not only been obliged to bribe the Sheriff to keep their freedom, but had been forced to repay Harysone in full, with extra to ensure his compliance. He gave a wry smile. No wonder the Waits were so keen to remain at Michaelhouse. They were still reeling from the disastrous financial effects of their brief foray into crime.

'The Chepe Waits seem to be connected to everyone,' said Bartholomew thoughtfully, as he and Michael walked back to Michaelhouse.

They had eaten the King's Head pig, which had not tasted nearly as bad as the landlord had made it sound. A shallow bowl had been provided, and when Michael had finished gnawing the bones, the remaining grease and juice on the platter was poured into it and presented to the monk to drink in lieu of bread to sop it up. Michael was still dabbing his oily lips with a piece of linen as they passed through the Trumpington Gate and walked down one of the alleys that led towards Milne Street, which, as the thoroughfare where many wealthy merchants lived, was more clear of snow than the High Street.

'Philippa and Turke hired them,' Bartholomew went on

when Michael did not reply. 'And Quenhyth saw them with Giles, Harysone and Norbert.'

'Frith has already admitted he was touting for business and says he spoke to a good many people in an attempt to secure work,' said Michael. 'And they touted even harder when Christmas was upon them and they still had not found employment. However, we must not forget the fishy connections you brought to my attention: Harysone penning a "book" on piscine matters; Turke being a fishmonger and Gosslinge a fishmonger's manservant; and Norbert winning a tench from Harysone the night he died.'

'It seems to me Harysone's "fishy connections" are incidental. I had the impression Turke shunned him at the King's Head – or they shunned each other. And the dicing game where Norbert won his tench – just like the bet Harysone had with Ulfrid when the lad won his dice – was designed to attract onlookers, so that Harysone could tell them about his book. I am not sure any of it is significant. But more importantly, Brother, what do you think of the accusation Harysone has made against our students?'

'Ridiculous,' said Michael, as Bartholomew knew he would. 'But, having seen him dancing, I can understand why someone sought to put an end to the misery with steel. I shall have words with our Franciscans – especially Ulfrid, who freely admits to debating about crabs and oysters with Harysone – and I shall learn the names of the other friars who were present that night. But I cannot see anyone confessing to stabbing the man, and, unless I find an obliging witness, it will be difficult to catch the culprit. Do you think Harysone was telling the truth about Morice returning his gold with interest?'

'I do not know, but I have the impression Morice encouraged him to be "compassionate". Morice's motives are the questionable ones, not Harysone's. All Harysone did was accept the return of his lost property and agree to let the matter rest. God only knows what sordid connivance Morice engaged in to make the effort worthwhile for himself.'

'I think Harysone agreed far too readily for the charges against the Waits to be dropped,' argued Michael. 'Which means either that he enjoys a more meaningful acquaintance with them than either has acknowledged, or that the gold was ill-gotten and he does not want the Sheriff looking too closely at where it came from.'

'Or that he was feeling generous – or greedy – and decided to accept the Sheriff's "interest" and end the matter,' said Bartholomew reasonably. 'Not everyone wants to take a stand against a corrupt Sheriff: it can be dangerous. I do not blame Harysone for taking the money and asking no questions.'

'Harysone's book is riddled with errors,' said Michael, declining to acknowledge that Bartholomew had a point and shifting the emphasis of the conversation instead. 'I doubt he has peddled many, so where did this gold come from?'

'Perhaps he sold copies on his way to Cambridge. They cost two marks when he arrived, and they are now three, so, he must have sold some, or he would not have raised the price.'

'Only a fool would buy one,' said Michael authoritatively.

'Very possibly. But he sells them in taverns, where men gather to drink ale and wine. I imagine some only realise they have made a poor purchase when they are sober.'

'There is Oswald Stanmore,' said Michael, pointing to the merchant, who was hurrying towards them. 'What is he doing out on a cold day when he could be by his fire?'

'I hoped I would meet you,' said Stanmore breathlessly. He cast a nervous glance behind him, as though worried that he might have been followed. 'I need to tell you something.'

'In here, then,' said Michael, opening the door to a small tavern called the Swan, which was famous for the size of its portions of meat. He leaned inside and inhaled deeply, detecting roast boar and spiced apples among the enticing odours that emanated from within. The King's Head pig seemed to have been totally forgotten.

'I do not have time,' said Stanmore, drawing him back out again. 'Edith is expecting me home, and I do not want to leave her for long. I have asked Cynric to stay with her while I am out.'

'Why?' asked Bartholomew, bewildered by his brother-in-law's rapid gabble.

Stanmore peered around him again. 'I do not think the deaths of Turke or his manservant were natural,' he said, agitated. 'I am sure Philippa knows something that she is not telling us.'

Bartholomew exchanged an uneasy glance with Michael. It was not long since they had discussed that very issue themselves.

'Such as what?' asked the monk.

'I do not know,' said Stanmore. He ran a hand through his hair and Bartholomew felt a lurch of alarm when he saw that the normally sanguine merchant was shaking. 'Turke's death has been on my mind. Perhaps I am just unused to seeing men die, but it has plagued my every waking thought. Because of this I found myself drawn to the Mill Pool, where he fell in. The more I studied it, the more I was certain no sane man would have skated there. I can only conclude that Turke never intended to go skating, and that something terrible happened to him.'

Michael regarded the merchant with sombre green eyes. 'I remarked at the time that the skates were improperly tied, and Philippa herself told us that Turke was not a man to go gliding across the river at a moment's notice. However, Matt examined the corpse, and he says Turke's death was exactly as it appeared: the man fell in the river and died of the cold. It does not matter whether he did so while he was skating or while he was doing something else.'

'I think it does matter,' insisted Stanmore. 'You see, if he was not skating, then it means that someone tied the bones to his shoes – wrongly, as you say – *after* he was dragged from the water. And that means someone wants us to believe that he died skating when he did not.'

'Perhaps he was just inept with his laces,' Bartholomew suggested.

Stanmore waved a dismissive hand. 'Then what about Gosslinge? You said yourself it is unusual for two members of the same household to die in such rapid succession, and you must see that neither death was exactly normal.'

'It is winter,' Bartholomew pointed out. 'People do freeze to death and fall through ice at this time of year. It is unfortunate that both are dead, but not necessarily sinister.'

'"Necessarily",' pounced Stanmore. 'You have already considered the possibility that there is something odd here, and you are right: there *is* something sinister – to use your word – going on. Think about what Turke muttered as he died. It clearly meant something to Philippa, because she was a different woman afterwards.'

'That is true,' acknowledged Michael. 'But what do you suggest we do about it? I cannot begin an official investigation, because Turke's death is outside my jurisdiction.'

'Jurisdiction can be bought these days,' said Stanmore grimly. 'Leave Morice to me.'

'I suppose corruption has its advantages,' said Michael with a sigh. 'I was obliged to offer him some money myself recently. His men were trailing my every move while I investigated the death of Norbert, and were making it impossible for me to work. The only way to get rid of them was to pay Morice with coins from William's fines chest.'

Bartholomew was unhappy that either of them should be involved in bribing one of the King's officers. He knew such matters had a habit of being raised at later dates – such as when Morice decided he had not been paid enough and demanded more, or when Morice himself was eventually called to explain his dishonesty to the King's justices. 'Even if you do buy Morice, Philippa will not want us prying into her business,' he warned.

'I do not care,' said Stanmore. 'I want you to look into it. You have solved so many cases before that I am sure this one will present you with no problems.'

'Where do you want us to start?' asked Michael.

'With Giles,' said Stanmore, glancing up the road again,

as though he imagined Abigny might be listening. 'Philippa never leaves the house unescorted – she is a nuisance actually, always wanting someone with her – but Giles is in and out like a bishop in a brothel, despite the pain he is in from his chilblains.'

'Where does he go?' asked Michael.

'Taverns, I imagine. The man lives in Turke's house, but is clearly discontented. Perhaps *that* is why he insisted on joining this pilgrimage – to dispose of the brother-in-law he despises, well away from other fishmongers who might ask awkward questions. By killing Turke he has relieved Philippa of a tiresome husband and improved his own lot in the process.'

'How do you know Philippa regarded Turke as tiresome?' asked Bartholomew. 'I thought she seemed fond of him. Even though she was uncomfortable with the notion of Fiscurtune's cold-blooded murder, she said nothing disloyal about Turke. And anyway, Giles might lose a good deal by dispensing with his brother-in-law. Without Turke to protect him, he may lose his post at the law courts. And he may have condemned Philippa to a life of destitution, if Turke's sons inherit their father's wealth and she does not.'

'Philippa was fond of Turke's money, not of Turke himself,' asserted Stanmore dogmatically. 'She chose an elderly fishmonger over you and, unless she is blind or deranged, she did not make that choice based on looks or character. It was his wealth she loved.'

'Many people marry for money, but that does not mean they are all biding their time to dispense with their spouses,' countered Bartholomew.

'Then prove me wrong,' urged Stanmore, glancing around him once more. 'Convince me that the deaths of Turke and Gosslinge are what you say – bizarre and tragic accidents. Look at Giles's role in the affair. Find out where he goes when he slips away wearing that plumed hat and that dark cloak. But do it soon, Matt. The weather shows no sign of breaking, and Philippa and Giles might be here for weeks.

I do not want Edith living under the same roof as ruthless killers until the spring brings a thaw and our unwanted guests transport their victim for burial in London.'

Bartholomew was unsettled by Stanmore's claims and felt a nagging concern for Edith, despite the fact that he thought Stanmore was over-reacting. He tried to convince himself that he did not seriously believe Philippa or Giles would do anything to harm her, but was aware that no amount of rationalising and reasoning would dispel the unease he felt. He knew he would have to do some probing into the affair, even if it was only to set his and Stanmore's minds at rest.

Since he had promised to take chilblain ointment to Abigny, he suggested they begin the investigation immediately by accompanying Stanmore home. Michael was willing, so they set off for Stanmore's business premises on Milne Street, stopping on the way at the apothecary's shop to purchase the ingredients necessary to make a soothing poultice for the clerk's painful kibes.

Philippa, Abigny and Edith were in the solar when they arrived. The building was not as comfortable as Stanmore's hall-house in the nearby village of Trumpington, but it was considerably nicer than Michaelhouse. Woollen hangings covered the plaster walls, and thick wool rugs lay on the floor. A fire blazed in the hearth, sending showers of sparks dancing up the chimney, and the room smelled pleasantly of wood-smoke and the dried flowers that Edith had placed in bowls along the windowsills. The shutters were closed against the chill, even though the windows were glazed, and the room was lit yellow and orange by the fire and the lamps in sconces on the walls.

Abigny was sitting near the hearth with his boots off and his toes extended towards the flames, while Philippa perched next to him, attempting to sew in the unsteady light. The garment was long and white, and Bartholomew saw it was a shroud for her husband to wear on his final journey. She was dressed completely in black, following the current fashion for widows who could afford it. Edith was at the opposite end of the room, sitting at a table as she wrapped small pieces of dried fruit in envelopes of marchpane. Michael went to sit next to her, and it was not long before a fat, white hand was inching surreptitiously towards the sweetmeats.

'Those are for the apprentices,' came an admonishing voice from the shadows near the door. Michael almost leapt out of his skin, having forgotten that Cynric had been charged to stay with Edith while Stanmore was out.

'God's blood, Cynric!' muttered the monk, holding a hand to his chest to show he had been given a serious fright. 'Have a care whom you startle, man!' He helped himself to a handful of the treats, indicating that he needed them to help him recover from the shock.

'Did you bring that potion for my feet?' asked Abigny eagerly of Bartholomew. 'I long to be relieved of this constant pain. I know you dislike calculating horoscopes, Matt, but I am your friend and my need is very great, so I am sure you will not refuse me. Do you know enough about me already to determine the course of treatment, or are there questions you need answered?'

'The latter,' said Michael, not very subtly. 'He needs to know whether you have spent much time walking in the snow of late.'

'Of course I have,' said Abigny, surprised by the question. 'First there was the journey to Cambridge, and then there have been old friends to see and arrangements to make.'

'Arrangements?' asked Michael innocently.

'Now that Walter is dead I may lose my post,' replied Abigny, apparently unconcerned by Michael's brazen curiosity. 'So, I went to see a Fellow at King's Hall, who has agreed to provide testimony that I am an honest and responsible citizen. And I have been obliged to visit coffin-makers and embalmers.' He regarded Bartholomew with innocent blue eyes. 'Are these the kind of things you need to know for my stars, Matt?'

His answers came a little too easily, and Bartholomew

could not help but conclude he had been thinking about what to say. Abigny continued to talk, regaling them with dull and unimportant details of a meeting he had had with the Warden of King's Hall, and giving details of various important dates in his life, which Michael pretended to write down so the horoscope could be constructed later.

Meanwhile, Bartholomew inspected Abigny's feet, wincing when he saw the huge chilblains that plagued the man's toes and heels. He was not surprised Abigny limped, and set about making a poultice of borage and hops to ease the swelling. He also prescribed a soothing comfrey water that would reduce Abigny's melancholic humours and restore the balance between hot and cold, and recommended that his friend should avoid foods known to slow the blood. Philippa offered to purchase her brother warmer hose to prevent his feet from becoming chilled in the first place.

She rose from her seat when Bartholomew had finished examining Abigny, and asked to be excused. She was pale, and there were dark smudges under her eyes – as expected in a woman who had recently lost her husband. Before she left, she fixed Bartholomew with a worried frown.

'You will not disregard my request, will you, Matthew? Walter is dead, and nothing can bring him back. He was not popular and did not always treat people with kindness or fairness. If you ask questions about him you will certainly learn that, even here in Cambridge where he was not well known. But I do not want you to encourage people to speak badly of him. I want him to rest in peace. It is no more than any man deserves.'

'Men deserve to have their deaths investigated if there are inconsistencies and questions arising,' said Michael gently. 'Walter will not lie easy in his grave if these remain unanswered.'

'There *are* no questions,' said Philippa stubbornly, her eyes filling with tears. 'He drowned. You saw that yourselves.'

'He died from the cold,' corrected Bartholomew. 'The water in his lungs did not—'

Philippa turned angrily on him, and the tears spilled down her cheeks. 'It does not matter! He died, and whether it was from the cold or by water is irrelevant. This is exactly what I am trying to avoid – pointless speculation that will do nothing but disturb his soul.'

'If there are questions, then they originated with you,' Michael pointed out, unmoved by her distress. 'You were the one who insisted that Walter would not have gone skating.'

She stared at him, tears dripping unheeded. 'I was distressed and shocked, and I said things I did not mean. Walter was *not* a man for undignified pursuits, like skating. But then he was not a man who undertook pilgrimages, either – yet that is why we are here. Perhaps the religious nature of his journey made him behave differently, but it does not matter because we will never know what happened. All I can do is console myself that he died in a state of grace, because he was travelling to Walsingham, and pray that God will forgive him for the incident regarding Fiscurtune.'

'The "incident" would not have led him to take his own life, would it?' asked Michael, beginning a new line of enquiry. Philippa was right, in that pilgrimages sometimes had odd effects on people and it was not unknown for folk to become so overwhelmed by remorse for what they had done that they killed themselves.

Philippa shook her head. 'Walter was not a suicide, Brother. The Church condemns suicides, and Walter would not have wanted to be buried in unhallowed ground.'

Bartholomew did not point out that securing a suitable burial place was usually the last thing on a suicide's mind, but agreed that Turke had not seemed the kind of man to take his own life. He watched her leave the solar, then turned to stare at the flames in the hearth, while Abigny hobbled after her in his bare feet. Was she hiding information about her husband's death, either something about the way he had died or some aspect of his affairs that led him to his grim demise in the Mill Pool? Was Stanmore right: that Philippa or Abigny – or both – had decided to kill Turke while he was away from his home and his friends? Had Turke been skating, or did someone just want everyone to believe he had?

He reached for his cloak, nodding to Michael that they should leave. Answers would not come from Philippa or her brother, since neither was willing to talk. He and the monk needed to look elsewhere.

That night was bitterly cold, with a frigid wind whistling in from the north that drove hard, grainy flakes of snow before it. The blankets on Bartholomew's bed were woefully inadequate, and he spent the first half of the evening shivering, curled into a tight ball in an attempt to minimise the amount of heat that was being leached from his body by the icy chill of the room. In the end, genuinely fearing that if he slept in his chamber he might never wake, he grabbed his cloak and ran quickly through the raging blizzard to the main building in the hope that there might be some sparks among the ashes of the fire that he could coax into life.

A number of students were in the hall, wrapped in blankets, cloaks and even rugs as they vied with each other to be nearest the hearth. The door to the conclave was closed and Bartholomew hesitated before opening it, suspecting that Deynman and his cronies would be within, plotting his next move as Lord of Misrule. But an ear pressed against the wood told him no one was talking, so he opened it and entered, tripping over the loose floorboard as he went.

He was surprised to find most of the Fellows there, even the ailing William, who was snoring loudly enough to cause several of his colleagues to toss and turn restlessly. Rolled into blankets or their spare habits, they looked like soldiers in a field camp as they lay close together to draw on each other's warmth. Michael was nowhere to be seen, and Bartholomew guessed the monk had found a more pleasant place to spend the night than on a hard, stone floor in Michaelhouse.

The physician noted wryly that even in the season of misrule some customs were hard to break: at night, the conclave remained the Fellows' refuge, while the students used the hall. He was grateful, since the hall was large and draughty.

'Where have you been, Matthew?' asked Kenyngham softly. He was sitting at a table, struggling to write in the unsteady light of a candle. 'Out to tend poor Dunstan? I hear he is suffering sorely in this cold weather.'

'His lungs are failing. What are you doing, Father? It is too late for work, and you should rest if you intend to say all those masses for Walter Turke tomorrow.'

Kenyngham shuffled together the parchments he had been studying and stuffed them into a pouch. 'You are right. Earthly matters should not interfere with my ability to say prayers for a man's soul.'

'What earthly matters?' asked Bartholomew, intrigued. The elderly friar should not have had any responsibilities that necessitated writing in the early hours of the morning, especially since he had resigned as Master and was supposed to be enjoying his retirement. 'Your teaching?'

'Something like that,' whispered Kenyngham with a gentle smile. 'But we are both tired, and it is too late for talking. Sleep – if William's snoring will let you.'

It was some time before exhaustion finally allowed Bartholomew to ignore William's roaring. He wedged himself between Wynewyk and Clippesby for warmth, and his last thoughts were for those of his patients whose homes comprised woven twig walls packed with mud, where a fire that burned all night would be an unimaginable extravagance.

'The river is frozen like a plate of iron!' exclaimed Deynman, bursting into the conclave before dawn had broken the following day, as the Fellows were just beginning to stir. 'And it has snowed so hard that the High Street is more than waist deep in drifts!'

'Go away, Deynman,' growled William, trying to manoeuvre himself into a position that was comfortable for his splinted leg. 'It is too early to listen to your cheerful voice.'

William was wearing a handsome grey robe made from soft, thick wool. The sleeves were the correct length and so was the skirt, so that his ankles and wrists no longer protruded in a ridiculous manner. He cursed it soundly, claiming it was inferior to the one the students had ceremonially burned in the yard, but Bartholomew knew the friar well enough to see he was delighted with his fine new acquisition. However, the physician could not help but notice the garment already bore signs that William owned it – a wine stain on one sleeve and a chain of greasy splatters across the chest.

'How are you feeling?' Bartholomew asked, rubbing the sleep from his eyes as he addressed the Franciscan. He shivered. Suttone was stoking up the fire, but it was still cold in the conclave. He stood, trying to stretch the aching chill from muscles that had not enjoyed a night on the floor.

'I am in pain,' declared William peevishly. 'But a cup of wine will ease my discomfort. Wine has a remarkable effect on the body, Matthew. You should recommend it as a tonic for good health. It tastes better than all those foul purges you physicians like to dispense, too.'

'I am sure it does,' said Bartholomew, crouching next to him to examine the afflicted leg. 'Shall I remove the splint today? A few days of immobility may have done you good, but you should not prolong it unnecessarily.'

'But it is broken,' argued William in alarm. 'You cannot remove the splint until it has properly healed or I shall spend the rest of my days as a cripple.'

'It is not broken,' said Bartholomew firmly. 'I saw you walking on it yesterday, when you thought no one was watching. It is not healthy to bind a limb that does not need it.'

'It *does* need it,' declared William, equally firmly. 'It is my leg, and I know it is broken. The splint stays where it is – at least until the cold weather has broken.'

'I see,' said Bartholomew wryly. 'That is the real reason for this malingering, is it? You want an excuse to be out of the cold?' He gave a wicked smile. 'And it was only on Christmas Eve that you told me you had exonerated the Dominicans of Norbert's murder, because they are too

210

feeble to set foot outside while the weather is icy. Now I learn a certain Franciscan is doing likewise.'

'I am not malingering,' hissed William, glancing around him, afraid someone might have overheard. 'You saw me fall; you know my injury is genuine. Besides, I would be certain to stumble and do myself far more serious harm if I were to go out in all this snow. My tripping over that loose board was a blessing.'

Bartholomew stared at him. 'You are afraid of falling? Is that what this is all about?'

William gave a shudder and, for a moment, there was a haunted expression in his eyes. Bartholomew had only ever seen the more base of human emotions in William – rage, indignation, fanaticism – and he was intrigued to see that William was genuinely afraid of something.

'I do not like ice,' whispered the friar hoarsely, looking furtively over his shoulder. 'I saw a man fall through some once. He struggled, and it cut through his hands and arms like daggers. I was standing on a bridge, and I could see him quite clearly screaming for help under the surface as he was swept to his death, scrabbling with bloodied hands as he tried to break through.'

'I am sorry,' said Bartholomew sympathetically. 'It must have been terrible.'

'It was,' agreed William fervently. 'His body was never found, and he was wearing three perfectly good emerald rings. But you understand, do you not, why I dislike bitter winters?'

'People say it is the worst they can recall,' said Bartholomew, not sure the traumatic loss of three emerald rings was really a valid excuse for William abandoning his University duties.

William snorted in disdain. 'Then they are wrong. I recall many winters that have been worse than this one, and I remember them better than most, since I hate them so. So, if you leave my splint until I tell you my leg is no longer broken, you will make me a happy man.' He noticed

211

Bartholomew's reluctance to condone a lie and his expression became crafty. 'The Franciscan Friary has a copy of Thomas Bradwardine's *De proportione velocitatum in motibus* that is seldom used. I can suggest it be given to you.'

Bartholomew was tempted. Bradwardine was a famous scholar at Oxford University's Merton College, which had been producing new and dynamic theories relating to the natural universe for the past fifty years. Bartholomew was a great admirer of Bradwardine's work, but what William was asking . . .

'It is all about successive motions and resistance,' added William enticingly.

Bartholomew wavered, and recalled that Bradwardine was the man who had challenged the traditional Aristotelian principle that half the force that caused an object to move would not necessarily mean half the velocity, and that twice the resistance that caused an object to slow down would not necessarily mean the speed was twice as slow. It was heady stuff, and even thinking about it sent a thrill of excitement down Bartholomew's spine. But even so . . .

'It is illustrated,' said William desperately. 'In colour.'

'Done,' said Bartholomew, offering the friar his hand.

'You timed your injury well, Father,' said Langelee, coming up to them. 'You can spend your day here, next to a blazing hearth, while the rest of us have business to attend out in the cold.'

William nodded smugly. 'I know.'

'Deynman gave me this for the College library,' said Langelee, reaching across to the table to retrieve a book that had been lying there. Bartholomew immediately recognised the cheap wooden covers and sparse pages, and wondered what his student had been doing in the King's Head associating with Harysone. 'Perhaps you can read it, Father, and let me know whether it is suitable material for us to keep.'

'You mean you want me to work?' asked William indignantly. 'I have a broken leg, man!'

'We do not need our legs to read,' said Langelee. He

glanced uncertainly at the friar, as though he was not sure that such a generalisation applied to the Franciscan. 'It is not long, and it will only take you an afternoon. You do not want heretical books in our library, do you?'

William growled something under his breath, unable to think of a suitable answer, and began to flick listlessly through the pages.

'*Cann a Fishe enterr Heaven?*' read Clippesby, peering over his shoulder. He appeared especially manic that morning, with his hair standing up in all directions and his eyes wide and bright in his pale face. Bartholomew could not help but wonder whether he cultivated the look just to unsettle William, who was eyeing him nervously, not liking the sensation of a Dominican so close behind him. 'Yes, read that, William. You may learn something.'

'Did everyone survive the night?' asked Langelee, cutting off William's indignant response. 'Wynewyk should check each staircase to make sure no one froze to death, while I imagine Bartholomew will want to visit his patients to do the same. We shall keep fires burning in the hall and conclave today, and I recommend we all stay inside as much as possible. This is no weather to be out unnecessarily.'

'We will all go skating on the river,' declared Deynman excitedly in his capacity as Lord of Misrule. 'I have already been to inspect it. It is set like stone, and it is possible to walk from one side to the other. And then we can go sliding.'

'Sliding?' asked Wynewyk doubtfully. 'I do not like the sound of that.'

'It is where you sit on a flat piece of wood and skid down a hill,' explained Clippesby. 'Cows do it all the time.' He glanced out of the window. 'However, there is not much scope for that activity in Cambridge, Deynman. It may have escaped your notice, but there is a paucity of hills around here.'

'There is the one at the Castle,' said Deynman.

'True,' said Langelee. 'But that is part of the town's defences, and is manned by soldiers with bows. They would shoot you. Now, I know I agreed not to interfere, but I cannot allow anyone to venture on to the river yet. Did you not hear what happened to the husband of Bartholomew's lover? He fell clean through the ice and died.'

'But that was two days ago,' protested Deynman, crest-fallen, and speaking before Bartholomew could object to Langelee's description of Turke. 'It is different now – harder and firmer. None of us will fall in. Turke was fat and heavy, but we are not.'

'No one skates on the river,' said Langelee firmly. 'We do not want anyone to end up like Turke – or like Father William.'

'No,' agreed Clippesby in distaste. 'Or you might make us read that horrible book!'

Michael was already in the church when the rest of the scholars arrived for prime. He declared he had had no intention of freezing in his bed the previous night, and had visited his fellow Benedictines at Ely Hall, where there were plenty of fires and an abundance of warm woollen blankets. He had even inveigled himself the use of half a feather bed, as evidenced by the fact that he was still picking down from his habit when the mass had finished, breakfast had been eaten and the scholars were free to spend their day – the Feast of the Holy Innocents – as they chose. The physician went to his room to don as many clothes as he could fit under his cloak in anticipation of a morning outside.

'What shall we do first?' Michael asked, watching Bartholomew struggle to pull his Michaelhouse tabard over his thickest gipon and two wool jerkins. It was a tight fit, and the physician could barely move when he had finished. 'Shall we investigate the death of Gosslinge by hunting down his missing clothes? Shall we see whether anyone saw Turke skating on the Mill Pool? Or shall we continue to probe into the insalubrious affairs of Harysone or Norbert?'

None of the options appealed to Bartholomew. 'There are patients I need to see, Brother. Langelee is right: this weather may well have killed some of the less hardy.'

'Then there will be little you can do for them,' retorted Michael practically. 'So I shall come with you, lest any of them need my services, rather than yours.'

Since the physician could not move his arms high enough to fasten his cloak without the sound of tearing stitches, the monk helped him, then they walked together across the yard. The gate's leather hinges had frozen solid, and needed to be treated with care to prevent them from snapping off completely.

There was a narrow gorge in St Michael's Lane, where the scholars had trodden a path through the drifts when they had attended mass that morning. On either side, the snow reached head height or more, towering above them in uneven white cliffs. Bartholomew and Michael trudged along in single file until they reached the High Street. It was now fully light and, for the first time that day, Bartholomew could see how much the storm had changed the town.

Snow had been blown in great white waves against buildings, and some of them were virtually invisible. Here and there, people toiled with shovels or bare hands, trying to dig their way out of – or into – their homes. Carts had been abandoned, and formed shapeless white humps all along the road. Some had been excavated by looters, in the hope that their owners had not had the chance to unload their wares before the blizzard had struck. A woman darted along the street with a tear-stained face, asking whether anyone had seen her father. From the way she eyed various lumps under the snow, it was clear she expected to find him dead.

Bartholomew had not gone far before he was spotted and urged to attend the home of a potter who had slipped on ice and damaged his arm. When he had finished, a scruffy boy clamoured for him to visit the shacks on the river bank, where he said he could hear horrible moans coming from the home of Dunstan and Athelbald.

It was impossible to run on the slippery, treacherous streets, but Bartholomew and Michael struggled along as quickly they could. When they reached the hovels that overlooked the river, well away from the sensitive eyes of the wealthy merchants of Milne Street, Bartholomew's heart sank. There was smoke shifting through the walls of most of the houses – not the roofs, because these were blanketed by snow – indicating that warming fires burned within, but not from the one occupied by Dunstan and Athelbald.

'Oh, no!' breathed Michael, his green eyes huge with horror. 'Not Dunstan!'

'He has been ill for weeks now,' said Bartholomew, wanting his friend to be prepared for what he was sure they would find. 'A cold winter is hard for a man well past three score years and ten.'

He tapped on the screen of woven willow twigs that served as Dunstan's door, and pushed his way into the hovel's dim interior, waiting for his eyes to become accustomed to the gloom. The shack was freezing, and smelled of ancient smoke and rancid grease. The beaten-earth floor was sticky underfoot, and Bartholomew thought he saw a rat glide through some of the darker shadows. A soft sob in the darkness made him turn to where two shapes were sitting together on a bench. One was crying, and the other was frozen where it sat.

Oddly, it was not the ailing Dunstan who had died, but his brother. Bartholomew closed his eyes in despair, wondering how the old man would possibly manage without his lifelong friend and companion. Behind him, Michael coughed and left the house quickly, pretending a tickling throat so that no one should witness his own distress.

Bartholomew gathered the blankets from the beds and wrapped them around Dunstan's shaking shoulders. Then he gave the urchin a penny for firewood and told him to hurry. While he waited, he lifted the light, ice-hard body from the bench and laid it gently on one of the wretched straw pallets, wishing he had something to cover it with.

Athelbald looked peaceful in death, and there appeared to be a slight smile on his face, as though his last thought had been an amusing one. In one hand he clutched an

216

inkpot, and Bartholomew supposed he had been telling some tale about it when he had died. Without knowing why, he prised the thing from the rigid fingers. Dunstan took it from him and cradled it to his chest like a talisman.

Michael forced himself to return and began to chant a final absolution in an unsteady voice, anointing the body with a phial of chrism. Dunstan's sobs grew louder, and Bartholomew sat next to him, drawing him close as he attempted to offer warmth as well as comfort.

'We shall bury him in St Michael's churchyard,' said Michael hoarsely, keeping his face in the shadows. The boy arrived with the kindling, and the monk set about lighting a fire that was so large in the tiny room it threatened to choke them all. 'He was in my choir from the very beginning, and he deserves that honour.'

'With a cross,' whispered Dunstan, raising watery eyes to look at him. 'Just a small, wooden one. And all the choir to sing for him. He would like that.'

'I shall arrange it,' promised Michael.

'What shall I do without him?' asked Dunstan, clutching Bartholomew's sleeve. With a shock, the physician saw the man expected an answer. Dunstan needed someone to tell him how to pass his days now that his brother had gone.

'You should not be alone,' Bartholomew said feebly, evading the question. 'Can I fetch someone to be with you?'

'There is no one I want,' said Dunstan bleakly. 'No one understands me like he did. He liked to talk with me, and speculate on all manner of things that happened in the town. Like that lad you found buried in the snow before Christmas Day. Athelbald had his ideas about *him*.'

'What were they?' asked Bartholomew, more to encourage Dunstan to speak than for information. Both the old men had enjoyed regaling the physician with grossly speculative rumours when he had visited them in the past, most of which he disregarded for the nonsense they were. But if Dunstan gained solace from repeating what he and Athelbald had fabricated about Norbert's death, then Bartholomew was

217

prepared to listen for as long as the old man wanted to talk. He emptied his flask of medicinal wine into a pot, and set it over Michael's fire to warm. There was not much of it, but he thought it might drive some of the chill from the old man's bones.

'Norbert,' said Dunstan, valiantly trying to reproduce the salacious tones he had used while gossiping with his brother. 'He was a fellow who did his family no credit.'

'No,' agreed Michael, forcing himself to smile. 'Athelbald was right about that.'

'He guessed what happened to the weapon that killed Norbert,' said Dunstan, his eyes glittering with proud tears. 'The beadles have spent days looking for it, but Athelbald knew where it went. He used logic, you see, like you University men.'

'What did he reason?' asked Michael, lowering his considerable weight gingerly on to the bench and sharing his cloak with Dunstan while Bartholomew tended the fire.

'He heard the killer used a knife,' said Dunstan, carefully wiping his runny nose on the inside of Michael's cloak. 'Because Norbert was stabbed. And he concluded that the killer had to get rid of it. But the killer knew if it was thrown away in the snow, it would be discovered – if not by beadles, then when the thaw came. Knives are personal things, and it would have given him away instantly.'

'True,' said Bartholomew, who had reasoned much the same thing. Dunstan started to cough, so he opened the door a little, to let some of the smoke out. 'But the killer may just have wiped it clean and put it back in its sheath. Daggers are expensive, and people do not discard them just because they have been between someone's ribs.'

'If you believe that, then you are wrong,' said Dunstan knowledgeably. 'Athelbald and I have seen many murders in our time, and we know people do *not* want to keep weapons that have killed. Some believe it was the weapon, not them, that performed the foul deed, you see.'

'Very well,' said Bartholomew, nodding acceptance of the

point. He poured some of the warmed wine into a beaker and watched the old man sip it. 'So, the killer dispensed with the knife. Not in the snow, where it would be discovered, but somewhere else.'

Dunstan nodded. 'And where would you throw a weapon, to get rid of it for ever? He gazed meaningfully towards the open door.

'The river,' said Bartholomew, understanding. 'Of course! All the killer needed to do was toss the thing in the water. Is that what you think happened?'

'It is what *Athelbald* thought happened,' said Dunstan, glancing at the frozen form on the pallet. 'He heard that commotion when you were here to visit me last week. Remember? The bells were chiming to mark the late night offices. He believes the commotion was Norbert's murder.'

'The timing ties in with what I know from my other enquiries,' acknowledged Michael. 'We have been reliably informed that Norbert left the tavern around midnight.'

'It was cold that night,' Dunstan went on. 'So, not many folk attended the mass, including Ovyng's other scholars. If they had, then Norbert would have been discovered sooner – before he was buried by the snow that fell later that night.'

'But it was clear then,' interrupted Bartholomew. 'The moon lit the towpath. I remember it very well.'

'It clouded over and snowed before dawn,' corrected Dunstan impatiently. '*I* was awake for the whole night, whereas you went home to sleep. Now, to continue. Athelbald heard from the servants at Ovyng that Norbert was injured but travelled some distance before he was struck on the head. He reckoned what happened was this: Norbert met his attacker nearby, probably at the Mill Pool, which is deserted at that time of night, and had some kind of discussion. They argued and Norbert was stabbed. Norbert struggled along the towpath to Ovyng, but was brained just as he reached the door. Athelbald said that would explain all the sounds he heard.'

'And what about the man who pushed me over, and the tench?' asked Bartholomew.

'The fish was Norbert's,' replied Dunstan confidently. 'Athelbald heard he won it in a game of dice. Obviously, if Norbert was stabbed and was fleeing for his life, then he would drop such a burden as soon as he could. It was then retrieved by a beggar.'

'Athelbald was undoubtedly right,' said Michael kindly. 'His theory fits the facts precisely.'

The conversation ended when Dunstan began to sob again. Bartholomew looked helplessly at Michael, then tried to persuade the old man to go to Michaelhouse with them, sure Langelee would let him stay until the weather broke. But Dunstan refused to leave his home, claiming he could never rest easy under a strange roof. In the end, sensing he would bring about the elderly fellow's demise even sooner if he forced the issue, Bartholomew relented. He checked the contents of his bag, and found he had enough money to buy firewood for another day. Michael said he had more at Michaelhouse, which could be stretched for a week if used prudently.

'What do we do when we run out?' asked Bartholomew unhappily, watching Dunstan kneel next to his brother and weep. He moved towards the door, where the smoke from the fire was less choking. 'It is not just fuel that he needs, but food, too. Meat and eggs. Agatha will give us some and Matilde will help, but neither can be expected to do it for long.'

'You are a physician, Matt,' said Michael softly. 'You must see that it will not be for long.'

'Do not worry,' came a voice at his elbow. Bartholomew was surprised to see the surgeon Robin of Grantchester standing there, the tools of his trade hanging in a jangling bracelet around his waist. He wore a thick cloak of what appeared to be ferret pelts, although it was matted with the blood of some unfortunate patient. Yolande de Blaston, the carpenter's wife, stood behind him holding a large basket. 'I am here to supply everything you need.'

'He does not need the services of a surgeon,' said Bartholomew quickly, assuming Robin had heard about Dunstan's misfortune and was there to offer a little phlebotomy.

Robin's ugly face creased into an expression of indignation. 'I am here to help!'

'I thought you were in prison,' said Michael. 'Ailred of Ovyng told me you had been arrested for Norbert's murder.'

Robin scowled. 'So has every other respectable man who can produce a noble for his release. So far, Morice has confined his extortion to townfolk, but it will not be long before he fixes greedy eyes on scholars, you mark my words. But enough of my affairs: I have brought Dunstan kindling, mutton and eggs. And Yolande de Blaston, the whore, has been paid to cook twice a day.'

'I am not a whore,' objected Yolande, pushing past him and bustling into the small space beyond. 'I am a businesswoman, making an honest penny, just like you.'

Bartholomew gaped at them. 'What is happening? Who is paying for this?'

'That is none of your concern,' said Robin severely, beginning to walk away, satisfied that his duties had been properly discharged. 'Dunstan will have peat faggots, wood, meat, bread and wine for the next week. By then, the weather may be warmer and he may be better.'

'I do not understand,' said Bartholomew, bewildered. 'How do you know about Dunstan?'

'I listen to gossip in the Market Square, and everyone knows Athelbald died last night,' said Robin superiorly. 'I do occasionally arrange for folk to have necessary victuals, as you may have heard. Good morning, gentlemen. Do not stay out too long, or you will be calling on me to sever ice-eaten fingers.'

'God forbid!' muttered Michael, tucking his hands quickly inside his cloak. He gnawed on his lip thoughtfully when the surgeon had gone. 'This is not the first time Robin has been associated with acts of mercy recently – ungraciously, it is true, but acts of mercy nonetheless. That is why Langelee invited him to the Christmas feast, hoping he might bestow a few merciful favours on Michaelhouse. Still, they say God moves in mysterious ways. This must be one of them.'

'This has nothing to do with God,' said Bartholomew. 'There is a human hand behind Robin's charity – and it is not his own. Still, since it has lightened Dunstan's life, I am not inclined to question it. Come on, Brother. You and I have a river to skate across.'

Michael stared at him. 'Skate? Are you insane? After what happened to Turke? I know Deynman said the river had set like stone, but I am not prepared to stake my life on *his* judgement.'

'Athelbald is right about the knife that killed Norbert,' said Bartholomew. 'The killer probably did throw it in the river. But the river was partially frozen that night, and with luck, the dagger may still be on the surface.'

Searching the river for murder weapons was a dangerous business. A layer of ice lay across the surface, mottled like marble. In places it was as thick as a millstone, while in others it was so brittle and thin that the smallest of pebbles dropped straight through it. The strongest parts were at the edges, where the current was slackest, and it was here that Bartholomew decided they should begin their search. For want of a better idea, he accepted Althebald's thesis that Norbert had been killed near the Mill Pool, and concentrated his hunt there. He gathered stones and hurled them, as the killer might have done with his knife, until he had a rough idea of where the weapon might have fallen.

The biggest problem they faced was the fact that the ice was covered with a layer of snow, which effectively blanketed everything from sight. Michael regarded it in dismay and suggested they should wait until it had melted. Bartholomew pointed out that if the knife had indeed fallen on ice and not in the water, then a thaw would simply send the weapon to the place it had been destined to go in the first place: the bottom of the river. If they wanted it, he argued, then they needed to search while the river was still frozen.

Once they had started, however, they realised it was not

as difficult as they had feared. The previous night's blizzard had deposited vast quantities of snow, but it had also brought fierce winds, which had scoured flakes from the hard surface of the river and piled them in drifts near the banks. Because the wind had been northerly, it had effectively cleared the area they wanted to search.

'It does not seem possible that just four months ago we went swimming in this,' said Michael, poking about with a long stick among the reeds as he recalled their visit to Ely in the summer.

Bartholomew was walking, very carefully, on the ice that covered the river, testing it with a heavy staff that Michael used for excursions outside the town before he entrusted his weight to it. There was a rope around his waist, the other end of which was tied to the monk. The wind was bitterly cold, and he felt the frigid river begin to send chilly fingers through his boots and up his legs. He could do little to warm himself, since any sudden movement might send him crashing through the ice. The current ran powerfully at that point, and he did not relish the prospect of being swept along with it. The rope would stop him from being dragged too far, but he was not sure that Michael would be able to rescue him soon enough to prevent him from drowning.

He stopped for a moment to stretch shoulders that ached from tension, and looked around, admiring the jumble of roofs that formed the nearby colleges and the Carmelite Friary. Most were dusted with snow, but here and there heat from fires had resulted in exposed patches of red tile and manure-brown thatch. A thick pall of smoke hung over the whole town, formed by the hundreds of fires that warmed houses and cooked food, and the stench of burning wood and peat was throat-searing, even down by the river. Suddenly, as he allowed his mind to wander, a horrible thought struck him like a thunderbolt.

'Turke died here.'

Michael nodded. 'Doing what you are doing – walking on

the river – so be careful. I do not want you to go the same way.'

'Doing what I am doing,' repeated Bartholomew slowly. 'Looking for a murder weapon.'

Michael stared at him in startled disbelief. 'You think Turke was looking for the knife that killed Norbert? Why should he do that? They did not even know each other, and it is not as if we are short of suspects for Norbert's murder. Rather the reverse, in fact.'

'How do you know they did not know each other?'

Michael sighed. 'Why should they? Turke was a stranger here and Norbert was dead before Turke arrived in Cambridge.'

'Norbert died *after* he arrived,' corrected Bartholomew. 'Turke came on the fifteenth of December, and Norbert died on the twentieth. And do not forget that Norbert received a summons to meet someone called Dympna, while Turke muttered that name as he died.'

'He did not,' objected Michael. '*You* thought you heard him say Dympna, but *I* heard him say Templar. But even if you are right about Turke's last words, the association between him and Norbert is a little far-fetched, if you want the truth.'

'Then what was Turke doing here?' demanded Bartholomew, irritated by Michael's reluctance to accept his reasoning. 'Philippa said he was not the kind of man to go skating. So, if he was not here for pleasure, then it means he was here for some other purpose. I do not see why you think looking for a knife is so improbable.'

'Because if he was looking for the knife, then it implies that he was Norbert's killer,' said Michael, equally exasperated. 'And I do not see how that can be possible.'

'We already know that Turke had a murderous streak,' Bartholomew pointed out. 'He slew Fiscurtune quite casually. And Fiscurtune was stabbed, just like Norbert.'

'Do you have any idea how many people are stabbed each year?' asked Michael archly. 'Since virtually every man, woman and child carries a knife for everyday use, it is the weapon of choice when ridding yourself of enemies. That both Norbert and Fiscurtune were stabbed means nothing.'

'This is getting us nowhere,' said Bartholomew, seeing they had reached an impasse, and neither was prepared to accept the other's point of view. 'Ah! Here it is.'

'You have the weapon?' asked Michael, moving forward eagerly, as Bartholomew stooped to retrieve something. He grinned in triumph when the physician held up a dagger that was far too highly decorated and expensive to have been thrown away for no good reason. 'Give it to me.'

'Michael, no!' cried Bartholomew. But it was too late. The monk's bulk was already on the ice, which immediately began to bow. Both scholars watched in horror as a series of small cracks began to zigzag away from him, accompanied by sharp snapping sounds. For an instant, nothing happened. And then the ice broke.

Bartholomew felt the surface under his feet begin to tip as though it were a small boat on a stormy sea. Instinctively, he hurled himself forward, landing flat on his stomach on a part that was solid. From Michael's direction he heard a splash, and the rope around his waist was tugged so sharply that it took his breath away. A distant part of his mind noted that it was ironic that he had borrowed the rope so that Michael would be able to pull him to safety, not the other way around. He glanced behind him, expecting to see the top of the monk's head bobbing among shards of ice.

Michael, however, had apparently broken through at a point where the river was shallow, because the water did not even reach the top of his boots. He stood among the ice like some vast, black Poseidon, and began reeling in the rope that connected him to Bartholomew. There was a sharp tug around the physician's waist, and then he felt himself begin to move.

'Do not worry,' the monk called, as he hauled on the line in powerful hand-over-hand motions that made Bartholomew feel like a landed fish. 'I have you.'

He certainly did, thought Bartholomew, powerless against the mighty force that was heaving him shoreward. He wanted to stand, to make his own way to the bank, but his fingers scrabbled ineffectually on the slick surface and there was no purchase for his feet. With a grimace, he gave up his struggle and submitted to Michael's 'rescue' with ill grace, sighing with irritation when a sharp piece of ice ripped a gash in his best winter cloak. By the time he was on the river bank, he had ruined a perfectly good tabard, his cloak would need some serious attention from the laundress's needle, and the knee was hanging from his hose. Still, he thought wryly, at least the ice was hard and dry, and his uncomfortable journey across it had not rendered him soaking wet.

'You should have been more careful,' said Michael, looking him up and down critically.

'Me be careful?' demanded Bartholomew indignantly. 'It was you who started to surge forward like Poseidon emerging from the deep.'

'Where is the knife?'

'I dropped it,' said Bartholomew, recalling how it had slipped from his fingers when he had made his headlong dive for safety.

'You did what?' demanded Michael, aghast. 'How?'

'While trying to save myself from drowning,' Bartholomew replied tartly. 'You should not have tried to come for it.'

'I only wanted to look,' said Michael sulkily, realising that the fault lay with him, but not prepared to admit it. 'Where did you drop it? Is it retrievable?'

Bartholomew shook his head. 'I saw it go into the water at a point where the river runs fast and strong. It will have been swept forward, and I have no idea where it will be now.'

'Damn!' muttered Michael angrily. 'That thing might have allowed us to trace Norbert's killer. And now it has gone.'

'I can describe it,' offered Bartholomew.

'Well, that is something, I suppose,' said Michael ungraciously. 'Go on, then.'

'The hilt was decorated, but not with precious stones. I think they were glass, because the thing looked well used. You do not have a jewelled knife for everyday use.'

'That very much depends on who you are,' said Michael sourly. 'But, in this case, you may be right. Continue.'

'The blade was scratched, again suggesting it was a favoured, much-used item, and wide – which is consistent with the wound in Norbert's back. And finally, and perhaps most importantly, there was blood on it.'

'Then damn it again!' snapped Michael. 'It must be the murder weapon, and you lost it!'

Bartholomew ignored the accusation. 'I can make a drawing with coloured inks, and we can see if anyone recognises it. Philippa, for example.'

Michael shrugged. 'Very well, if you do not mind offending her by suggesting that her recently dead and much-lamented husband crept around the town at night knifing students in the back. More usefully, though, I can ask Meadowman to show it in the taverns when he does his rounds tonight.' He gave the physician a rueful smile. 'I suppose something may emerge from our incompetence.'

CHAPTER 7

WHILE BARTHOLOMEW SAT IN HIS ROOM WITH A BLANK piece of parchment and several pots of coloured ink – borrowed from Deynman, who never wrote in black when blue, yellow, red or green was available – Michael perched on the physician's windowsill and complained that the river water had stained his best riding boots. It was so cold that a rime was starting to form on them, and Michael hastily removed himself to the kitchens, where there was a fire to thaw them and perhaps even freshly baked oatcakes for the taking. It was true it was not long since he had eaten, but everyone knew that cold weather increased the appetite.

Agatha was there, presiding in her wicker throne near the fireplace, from which she oversaw the preparations for the evening meal with critical eyes. Deynman had provided a hundred eggs, and had decreed that no dish should be served that did not have egg of some form in it. Agatha's infamous egg-mess was already mixed, and was busily transforming itself into rubbery lumps near the fire where it was being kept warm. The undercook was struggling with a vat of custard, which was lumpier than the egg-mess and smelled sulphurous, and the butler was patiently shelling hard-boiled duck eggs, humming as he did so.

'No meat?' asked Michael, surveying the preparations with disappointment. He found a stool and three boiled eggs, and carried them to the hearth, settling himself comfortably with legs splayed in front of him and his habit rucked up around his knees so that his boots could dry.

'Hens,' said Agatha, jerking a powerful thumb to one of the back kitchens, where a number of hapless birds were being roasted to dryness on spits that would have benefited from the occasional turn. 'They had eggs in them, did they not?'

Michael laughed. 'You are a clever woman, Agatha. Yes, they did. It will be interesting to see whether Deynman understands such a fine point.'

'I saw you in the King's Head yesterday,' said Agatha conversationally. 'You were watching that Harysone dancing. At least, I assume that was what he was doing. It looked obscene.'

'It was obscene,' agreed Michael, shelling an egg and then sliding it whole into his mouth. He spoke around it with difficulty. 'Have you seen him in the King's Head before?'

'I have not eaten bear liver since I was a child,' said Agatha, answering whatever question she thought Michael had asked. 'But we were discussing Harysone. I have seen him in the King's Head on several occasions, you know.'

'Doing what?' enunciated Michael carefully.

'He likes to show off his dancing "skills", and he has been hawking his book at reduced prices: three marks, and a bargain, he claims.' Her strong face turned angry. 'He is a pardoner, and he asked if I cared to buy a pardon for the seven deadly sins, because he had one that would take care of them all in one go.'

'That was rash of him,' said Michael, meaning it. The man was lucky to escape with all his limbs, given that Agatha had evidently considered herself insulted. He peeled another egg, and thought about Harysone's claim that he had come to Cambridge only to sell his books. He had not mentioned to the guards that he was also a pardoner. The monk mulled over the possibility that misleading town officials might be sufficient grounds to expel the fellow.

'Harysone gambles,' said Agatha disapprovingly. 'I saw him dicing with Ulfrid – who should know better. And I saw him gaming with Norbert the night he died.'

'Did you now?' mused Michael, realising he should not have bothered to send his beadles to the King's Head to question uncooperative townsfolk when he had a fine source of information under his very own roof. 'Did you see him win a fish?'

She nodded. 'They are two of a kind: sly, lecherous and nasty. Harysone also asked whether I knew a person called Dympna. I told him that even if I did, I would not tell him!'

'He asked that?' said Michael. The third egg rolled from his lap and landed unnoticed on the floor. 'He asked about a *person* called Dympna? Not a man or woman?'

'A person,' said Agatha firmly. 'He did not specify whether it was a man or a woman, and when I asked why he wanted to know, he became vague. He said it was a matter of money he was owed. Of course, I said nothing more after that. I would not like to think of some poor soul owing that evil character a debt, and me being responsible for setting him on his trail.' She shuddered.

'Do you know Dympna?' asked Michael, hopeful that she might have answers to questions that had been plaguing him for days.

'No,' came the disappointing answer. 'But I have heard of him.'

'Him?' asked Michael, surprised. 'I thought it was a woman. Norbert received messages from Dympna before he died, and Matt and I made the assumption they were from a lover.'

'Norbert!' spat Agatha in disapproval. 'You should not make any such assumption about him. He did have a lover, although it was not a woman. There is a certain pig that was the object of his amorous attentions. Doubtless Helena will be relieved now that he is gone.'

'Helena?'

'Robin of Grantchester's pig. Folk saw Norbert slipping into the back of Robin's house at odd hours to visit her. Poor creature!'

'How do you know he was not going to meet Robin?' asked Michael curiously.

Agatha regarded him in horror. 'That is a disgusting

notion, Brother! Call yourself a monk? You should see Master Kenyngham and ask him to say prayers that will cleanse your mind of such vile thoughts. Robin of Grantchester and Norbert!'

'It is no worse than you accusing him of courting a pig,' objected Michael indignantly. 'And I was not suggesting Norbert went to see Robin with "amorous intentions", as you put it. They may have had business to arrange.'

'Then why did Norbert not knock at the front door, like Robin's patients do?' demanded Agatha. 'You are wrong, Brother. It was the pig that Norbert went to see.'

'And this pig is definitely called Helena?' asked Michael. 'Not Dympna?'

'You said Dympna sent Norbert messages,' said Agatha, giving him a glance that indicated she thought he was short of a few wits. 'Pigs do not write. Well, Clippesby says they can but choose not to. He said they dislike the sensation of spilled ink on their trotters. Do you think he will remain insane for ever, Brother, or will he become as normal as the rest of us one day?'

'Lord knows!' muttered Michael, declining to answer a question that might lead to so many pitfalls. 'So, what have you heard about Dympna? You referred to this person as "him".'

'I do not know whether it is a man or a woman,' admitted Agatha. 'But I have only ever heard him associated with good things – never bad. That is why I was surprised to hear the name on the lips of a foul beast like that Harysone. What is that egg doing on the floor?'

Michael retrieved it and began to remove its shell while he pondered what Agatha had told him. Dympna, whoever she – or he – was, now provided a definite link between Harysone and the dead Norbert, along with the tench Norbert had won. Michael decided that as soon as Bartholomew had finished his sketch, he would make it a priority to show it to anyone who knew Harysone. The physician could show it to Philippa and her brother if he liked, but Michael was certain he would be wasting his time.

'Did you know Harysone has accused Michaelhouse students of stabbing him?' he asked casually, aware that such information would turn Agatha against the pardoner even more.

'I heard,' said Agatha shortly. 'And so did Sheriff Morice. He visited Harysone just after you did, and tried to force him to make an official complaint. Harysone declined.'

Michael was astonished. 'Harysone refused to allow the Sheriff to investigate the fact that he was stabbed? Why? I anticipated we would have problems with that – I thought Morice would claim that it was a town crime, committed against a visitor, and that the culprits should be turned over to him for sentencing. And you can imagine what would happen then.' He ate the egg.

Agatha nodded. 'The scholars would scream that no member of the University should be tried by a secular authority – especially if the culprit is a friar, as Harysone claims – and there would be a riot. Morice would yield – in return for a certain amount of University money passed directly to his personal coffers – but the ill feeling between scholars and townsfolk would fester anyway.'

'Exactly,' said Michael, thinking she had summed up the situation very well. 'But Harysone declined to allow the Sheriff to look into the matter?'

Agatha pursed her lips. 'Not because he wanted to avoid riots and mayhem. He said he could not afford a second investigation by Morice, and I am sure he meant it literally. Anyone who deals with Morice can expect any help to cost him a noble or two.'

Michael sucked egg from his teeth as he stared into the fire and considered. So, it was likely that Harysone *had* paid Morice something when the Sheriff had recovered his stolen gold, and had not received the entire sum back with interest as he had claimed. But if Harysone's gold had been honestly won, then he would not have needed to give Morice anything. That meant Morice had discovered it was not, and had taken advantage of that fact. Had Harysone stolen the gold from someone else? Or had the Sheriff decided Harysone was overcharging for his book, and threatened to arrest him for fraud? Michael stood, shaking the eggshells from his habit into the fire, where they hissed and popped as they were consumed by the flames.

Michael knew Harysone was unlikely to confess to Norbert's murder if he just marched up to the man and demanded to know whether he was the owner of the jewelled dagger that was now lost for ever in the river. He decided the best way to gain Harysone's confidence would be to act as if he was making a serious attempt to find whoever had stabbed him – to present him with a culprit and show that justice would be done. Harysone would be impressed that the University took accusations of assault seriously, and that it, unlike Morice, did not charge for its services. Once he had the pardoner's trust. Michael would be in a position to talk to the man, in the hope that he could be tricked, flattered or cajoled into saying something incriminating.

The first thing the monk needed to do, therefore, was identify the Michaelhouse friars who had been in the King's Head when Harysone was demonstrating his dancing skills. It would not be difficult: Father William and his five students were the only Franciscans in the College. William had already 'broken' his leg when Harysone was attacked, and everyone knew he had not set foot outside since. That left his students, all of whom might very well have enjoyed an illicit drink in a tavern, although Michael could not see any of them knifing a man in the back.

It was almost dusk, and time for the evening meal, so the monk enjoyed his chicken, egg and custard first, then approached the Franciscans as they were heading to the conclave for an evening of entertainment organised by Deynman.

'We are growing bored with the Waits,' grumbled Ulfrid, when the monk asked why the students were reluctant to follow Deynman that evening. 'Makejoy can dance, and Yna and Jestyn can juggle, but Frith is dire with the pipe and tabor.' His fellow Franciscans gathered around, pleased by an opportunity that would excuse them from the dull festivities for a little longer.

'Frith is a poor musician,' agreed Michael, which was damning indeed coming from a man whose standards were based on the Michaelhouse choir. 'He cannot hold a beat with his drum, and his piping is noise rather than proper tunes. His "Kalenda Maya" was unrecognisable last night.'

'We have had nothing but tumbling and juggling for days now,' Ulfrid continued bitterly. His friends murmured their agreement. 'We want something else. Christmas is a time for things like closh, kayles and quoits, not sitting around indoors watching Waits.'

'You cannot bowl on snow, which eliminates kayles,' Michael pointed out. 'And you would lose your horseshoes and balls if you were to try quoits or closh. But there is always the camp-ball tomorrow to look forward to. And then there are the First Day of the Year games, where there will be ice-camping, wrestling, tilting and all manner of fun.'

'I suppose,' conceded Ulfrid reluctantly. 'But we should have voted for Gray. He is more imaginative than Deynman.'

'Deynman said he paid in advance for the Waits, so he wants his money's worth out of them,' said another of the novices, a prematurely balding youth with a square jaw who possessed the unlikely name of Zebedee.

'The Waits are getting their money's worth out of us,' muttered Ulfrid bitterly. He turned to Michael. 'I caught Frith leaving my room this morning, and later I could not find some pennies I'd left there. I cannot say for certain that he took them, but I am suspicious.'

'Deynman is a fool to retain their services,' agreed Zebedee. 'Agatha said things have gone from the kitchen, too – a pewter spoon, a glass dish for salt, a brass skewer. Little, unimportant items that you do not miss until they cannot be found.'

Ulfrid frowned in puzzlement. 'But, conversely, Cynric accidentally left the College silver out after the Christmas Day feast, and it sat unmolested for a whole day before it was returned to the chest in Langelee's room. Frith could have had that easily, yet he did not touch it.'

'And William has three gold nobles that he always leaves in full view on his windowsill,' added Zebedee. 'They are worth six shillings and eightpence each, and it would be a simple matter for someone to reach in and grab them. I know Frith has seen them, and there have been plenty of opportunities when they could have been his. But he ignores them.'

'Then perhaps we are misjudging him,' suggested Michael. 'It is easy to think the worst of people we do not know, and the fact that he is able to resist gold nobles and silver plates tells me he is probably not interested in pennies and salt dishes. But there is another matter I would like you to help me with. It involves the King's Head.'

Ulfrid was suddenly the recipient of a lot of stares that were far from friendly, and he squirmed uncomfortably. 'You did not have to come,' he blurted defensively, glaring back at his colleagues. 'You could have stayed in the Swan.'

'We could not let you go on your own,' said Zebedee. 'What if Godric and the others had not turned up? You would have been alone in an apprentice-filled tavern.'

'Godric from Ovyng?' asked Michael. 'You went to the King's Head to meet him?'

'Now look what you have done.' Ulfrid rounded on his friend. 'You have dragged Godric into trouble, too, and he has enough to worry about, what with the Tulyets not giving his hostel any more money, and Ailred fretting over this Norbert business.'

Michael crossed his arms and listened. Questions he would have asked were answered by the bickering students without any intervention on his part. He learned that the Michaelhouse Franciscans preferred to drink their illicit ale in the Swan, which was quieter and more peaceful than most of the town's inns, while the Ovyng Franciscans favoured the noisy, lively atmosphere of the King's Head. The students of most Colleges and hostels tended not to mix, but the building Ovyng used was owned by Michaelhouse, and the Franciscans were on friendly terms with each other, occasionally meeting for a companionable drink.

Early on the night Norbert had been killed it had been Godric's turn to buy the ale, and he had suggested the King's Head as the venue. The Michaelhouse lads had demurred, nervous of patronising such a disreputable place at a busy time like Christmas, but Ulfrid had later decided to go anyway, if only to tell Godric not to expect them. Reluctantly, the others had gone with him, but it had been their first and last visit. Ulfrid had won some dice in a bet with the boastful Harysone, and they had all witnessed the pardoner's individual dancing style. However, although they had passed an enjoyable evening with their Ovyng friends, they knew that the King's Head was more likely to be raided by beadles than other taverns, and had declined to go a second time. All the student Franciscans had left the inn before compline, and had returned to their respective homes fairly sober and long before the gates and doors had been secured for the night.

'Did you see Norbert in the tavern that evening?' asked Michael.

The friars nodded. 'But we were in a small chamber at the back, and he was in the public room at the front,' replied Ulfrid.

'We saw him gambling with Harysone,' offered Zebedee helpfully.

'This is interesting,' said Michael. 'Your Ovyng friends have not mentioned this.'

'That is because they were not there at that point,' said Ulfrid, sounding surprised that Michael did not know. 'We arrived first, to make sure of grabbing seats in the back room. Godric and the others are not so fussy about where they sit, and they were late that night, because they were at some public lecture that went on for longer than they expected.'

'After Norbert won the fish, he took his winnings and a woman, and retired upstairs,' continued Zebedee. 'Godric and the others arrived a few moments after that. Norbert was still up there when we all left, so none of the Ovyng students could have seen him. They did not even know he was there. None of us mentioned the fellow, because talking about him would have spoiled their evening. So, I think we can safely say that none of them had anything to do with the murder.'

'I see,' said Michael noncommittally, thinking that it was not impossible for an Ovyng student to have slipped out of his hostel later and killed Norbert. He turned the subject back to Harysone and his stabbing, and learned that the Michaelhouse students' only visit to the King's Head had been several days before Harysone was attacked.

'I expect Harysone remembered that Ulfrid was from Michaelhouse,' said Zebedee. 'He would recall Ulfrid, because he lost his dice to him. He then made the erroneous assumption that all Franciscans are from the same College. But we know nothing about any stabbing, Brother. How is it that Harysone did not see his assailant, anyway? I would remember a man who had knifed *me*!'

'Whoever assaulted him made the mistake of aiming for the hard bones at the base of the spine, instead of the soft bits higher up. Or perhaps Harysone moved suddenly, and the would-be killer's dagger found itself embedded lower than was intended. Can I see your knives?'

The students obliged, and Michael was presented with a mixture of implements. Most were tiny, intended only for cutting up food at the table, although Zebedee's was larger, and Ulfrid's was more ornate than it should have been.

'I lost mine,' admitted Ulfrid. 'So William lent me his spare one. It is a little fancy, but it will suffice until I have the money to buy another.'

Michael nodded his thanks and walked away. Had Ulfrid really lost his original knife, or had he thrown it away when he realised the tip had been left in his victim? The monk shook his head impatiently. The novices had just told him they had only visited the King's Head once, and that had been before the attack on Harysone. Or was Ulfrid lying? Had he returned alone at a later date, thinking he might win something more interesting than a pair of dice? And had he been disappointed in his hopes and had then taken revenge on Harysone?

And was Ulfrid the owner of the knife that had killed Norbert? The friars of Michaelhouse and Ovyng were friends, so was it possible that Ulfrid disliked Norbert for bringing Ovyng into disrepute and had decided to solve the problem for his comrades once and for all? Or was the merry-faced Ulfrid innocent of both crimes, and had just lost his knife, as he claimed? People mislaid items like knives, pens and inkwells all the time.

His instincts told him that the Michaelhouse lads were honest in their denials about Norbert's murder, although he was less certain about their Ovyng colleagues. Perhaps they *had* seen Norbert in the King's Head, and had merely declined to enter the tavern as long as the man was flaunting himself in the main chamber. It was also possible that one had doubled back and had lain in wait for him, stabbing him by the Mill Pool. And perhaps it had been another of them who had finished what the first had started, using a stone when Norbert had finally crawled to where he thought he would be safe. Michael's sense of unease intensified, and he saw he would have no peace until he had Norbert's killer under lock and key – whoever he transpired to be.

Bartholomew presented his finished illustration to Michael with a flourish. The monk was impressed. The drawing was very precise, even down to the way the blood had crusted where the hilt met the blade, and he realised the physician had quite a talent for sketching. The monk studied the diagram carefully. The dagger's handle was depicted as relatively plain, but there was green and yellow glass that would make the thing very distinctive.

'You saw all this before you dropped it?' he asked, hoping that his friend had not added the beads to the picture to make it more attractive.

Bartholomew shot him a withering glance. 'I have included nothing I did not see. Will it do?'

'It will do very nicely,' said Michael, nodding his satisfaction. 'And the first people we shall try it on are the Franciscan friars of Ovyng, who may know more than they are telling about this peculiar business. I have just learned they were in the King's Head the night Norbert died, although Ulfrid believes the friars and Norbert did not see each other. However, I shall reserve judgement on that.'

'I think you will achieve more success when you show it to Philippa and Giles. You know what I think Turke was doing when he fell through the ice.'

Michael gave a hearty sigh. 'You cannot be more wrong. In order to kill someone you need a motive, and Turke had no reason to murder Norbert. However, now Agatha has revealed that Harysone was asking after Dympna, we can conclude *he* had a connection with Norbert – more than just two men dicing for fish together. I shall show your picture to him, too.'

'Agatha's information must have pleased you. You have had Harysone marked down for a criminal act ever since he arrived.'

'Yes,' agreed Michael happily. 'And it is good to know my instincts have not misled me. But we should hurry, or the Ovyng lads will be in their beds. These Franciscans retire early in the winter, and it is almost six o'clock already.'

They walked briskly to Ovyng. The temperature had fallen dramatically with the approach of night, and the air almost cracked with cold. The ground underfoot was as hard as stone, and any moisture had long since frozen like iron. Few people were out, and those that were huddled deep inside their cloaks.

239

'Another beggar froze to death last night,' said Michael as they struggled through the snow. 'I am going to ask Langelee to keep St Michael's open. Beggars are useful sources of information for us proctors, and I do not want to lose them all this winter.'

Bartholomew smiled, knowing Michael was hiding his compassion for the poor by pretending their welfare was in his own interest. 'We should visit Dunstan before we go home,' he said, thinking it might take more than Robin's provisions to keep the old man alive that night. 'I want to make sure Yolande has banked the fire.'

They knocked on Ovyng's door, and were admitted by Godric, who had a smear of ink on his face and held a sheaf of parchment. He wore thick hose and outdoor boots against the cold, and his woollen habit looked bulky, as though he had pulled on as many clothes as he could underneath it. Even so, his fingers had a bluish tinge at their tips, and he was shivering as he stepped aside to let Bartholomew and Michael in.

A small fire was burning in the hearth of the main hall, but it was wholly inadequate to warm a large, stone-built room that had gaps in its window shutters and a wide chimney, both of which allowed the wind to blast through them. All the student friars and Ailred were present, sitting around a table that had been placed as close to the fire as possible, and looking as chilled and miserable as did Godric. Ailred had a pile of sad-looking fish in front of him, which he was patiently gutting. He was leading a debate on the sermons of Thomas Aquinas at the same time.

Some of the fish were cooking over the meagre flames, and the distinctive aroma of food that was past its best pervaded the hostel. Two loaves of bread were being warmed in an attempt to disguise the fact that their outsides were blue with mould, and a bucket of cloudy ale stood behind the hearth, so that some of the chill might be driven from it. Godric kept glancing towards the fire. Bartholomew had the feeling he was hungry, and the visit from the Senior

Proctor meant that his meal was being delayed.

'Finances,' he said in a subdued voice, seeing the Michaelhouse men absorbing the details of their frigid room and paltry meal. 'I know we friars are supposed to seek ways to deny ourselves bodily comforts, but freezing solid and eating food unfit even for animals is not generally recommended by our Order. Norbert's death has been a bitter blow for Ovyng.' He scowled at Ailred.

'Tulyet has stopped paying for Norbert's education,' said Bartholomew in understanding, thinking the dead man's family must have been charged some very princely fees if their cessation resulted in such sudden and abject poverty at Ovyng. 'But you must have anticipated their loss when he died, so you cannot be surprised.'

'We are not surprised,' said Ailred, a little testily. 'But we did not expect the weather to turn quite so bitter before we could think of ways to manage the shortfall. We have food, but little fuel.'

'Food of sorts,' muttered Godric under his breath. 'Stinking fish that even the cat would not touch, and blue bread.'

'You should mention your plight to Robin of Grantchester,' said Bartholomew to Ailred. 'He conjured peat faggots and wood from thin air when Dunstan the riverman was in need.'

'That is different,' said Ailred stiffly. 'Dunstan's is a case of genuine hardship, whereas we are merely uncomfortable. We will not die from the cold.'

'We might,' muttered Godric resentfully, and Bartholomew concluded that their reduced circumstances were something about which the two men did not agree. Some of the students nodded, and the physician saw that they definitely sided with Godric.

'We shall have to get out our begging bowls,' said one, while the others muttered rebelliously. 'We will not survive the winter if we do not do something to help ourselves.'

'We shall manage,' said Ailred sharply. 'You must remember that however cold and hungry you feel there is always someone worse off than you. Do not complain unnecessarily, and give the saints cause to increase your hardship.'

'I have come to ask you about Master Harysone the pardoner,' said Michael conversationally in the silence that followed. 'He speared himself while dancing in the King's Head, and has accused a Franciscan of holding the knife. Does anyone have anything he would like to tell me?'

Ailred looked horrified. 'I can assure you that no one here would set foot in a house of sin like the King's Head.'

'Which houses of sin do you set foot in, then?' asked Michael, aware that the students were not so quick to deny the accusation. They were exchanging guilty, anxious glances, and clearly wondering whether their Michaelhouse colleagues had betrayed them.

'None!' protested Ailred, appalled at the notion. 'Such behaviour would break University rules. I do not need to tell you that, Brother.'

'What about you, Godric?' asked Bartholomew. 'We are not interested in whether you imbibe in the King's Head regularly, just whether you were there on St Stephen's Day, when this particular incident occurred.'

'I do recall a brief sojourn in a tavern around that time,' replied Godric ingenuously, making it sound as though it was of so little importance that it had all but slipped his mind. 'And I do recall a pardoner doing strange things with his body. It was why we left, actually.'

'We?' pounced Michael. 'Who was with you?'

Godric grimaced, angry with himself at being caught out so easily. 'A few of us,' he replied, deliberately vague. He turned defensively to Ailred. 'Well, what do you expect, Father? It is Christmas, and our hostel is as cheerless and cold as a charnel house. All we wanted was a little spiced ale to drive away the chill, and a taste of plum cake.'

Ailred closed his eyes, disgusted. 'But look where it has brought you, boy. You break the rules and bad things happen. Now you are accused of letting a pardoner dance on to your knife.'

'We had nothing to do with that,' declared Godric vehemently. 'We listened to him spouting all manner of nonsense about fish, but we did not argue with him. He offered to sell us his book, and we declined politely. We watched – appalled – when he began to twist and turn to music, but we did not linger long.'

'Neither did many other patrons,' added one of the students helpfully. 'We were among a number of folk who left when he began his display.'

'Did you notice anyone taking a particular interest in him or his dancing?' asked Michael. 'You say people left, but was the reverse true?'

'The other pardoners left immediately,' said Godric thoughtfully. 'But one stayed. He watched intently when it started, and was still staring when we slipped away.'

'One of the pardoners,' said Michael, sounding pleased. Bartholomew was sure the monk would love to arrest a pardoner for the attack on Harysone. 'What did he look like?'

Godric frowned. 'I am not sure. He was smaller than me. He wore a dark cloak and a hat.'

'Disguised?' asked Bartholomew, thinking it was odd for someone to be swathed in hat and cloak in a crowded tavern that was likely to be stuffy. And being smaller than Godric was no kind of description – Godric was a sturdy man.

'The landlord was having problems with snow in his chimney, so the fire was unlit. It was cold, and a number of us were wrapped in outside clothes, with hoods or hats pulled down.' He gave an apologetic shrug. 'That is all I remember: one man watching Harysone from under a hat.'

'Whoever attacked Harysone left the end of his blade in his victim's back,' said Bartholomew. 'Can we inspect everyone's knife, to see whether one matches the break?'

'Please do,' said Ailred, gesturing to his friars to comply, although most were already producing blades from belts and scrips. Michael studied each one in turn, but, like those belonging to the Michaelhouse Franciscans, none were

243

missing their tips. Godric's knife was of a better quality than the rest, and the monk regarded it thoughtfully.

'It *is* new,' said Godric, seeing what Michael was thinking. 'But I have had it for about a week, not two days. I threw the old one away, because the hilt was cracked. My sister, who is Prioress at Denny Abbey on the Ely road, sent me another.' He brightened as a thought occurred to him. 'She is a kind and generous lady. If I were to write to her about our condition—'

'No!' snapped Ailred. 'We cannot accept alms from nuns. Supposing they deprive others in order to help us? It would be unconscionable.'

'I do not suppose this is the knife you discarded?' Michael extracted Bartholomew's drawing from his scrip and passed it to Godric, watching him intently for a reaction.

'No, mine was plain,' said Godric. He held up the picture for the students to see. 'Have any of you seen this before?'

There were shaken heads all around, and if any recognised it as being the one 'with the cracked hilt' that Godric had discarded, no one said so. Most huddled deeper into their cloaks and denied knowledge of the thing with polite uninterest. Others made more of an effort, and at least examined the parchment first.

'What about the blades used for cooking?' asked Bartholomew, thinking the metal he had extracted from Harysone was from a fairly substantial implement, not from something small like the knives the friars carried for cutting their food.

'Please look,' invited Ailred. 'Godric will help you. And while you play with our greasy cooking utensils, Brother Michael can tell me about the progress he has made with Norbert's case.'

Godric took Bartholomew across to a bread oven set into the wall near the hearth. Two pots stood there, one scrubbed, clean and ready for use, the other half full of some grey material that was evidently the remains of the meal the friars had eaten the day before. It looked worse

244

than the fish they planned to dine on that evening, and Bartholomew was not surprised that Godric and his students sought edibles from outside. The knives were hanging on the wall and the physician inspected each one with care: none was missing its end.

'We still know very little about Norbert's death,' Michael admitted to Ailred. 'Although we think we have discovered the weapon that killed him.' He nodded to the illustration lying on the table, where the last of the friars to inspect it had set it down.

'That?' asked Ailred eagerly, moving forward to look at the picture again. 'Are you sure?'

The friars craned towards the diagram a second time, more interested now they knew it had caused the death of their colleague and was not just a weapon used to injure a pardoner. But despite their apparent willingness to help, no one was able to say he had seen it before.

'You can take it to the taverns,' suggested Ailred. 'Someone there might recognise it.'

'I know,' said Michael sharply, not needing to be told how to do his job. 'The King's Head is a good place to start.' He looked hard at the novices. 'Why did you not tell me you were all there the night Norbert was killed?'

'What is this?' cried Ailred in horror. 'What are you saying?' He turned to his students. 'Tell him this is not true.'

'It is true,' said Godric softly. 'But the reason we did not mention it was because we did not know Norbert was there. Ulfrid has since told us he was frolicking in a private chamber with a lady while we drank our ale, but, as God is my witness, none of us set eyes on him that night.'

'You should not have concealed this,' said Michael sternly. 'You must see how it appears.'

Godric hung his head. 'I know we were wrong to visit the King's Head. But since we could tell you nothing about Norbert's death, we saw no point in confessing that we had broken the University's rules. We have enough spare coins for the occasional hot ale, but we cannot afford to pay the kind of fines Father William will now levy on us. *He* is the reason we have remained silent on the matter.'

There was a growl of agreement from the others. 'I shall say nothing about it to William,' said Michael tiredly. 'However, more important than your rule-breaking at the moment is gathering information about Dympna. I am sure she is relevant.'

'Not this again,' groaned Ailred. 'How many more times will you raise this subject? We have told you all we know, and I cannot see how she relates to Norbert's death.'

'I think she does,' countered Michael. He eyed the students coolly. 'So, I repeat: what can you tell me about her?'

'No more than we told you the first time you asked,' said Godric, watching Bartholomew take a meat knife and examine it, while Ailred sighed his annoyance at the monk's persistence. 'Surprisingly, her notes to Norbert were not romantic or filled with affection; they just told him to be in St Michael's at a particular time, and were followed by a set of numbers.'

'Why surprisingly?' asked Michael.

Godric gave an abashed grin and gazed down at his booted feet. 'Well, if a woman takes the trouble to write to a man, you assume she would pen something loving, to encourage him to meet her and sample the delights of her company.'

'You have very colourful ideas about courtship,' said Michael, eyeing him sceptically.

'Godric believes in romantic love,' said Ailred wearily to Michael. 'I mentioned that before. It is as well he decided to become a friar and forgo relationships with women, because otherwise he would have been wounded deeply when he learned that not all are virtuous virgins.'

'Many are,' protested Godric, offended. 'Dympna must be. She could have dispatched some grubby boy with a spoken message to Norbert, but she chose to write. That shows she cared for him: she took time and trouble to pen a message – or she hired someone to scribe it for her.'

246

'Did any of you ever follow Norbert to see what happened when he met this paragon?' asked Michael, more interested in Norbert than in Godric's misguided ideas. Ailred made an impatient sound at the back of his throat, as though he could scarcely credit that Michael was still pursuing the subject when there were far more relevant and important issues to be considered.

'Several times,' replied Godric, ignoring his principal's reaction. 'But whomever he met was elusive. We shadowed him to the church, but when we entered through the north porch, she left through the south entrance, and when we had someone posted at both doors, she slipped away through the tower. I glimpsed a hooded figure once, but could tell nothing about her.'

'Could it have been a man?' asked Michael.

Godric gazed uncertainly at him. 'Are you saying Norbert's heart was captured by a man?'

'Better than by a pig,' muttered Michael, thinking of Agatha's theory. 'But can you say for certain that this hooded figure was a woman?'

'Well, it was not a pig,' said Godric firmly. 'But it could have been a man, I suppose. It is possible it was not Dympna at all, but someone else who just happened to be there.'

'Enough of this,' said Ailred irritably. 'It is taking us nowhere. You will find some tavern patron will be your culprit, Brother, not this mysterious figure who vanishes from churches. You should look into anyone who has connections to the King's Head – including wealthy folk who hire the best chambers. Rich men murder just as capably as poor ones.'

'Are you thinking of Harysone?' asked Michael immediately.

Ailred shook his head crossly. 'I am not thinking of anyone specifically. I am only saying you are wasting time with Dympna when you could be investigating the real culprit.'

'You did not try very hard to discover the identity of the person Norbert met,' said Michael to Godric, sounding accusatory and ignoring the principal's advice. 'It could not have taken much skill to catch her, once she was inside.'

'It took more than we had,' said Godric ruefully. 'We are not experienced at that kind of thing. We were just being nosy – to see what kind of wench would be attracted to Norbert. Had we known it would lead to a line of enquiry relating to his murder, we would have tried harder.'

Michael pursed his lips. 'So, none of you stabbed Harysone, and none of you can tell me about Dympna?' He sighed. 'Then I suppose I shall bid you goodnight.'

Bartholomew and Michael walked to the hovels on the river bank, feeling frozen snow crunch under their feet. For the first time in many days, the evening was clear, and millions of stars glittered overhead in a spectacle of indescribable beauty. The beauty had its price, however, and the temperature had plummeted even further. Sudden cracks rent the air when water expanded into ice and split walls, wood and stone, and the still night air was thick with smoke from hearths.

Michael sat with Dunstan, holding his hand and allowing him to reminisce about his brother, while exaggerating the quality of Athelbald's singing. Bartholomew banked up the fire so its heat filled the single room, then made sure the blankets were tucked around Dunstan's thin shoulders. He tried again to persuade the old man to stay at Michaelhouse, but Dunstan claimed his brother's soul was still in the house, and said he would not leave until it had gone.

They had not been there for long before there was a perfunctory knock on the door and Matilde entered. Bartholomew felt a lurch of pleasure when he saw her, standing tall and graceful in the centre of the shabby hut. She wore her cloak of bright blue with the silver clasp, and her feet were clad in stout, practical boots. Robert de Blaston was with her, flapping his arms and stamping in an attempt to warm himself. Bartholomew recalled that Matilde had taken the carpenter and his brood into her house when it became apparent that their own home was unsafe, and had probably saved their lives by doing so. Matilde greeted the scholars, then indicated Blaston, who had declined to enter the crowded hut.

'Rob insisted on accompanying me, because you know what this town can be like for a lone woman after dark. I wanted to make sure Dunstan was settled for the night, but it seems you have already done that. How is Philippa?'

Bartholomew was startled by the abrupt question. 'Well enough, I suppose. Her husband is being embalmed and prepared for travel, so I imagine she will go home when the weather breaks.'

'Good,' said Matilde. She blushed when she realised how that sounded. 'I mean it is good for her to complete this grim business and be about her life. She will be obliged to search for new suitors soon and will want to make a start.'

'Will she be courting you, Doctor?' asked Dunstan. But his eyes lacked the mischievous sparkle such teasing usually brought, and his voice was lustreless and flat.

'I do not think she is in a hurry to remarry,' said Bartholomew, aware that Matilde was waiting for his answer. 'She will not think it seemly for a widow to be soliciting husbands until a decent amount of time has passed.'

'That depends on what Turke left her in his will,' said Matilde practically. 'She may have time for a leisurely approach, but then she may be obliged to begin the hunt immediately.'

'I hope she does not hunt around here,' said Michael fervently. 'I do not think she would make a good wife for Matt. She has changed since we first met, and I cannot say I like her as much as I did. Besides, I do not think she would welcome my visits to her home or offer me the best food in her larder.'

'I do not think she would appreciate visits from Matthew's other friends, either,' said Matilde meaningfully. 'And I would miss his company terribly.'

'You need not worry,' said Bartholomew, amused by their

249

flagrant self-interest. 'I doubt I am any more Philippa's idea of the perfect husband now than I was five years ago. We are not as easy in each other's company as we were, and she is often irritable.'

'She is not a happy woman,' agreed Matilde. 'And it is not because she has lost her husband. Her sadness goes deeper than that, and has lasted for more than a few days.'

'She was not sad at the feast,' said Bartholomew, surprised by Matilde's assertions. 'And that was before Turke died. She is not the woman I remember – who laughed a good deal – but she did not seem despondent. Just older and wiser, like all of us.'

'You are wrong,' said Matilde. 'She is carrying a burden that is hard to bear. I noticed it when Edith introduced us days ago, when Turke was still alive. Perhaps she realised what a mistake she made in declining you in favour of him. I am sure it is something to do with love – or the lack of it. We women can tell these things.'

'It is probably indigestion,' said Michael, eliciting a husky chortle from Dunstan. 'God knows, the woman eats enough!'

Amused by the monk's unashamed hypocrisy and Matilde's wild assumptions about a woman she did not know, Bartholomew mixed Dunstan a mild dose of laudanum to induce the sleep he felt the old man needed. Then he sat in mute sympathy when Dunstan's laughter dissolved into tears. When he began to doze, Bartholomew and Michael left him with Matilde, and slipped away. Michael sniffed hard as they walked along the towpath, and when he spoke his voice was unsteady.

'I hate winter, Matt. It is a cruel and uncaring season.'

'Summer can be as bad,' Bartholomew replied sombrely. 'Hot-weather agues claim people, too, and so does marsh fever.'

Michael took a deep breath and tilted his head to look at the bright stars overhead. 'We have so much to do,' he said eventually. His voice was steadier, and he was evidently finding solace in thinking about his duties, pushing

Athelbald and Dunstan from his mind. 'We have the picture of the knife to show folk in order to identify Norbert's killer. And I should speak to the town's other Franciscans about Godric – I am suspicious he has a new knife just after Norbert's murder.'

'And there is Harysone's stabbing. We have to prove beyond the shadow of a doubt that the Michaelhouse lads did not do it before he complains to the Chancellor. Tynkell will do almost anything to avert a riot, and may order Michaelhouse to pay Harysone to keep him quiet. We cannot afford to compensate the man for his injury – unless we want to spend the rest of the winter living like Ovyng.'

'You are right. But things are beginning to come together and I can see connections now that were not obvious before. For example, we know Harysone played dice with Norbert and lost a tench to him. Meanwhile, Harysone has also been asking about Dympna, who we know sent missives to Norbert.'

'Dympna connects Norbert to Turke, too. He said her name as he died. And fish links all three men to each other: Norbert's tench, Harysone's book, and Turke's chosen trade.'

'I disagree with you about Turke's dying words, as you know,' said Michael pompously. 'But your fishy associations look promising. However, I will not accept that Turke killed Norbert. The culprit is far more likely to be Harysone.'

'Then there are the Chepe Waits,' added Bartholomew, not wanting to argue about it. His conclusions had been built solely on the fact that Turke had died near where the murder weapon had been found, and he knew this was a weak foundation for any theory. He also accepted that the visiting fishmonger had no reason to murder Norbert. Although he did not want to admit it to Michael, he had reconsidered the hasty suppositions he had made relating to Turke's place of death, and was inclined to believe that the monk was correct after all. Turke did not kill Norbert.

'What about the Waits?' asked Michael.

'Quenhyth saw them conversing with Harysone in the King's Head; they played in Turke's house and admitted talking to Gosslinge in Cambridge; and they spoke to Norbert. They have connections to the three dead men, too.'

'We know they were desperately looking for someone to employ them, so they probably spoke to lots of people,' said Michael, unconvinced as he mulled over the information. 'I think that particular connection is spurious.'

'But it is odd that Philippa should not mention she had hired them – and that Giles immediately left when they appeared. And what about Quenhyth? He is a connection, too. He knows the Waits, he hails from near Chepe, and he is the son of a fishmonger.'

'That must be coincidence,' determined Michael. 'I can accept he might kill a Wait, but he, like Turke, has no motive for murdering Norbert. So, we are left with a lot of questions. It seems there are strands linking Norbert, Harysone and the Turke household together, but we cannot be sure what – if anything – they mean. Meanwhile, Stanmore believes – and I concur – that the circumstances of Turke's death warrant a little probing by the Senior Proctor. You yourself said it is odd that he and his servant should die in quite such quick succession.'

'But there is nothing on either body to suggest foul play: Turke died because he fell through ice, and Gosslinge seems to have been a victim of the cold weather.'

Michael's expression was crafty. 'Both still lie in the church, because there is too much snow to bury one, while the other is awaiting transport to London. Will you look at them again? To make sure there is nothing you missed?'

Bartholomew sighed. 'I can look at them until I am blue in the face, but I still will not be able to tell you more than we already know.'

'You think Turke was looking for the knife that killed Norbert,' pressed Michael, still unaware of Bartholomew's recapitulation on that point. 'We need to continue our search for connections, and the best way to do that is to examine the bodies again. Tonight.' He raised a hand to quell Bartholomew's objections. 'I know you promised Philippa you would not tamper with Turke, but it is obvious she has her own reasons for making such a request, and they may not be innocent.'

'But it is freezing tonight,' objected Bartholomew. 'If I die of an ague brought on by cold, you will have no one to inspect your corpses when it is really necessary.'

'I think it is really necessary now,' argued Michael. 'And it is an excellent time for looking at corpses. It is late – probably long past eight o'clock – and no one will be looking.'

'You make it sound so underhand,' grumbled Bartholomew, reluctantly turning towards St Michael's. 'Looking at bodies in the dark, when no one can see what we are doing.'

The air was so cold that it hurt Bartholomew's throat when he inhaled, exacerbated by the thick wood-smoke that clogged the town. The physician was revolted to note that, near the church, the fumes had all but blocked the stars from the sky, and he could taste soot and cinders in his mouth, crunching between his teeth. He unravelled part of his hood turban and used it to cover his mouth. His ears ached from the chill, while his nose was so numb he could not tell whether it was dripping. He longed to be back in Michaelhouse, even if it meant another evening of the Waits. They reached the church, squat and mysterious in the smoke that swirled down the High Street from the great fires in King's Hall. Michael fumbled in his scrip for the key, but when he inserted it the door swung open of its own accord.

'That is odd,' said the monk. 'I have not spoken to Langelee about the beggars yet, and I doubt he would leave the church unlocked without being prompted.'

Bartholomew inspected the latch. 'It is not unlocked, Brother. The mechanism has been smashed. And there is a light inside. Someone is in there!'

'Stay here and make sure he does not escape, while I fetch the beadles,' instructed Michael. 'We will not attempt to apprehend this intruder by ourselves. We tried that last summer in Ely, and we allowed a killer to go free and claim more victims. This time, we will do it properly. If he comes out, hide. I do not want to return and find you dead.'

He slipped away into the night, leaving Bartholomew alone. The physician huddled into his cloak and tried not to think about his icy feet. The monk had not been gone for more than a few moments before the door opened and two people emerged. Bartholomew cursed softly. What should he do? Hide himself, as Michael had instructed? Or should he try to grab one?

Boldly, but rashly, he opted for the latter. With an ear-splitting yell that he hoped would bring Michael rushing back, he launched himself at the shadowy figures. Both were startled into releasing howls of their own, voicing their terror at being assailed from a shadowy graveyard. One began to lay about him with clumsy, panicky punches, none of which met their intended target, while the other dropped to his knees and began a prayer. Bartholomew recognised the voice and promptly abandoned his attempts to seize the fellow's companion.

'Kenyngham?' he asked in confusion. He reeled backwards, as the second man found himself with a stationary target and a fist grazed the physician's right ear.

'Got him!' yelled Suttone victoriously, jumping up and down in glee. He stopped jigging and shrank back in alarm as Bartholomew turned to face him. 'No! Please do not hit me back! It was an accident. I will give you anything – the key to Michaelhouse's silver chest, if you would like it.'

'No, thank you,' said Bartholomew stiffly, rubbing his ear. 'And you should not have it, either, if you are prepared to give it up so easily. What are you doing here at this time of night?'

'Matthew! Thank the Lord!' Kenyngham pulled himself up from his knees and gave a sigh of relief, crossing himself vigorously. 'I thought you were a robber. What made you throw yourself at us with that unholy screech? I feared it

254

was Turke's tortured soul, come to haunt us for not saying more masses.'

'I assumed you were burglars,' said Bartholomew lamely. Since the scuffle, the door had swung open, illuminating them with faint candlelight from inside. It seemed impossible that he could mistake Kenyngham and Suttone, with their wide-sleeved habits and pointed cowls, for thieves. He could only plead that it had been very dark. 'The latch has been smashed.'

'I noticed that when we arrived,' said Kenyngham, sounding careless of the fact that it meant someone had forced an illicit entry. 'But you were the one who asked us to pray for Turke, so I am surprised that you should attack us for being here.'

'I am sorry, Father,' said Bartholomew tiredly. 'I hope I did not alarm you too much.'

'You did, actually,' said Suttone coolly. 'I do not like being screamed at by spectres that launch themselves from graveyards.' He turned to Kenyngham with accusing eyes. 'You did not mention the lock was broken. I assumed you used your key to enter.'

'I did not want earthly concerns to distract you from your meditations,' said Kenyngham. 'I planned to ask Langelee to mend it tomorrow.'

'But this means that the pair who are in there now are intruders,' said Suttone in a hushed, appalled whisper.

'I suppose so,' acknowledged Kenyngham, sounding as though he did not much care. 'They could also be folk who are weary of fiddling with our awkward latch. It seems to be much worse these days, and I am often obliged to use the south door when I want to leave.'

'How often?' asked Bartholomew, thinking of the day when Michael had discovered the south door open and had immediately drawn the conclusion that Harysone had done it.

'Once or twice a week,' came the alarming reply. 'Why? Have I done something wrong? I do not—'

'The people inside right now must have forced the lock,' said Suttone, rudely cutting across his words. His voice grew unsteady, as the implications slowly sank in. 'I wondered why they seemed nervous until we knelt and started to pray. They imagined they had been caught red-handed, and were anticipating a fight.' He swallowed hard and leaned against the door, unnerved by his narrow escape.

'Where are they now?' demanded Bartholomew, pushing past him. He advanced cautiously, not wanting to barge in and have his brains dashed out with one of the heavy pewter candlesticks from the altar. 'Who are they? And what are they doing?'

'There are two of them,' said Kenyngham helpfully, following him into the nave. 'They are cloaked and hooded, so we did not see their faces – and they were in the Stanton Chapel, anyway. They were there the whole time we were saying our prayers, moving about and muttering. I assumed they were troubled souls, seeking the peace only a church can offer.'

'Or the silver only a church can offer,' muttered Suttone, who appreciated that folk entered churches for reasons other than to pray, even if Kenyngham did not.

'Are you sure they are still here?' asked Bartholomew, inching down the nave, keeping well away from pillars that might conceal an attacker. 'They did not leave through the south door, as you have just confessed to doing?'

'Not as far as I know,' said Kenyngham. 'They were in the Stanton Chapel when Suttone and I completed our devotions and left.'

Heart thumping, Bartholomew headed towards the chapel. He held one of the knives he used for surgery, and was aware that his hand was sweating, despite the chill, so the weapon felt slippery in his grasp. Kenyngham began to remonstrate with him for drawing a dagger in a church, but the physician silenced him with an urgent order to remain behind a column, out of harm's way. The cowardly Suttone needed no such advice, and had chosen to remain outside while Bartholomew hunted the interlopers.

The physician reached the chapel and explored it carefully. But whoever had been there, 'moving about and muttering', had gone. Only Athelbald and Turke were there, shrouded and silent in their coffins.

Not sure whether to be relieved or disappointed, Bartholomew went to the south aisle, where the body of Gosslinge lay – as a mere servant and a stranger to the town, Gosslinge did not warrant use of the Stanton Chapel, like the wealthy Turke or members of the Michaelhouse choir. The south door had been unbarred and opened, and Bartholomew saw that the two intruders had slipped away quietly into the night.

Michael rounded up his beadles and ordered them to make a search for the two people who had been in the church, but he held no real hope of finding them. It was not difficult to remain undetected at night in a place like Cambridge, where there were plenty of cemeteries in which to hide, and taverns and alleyways into which to duck. Briefly, the monk entertained a notion that the snow might help, and that the intruders might have left footprints that could be followed, but the ground was frozen so hard it was barely possible to make an imprint by stamping. Normal walking made no kind of mark at all.

'Damn Suttone!' muttered Michael, watching Meadowman escort the two friars back to Michaelhouse. 'I expect eccentric, gullible behaviour from Kenyngham, but if Suttone had been more observant, we might have had this pair by now. What were they doing, do you think?'

'I have no idea,' said Bartholomew. 'There is nothing in the Stanton Chapel that could interest them, so I suspect they were disturbed when Kenyngham and Suttone arrived and hid there.'

'Then they heard you scuffling with Kenyngham in the churchyard, and realised they had better escape while they could.' Michael rubbed his chin, fingers rasping softly on

257

his bristles. 'However, the fact that they were prepared to linger suggests they had not finished what they were doing when Kenyngham came, but that it was sufficiently important to warrant them waiting for him to leave.'

'I recommend you post a guard and return in the morning, when you will be able to see. We should not look at the bodies of Turke and Gosslinge now, because we may miss or destroy clues about these intruders that will be obvious in daylight.'

'I suppose you are right,' conceded Michael reluctantly. 'Of course, the presence of these burglars may have nothing to do with our investigation. They may just be opportunistic thieves.'

'I disagree. It is common knowledge that St Michael's does not leave its silver lying around. Consequently, there is little for anyone to do here, except stand and pray. However, we are well endowed with corpses at the moment, and it seems to me that the intruders were here in connection with them. There can be no other reason.'

'In that case, we shall return at dawn tomorrow and search every nook and cranny of this building until we find the clues we need to sort out this mess. No shadowy figures who lurk in cold churches shall gain the better of *me*!'

'I am glad to hear it,' said Bartholomew tiredly, not liking the sound of the 'we' who would conduct the exhaustive survey the following day.

'So, which of the corpses do you think warranted this pair spending all evening here?' asked Michael. 'Turke or Gosslinge?'

'I have no idea. And I cannot imagine who the intruders were, either – unless you think Philippa and Giles have a penchant for this kind of thing.'

'Or Ailred and Godric,' suggested Michael. 'Or Harysone and an accomplice. But speculating will do us no good. Let us do as you suggest and come back tomorrow – at first light.'

* * *

It was too dark to explore the church at prime, so Michael declared they should wait until after breakfast. Meadowman was still on duty when they returned, and reported that no one had attempted to enter the church. Based on the fact that he believed the intruders were desperate to get what they wanted, Michael had 'mended' the lock in a way that made it easily re-breakable, and Meadowman had been told to remain hidden, so that he could catch anyone who arrived illicitly. But Michael's precautions came to nothing, and a weary, bored Meadowman had not heard a suspicious sound all night.

Although Michaelhouse's scholars had completed their devotions and eaten breakfast, the friars of Ovyng still had to say their morning prayers. Like the other hostels that paid Michaelhouse a fee to use the Collegiate church on a regular basis, Ovyng had been allocated specific hours, to ensure the various institutions did not impinge on each other. That week it was Ovyng's turn to pray at eight o'clock, and Ailred and his students began to file into the church as Bartholomew and Michael were finishing their examination of the chancel.

'Looking for coins between the flagstones, Brother?' asked Ailred amiably, not seeming at all surprised to see the fat Benedictine on his hands and knees. 'You may be fortunate. I often find farthings by doing just that, and such explorations are frequently worthwhile.'

'I do not suppose you came here last night, did you?' asked Michael hopefully. 'To look for pennies in the church, after everyone else had gone home?'

Ailred was astonished by the suggestion. 'I would not do it in the dark; I would not be able to see. Once you left us, I barred our doors and allowed us the luxury of an extra log on the fire. It was a bitter evening, and no one in his right mind would have ventured out unless he had no choice.'

'What would give him "no choice"?' asked Michael, detecting a caveat in Ailred's denials.

Ailred was becoming impatient, although whether it was

259

because he genuinely did not understand why Michael was questioning him, or because he had something to hide, Bartholomew could not decide. 'A number of things,' the friar snapped. 'Bartholomew has no choice when he is summoned by a patient; I have no choice when there are sacred offices that need to be recited.'

'But not last night?' asked Michael.

'Not last night,' replied Ailred firmly. 'We had our evening meal at six o'clock, which was fish stew, then we sat around the fire playing merels – the board game, where you have nine holes and must use wit and cunning to prevent your neighbour's pieces from occupying them. Since it is the Twelve Days, and given that my previous policy of austerity seemed to produce in my students a desire to visit taverns, I decided I should relent and allow them a little fun.'

'Merels!' said Michael scathingly. 'That must have made for a thrill-filled evening.'

'It was most entertaining,' said Ailred, evidently unaware of Michael's sarcasm. 'We all enjoyed it very much, and tonight we shall play backgammon. I have borrowed a board and game pieces from Robin of Grantchester for the occasion. But why do you ask about our whereabouts? Have you learned something new about the death of Norbert?'

'Two people visited St Michael's last night, and we do not know why. It was a passing thought that you might have been one of them, perhaps with a student. We do not know what these folk were doing, so we are not accusing anyone of anything untoward.'

'Good,' said Ailred firmly. 'Because it was not me – or any of us, for that matter. You can ask my students, and they will all tell you the same thing: we were at home last night. But now you must excuse me: I have a mass to celebrate.'

He turned abruptly, and began to lay out the vessels he would need for his devotions. Meanwhile, Godric and his students waited patiently some distance down the chancel, whispering in low voices as they stood with their hands tucked inside their sleeves and their cowls thrown back to reveal their tonsures. Michael caught Godric's eye, and beckoned him over, confident both that Ailred was too absorbed in his preparations to notice what the monk was doing and that the student had not overheard the exchange with his principal.

'What transpired at Ovyng last night?' said Michael. 'What did you do? Where did you go?'

'We played merels,' replied Godric heavily. It was evident that while Ailred considered the board game a risqué form of enjoyment, Godric did not share his enthusiasm. 'I have not played merels since I was a child, and I confess it is not what I had in mind when I pressed Father Ailred to allow us a little levity during the Christmas season. Still, merels will be better than backgammon, which is what he has planned for tonight.'

'When did you start these games? Immediately after your meal?'

'Later. Ailred had some errands to run, and I wanted to go the Market Square, to see whether the traders would sell me anything cheaply, since the day was over.'

'Really,' said Michael, his eyes gleaming. 'And what time did you all return?'

'I do not know. Ailred buys cheap hour candles, and they burn at variable rates, so we never really know what the time is. But I think we barred the door, with all inside, by perhaps half-past eight or a little later.'

'Thank you, Godric,' said Michael, grinning wolfishly. 'However, this is not what Ailred told me, so we had better keep this discussion between you and me, eh?'

'What did he tell you?' asked Godric in alarm, horrified by the notion that he might have done something wrong. He shot an agitated look at his principal, but Ailred had not yet noticed that the monk had taken him at his word and was indeed asking the scholars to confirm his story.

'He told me you all stayed in,' said Michael. 'Return to your prayers, lad, before Ailred sees that you have gone.'

Godric hurried back to his friends, but his mind was no

longer on his devotions. He seemed pale in the dim light, and nervous fingers twisted one of his sleeves. He was late with his responses, and his thoughts were obviously elsewhere. Bartholomew watched him thoughtfully, thinking he seemed more dismayed than he should have been by Michael's mention of discrepancies between his and his principal's stories. Did he know that Ailred or one of the other students had been doing something he should not have been, and was aware that he had just ruined what could have been a perfectly sound alibi? Or was he afraid for himself, realising that the differences in stories revealed him to be a liar?

Ailred completed his preparations, then turned to the waiting scholars. 'Before we start, Brother Michael would like to ask about our activities last night. He wants to know what we did after we ate our fish and immediately turned to our games of merels.'

'Nicely put,' murmured Michael to Bartholomew. 'No leading statements here.'

'Nothing,' came a quiet chorus of voices.

'Did any of you go out after the meal?' asked Michael.

Godric stared ahead and did not answer, and Bartholomew saw his hands were clenched so hard that his knuckles were white. No such agonies afflicted the other friars. They glanced at each other as though they were mystified, and shook their heads to deny that they had left Ovyng.

'And after the merels?' asked Michael, raising his eyebrows.

'We retired to bed,' said Godric, meeting his eyes. The others chorused their agreement, and Bartholomew supposed they were telling the truth about that, at least. However, according to Godric's initial statement, the games could have started relatively late – perhaps even after the escape of the two intruders from the church. It was entirely possible that they had fled immediately to Ovyng and settled down to play merels until it was time to sleep.

'And what about the interval between the meal and the games?' pressed Michael, to be sure of his facts.

There was a brief pause as the friars exchanged more uncertain glances, and then someone seemed to recall that Ailred had already told them the answer he wanted them to give. 'There was no interval,' he said, and everyone obligingly agreed, although there were a few downcast eyes and shuffling feet: some of the friars were uncomfortable about lying in a church. Godric was one of them; he gazed at the floor with his cheeks burning. Ailred, however, was smiling his victory at Michael, and did not notice his colleagues' discomfort.

'Interesting,' murmured Michael to Bartholomew as they went to continue their search of the north aisle. 'I think Godric is telling the truth and Ailred is lying. Now, why would Ailred lie, do you think? I did not seriously imagine last night's intruders would be from Ovyng, because I cannot imagine why they would feel a need to enter by force when they own a key, but something odd is going on. Something very odd indeed.'

When their devotions were completed, the Franciscans lined up to walk back to Ovyng, leaving the church deserted and silent again. Bartholomew and Michael turned their attention to the nave and then the Stanton Chapel. The nave was basically bare, and there was not so much as a leaf on the flagstones, since it had been swept and cleaned for the Christmas season. There was a bench against the back wall, set there for the old or the infirm who were unable to stand, but there was nothing else except the line of smelly albs and a chest so ancient and fragile that only water jugs for flowers were kept in it.

The Stanton Chapel was much the same. There was the founder's elaborate tomb, which had been decorated with holly boughs and a sprig of ivy, and on a windowsill stood a tiny chest containing pebbles that were supposed to have come from Jerusalem – although Bartholomew thought they were identical to ones in the river near the Great Bridge. He rummaged through the box, wondering whether something might have been stored among the stones, but found nothing there.

'This is hopeless, Brother. What did you think you might find? Documents? A knife with a broken blade? What?'

'It was your idea to return this morning and search, not mine,' Michael pointed out testily. 'And I have no idea what I expected to find. All I know is that it must have been fairly important to warrant that pair waiting until Kenyngham finished his prayers. You know how long-winded he can be while he is about his devotions.'

'But the intruders would not necessarily know that. Perhaps they imagined it would be a matter of a few moments, and found themselves waiting a good deal longer than they anticipated.' Bartholomew sighed. 'I have finished, Brother. There is nothing here and nowhere left to look.'

'There is one thing we have not examined,' said Michael, his eyes straying to the mortal remains that inhabited the chapel.

Bartholomew stared at him. 'You think they wanted something from Turke's body?'

Michael raised his shoulders in a shrug. 'Why not? We were going to have another look at it last night, so perhaps they were, too. Maybe there is something hidden on it, which you missed when you gave Turke that very cursory examination the day he died.'

Bartholomew lifted the sheet that covered the fishmonger and pointed. 'He has been washed and dressed in a shroud. We will find nothing here.'

'Look anyway,' instructed Michael.

Hoping Philippa would not choose that moment to pay her respects to her husband, Bartholomew began a careful examination of Turke. The corpse's skin was icy to the touch, and in places it felt hard, where it was partially frozen. There were ancient scars on the calves, although Bartholomew could not begin to imagine what had caused them – short of riding a horse through knife-brandishing foot-soldiers. He found cuts on the hands and a mark on Turke's face that had probably occurred when he had fallen through the ice and attempted to claw his way clear. Bartholomew completed his examination, replaced the sheet and shroud, and gave Michael a helpless shrug.

'Damn!' muttered Michael. 'Turke's corpse was my last hope. I thought that someone might have left something with it – a letter or some message – that last night's intruders wanted to collect, but I see I was mistaken.'

'I suppose there is always Gosslinge's body,' suggested Bartholomew, unable to think of anything else. 'I cannot see why anyone would leave a message with him, but it may be worth looking. But then I am leaving this freezing church. There is nothing here, and I think we should go elsewhere for clues – like trying to find out what Ailred was up to last night, or interviewing Harysone again.'

Gosslinge was in the south aisle, tucked out of sight behind a pile of broken benches. Bartholomew noticed that candles had been placed at his head and feet, although these had already burned away, leaving nothing but a saucer of cream-coloured wax and a mess on the floor. A piece of cloth had been tucked around him, but he was still dressed in the mean clothes he had worn when they had first discovered his body. Someone had pressed a flower into his hands. It was a Christmas rose – Edith's favourite – and Bartholomew suspected that the small kindnesses to his body were her work.

It was gloomy in the aisle, almost as dark as it had been when Bartholomew had first examined Gosslinge, so he opened the south door to allow the daylight to flood in. It made a huge difference. He noticed for the first time that Gosslinge's nose and mouth had a blue tinge, and that his lips looked bruised. They were small things, but they made Bartholomew's stomach feel as though it had been punched. He rubbed a hand through his hair and closed his eyes.

'Lord help us, Brother!' he muttered. 'I think I have made a terrible mistake.'

'Why?' demanded Michael. 'What is wrong with you? You

look as though you have seen a ghost. Have you found what that pair were looking for?'

'Something more important than that. Now I can see Gosslinge in good light, I think his death was not from natural causes, as I told you days ago.'

'You mean he was murdered?' asked Michael in disbelief. 'But you said that he had died of the cold.'

'I said the cold had *probably* killed him. But now I see signs to suggest that was not the case.'

'God's teeth, Matt!' exclaimed Michael, horrified. 'We could have been looking for his killer days ago!'

'I know,' said Bartholomew miserably. 'You do not need to tell me that.'

Michael sighed irritably. 'You had better tell me what you think now, then. Is it his swollen lips that made you change your mind? Or the fact that one of his fingernails is ripped?'

'Is it?' asked Bartholomew weakly. He lifted the stiff limb and saw that Michael was right. Gosslinge had possessed long, yellowish nails, and one of these had ripped jaggedly near the top of one finger. It was only a broken nail, not an actual injury, but no living person would have left it sticking at right angles to his finger; he would have pulled it off completely. It indicated the damage had probably occurred at about the time of Gosslinge's death, and that he had been involved in something physical.

Bartholomew gazed at Gosslinge in disbelief. He knew he had not conducted a thorough examination of the body when they had first discovered it; the church had been too dark and he had been tired from watching over Dunstan the two previous nights. He had also been cold, and recalled that his numb fingers and feet had felt like lumps of wood. But these were no excuse. He saw now that he should have moved the corpse out of the church and examined it in the cemetery, where he would have been able to see. He also knew he should have pushed his physical discomfort to the back of his mind, and done his duty properly. He felt sick with self-recrimination.

'Are you going to examine him now?' asked Michael, growing tired of waiting while the physician did nothing but stare. 'Or are you hoping he will sit up and tell you what happened?'

Bartholomew forced himself to move. He removed the poor clothes that covered Gosslinge, cutting them with his knife, since there seemed to be no next of kin who would claim them. Then he assessed every part of the body, beginning with the feet and working up. He palpated to test for broken bones, and looked at the corpse from every possible angle, to ensure he missed no abrasions. Carefully, he ran his fingers through the hair, to see whether he could detect a blow to the head, and finally, he spent a long time exploring Gosslinge's neck.

'Now you are going too far the other way,' complained Michael, stamping his feet in an attempt to keep warm. 'You missed evidence last time, so you are compensating by being overly fussy now. What can you tell me? How did he die?'

'I do not know,' said Bartholomew, puzzled. 'I doubt it was from natural causes – because of the swelling around his mouth and that chipped tooth. And there is the fingernail. Everything points to some kind of suffocation – smothering, perhaps – but I cannot pinpoint it.'

'Suffocation will do,' said Michael. 'How do you know he did not do it himself?'

'It is not easy to suffocate yourself. You lose consciousness before you die, and whatever you are pressing against your face falls away. And I cannot see him choking himself while wrapped in the albs, anyway. I think the lack of air would have driven him away from them.'

'Not if he intended to die, and he hid so his body would not be discovered before he was dead. You said yourself that you had no idea how long he had been there.'

'We know he disappeared shortly after arriving in Cambridge,' said Bartholomew. 'Turke told us at the Christmas Day feast that he had been missing for five days.'

'That means he disappeared on the twentieth of December,' said Michael. 'A Tuesday, and – coincidentally – the day Norbert went missing. I wonder whether that is significant. But what was Gosslinge doing to warrant ending up smothered in St Michael's mouldy robes? Does this mean his corpse stood hidden in here for two whole days before we happened to come across him?'

'It looks that way, Brother.'

'You do not think these marks – I hesitate to call them injuries, since they are so minor – were caused by Gosslinge himself in his death throes?'

'There is no way to tell, but I would imagine not. I think it more likely someone harmed him – but I could be wrong.'

'Perhaps he was lonely,' suggested Michael, reluctant to abandon the suicide theory. 'Perhaps he did not want to go to Walsingham. Perhaps Turke drove him to take his own life. Gosslinge knew no one else here, so if anyone drove him to suicide, it must have been his master.'

'Or Giles or Philippa,' said Bartholomew. 'But do not forget he knew the Waits. Quenhyth saw them with Gosslinge, and so did Harysone. And the Waits said Gosslinge ate a meal with Harysone – something Harysone admitted, too.'

'I do not see why the Waits should drive him to take his own life – unless they threatened to inflict their juggling on him. But Harysone is another matter. I knew he was up to something when we saw him trying to get into the church, just a short time before we discovered Gosslinge's corpse.' Michael's eyes gleamed with triumph, and Bartholomew saw the monk thought he had a workable theory.

'No one in the Turke household mentioned any malaise or unhappiness on Gosslinge's part,' the physician said, still trying to think of reasons why Gosslinge might have killed himself. Some instinct told him that Gosslinge had not intended to die and, because of his earlier negligence, he felt obliged to give the matter his best attention now. He sighed despondently as he considered the scant evidence. 'Suicide makes no sense. If Gosslinge took his own life, why was he not wearing his livery? And how did he end up among the albs?'

268

Although he was too embarrassed to admit it to Michael, Bartholomew was painfully aware that he had not taken the time to assess the nature of the folds that had held Gosslinge in the rotten robes. He knew now that he should have unravelled them slowly, so that he could have seen whether Gosslinge had tied them himself or whether someone else had done it for him. He had been careless and irresponsible, and that knowledge would haunt him for a very long time.

Michael sighed. 'It would help, of course, if we knew for certain whether this was a suicide or murder. Are you sure there is nothing lodged in his mouth that may tell us one way or the other?'

Bartholomew was sure, but his confidence had suffered a serious blow, so he looked again. There was nothing. He tipped Gosslinge's head back, and peered down the corpse's throat for so long that Michael began to mutter in exasperation. Eventually, he rummaged in his medical bag and produced a knife, which he placed against Gosslinge's windpipe.

'What are you doing?' cried Michael in alarm. He glanced around in agitation. 'Put that thing away, man! You cannot start carving up Christian men as though they were slabs of meat on a butcher's stall! I know you enjoy indulging in surgery now and again, but you cannot do it here, and you cannot do it on him. Someone will be sure to notice.'

'But I want to see whether there is anything stuck in his throat,' objected Bartholomew.

'Then use tweezers, and go to his throat via his mouth. Do not start hacking him about in places where it will show. God's teeth, Matt! You should not need me to tell you this.'

Reluctantly, Bartholomew complied, declining to point out that if Michael wanted answers to his questions, then he should not be squeamish about the ways in which those answers were provided. He found a fairly long pair of forceps and inserted them into Gosslinge's mouth, pushing them as far to the back of the throat as he could.

'There *is* something here,' he exclaimed, leaning to one side to gain a better purchase on the object that was lodged just beyond his reach. He pressed harder, hoping Michael did not hear the snap as Gosslinge lost another of his front teeth.

'I sincerely hope you did not submit my husband to this kind of treatment,' came a cold voice from behind them.

CHAPTER 8

BARTHOLOMEW JUMPED SO MUCH WHEN PHILIPPA SPOKE IN the silence of the church that he dropped his tweezers, which clattered across the floor with a sound that was shockingly loud. Stanmore was with her, looking from the dead servant to his brother-in-law with an expression of horror. To hide his consternation, Bartholomew bent down and took his time in retrieving the dropped implement, irrationally hoping that both Philippa and Stanmore would be gone by the time he straightened up. Philippa, meanwhile, waited for a response.

'Matt made you a promise,' replied Michael suavely, when he saw Bartholomew did not know how to answer her. 'It is Gosslinge he is examining, not your husband.'

'Did you ram metal objects down Walter's throat, too?' asked Philippa icily, addressing Bartholomew. She was too intelligent not to see that Michael had deftly side-stepped the issue.

'I did not,' replied Bartholomew, standing and thrusting the forceps into his bag.

Philippa made a grimace of disgust. 'I thought you kept your clean bandages in there. If you throw things that have been inside corpses on top of them, then it is not surprising your patients sicken and die. I heard about the deaths of the two old men who live by the river; Edith told me.'

'One,' said Bartholomew defensively. 'Dunstan is still alive.'

'He was dead this morning,' said Stanmore, still regarding Bartholomew askance. He started to edge towards the door, deciding that if his brother-in-law had a good explanation for his ghoulish activities then he did not want to hear it.

271

He saw Bartholomew's distress at the news about Dunstan and stopped. His voice was gentle when he spoke again. 'Matilde came to tell Edith, Matt. She said she left him asleep but alive shortly after you went home, but he was dead when she returned at dawn.'

Bartholomew turned away, embarrassed by the sudden pricking of tears at the back of his eyes. He was fond of the two old rivermen, and would miss their cheerful gossip on summer evenings, when he had sat with them outside their hovel. He had known it would not be long before Dunstan followed his brother, but he had not anticipated it would be quite so soon. He wondered what more he could have done to help, and felt grief threaten to overwhelm him.

'I will say his requiem mass,' said Michael in a voice that was hoarse with emotion. 'He sang in my choir, and I have known him for many years.'

Philippa looked from one to the other in sudden consternation. 'I am sorry,' she said, sounding contrite. 'I see they were dear to you. I did not know, and you must forgive me. I would not have broken the news so baldly had I known.'

Her sympathy was more than Bartholomew could bear. He walked away, saying he was going to wash his hands in water from the jug at the back of the nave. Memories of the old men's chatter in the summer sunlight returned to him, and it was some time before he was sufficiently in control of himself to rejoin to the others. Michael's reaction had been much the same. He was in the Stanton Chapel, standing over Athelbald with sad eyes and a down-turned mouth.

Philippa and Stanmore waited together in the nave, standing stiffly side by side, as though neither was comfortable with the other's company. With a distant part of his mind, Bartholomew wondered whether Philippa knew Stanmore suspected her and Giles of foul play in the deaths of Turke and Gosslinge and resented him for it. Stanmore, meanwhile, was edgy and restless, and looked as though he could not wait to escape from her presence. Eventually, Michael muttered a benediction, then took a deep breath before turning to Bartholomew.

'Obviously there is no more you can do for Dunstan, but I need to make arrangements for him to be buried with his brother.'

'Will you wait a moment while Philippa lights some candles?' asked Stanmore, abandoning the widow with relief as he headed for the door. 'I escorted her here, but I have a guild meeting to attend and cannot see her home again. It is on your way – more or less.'

He had opened the door and left before they had had the chance to reply, transparently grateful to be about his own business. He slammed the door behind him, sending a hollow crash around the building. Bartholomew wished that Stanmore had made as much noise entering the church; then he would not have been caught with a pair of forceps in the throat of a corpse.

'Cambridge is reasonably safe during the day,' he said, thinking Philippa was being overly sensitive by not wanting to walk alone. 'You are unlikely to come to harm, and it is not far from here to Milne Street.'

'Actually, Cambridge is a very odd little town,' she countered. 'And do not try to convince me otherwise, because I remember it from when I was here during the plague – bodies hidden in attics, Masters burned alive in their rooms, men murdered and their deaths made to appear natural. But my insistence on an escort is not because I am afraid, but because it is not seemly for a recent widow to wander the streets on her own.'

'London manners,' remarked Michael. 'No one would condemn unescorted widows here.'

'Perhaps so, but I do not want to abandon my principles just because I am travelling. What are you doing here anyway? Do you not have better things to do than thrusting pincers down dead men's gullets?' She turned and flounced into the Stanton Chapel without waiting for a response.

'It is a good thing I did not allow you to slice Gosslinge open,' muttered Michael, watching her leave. 'Otherwise she and Oswald would have rushed screaming from the church and we both would have been burned as warlocks in the Market Square. Next time you want to do something so excessively unpleasant, we shall have to remember to lock the door.'

'I am done with bodies, Brother,' said Bartholomew, covering Gosslinge with the sheet. 'First I conducted an examination so superficial that I missed important evidence, then I held one so thorough I shocked and dismayed a widow. I do not enjoy it anyway, and you will do better to find someone else.'

'You made a mistake,' acknowledged Michael. 'But few of us are perfect, and you will do until someone better comes along. Did you retrieve whatever it was you located in that poor man's throat? Or do we have to return at midnight with satanic regalia and do it all over again?'

'It is in my bag. It fell on the ground when Philippa made me jump, and I did not want her to see it – that is why I put the tweezers on top of all my clean bandages, not from any habit of poor hygiene. I wanted to keep the thing a secret.'

'Intriguing,' mused Michael, regarding his friend with interest. 'Your responses to Philippa are difficult to fathom, Matt. I cannot decide whether she still means something to you, or whether you are just relieved she is not Mistress Bartholomew. And although you balked at examining Turke because she asked you not to, you are suspicious of her contradictory statements about the Waits and her odd reaction to her husband's death. So, what is she to you: innocent widow or sly trickster?'

'Neither,' said Bartholomew, sensing that Michael's assessment was correct: his feelings towards Philippa were definitely ambivalent. His memories of her were pleasant and she represented a happy phase in his life, yet there were

274

things about her now that he did not understand and that he did not want to probe.

'So, you are not still half in love with the woman, then?' asked Michael nosily.

'No,' said Bartholomew, certain that any spark of passion that he might have harboured was now well and truly extinguished. It was not romantic love that was at the heart of the complex gamut of emotions he felt for her.

'Good. I confess I held hopes that she might be just what you needed when I first heard she was here, but she has changed and I have revised my opinion. You are better off with Matilde.'

'I shall bear it in mind,' said Bartholomew dryly.

'Be sure you do. Philippa may come after you now she is free, and I do not think you should succumb. Remember that she is no longer the woman you loved. So, tell me why you hid the object you found in Gosslinge's throat. Do you suspect her of foul play, like Oswald does?'

'No,' replied Bartholomew. 'Yes.' He sighed. 'I do not know, Michael. I *am* confused by the fact that she denied knowing the Waits, and Giles has been acting very oddly since he arrived. I think something is going on, but I have no idea what it might be. It could be wholly innocent. I do not know why I felt the need to hide the thing I found in Gosslinge. I acted on instinct.'

'What was it?'

'I do not know that, either. It was too covered in—'

'Tell me later, interrupted Michael hastily. 'Or even better, do not tell me at all. Just present it nicely cleansed of all signs that it has been residing in a corpse for the last few days. Here is Philippa. Shall we go?'

Philippa refused Bartholomew's arm as they left the church, and took Michael's instead. They started to walk towards Milne Street, their progress slow because of the ice and filth that covered the roads. The deep snow meant the dung carts had been unable to collect, and the festering piles along the edges of the street added a sulphurous stench to the choking palls of smoke from wood and peat fires. Dogs foraged enthusiastically in the sticky brown heaps, gorging themselves on objects that even starving beggars had passed over.

'Did you ignore my wishes and examine my husband's body anyway?' asked Philippa, looking briefly at Bartholomew before returning her attention to the demanding task of watching where she placed her prettily clad feet.

'Yes,' said Bartholomew bluntly. He imagined she would find out, since the shroud had probably not been replaced exactly as he had found it, and he disliked lying. 'But I only looked at him. I did not touch him with instruments.'

'Well, that is something, I suppose,' she said coolly. 'And did this examination tell you anything you did not already know?'

'No,' admitted Bartholomew. 'It told me he had died of the cold, after falling in the river. There were some old scars on his legs, though. Do you know how he came by them?'

'He never told me. They derived from something that happened long before we met. He disliked anyone seeing them – which was why I was careful how I removed his hose when we were stripping off his wet clothes. I did not want him to wake up and find them bared for all to see, because it would have distressed him. What did your gruesome treatment of Gosslinge tell you?'

'Nothing,' said Michael, before Bartholomew could reply. 'But you should not take our investigation amiss. The Sheriff or the proctors examine anyone who dies unexpectedly or suddenly. We would be remiss if we did not ensure there was nothing odd about a death.'

'But there was not – for either of them,' said Philippa. 'You just said so.'

'We had to be certain,' said Michael. 'It would not do to bury a man, then have his grieving kin arrive months later clamouring there was evidence of murder.'

'Murder?' asked Philippa in alarm. 'Who said anything about murder?'

276

'No one,' said Michael, startled by her outburst. 'I was only explaining why these examinations are necessary. Matt did not want to do it, but I insisted.'

'Well, it is done now, and it is a pity to argue,' said Philippa, giving Bartholomew a reluctant smile. 'Let us be friends again.'

'Good,' said Michael, patting her arm. 'But here comes your brother. Perhaps he can escort you home, so we can go and see what can be done for poor Dunstan. That is where our duty lies this morning.'

Abigny smiled as he approached, but would have walked past if Michael had not stopped him. The clerk did not want to return the way he had come, and said his feet hurt too much for all but the most essential journeys. Curtly, Philippa informed him that escorting her was essential, since she was a recent widow and in need of such attentions. Abigny offered her his arm in a way that suggested he wanted her delivered home as soon as possible, so he could go about his own errands.

'Since you are both here, perhaps you can answer a few questions while Giles rests his feet,' said Michael artfully. He drew the picture of the knife from his scrip and held it out to them. 'Do either of you recognise this?'

'No,' said Philippa, glancing at it without much interest. 'Why? Have you lost it?'

'It is not mine,' said Michael. 'I believe it is the weapon that killed Norbert.'

'Norbert?' asked Philippa. 'Who is he?'

'The student who was killed outside Ovyng,' replied Michael. 'Dick Tulyet's cousin.'

Philippa nodded understanding, then looked at the parchment again. 'No,' she said after a moment. 'It is not familiar. I wondered whether it might have been Gosslinge's, but it is not.'

'It is only a picture, not the real thing,' pressed Michael eagerly. 'So there are bound to be errors. Are you sure it did not belong to Gosslinge?'

'It is not the same,' said Abigny, taking the parchment and turning it this way and that as he assessed it. 'Gosslinge's had three glass beads in the hilt, and this only has two.'

'You seem very well acquainted with your servant's knife,' remarked Michael curiously.

Bartholomew agreed, and thought Gosslinge's dagger and the one in the river sounded remarkably similar. It also occurred to him that while there were only two glass beads when he had seen the weapon, one might well have fallen out after it had been abandoned. He recalled a previous discussion he had had with Abigny about Gosslinge's knife: when Turke had identified his servant's body Abigny mentioned that Gosslinge had indeed possessed a knife, and had said it was too large a weapon for him. Michael was right: Abigny did seem well acquainted with the dead man's personal arsenal.

Abigny gave a pained smile. 'I forgot to bring my own dagger on this journey, and I have been obliged to borrow Gosslinge's – for the dinner table and suchlike. It is embarrassing to be in debt to a servant, especially for something as essential as a knife. Turke was scathing in his criticism, of course.'

'Let us remain with Gosslinge for a moment,' said Michael, shooting a brief but meaningful glance at Bartholomew to suggest that Abigny's statements had raised all sorts of questions that would later need to be discussed. 'Was he of sound mind when you last saw him?'

'What do you mean?' asked Philippa warily. 'He was not insane, if that is what you are asking. Not like your Clippesby. Gosslinge complained a lot – about the cold, his clothes, the food we ate, his pay. Especially his pay. Is that what you wanted to know?'

'He was very feeble,' added Giles. 'I was surprised when Walter chose him to come with us when he had better men at his disposal. But Walter did make odd decisions on occasion.'

'What do you mean?' demanded Philippa, voicing the question that was also on Bartholomew's lips. 'Everything Walter did was careful and prudent.'

'Careful, yes,' said Giles. 'But not always prudent, and they are not the same thing. You cannot say that killing Fiscurtune was prudent – and neither was going skating on thin ice.'

'He was prudent in business matters,' she said defensively. 'It made him rich. And he owned two relics – St Zeno's finger and the snail from Jesus's tomb. That made him special, too.'

'But he gave them both away,' said Bartholomew. 'The finger is at Michaelhouse and Sheriff Morice has the snail.'

'He planned to buy more relics at Walsingham,' said Abigny. 'He had his heart set on purchasing something really impressive, like a piece of the True Cross or a lock of the Virgin's hair – some very holy item to flaunt at his colleagues in the Fraternity of Fishmongers.'

'That does not explain why he parted so readily with the old ones,' pressed Bartholomew. 'Surely it is more impressive to own three relics than one?'

'I do not think he ever felt comfortable with that finger, despite the fact that he usually carried it with him,' said Abigny. 'And he, like me, thought the snail was fraudulent. It was a clever ploy to give it to Morice.'

'He did not care for the finger,' agreed Philippa. 'I think he was afraid of St Zeno. But the snail *was* a real relic. He bought it from a Knight Hospitaller for two gold nobles. It must have been genuine to be that expensive.'

'Gosslinge,' prompted Michael, to bring the discussion back to the dead servant and declining to comment on the fact that price had little to do with authenticity in the world of relics. 'Was he upset about anything? Lonely? Worried about the journey that lay ahead? And in what way was he weak? Easily bullied?'

'Oh, no!' exclaimed both Philippa and Abigny at once. Philippa continued. 'Despite his size, Gosslinge was very confident. Walter was the only man he ever heeded; he ignored everyone else.'

'He was rude and lazy,' murmured Abigny.

Philippa did not hear him. 'But he was not strong physically. I do not mean he was sickly, just that he seemed unable to lift even fairly light loads.'

'That was because he did so little work,' muttered Abigny. 'His muscles were wasted.'

'But he was not upset about anything,' said Philippa, ignoring her brother's aside. 'On the contrary, he was looking forward to the journey we were about to make.'

'He saw opportunities,' said Abigny darkly. 'Him and his dice. I think he had done something to the balance, so they would fall more often in his favour. While I have no idea what led him to die in a church wearing someone else's clothes, I would not be surprised to learn that he did it for reasons that would benefit him financially.'

'Giles!' admonished Philippa tiredly. 'It is not kind to tell tales now the poor man cannot defend himself.' She turned to Michael and made a helpless gesture, raising her hands palms upward. 'Gosslinge was not the best servant we had, but he was loyal, and Walter valued loyalty.'

'I never understood that,' said Abigny. He looked at Philippa. 'Even you cannot pretend Walter treated his servants well – he was demanding, mean and critical of their efforts. Yet Gosslinge stayed for years, when we were lucky if others managed more than a few months.'

'They liked each other,' said Philippa stubbornly. 'Walter was kinder to Gosslinge than to the others, and Gosslinge repaid him with devotion.'

'No,' said Abigny, shaking his head. 'It was more than that. I always felt there was some bond that went deeper than a master – servant relationship.'

'But Walter did not seem particularly distressed when he learned that Gosslinge was dead,' Michael pointed out. 'Rather, he was irritated, because it meant he had to find a replacement.'

280

'You did not know Walter,' said Philippa, angered by the comment. 'He was upset; he just did not show it with tears and lamentations. He would have missed Gosslinge very much.'

'Can you think of any reason why they should both die in Cambridge?' asked Michael, unruffled by her ire. 'Is it possible that Walter was so distressed by Gosslinge's death that he skated on the Mill Pool, knowing that it might crack under him and bring about his death?'

'Suicide?' asked Abigny with a startled laugh. 'Walter? I do not think so!'

'No,' said Philippa firmly. 'It is winter, and men do die of cold or falling through ice. You are trying to read something into these deaths, when there is nothing. Now, the best thing you can do is leave my husband and his servant in peace, and let me grieve for them.'

She took her brother's arm and marched away towards Milne Street, so Abigny was obliged to hobble and stumble to keep up with her. Bartholomew could tell by the set of her shoulders that she was agitated, and he was curious. Was it because she did not like Michael probing into secrets she would rather keep concealed? Did she know Gosslinge's death had not been natural, as had first been assumed, and was determined the truth should not come out? What was the nature of the odd relationship between Turke and his servant? It did not sound as though either was a man who inspired or gave loyalty for no reason. Bartholomew wondered what that reason might be.

Deynman decreed that all Michaelhouse scholars and servants should take part in a game of camp-ball that had been organised for the town that afternoon. It was not good weather for such an activity, and Bartholomew anticipated he would be busy later with patients who had cuts and broken bones. Camp-ball was a vicious event anyway, but it would be worse with ice on the roads and piles of hard snow everywhere.

The game had been Sheriff Morice's idea, and had been planned for weeks. People were looking forward to it, although Bartholomew could not imagine why. To him, camp-ball was another word for 'riot', and it was not unknown for folk to be killed while taking part. The game was played with two sides, and the aim was to put an inflated leather bag between twin posts that marked the 'goal' of the opposing team. There was no limit to the number of people who could play, and the teams were sometimes hundreds strong. The ball could be kicked, but it was mostly thrown. This year, Morice had set one goal at the Barnwell Gate, and the other at the Castle. People complained these were too close together – in the past, the goals had been as far apart as the Castle and the village of Trumpington, some two miles distant – but the Sheriff pointed out that most roads were closed by snow, and if folk wanted to play, then the event had to take place in the town, where at least some of the streets were navigable.

Knowing the game could turn into a competition between townsmen and scholars – and then into something that had nothing to do with sportsmanship – Michael petitioned Morice to ensure both sides contained a mixture of town and gown. Michaelhouse scholars were to play for the side called 'Castle', who were supposed to drive the ball to their opponents' goal at the Barnwell Gate. Meanwhile, 'Gate' were supposed to stop them, and carry the ball to Castle's goal. Any method to achieve this was acceptable, although use of weapons was not permitted. There were no other rules.

The teams massed in the Market Square, where there was some reasonably good-natured shouting and bantering, and much quaffing of the powerful church ale that was for sale in the graveyards of St Mary the Great and Holy Trinity. The apprentices were out in force, and so were scholars, all wearing their warmest clothes in anticipation of a long afternoon in the cold. Morice sat on his horse, and addressed the crowd, informing them it was illegal to use anything other than fists while attempting to gain possession of the ball – and anyone aiming a crossbow or drawing a sword could expect to be arrested on sight – and everyone should take care not to trample small children. The prize to the winning team was a groat for every man, half a groat for every woman, and a penny for boys. Girls, Bartholomew assumed, should expect to be disappointed or should lie about their age or sex.

There was a cheer of delight as the Sheriff raised the camp-ball over his head. Michael glanced around warily, watching the vintner's apprentices fix the scholars of Valence Marie with meaningful intent that had nothing to do with a leather bag. He nodded to Meadowman, and several beadles appeared, jostling the scholars until they were obliged to move away. The vintners were deprived, at least temporarily, of their prey.

Bartholomew saw the Michaelhouse contingent instinctively move closer together. Everyone was there: every student, all the Fellows (except William) and the servants. Cynric had dispensed with the Welsh hunting knife he always carried – it was not unknown for folk to be stabbed by scabbarded weapons when there was a scrum for the ball – and had replaced it with something smaller and less menacing. Agatha clutched a heavy stick, pretending to use it for walking through the snow, although it was obvious that the 'Gates' had better watch themselves when she was near.

'I think I must be the oldest player here,' said Kenyngham, glancing around in dismay. 'Spending a whole afternoon chasing a ball is not a good use of my time. I would rather pray.'

'So would I,' said Michael fervently. 'So, why are you here, Father? This is too rough for you.'

'Deynman ordered everyone at Michaelhouse to take part,' said Kenyngham. 'Even the Waits. He wants us to be on the winning team, and thinks numbers may make a difference.'

'This was not what we had in mind when we agreed to work for Deynman,' said Frith the musician resentfully. 'I do not like games of violence.'

'I do,' said Agatha, brazenly confrontational. 'They sort the men from the boys.'

'Oh?' Frith's eyes travelled insolently over Agatha's formidable bulk. 'And which are you?'

Agatha's eyes narrowed, and powerful fingers tightened around her cudgel. 'I am more man than you will ever hope to be. *I* do not skulk around the College, looking for things to steal.'

Frith's lips compressed into a hard, straight line. 'Neither do I. Michaelhouse folk keep accusing us of stealing, but then the objects turn up a few days later, and it transpires they were just misplaced. You should watch what you say, woman. Defaming the character of innocent people is an offence that I am sure Sheriff Morice will prosecute.'

'I am quite sure it is,' murmured Michael to Bartholomew, so Frith would not hear. 'Morice knows Colleges will pay to drop any charges that might bring them into disrepute.'

Bartholomew suspected the monk was right. However, the Waits were not stupid, and they had already weathered one encounter with the greedy Sheriff that had probably left them the poorer. They would know that levelling accusations against Michaelhouse would cost them money – especially since they had already demonstrated a fondness for other folks' gold, so their honesty was compromised.

'Morice will throw you in his gaol for thieving,' declared Agatha hotly, glowering at Frith in a way that should have made any sane man back down. 'And you and your friends will hang.'

'Prove us thieves, then,' challenged Frith, his voice dripping with disdain. 'Search our possessions. You will find nothing amiss.'

'I have already done that and he is right,' murmured Cynric in Bartholomew's ear. 'The salt dish, Wynewyk's inkpot and Ulfrid's missing knife were not there. I do not

284

understand: it is obvious they are the culprits, yet I cannot discover where they have hidden what they stole.'

'Are you sure they are dishonest?' asked Bartholomew. 'I was under the impression that valuable things have been left lying around, but have been ignored. Why take a salt dish when they could have William's gold nobles or the College silver?'

Cynric shook his head. 'As I said, I do not understand them at all.'

'You should leave Michaelhouse,' said Agatha imperiously to Frith. 'You are no longer welcome. I shall speak to Deynman, and have him dismiss you.'

Frith sneered. 'Deynman cannot dismiss us. He signed a document that promised us food, shelter and employment for the whole Twelve Days. We will take it to Morice if you renege.'

'That document was clever planning on their part,' remarked Michael to Bartholomew. 'Previous employers must have found them lacking, so they learned to draw up legal contracts outlining their terms in advance. Langelee would never have signed it, so they are lucky Deynman was elected Lord of Misrule: he is the only one stupid enough to put his mark to such a thing.'

'Evicting them in this weather would be wicked, anyway,' said Bartholomew gloomily. 'We shall have to keep them until it breaks.'

'We shall have to do no such thing,' declared Agatha, overhearing him. 'I do not care what happens to thieves. If they kept their hands to themselves and put on decent performances, we would not be having this discussion in the first place.'

'Our performances are good,' objected Makejoy, offended. 'We are professionals!'

'*You* are all right,' acknowledged Agatha. 'And Yna and Jestyn are adequate. But Frith is wholly without talent. You should dispense with him – you would do better without the racket he dares to call music.'

Makejoy regarded Frith unhappily, and Bartholomew was under the impression she thought the aggressive laundress was right. Frith did not, however, and he moved up to Agatha until his face was only inches from hers. His voice was low and hoarse with menace.

'Leave me alone, woman. And keep your nasty opinions to yourself.'

'I think you should—' began Bartholomew, wanting to warn Frith to back down before it was too late. Next to him, Cynric was laughing softly, while Michael watched Frith step into mortal danger with folded arms and an amused smile. Bartholomew never had the chance to complete his sentence. Agatha's stick moved so fast that it was a blur. There was a sharp crack, and Frith crumpled to the floor at her feet.

'Whoops,' she said flatly. 'How clumsy of me.'

'He will be all right,' said Bartholomew, kneeling quickly to inspect the fallen man before Makejoy could make a fuss. 'He is just dazed. Take him back to Michaelhouse and tell him to spend the rest of the day quietly. He glanced up at Agatha. 'You should watch what you do with that thing. You do not want to be charged with assault.'

'It was an accident,' said Agatha archly. She turned to the Fellows and servants, who were watching her antics with unconcealed approval. Langelee was chortling with delight, and even the dour Suttone was laughing. 'Well? Was it not?'

'Yes,' agreed Cynric gleefully. 'The stick just slipped.'

'It was a shame Frith walked into it,' added Langelee. 'I imagine he will be unable to entertain us with music tonight. Pity.'

Makejoy helped the stunned piper to his feet. 'I am sorry,' she said to Agatha, seeing where the sympathy lay and determined to make the best of a bad situation. It would not do for Michaelhouse to ignore the contract and dismiss them when they would be unlikely to find alternative employment that season. 'This will not happen again.'

'It had better not,' said Agatha ungraciously. 'Keep him away from me, or I shall do more than give him a bump on the skull next time.'

'She will, you know,' said Deynman cheerfully. 'You should hide him away, if you want him to live to see his old age.'

'I shall try,' said Makejoy. She slipped Frith's hand over her shoulder and led him away. He pulled away from her in an attempt to regain some of his dignity, but staggered on rubbery legs.

'Oh, dear,' said Kenyngham, watching him in dismay. 'Violence already, and the game has not even started yet. I do not want to be here!'

'Do not worry,' said Bartholomew, giving Deynman a withering glare for inflicting camp-ball on someone like the Gilbertine. The student looked surprised, as though he could not imagine what he had done wrong. 'Wait until the game begins, then slip away. You will not be missed. This is a game for the strong and the fast, and the chances of you even seeing the ball once the game has started are remote. Let the likes of Deynman and Agatha compete, if they will.'

The Sheriff abruptly concluded his opening speech, then tossed the leather bag with all his might into the waiting crowd. There was an almighty cheer, and all eyes followed it as it rose, then arced downwards – straight into the astonished arms of Kenyngham.

'Lord!' cried the Gilbertine in alarm. 'I do not want it. Here!'

Before Bartholomew could stop him, Kenyngham had given him the ball. Large and determined men were already beginning to converge on the spot where the ball had landed, thrusting the smaller and weaker out of the way. An old woman was battered to the ground, where she covered her head with her arms as feet trampled heedlessly across her. A child screamed in terror at the chaos, and everywhere, people started to shout with excitement.

'To me! To me!' yelled Deynman, beginning to dart away,

and raising his hands to indicate he was ready for Bartholomew to pass him the ball.

'No! Me!' howled Gray, dashing off in the opposite direction.

'Here!' shouted Langelee, jumping up and down with excitement. 'Throw it to me!'

'Not me!' shrieked Michael, as the physician glanced in his direction. 'I do not want it, man!'

'I will take it,' announced Agatha, snatching the ball from the physician. She drew back one of her mighty arms and precipitated the ball high into the air, far higher and further than Sheriff Morice's paltry effort. The crowd howled in delight, the burly men abruptly changed the direction of their charge, and the Michaelhouse Fellows were reprieved. The students rushed into the affray, Cynric and the other servants among them, while Bartholomew heaved a sigh of relief that his part in the game was over.

'I am going to the church,' said Kenyngham shakily. 'I did not enjoy that at all.'

'Neither did I,' said Suttone fervently. 'I thought we were all about to be bowled over like kayles. I was terrified. I am going to Michaelhouse, where I shall bar the door to my room and spend the afternoon thanking God for my lucky escape.'

'The ball is still in the air,' yelled Langelee admiringly. 'That was quite a throw, Agatha. We shall have to make sure you are on our team again next year. But I am away to join the fun.'

He shoved through the jostling crowd, becoming one of the large, tough men whose only aim was to grab the ball and play, careless of anyone who happened to be in his way. Bartholomew could see the bag as a black dot in the distance, sailing towards St Mary the Great. He wondered whether it would ever return to the ground. The crowd was still cheering when it smacked into the church like one of the new fire-propelled missiles that the English were currently using to frighten the French in the wars.

Then there was a disbelieving silence, as every eye was fixed on the spectacle of the town's one and only camp-ball firmly embedded in the mouth of one of St Mary's more impressive gargoyles. It was so high up that Bartholomew suspected there were few – if any – ladders that would reach it. Gradually, people looked away from the ball and turned to Agatha. There was discontented mumbling, and bitter disappointment was written clear across the face of every man who had been looking forward to an afternoon of violent fun. Michaelhouse's laundress suddenly found herself the centre of some very hostile attention.

'What?' she demanded belligerently, hands on hips.

That evening, while the students caroused in the conclave, Bartholomew and Michael sat in the kitchen to avoid being asked by the Lord of Misrule to provide musical entertainment. Once settled with mulled wine and a dish of dried fruit, they discussed the day's events. Bartholomew was tired and distressed about Dunstan, and was grateful that Agatha was not in her domain that night, sewing by candlelight as was her habit on winter evenings. She had gone to the King's Head, to give her own version of the camp-ball incident to a host of wary admirers.

Michael was in Agatha's wicker throne, while Bartholomew had drawn a stool as close to the fire as it was possible to be without actually setting himself alight. It was another bitterly cold night, and the physician felt he should probably be grateful that Dunstan did not have to live through it with lungs that were irritated both by the cold and by the smoke from his fire.

The Waits were also out, having been offered a non-optional night off. Gray had bluntly informed Deynman that he needed to provide a change in entertainment, because everyone was bored with poor music and lack-lustre juggling. Agatha had wholeheartedly agreed, and informed Deynman that even the Fellows could put on a better show than the Waits. Deynman had taken her literally, and the

Fellows had been instructed to perform that night.

Surprisingly, most were pleased to be asked. William offered to sing some troubadour ballads, learned while persecuting heretics in southern France. Kenyngham read a religious poem – but just the one; the students declined a second on the grounds that they only had until dawn before the evening's entertainment was over. Clippesby's tavern songs were by far the most popular turn, while Suttone's peculiar jig, he claimed, had been copied from a Castilian sailor. Wynewyk played his lute to the Carmelite's ponderous, uncoordinated moves.

Deynman wanted Michael to sing, and Bartholomew to perform the magic tricks he used to distract or cheer sick children. Gray, however, had heard about Dunstan, and with uncharacteristic sensitivity had instructed Deynman to excuse them. Bartholomew had experienced a profound sense of gratitude towards Gray as he and Michael left the noisy revelry of the hall for the steamy, yeasty warmth of the kitchen.

There were cobwebs on the ceiling, Bartholomew noticed, as he tipped his head back and listened to the distant rumble of William's singing. Bunches of herbs hung there, too, tied with twine and drying for future use. The wall behind the hearth glistened black with grease and soot, and the kitchen smelled of ancient fat, wood-smoke and burnt milk. All around were pots and pans, some half filled with the remains of the evening meal, and others already scoured clean for the following day. Vast ladles lay in a neat line on the scrubbed table, and flour had been weighed and sifted into bowls, ready for baking the morning's bread. It was a scene simultaneously chaotic and organised.

The College cat rubbed itself around Bartholomew's legs, so he picked it up and set it on his lap. Immediately it began digging its claws into his thigh. Bartholomew had always been puzzled by the fact that cats often found themselves a comfortable spot, only to lose it by their painful habit of clawing. He set it back on the floor, and it went to try its luck with Michael. The monk allowed it into the cradle formed by the sagging habit between his knees and at once began to sneeze. He chuckled as he wiped his nose on a piece of fine linen.

'It was dusk by the time they retrieved the camp-ball. Agatha will be remembered for that particular trick for a very long time. Apparently, when Cynric finally managed to reach it, it was so deeply jammed into the gargoyle's maw that he was obliged to use his knife to prise it out.'

'I heard that Morice declared the game a draw, and said neither Castles nor Gates should have the prize money. He was almost lynched, and has been obliged to set a date for a rematch.'

'He was going to keep the money for himself. Foolish man. Some of his unorthodox ways of accumulating wealth can be ignored, but not brazen appropriation of funds on that scale. People will be watching him constantly now he has revealed himself to be openly dishonest. He has done himself a grave disservice.'

'I am glad we were able to bury Dunstan and Athelbald today.' Bartholomew stared into the flames.

'Thanks to you,' said Michael. 'I thought you were being ghoulish when you persuaded each church to dig graves before the weather turned foul. But it was good to lay my old tenors in the ground today, rather than storing them in the charnel house to wait for a thaw. It is a pity you did not demand more holes: it is time Gosslinge was gone, too.'

Now that the day was spent, and Bartholomew was free to let his mind dwell on what had happened during it, he was weary and dispirited. There was a nagging ache behind his eyes, and he found it hurt to think about the two old men they had buried. He was also still disgusted with himself for failing to see the signs that Gosslinge had choked, and for being caught by Philippa with his tweezers down a corpse's throat. All in all, it had been a miserable day, and he was heartily glad it was over.

291

'We need to talk to Giles when his sister is not there,' said Michael, sneezing so violently that the cat was catapulted from his lap. 'He seems to have a different view of Turke and Gosslinge than she does, and I would like to hear his side in more detail.'

'Tomorrow,' said Bartholomew without enthusiasm.

'The more I see of your old sweetheart, the more I sense she is not as honest as she was. She was angry with you for examining Turke's body, but her ire dissipated as soon as you said you had found nothing amiss. She was anticipating you would, and was relieved to learn you had not.'

'You are reading too much into it,' said Bartholomew, wincing as the cat ascended to his knees again, claws at the ready. 'She was cross at first, but I think she saw there was no point in remaining angry as long as she is obliged to stay with my sister.'

'No, I am right. She was worried you would find something when you looked at Turke.' Michael fixed the physician with a penetrating look. 'You did not miss anything, did you?'

'Now you do not trust me,' said Bartholomew glumly. 'I made a mistake with Gosslinge, and you are wondering how many more I have made – starting with Turke.'

'I am merely ensuring we should not return to St Michael's and shove a pair of tweezers into Turke's lungs, as you did to Gosslinge's.'

'Turke spoke. He could not have done that if something had been lodged in his throat. I wonder if those scars on his legs were what she did not want us to see.'

'But we did see them, and you even asked her about them, but she did not react suspiciously when they were mentioned. She merely said he had come by them before they met. Is that true? Are they old wounds?'

'Some years. I have seen nothing like them before. What do you think about the knife? Was it Gosslinge's, do you think?'

Michael sighed heavily. 'Who knows? Your picture is

detailed, but it is not like showing folk the real thing. I could not decide whether Giles recognised it or not, and the differences he mentioned might have been due to errors in your illustration. However, just for argument's sake let us assume they are one and the same. So, how did Gosslinge's knife come to kill Norbert? We believe Gosslinge and Norbert met their Maker on the same day, so was Gosslinge killed just to provide the killer with a suitable weapon to use on Norbert? That seems harsh!'

'Perhaps Gosslinge was the killer,' suggested Bartholomew. 'That would be the simplest solution. Then he went to the church dressed in rags as some kind of atonement.'

'Perhaps we should ignore the knife and its implications for now,' said Michael, seeing an infinite range of possibilities, none of which could be proven one way or another. 'Where is that thing you extracted from Gosslinge? And, more importantly, what was it?'

'It was crushed into a ball and frozen solid, and is now in my room, being thawed slowly over a candle. We can unravel it when it is pliant.'

'When? Tonight?'

'Recent experience has shown that we should do this kind of thing in daylight, when we can see. So, we will do it tomorrow morning. Damn this cat! It has claws like daggers.'

'How did this ball get inside Gosslinge?' asked Michael. 'Did someone put it there?'

Absently, Bartholomew ruffled the cat's fur, making it purr and ready its claws for more kneading. 'I was thinking about that all through dinner. The answer is that I am not sure. Gosslinge's lips were bruised and his fingernail was damaged, so he was probably involved in some kind of struggle. Perhaps someone rammed it down his throat – literally. Giles and Philippa said he was not strong, so it probably would not have been difficult.'

'Nasty,' said Michael in distaste. 'You do not think he did it himself? Tried to eat it and choked, and the bruises were made by his desperation to breathe?'

'It is possible. What do you think happened? Gosslinge went to St Michael's, dressed in his livery, and ate the ball of material. Then he ran to the albs, wrapped himself up and died?'

'Changing his clothes as he did so,' mused Michael. 'It does not make sense, does it? How about if he entered the church and met someone there. Let us say Harysone, for the sake of argument. He and Harysone fought, and Harysone rammed this ball into Gosslinge's throat. Gosslinge died. Harysone stole his clothes and concealed the body among the albs.'

'But that solution would have Harysone carrying a full set of beggarly clothes when he went to meet Gosslinge.'

'Perhaps that was why Harysone visited St Michael's Church the time we followed him: he had already killed Gosslinge and was returning to exchange the clothes. I *knew* he had something to do with Gosslinge's death!' Michael rubbed his hands together, pleased with his reasoning.

'First, Harysone was not carrying anything when we saw him,' Bartholomew pointed out. 'His hands were empty, except for the ink and parchment he had bought in the Market Square. And second, we saw him enter St Michael's on the Thursday, whereas we have reasoned that Gosslinge died on the Tuesday. Why bother to change the clothes two days later?'

Michael said nothing, although the very fact that he declined to argue suggested he was aware there was a flaw in his reasoning. 'What do you think about the people who broke into St Michael's last night?' he asked eventually. 'Were they Philippa and Giles? Ailred and Godric? Frith and one of his friends? Or was it Harysone and an accomplice?'

'There is nothing to suggest Harysone has an accomplice.'

'He has enemies, though,' said Michael. 'Someone put a knife in his spine, do not forget.'

'Perhaps we should not read too much into the attack on Harysone, either. The King's Head is famous for its fights, and stabbings are not infrequent there, as you know.'

'People do not get stabbed because they dance badly,' said Michael irritably.

'He is not a bad dancer, but his movements are provocative. Sexual. Perhaps he aimed his hips at someone's wife or daughter, and that person took offence. Or perhaps he writhed into someone, and stabbed himself accidentally. His movements are very powerful.'

'No,' said Michael, giving the matter serious thought. 'Someone stabbed him. But tomorrow, we shall do three things. First, we shall look at the ball thawing in your room. Secondly, we shall talk to Harysone again – I want to know where he was when those intruders were in our church. And thirdly, we shall have words with Ailred of Ovyng and ask why he lied to us.'

Bartholomew slept poorly that night. The students were carousing in the conclave, and he knew he would have no rest if he used the hall or the kitchens. There was little choice but to stay in his room. It was bitterly cold, and another blizzard raged, making him reluctant to move across the courtyard to the hall, even when it was so late he knew the students would be sleeping.

Snow worked its way under the window shutters to powder the floor white, and sometimes flakes caught in the draught from the door and went spiralling upwards to land on him. His blankets had been dusted with a thin layer of frost when he had first gone to bed, and the heat from his body melted it to release a clammy dampness. He curled up, trying to conserve warmth, and if he moved so much as a muscle, he felt tendrils of cold begin to attack.

When he did manage to doze, his dreams teemed with disjointed images. He had innumerable conversations with all manner of people, including the two dead rivermen, Michael, Philippa and Abigny. He grew confused, knowing that he was dreaming, but becoming uncertain about what had actually happened and what had not. He watched cold earth shovelled on the stiff, brown sacking bundles that represented Dunstan and Athelbald again and again, and he argued with Michael about Gosslinge. Meanwhile, Gosslinge himself sat on his bier and fixed Bartholomew with baleful eyes, cursing the physician for failing to notice that his death was not from natural causes.

Bartholomew woke with a start, then shook his head half in disgust and half in amusement at the tricks a sleeping mind could play. His feet were so cold he could not tell whether they were still attached, and he felt as though he would instantly freeze if he moved so much as a finger outside the humid cocoon of blankets that encased him. A low, golden light filled the room, giving it a misleading sense of cosiness. The candle still burned, while above it, on a small tripod he had rigged with metal rods and a broken spoon, was the ball of material he had salvaged from Gosslinge. Bracing himself, he threw off the covers and went to inspect the object, leaping from foot to foot so neither would be in contact with the snow-covered flagstones for too long.

His patience had paid off and the ball was now pliable. He glanced through the crack in his window shutter in an attempt to gauge the time, to see whether it was too early to wake Michael. It was pitch black, but he knew he would not sleep any more that night. It was too cold and he was restless. He decided to dress and make an early start on his daily duties. Besides examining the ball and going to visit Harysone and Ailred, there were the following term's lectures to be prepared.

He scraped half-heartedly at his face with a knife, then rubbed a handful of snow over it, gathered from the miniature drifts that had piled up on the floor. Then he took every item of clothing he possessed from the chest at the end of the bed, and put all of them on with hands that shook almost uncontrollably with cold. By the time he had finished, he was so well wrapped that he could barely move and, with his black cloak thrown around his shoulders, he looked like Brother Michael. The candles he lit cast his shadow against the wall, making him look monstrously vast.

He drew a three-legged stool to the table and sat. Regarding the various tasks that awaited without enthusiasm, he found his thoughts returning to the mysteries that confronted him. Foremost in his mind was Philippa. He still could not decide whether the stricken distress she had first shown over Turke's death was grief for the loss of a loved protector and companion, or whether it was something else completely.

His thoughts turned to Gosslinge, at which point he cringed. He wondered whether he had missed clues on other victims, allowing their killers to go free. He inspected a large number of corpses for Michael – any member of the University who died, usually. Many did perish from natural causes: being near the marshes, Cambridge was an unhealthy place to live, and fevers and agues were commonplace. It was also smoky, with hundreds of fires belching fumes that became trapped in the dense fogs that plagued the Fen-edge town, and the choking, stinking mists took their toll on scholars with weak chests. And then, of course, there were the usual accidents that occurred with distressing regularity: falls from buildings, collapsing roofs, bites from animals that turned poisonous, bad food, crushings by carts, drownings and many more. He smiled ruefully. Perhaps his misdiagnosis of Gosslinge had a positive side: he knew he would never be complacent about a cause of death again.

Next, he considered the fact that Gosslinge had been trussed up among the albs wearing beggarly clothes. Did it mean a thief – not the killer – had come across the body and had taken a fancy to its fine clothes? But why bother to dress a corpse in the discarded items? Why not leave it naked, thus giving the thief more time to escape? Bartholomew frowned thoughtfully. Now he was getting somewhere. No thief would bother to dress a corpse – which was not an easy thing to do, nor a pleasant one – unless he had some powerful reason for doing so. But what?

Bartholomew pondered the question, but concluded it

was more likely that Gosslinge had dressed in the rags himself. Perhaps he had arranged to meet someone in the church and did not want to be recognised, so he dispensed with his livery and wore rags instead. People tended to ignore beggars and, since no one liked being accosted with demands for money, eye contact was usually avoided wherever possible. It would be a good disguise. And then what? Gosslinge had his meeting, choked on the ball and was wrapped in the albs by the person he was meeting? Or was he hiding in the albs anyway, trying to keep warm, because he was wearing thinner, cheaper clothes than he was used to and he was cold?

Bartholomew nodded in satisfaction, feeling he was finally deducing some acceptable answers: Gosslinge had gone to the church in his beggarly attire, and was so cold while he waited for his meeting that he wrapped himself in the albs. Then what? Had his assailant seized him while his arms were tangled and forced the ball down his throat? Or had Gosslinge put it in his own mouth? Bartholomew turned the question over and over, but was unable to come up with an answer that satisfied him. The evidence to point him one way or the other was simply not there.

Next, he thought about the scars on Turke's legs that Philippa had concealed when he was dying. Were the scars the reason for her request that her husband should not be examined? She intended to ensure that no one saw what he wanted to keep private? Or was there another reason? Idly, he sketched the wounds on a scrap of parchment. They comprised a series of small white marks that criss-crossed Turke's legs from the knees down. They were not especially disfiguring, and looked at least five years old. He racked his brains, but could think of nothing that would cause such injuries other than his original notion – that Turke had been hacked at with weapons while he sat on a horse. However, it did not seem to be a likely scenario, and Turke had not seemed like a warrior.

His mind flipped back to Gosslinge again. He had an

ancient injury, too – one that had deprived him of a thumb. Were the two connected? Had Gosslinge lost his digit at the same time as Turke had earned scarred legs? Turke had given Langelee a relic – a finger – that he claimed belonged to St Zeno. Bartholomew wondered whether it was Gosslinge's thumb, given away once the servant was dead. He grimaced. That would make the relationship between Gosslinge and his master a curious one. But Bartholomew decided that speculating on the thumb was pointless, and likely to lead him astray. Nevertheless, he made a note to ask Langelee whether he could inspect the relic later that day.

Then there was Norbert to consider. While there were many questions and snippets of information pertaining to the deaths of Gosslinge and Turke, there was virtually nothing to identify the killer of Dick Tulyet's kinsman. Bartholomew thought about Ovyng Hostel. Why had Ailred lied about his whereabouts the night the intruders had invaded St Michael's? The fact that he had felt obliged to tell untruths suggested something was amiss.

And what about Dympna, who wrote asking Norbert to St Michael's Church? The meetings obviously involved some unusual or illegal transaction, because she had eluded the nosy Franciscans when they followed Norbert. If the meetings were innocent, then there would have been no need for such subterfuge. Norbert had not cared whether he had broken other University rules, and certainly would not have minded being caught with a woman. Bartholomew supposed Dympna might have been protecting herself – perhaps she was married, or had other reasons why she did not want to be caught associating with him – but he thought it more likely she was trying to keep the *purpose* of their meetings a secret.

And finally, why did so many strands of the investigation lead to the Chepe Waits? They had been employed to play in Turke's home, and they had spoken to Gosslinge, Norbert, Harysone and Abigny in Cambridge. Were they merely trying to secure work for the Twelve Days, as Michael believed, or was their timely presence in Cambridge more than coincidence?

Bartholomew scratched his chin, thinking there were too many questions and too little information, and realised he could sit all night and ponder, but he would have no answers until he had more clues. Reluctantly, he turned his mind from the mysteries and concentrated on the mound of parchment that lay in front of him. He sharpened a pen and prepared to make a start.

Writing while wearing two pairs of gloves was not easy, but he managed. He produced a list of the texts that he wanted his students to read over the next few days, which would be discussed in classes once term had started, and then continued writing the current chapter of his treatise on fevers, concentrating on ailments that afflicted people during winter. With sadness, he used Dunstan as an illustration of specific symptoms and rates of decline. That done, he turned his attention to a public lecture he was to give in the new term, entitled 'Let us debate whether warm rooms in cold weather breed contagion.' He intended to base his argument on the works of Maimonides, the great Hebrew physician and philosopher.

He was pleased with the amount of work he had completed before any of his colleagues were out of their beds. He laid down his pen and listened, but the silence was absolute: there were no voices in the courtyard, no distant carts rumbling on the High Street and no dogs yapping. In fact the silence was unnatural, and he supposed it was due to the snow. He wondered what time it was, and with a shock he saw that the candle he had set under Gosslinge's ball of material had burned away to nothing. It had been new when he had set it there the previous evening, and should not have disappeared quite so soon – unless it was a good deal later than he thought. Puzzled, he left his room and went into the hall, which comprised the door to the cupboard he used to store his medical supplies and a wooden staircase that led to the two upstairs chambers, one of which was Michael's. He could still hear nothing.

Quietly, so as not to disturb anyone, he climbed the stairs. He pushed open the door to Michael's room and found it deserted. The same was true of the one opposite, which was usually inhabited by a trio of retired scholars. Bartholomew assumed they had all opted for the noisier – scholars snored – but warmer alternative of a night in the hall or the conclave.

He closed the door and walked back down the stairs, deciding to go to the kitchen and see whether there was any new bread to steal or a fire to sit near. He opened the door to the courtyard and stared in shock. A blank wall of snow faced him. He remembered the blizzard of the night before, and supposed he should not be surprised that it had drifted. He climbed the stairs again and went back into Michael's room, to look out of the window and assess the height of the drifts. He started in alarm when he opened the shutter only to find snow filling that opening, too. It must cover the entire building, and he was trapped inside!

A feeling of dull horror seized Bartholomew as he gazed at the dense whiteness outside Michael's window. Would anyone notice that he was missing, or would they assume he had gone to spend the night with Edith or Matilde? Would it be days before the snow melted, or someone started to dig? He seized the heavy staff Michael used for travelling, and began to hack at the snow. A good deal toppled inward, but he could detect no glimmer of daylight in the hollow he made. He wondered how the rest of the town had fared, if the drifts were deep enough to bury Michaelhouse.

The practical side of his mind began to assert itself and he devised a plan. First, he would light a fire. The smoke would alert his colleagues to his predicament and serve to warm him. Next, he would set water to melt and eat a piece of the cake he had downstairs, then he would use Michael's staff to begin to dig himself out. The snow was not so hard

301

packed that it could not be tunnelled, and he did not want to leave his rescue entirely to his colleagues, lest they had other disasters to manage. Visions of the Blaston house flashed through his mind, its roof crushed by the weight of snow. Michaelhouse's roofs were also in poor condition, so the same could happen here. The thought spurred him into action.

The fire was blazing nicely, and he was eating his second piece of cake, when it occurred to him that there was something to be said for the silence of being interred. He was free to allow his mind to wander, and it was pleasant sitting quietly without students wanting answers to questions or Michael ordering him to inspect bodies. He had just stoked up the fire and started a third slice of cake when the room was suddenly filled with light. He glanced up to see Michael's anxious face peering through the window.

'There you are,' said the monk accusingly. 'I have been worried. Why could you not sleep in the hall, like everyone else?'

Bartholomew gazed at him in surprise, then walked to the window to look outside. The sight that greeted him was one he would remember for the rest of his life. The blizzard had blown snow so high against the north wing that it came to the eaves, although the south wing had escaped more lightly, and drifts only reached waist height. Snow lay in great, thick pillows across the roofs, transforming Cambridge into an alien land of soft lines and curves that were a uniform white. In the courtyard below, Langelee was supervising a chain of students as they dug a path between the hall and the gate, while Clippesby and Wynewyk held Michael's ladder.

'Do not worry,' Michael called archly, glancing down at them. 'He is quite unharmed. He has made himself comfortable near the fire and is eating cake. We need not have hurried after all.'

'What time is it?' asked Bartholomew, offering Michael the remains of the slice he had been eating. The monk accepted ungraciously, and crammed it whole into his mouth.

'A little after ten o'clock, I should think. We have passed the morning digging ourselves back into civilisation. The whole town is like this.'

'I should see whether Edith needs help,' said Bartholomew, trying to push past Michael to reach the ladder.

'Edith needs no help from you,' said Michael, grabbing the windowsill as the physician's rough treatment threatened to unbalance him. 'It was Oswald's apprentices who came to rescue *us*. He wanted to make sure you were all right.'

'What about the students?' asked Bartholomew, looking towards the hall. 'Is everyone accounted for?'

'Yes – which we owe to the Lord of Misrule, who passed a decree last night that the first person to leave the hall was to buy the wine for the next feast. Needless to say, everyone remained. You were the only one missing. And now I know why: you intended to pass the night in great comfort, using my personal supply of firewood and eating cakes you ought to have shared. Give me another piece; climbing ladders is hungry work.'

Bartholomew saw his room was likely to remain inaccessible for some time, so he made a parcel of various essential medical supplies before he abandoned the building. One of the things he took was the ball that had been in Gosslinge's gullet, which he tucked inside his tunic to make sure it did not freeze again. He also collected his four books: they were the most valuable things he owned and he did not want them crushed or damaged should the roof collapse. Meanwhile, Michael's prized possessions comprised the rest of the cake, a casket of wine and a clanking bag that held his gold crosses and rings. When they had descended the ladder, Michael suggested they examine Gosslinge's ball at his office at St Mary the Great, where they would have some privacy.

The High Street was barely recognisable. One side was not too bad, but the other contained drifts so high that

303

many of the houses were completely submerged. Some roofs were poking out, but the single-storeyed ones were totally enveloped. People staggered and stumbled, some calling for missing loved ones, others enjoying the confusion. A group of children screamed with delight as a minor snowball fight developed into a massed battle, and a cow lowed balefully, confused and frightened by the strange white world in which it found itself. Dogs trotted here and there, sniffing out what they deemed to be edible morsels, while a cat sat on a wall and looked down on the chaos with aloof uninterest.

'We shall go to St Michael's instead,' gasped Michael. 'I do not think we will make it to St Mary the Great. Meadowman tells me that the drift outside Bene't College – which was already huge and causing problems for carts – is now the size of the Castle motte. We should stay away from that end of the town, in case we are asked to help with the digging. Now even *you* cannot say that this winter is not the worst that has ever been known in the history of the world!'

'I can,' replied Bartholomew mildly. 'I would never make such a wild statement. How can we know what the weather was like after the Flood or in the reign of the Conqueror? For all we know, the drifts could have been twice this size.'

Michael made no reply, and concentrated on hauling his bulk through the soft white snow, obliged to tug one leg free before lifting it to thigh height for the next step. It was strenuous work and left little breath for chatting, especially for a large man like Michael who was unused to exertion. To take the monk's mind off the exercise, Bartholomew regaled him with a summary of all he had reasoned while ensconced in his womb of snow. Michael listened without comment, although he acknowledged most of the physician's points with nods to indicate they were accepted.

In the gloom of St Michael's, Bartholomew lit three candles and used the top of the founder's tomb for a flat surface. He took the ball from his tunic and carefully unravelled it. Michael watched eagerly, anticipating some clue that would solve the mystery of Gosslinge's death once and for all. He was to be disappointed.

'Well?' he demanded, as Bartholomew teased the material into an irregularly shaped rectangle.

'I thought it was some kind of cloth last night, but it is only vellum. It probably swelled and distorted when the fluids from Gosslinge's throat wetted it.'

'You mean he did not choke within a few moments?' asked Michael, appalled. 'It took some time for him to die?'

'I do not know about that. It may have swollen later; it would not have done so instantly. I was hoping something would be written on it, but it appears to be unused.'

Michael rubbed his chin. 'So, Gosslinge choked on vellum. I suppose this means he *must* have been murdered – I can see no reason why he would willingly thrust vellum into his mouth.'

Bartholomew picked it up and held it near the candle. 'I have heard of messages being written in onion-juice ink or some such thing. They only appear when it is warmed.'

'Do not be ridiculous, Matt,' said Michael impatiently. 'No adult would write secret messages with onions these days. You . . .'

He faltered when a series of letters appeared as Bartholomew moved the material back and forth over the flame.

'Dympna!' exclaimed Bartholomew in excitement. 'It says "Dympna" quite clearly. And there are numbers, too. Three, eight and four.'

'Is there anything else?' asked Michael, snatching it from him and performing his own set of manoeuvres. In his impatience, he held it too close to the flame. There was a brief flash and he dropped it with a cry, raising singed fingers to his lips. Bartholomew stamped on it quickly, but what remained was too charred to be of any further use.

'You have just destroyed the only clue we have,' Bartholomew remarked irritably. 'I do not think there was any more written on it, but now we will never know for certain.'

'Damn!' muttered Michael wearily. 'You and I are not

having good fortune, Matt. First, you misdiagnose a death and lose a murder weapon in the river, and then I set a clue alight. Now it seems that neither of us is perfect, whereas yesterday I thought it was just you.'

'What do you think it meant?' asked Bartholomew, gazing at the blackened mess on the ground. 'Is it a reference to a book, do you think?'

'Or numbers in some court roll or legal document. You know – "37, Ed II" means the thirty-seventh section in the Court Rolls of Edward the Second.'

'That does not work, either. There are too many numbers.' Bartholomew shook his head in frustration. 'It could mean anything – from orders of cloth in ells, to astrological computations. We are no further along now than we were before.'

'It must have been important, though. Why else would it have figured so prominently in Gosslinge's death?'

'Who knows?' asked Bartholomew, dispirited. 'I certainly do not.'

The winds had raged so hard the previous night they seemed to have blown the cold away, and the weather had grown milder. This brought its own dangers, for it weakened the snow's grip on roofs and trees, and huge loads were constantly being precipitated downward. There were rumours that a potter's neck had been broken as he walked down Henney Lane, and people were vying for space in the very centre of the High Street, away from eaves and overhangs. The narrower lanes and alleyways were conspicuously empty of people.

A group of singers stood in the Market Square, performing secular and religious songs. Their faces were red from the cold, and all had their hands under their arms in an attempt to keep them warm. Their discomfort did not improve their performance, and what should have been cheerful, celebratory tunes sounded like dirges. Bartholomew felt sorry for them, and tossed them some coins as he passed. One detached himself from the group and followed them.

'Now look what you have done,' grumbled Michael disapprovingly. 'We will never be rid of the fellow now that he believes you have funds to spare.'

'We sing for private houses and institutions,' said the musician hopefully. 'All we ask is a little bread for our supper and a cup of warmed ale.'

'No, thank you,' said Michael stiffly. 'We have the misfortune of owning our own band of entertainers this season.'

'You mean the Chepe Waits?' asked the singer, his face displaying a good deal of disgust. 'You are from Michaelhouse? Frith said he had secured a good arrangement with Michaelhouse.'

'He certainly did,' grumbled Michael. 'Food, beds and, because they are not very good, they are not even obliged to perform that often.'

'Why keep them, then?' demanded the singer eagerly. 'Why not hire us instead?'

'Because we are loath to throw folk into the streets while the weather is bad.' Michael did not sound at all compassionate.

The singer sneered. 'You should keep your sympathy for those who need it. The Chepe Waits will never spend a night in the open. They will always inveigle themselves a bed somewhere, and if that fails, they can use their personal fortunes to hire a room in a tavern.'

'Their funds do not run to those sorts of expenses,' said Bartholomew, surprised that the singer needed to be told this. 'They are itinerants, like you.'

'No,' said the singer bitterly. 'They are not at all like me. If I had their money, I would not be standing here, losing my fingers and toes to the weather. I would be in a warm inn with a pot of spiced ale at my elbow and a hot wench on my knee.'

'What are you saying?' asked Bartholomew. 'That they are wealthy?'

'I know the Chepe Waits from when we perform in London. They have friends in high places, who arrange for them to play in the best houses. Then they steal small items – not jewellery or gold, you understand, but little things no one will miss immediately. These they deposit with a friend, so that when accusations are levied, nothing is ever found.'

'Quenhyth told me that,' said Bartholomew to Michael. 'He did not mention that stolen goods were deposited with a third party, but he said a chalice had disappeared from his father's home. He thought the Waits were responsible.'

'Well, your Quenhyth was mistaken, then,' said the singer. 'The Chepe Waits would never take something as valuable as a chalice. That would cause a stir, and would tell other households they should not be hired. They are cleverer than that and only take objects that can be sold with no questions asked.'

'Like glass salt dishes, knives, brass skewers and inkpots?' asked Michael, naming four of several items that had been reported 'lost' at Michaelhouse.

'Exactly!' said the singer. 'Everything they steal is small, unimportant, difficult to identify and can be sold openly. Not chalices.'

'But these paltry objects will not buy them warm beds and decent meals in taverns,' Bartholomew pointed out.

'A little stolen regularly over long periods will make pennies add up. Also, remember that all their meals and beds are provided by the people who hire them. When you have no living expenses you can amass a fortune quickly, even if you are only adding a few coins a day.'

'Ingenious,' said Michael. 'But it sounds a slow and tedious way to gain riches to me.'

'That may be so, but it is easy and, if you are careful never to take too much, it is safe. It is better than standing in icy marketplaces singing to people who would rather you were silent.'

'The Waits stole a sizeable sum of money at the King's Head,' said Michael. 'If they are only interested in pennies, then why did they take Harysone's gold?'

'That is obvious: because they had not been *hired* by the

King's Head,' replied the singer impatiently. 'The tavern was so full of travellers that it would have been impossible to pin the blame on any one person.'

'Sheriff Morice pinned it on the Chepe Waits,' said Michael. 'He knew the identity of the thieves immediately.'

The singer was suddenly furtive. 'I imagine someone must have slipped him a hint.'

'I see,' said Michael, raising his eyebrows and treating the singer to an amused smile. 'I wonder who that could have been.'

'If the Waits are known for petty theft, then why has no one denounced them?' asked Bartholomew.

The singer shrugged. 'I do not think their habits are well known – not here, at least – and who would believe me if I started making accusations? People would say I was just trying to steal their custom, or that I was jealous because my troupe has not been hired by a wealthy College.' He gave a rueful grin. 'And they would be right.'

'I do not think the Waits have friends in high places, though,' said Bartholomew, thinking about another of the singer's claims. 'They were the last to secure employment this year.'

'Not quite the last,' the singer pointed out bitterly. 'I have no idea why they are in Cambridge. They were doing well in Chepe, where they have their influential friends. They secured a lot of business there – to the exclusion of the rest of us, I might add – over the last five years or so. I cannot imagine why they abandoned such a lucrative situation to come here.'

'You said they give what they steal to a friend, who sells it for them,' said Bartholomew. 'Is this friend with them now? Is it the same person, or do they vary their "friends" between towns?'

'I have no idea,' said the singer. 'I only know what I do because Frith once confided in me when he had fleeced a particularly wealthy patron, and was of a mind to brag. Doubtless he has since wished he held his tongue.'

'Have you told anyone else all this?' asked Michael.

The singer grimaced. 'Several people, although none have listened as long as you. But you should hire us instead, Brother. I promise *we* will not take your salt dishes or your inkpots.'

'Perhaps next year,' said Michael. 'Here are a few coins. Buy yourself and your companions some spiced ale, and you may find your singing is the better for it.'

CHAPTER 9

'THAT WAS INTERESTING,' SAID BARTHOLOMEW, AS HE AND
Michael picked their way between the walls of snow
in the High Street. 'The Waits have been seen with
Norbert, Gosslinge and Harysone. I wonder if any of them
is the "friend" who takes their stolen property and converts
it to pennies.'

'Not Gosslinge,' said Michael. 'He was in the employ of
a respectable merchant. Why should he waste his time with
pennies?'

'It might explain why he was wearing rags,' suggested
Bartholomew. 'He exchanged his livery for shabby clothes
as a disguise while engaged in illegal activities.'

'It might, I suppose. And then he and the Waits had a
falling out, and Frith rammed the vellum down Gosslinge's
throat. But would they kill the man who was going to sell
their goods? I imagine you need to be very careful about
who you trust when you turn criminal, and new and reliable accomplices would not be easy to find.'

'Perhaps Gosslinge wanted more money, but they refused.'

'And killed him? Why? It is not as if Gosslinge could go
to the Sheriff with his information, because that would see
him hanged, too.'

'Then what about Norbert as the accomplice?'

'Norbert seldom left the town. He could not have helped
with stolen goods in Chepe.'

'The singer said he did not know whether the accomplice
travelled with them, or whether they had different help in
different places. Norbert may have been their Cambridge
man.'

'But, like Gosslinge, Norbert died five days after they arrived,' Michael pointed out. 'Does that mean he was not good at his job, and so they stabbed him?'

'Perhaps he tried to cheat them. Who knows what sort of arrangement they had?'

'But, again like Gosslinge, why kill their accomplice when replacement partners in crime would be difficult to come by? I am more inclined to believe that the accomplice is Harysone.'

'I wonder why that does not surprise me,' muttered Bartholomew dryly. 'On what grounds?'

'His behaviour, for a start. He told you about meeting the Waits when you went to treat his back. He wanted to make sure you understood it was a *chance* encounter. He anticipated someone would tell you they had been seen together, and he wanted you to believe the meeting was meaningless before it figured in our investigation. But he is our man. Why else would he be here?'

'To sell copies of his book?'

Michael pulled a face to show what he thought of Harysone's attempts at scholarship. 'His "book" is not worth the parchment it is written on. It is a ruse – an excuse for his presence here so no one will ask questions.'

Bartholomew gave a sudden laugh. 'Did you hear William complaining about it this morning, after you excavated me from the snow? He is supposed to tell Langelee whether it is suitable for the library, and is enjoying it because it is not. He does not know whether to be amused or shocked. He read me the parts he considered most damning.'

'What did they say?'

'All sorts of rubbish, but what really caused him to launch into one of his tirades was Harysone's statement that fish are angels. Harysone's logic is that fish have silver scales, but their brilliance fades after they die; this is because the angel's soul leaves the fish to go to Heaven. He also says angels are the only creatures on Earth that do not breathe air. *Ergo*, angels are fish.'

Michael gazed at him in open-mouthed astonishment. 'Harysone really wrote that?'

'You should borrow the book from William before he wears it out with his aggressive thumbing and browsing.'

'I could not bring myself to touch it,' said Michael primly. 'But all this merely confirms my suspicions: Harysone is the Waits' accomplice.'

'Because he writes heretical books?' asked Bartholomew, laughing. 'You will need something better than that to convict him! However, remember that if Harysone is the Waits' accomplice, they would not have relieved him of his gold in the King's Head.'

Michael was not pleased to see his argument thwarted. He muttered something incomprehensible, then declared they would pay Harysone a visit immediately. Bartholomew saw that the monk obviously preferred to trust his own instincts about the pardoner than the physician's scientific analysis of the facts.

It took a long time to reach the King's Head, partly because it was difficult to walk, but mostly because people kept stopping them to ask for help or to enquire whether they had seen someone who was missing. Matilde was out, taking bread and milk to those in need, assisted by Yolande de Blaston's older children. They struggled through the snow carrying baskets and jugs, putting their feet in her footprints, so that Bartholomew was reminded of the legend about the sainted King Wenceslas. She waved to him, but was too busy with her charity to stop and talk. They met Langelee near Bene't College. Looking pleased with himself, he waved a bag of coins at them.

'Five pounds,' he said with satisfaction, bracing himself against the monstrous pile of snow outside that College in order to let Robin of Grantchester slink by without touching him; the drift made the road very narrow at that point. A trail of red in the white after Robin had passed indicated the surgeon had been practising his trade that morning.

Michael grinned conspiratorially. 'You persuaded

Harysone to part with five pounds? That is five times what he wanted for one of his miserable books. I knew he would be unable to resist!'

'St Zeno's finger,' said Bartholomew, looking from one to the other. 'You sold Harysone the relic Turke gave you?'

'For a modest sum,' bragged Langelee, clearly delighted. 'I played on his love of fish, as you suggested, Michael. I thought I might have to exaggerate Zeno's association with fishermen to make him bite – so to speak – but he already knew all about the Saint of Anglers, and all I had to do was appear to be reluctant to part with the thing.'

'I was going to inspect that,' said Bartholomew, disappointed to learn it was no longer in Michaelhouse's possession. 'I thought it might be Gosslinge's thumb.'

'More than likely,' said Langelee carelessly. 'I had a good look at it myself, and it is definitely a human digit of some kind or other. It was blackened and covered in dried skin. I saw many relics when I worked for the Archbishop of York, and I sensed Turke's was a fake from the beginning. When I touched it, and was not struck down by the Wrath of God, I knew I was right.'

'That was a risky way to find out,' said Bartholomew, disapprovingly. 'You should have asked Kenyngham to assess it first. If anyone can identify saintly objects, it is him.'

'He did,' said Michael, shooting the Master an admonishing look for telling only part of the story. 'Kenyngham blessed it, but said it felt tainted. We decided to rid Michaelhouse of the thing as soon as possible. And who better than to a pardoner with an obsession for fish?'

Langelee jingled his coins in boyish glee. 'I must go – to consult with Agatha about how best to spend five whole pounds!'

Harysone was sitting in the main chamber of the King's Head when Bartholomew and Michael arrived. Lounging elegantly near the hearth, he was enjoying the company of two merchants who also wanted the warmth of a fire that winter day. He wore the relic bag around his neck, and was fingering it as he spoke. The merchants looked pleased when Michael beckoned Harysone away, glad to be rid of him. Bartholomew saw one of them held a copy of Harysone's book, and supposed the pardoner had been working on a sale.

'Cordwainers,' said Harysone, revealing his teeth in a predatory smile. 'They love to hear about my escapades in Chepe, among the best and most ruthless traders in the country.'

'They did not look as though they were loving it to me,' said Michael rudely. 'They looked bored to tears.'

'Chepe?' pounced Bartholomew. 'When were you in Chepe?'

'I do not remember precisely,' said Harysone carelessly. 'A year ago, perhaps. When you travel a lot, as I do, you tend not to recall details. Perhaps it was not Chepe at all, but Smithfield or the Fleet. They, too, have great markets.'

'But you said, quite categorically, that Chepe merchants are among the "best and most ruthless in the country",' pressed Bartholomew. 'How can you now say you may have been referring to traders from other markets?'

'I am tired, and my back is paining me,' snapped Harysone, irked at being caught out in a falsehood. He went on the offensive. 'What have you done about the student who stabbed me? You seem willing to quibble about the locations of markets, but have you caught the man who inflicted this grievous wound on my person?'

'Why do you frequent markets?' asked Michael, ignoring Harysone's questions and persisting with his own. 'You are a pardoner, so your trade will be in and around churches, where you can catch the conscience-stricken before they are obliged to make embarrassing confessions.'

'I like markets,' said Harysone defensively. He sipped wine from his goblet, and his teeth clanged noisily on the rim. Bartholomew wondered if the man had ever considered having them filed to a more manageable size. 'I like the smells and the atmosphere. It is not a crime.'

'You like fish, too,' said Michael, making it sound like an accusation.

Harysone smiled fondly, ignoring the monk's hostile tone. 'Yes, I do. Fish are God's glimpse into Heaven. You know the story of the loaves and the fishes – God made many fish out of an original two or three, because He wanted everyone to enjoy them and see how wonderful they are to eat. Fish are marvellous creatures, and so useful.'

'Useful?' asked Bartholomew warily, sure that Harysone's interpretation was not the message the gospel writers had intended to impart.

Harysone flashed his teeth. 'As a physician, you should know their myriad virtues. Fish oils can cure diseases, and they produce luxuriant and glossy curls, if applied to the hair.'

'I thought I smelled something odd,' remarked Michael, edging away from him.

'They are also tasty, and are better than meat for the digestion,' Harysone went on. 'They are in every sea, river and stream, providing an inexhaustible supply for human delight. And they make for good friends – better than dogs.'

'You have a lap-fish?' asked Michael wryly. 'Like rich widows have lap-dogs?'

'Of course not,' said Harysone scornfully. 'They die if you put them in air, and no one wants to sit around with a water-filled lap. You keep them in a jug or, if you are wealthy, in a pond in your garden. If you find one dull or unresponsive company, you can eat it and buy another.'

'Lord!' breathed Michael, regarding Harysone as though he had escaped from St John's Hospital, where the town's lunatics were housed. 'Have you always been a pardoner, or does your obsession with matters piscine stem from an earlier career as a fisherman or a fish*monger*?'

Bartholomew supposed that this none too subtle question was intended to raise the subject – again – of whether Harysone had known Turke or Gosslinge.

Harysone's face bore an expression of genuine regret. 'I wish I were a fishmonger, because I can think of no occupation that would suit me more. However, we cannot always do what we want, so I am obliged to make my living by selling pardons. My book – I have a spare copy for sale, if you are interested – is my little tribute to the creatures I revere.'

'I see you have a relic,' said the monk casually. 'Is it a fish, by any chance?'

'The best relic would be a fish Jesus caught in the Sea of Galilee,' declared Harysone wistfully. He fingered the pouch. 'But this is almost as good: St Zeno's finger.'

'May I see it?' asked Bartholomew politely, wondering whether his knowledge of bones would allow him to distinguish a finger from a thumb if the skin was withered away.

'You may not,' said Harysone haughtily. 'This is a sacred relic, and not for pawing by curious physicians who want to examine everything they see.'

'How much did it cost?' asked Michael wickedly. 'I am sure saints' bones are expensive.'

'Terribly,' agreed Harysone. 'This was five pounds, but worth every penny, even though its purchase has left me impoverished. I shall have to sell more books. Are you sure you do not—?'

'What about the gold Sheriff Morice returned to you?' interrupted Michael, as quick as lightning. 'Could you not have used that? How much was it, anyway? Morice is fond of gold himself, so I wager he took a small something for himself.'

'It was not small,' grumbled Harysone. 'He offered me all my recovered gold, plus interest, but then informed me he always keeps a percentage of any recouped stolen property for the needy. By "needy", he meant himself, I gather. However, I do not make a habit of contesting rules set by venal officials. I do not want to end up dead in a ditch over a mark or two.'

There was an element of wisdom in Harysone's position. It was not unknown for folk who spoke out against civic corruption to die in mysterious circumstances, and Bartholomew thought Harysone was probably prudent to pay what

317

Morice asked and forget about the loss – especially in a town where he was a stranger and friendless.

'You did not mention this before,' said Michael accusingly. 'You said Morice returned it all with interest. But I shall ignore your dishonesty for now, if you tell me how much was stolen.'

'Eight nobles,' replied Harysone, bristling at Michael's rudeness. 'And Morice took three of them. I suppose I should count myself fortunate that he did not steal them all.'

Bartholomew thought the same thing, and did some rapid calculations. Since a noble was a third of a pound, Harysone's returned gold would only have covered a third of the cost of the relic. He wondered whether the man's book sales had provided the rest.

'Do you know the identity of the culprits who stole your gold?' asked Michael.

'I do not,' said Harysone. He raised a dirty hand to prevent Michael from speaking. 'And I do not want to know, so do not tell me. There is nothing I can do about it now and I want to forget the whole miserable business.'

'You love fish, yet you did not take the opportunity to converse with Walter Turke or his servant,' Bartholomew observed, changing the subject. 'They stayed in this tavern before moving to be with friends. Surely, you would have enjoyed their company?'

'I have already told you Turke was not a gentleman,' said Harysone. 'And I doubt he loved fish anyway. For him, they would have been just a way to make money.'

'Unlike you,' said Michael, staring pointedly at the book. 'But you were seen with Gosslinge by reliable witnesses.'

'The inn has been busy since I arrived,' explained Harysone patiently. 'The man may have shared my table once, but we did not speak. I recall finishing my meal and leaving as soon as I could. I do not waste my time in discussion with illiterate menials.'

'How do you know Gosslinge was illiterate?' pounced Michael.

318

Harysone made an impatient noise. 'He was a servant, and servants do not read. I am here in Cambridge only to sell copies of my book, so there is little point in chatting to folk who are unlikely to want one.'

'You tried to sell Agatha the laundress a pardon,' said Michael immediately, recalling her outraged reaction when she mentioned Harysone had offered her one that would take care of all seven deadly sins simultaneously. 'So you are *not* here just to sell your book.'

'You cannot blame me for trying to help a soul in need,' said Harysone wearily. 'Suffer the little children to come unto me – for pardons. That is Revelations, of course.'

'It is the gospels, not Revelations,' corrected Michael. 'Your theology is very hazy for a pardoner.'

With some effort, Harysone drew his lips over his teeth and managed to purse them. 'You are not in a position to criticise the way I practise my profession. You are a proctor, yet you have not discovered the identity of the man who stabbed me. Who is the worst offender: the pardoner who makes an occasional mistake with his references, or the proctor whose ineptitude allows a would-be killer to walk free?'

'The Chepe Waits,' said Bartholomew quickly, thinking that Harysone had a valid point, but not wanting Michael to become involved in an argument when they had work to do. 'Have you met them before?'

'You have asked me this already,' snapped Harysone. 'And my answer now is the same as it was then: why would a respectable man like me know a group of ruffians?'

'Because you travel?' suggested Bartholomew. 'Because you said yourself you often meet interesting and unusual people in the course of your wanderings. And there is the fact that the Waits come from Chepe – where you profess to know the merchants.'

'We may have met,' said Harysone cautiously. 'I really do not recall. I see so many people that it is difficult to keep track of them all.'

'Are you sure?' asked Michael coldly. 'I would not like to learn later that you have misled me. Lying to the Senior Proctor is a serious offence in this town, and carries a heavy fine.'

This was the first Bartholomew had heard about a fine for lying, although he was certain Michael would love the introduction of such a measure, while Father William would make the University fabulously wealthy on it. The threat of parting with money had an instant effect on the pardoner. He appeared to reconsider.

'Perhaps I have met them before, but I do not recall whether it was in Chepe or elsewhere.'

'How did you meet them?' asked Michael, victory gleaming in his eyes, as he sensed he was getting somewhere at last.

'Perhaps I asked them to play for me. I like a little entertainment now and again, and employ musicians when I have funds to spare. I hired one the other night, so people could see me dance.'

'I do not suppose the Chepe Waits ever gave you anything in return?' asked Michael. 'And I do not mean the benefit of their musical talents. I mean things like salt dishes and inkpots.'

'Why should they do that?' asked Harysone, raising his eyebrows. 'Really, Brother! I am not surprised your investigations have been unsuccessful, if this is your idea of solving crimes. I may have passed the time of day with your Chepe Waits, and I may have encountered them on my previous travels, but I have certainly never taken anything from them. And now . . .'

'I hear you have been making enquiries about a certain Dympna,' said Michael smoothly, when the pardoner rose to his feet. 'What do you say to that?'

'Nothing,' said Harysone angrily. 'Because I do not know what you want me to say. I heard she is good with her hands, and was hoping she would heal my afflicted back, since your physician is incapable of relieving my pain. Why do you ask? Is she dead, too?'

320

'Not that I know of,' said Michael. 'Is there something you would like to tell me?'

Harysone sighed. 'Why do you persist in treating me like a criminal? I am the one who has been stabbed, yet you come here and demand to know inner meanings to every conversation I have had since I arrived. You would do better to interrogate those Michaelhouse boys, because if you do not charge one of them soon, I shall go to the Sheriff and demand justice. And that will cost you a good deal more than your time!'

'Harysone is hiding something,' said Michael, as he struggled through a particularly deep drift en route to the Trumpington Gate. 'I know he is.'

'Possibly,' said Bartholomew. 'Do you remember Langelee, when he first arrived here? He pretended to be a scholar, but all the time he was spying for the Archbishop of York.'

'What does that have to do with Harysone?'

'Perhaps it is no coincidence that Harysone arrived the same day as the Waits. Perhaps they made a powerful enemy by stealing from one particular household – someone who does not like his good faith abused and who wants revenge. In other words, Harysone is an agent, employed by some wealthy merchant from Chepe to catch the Waits and bring them to justice.'

'They would not be worth the expense,' said Michael. 'That singer said the Waits' light fingers land only on paltry items; he said they would never take anything valuable.'

'But he also said the money generated from these thefts was considerable. Would you want those kind of people wandering around the villages or land that you owned?'

'I do not think Harysone is here for any purpose other than to benefit himself. He is not some avenging angel, intent on putting right what is wrong in the world.'

'The Waits have made enemies, though. The singer disliked them enough to tell Sheriff Morice they had stolen Harysone's gold, while Quenhyth is positively rabid about

321

them. There must be others who feel the same way. Harysone may be one of them.'

'I suppose,' conceded Michael reluctantly. 'However, although you think it is highly suspicious that Harysone and the Waits all reached Cambridge on the fifteenth of December, do not forget that Turke and his household arrived that day, too.' He gave a grim smile as he recognised a familiar figure battling through the snow. 'And here comes Giles, limping almost as badly as our investigation and with his feathered hat looking as dishevelled and disheartened as I feel. I intended to visit him later today, but we can talk to him now instead. It will save me a journey.'

'It is too cold to chatter in the street,' grumbled Bartholomew. 'The snow has melted in my boots, and my feet are frozen. I shall have chilblains, like Giles, if I do not go home soon.'

'It is mild,' contradicted Michael, warmed by the mulled ale from the King's Head and the effort of walking. He shot out a powerful arm to prevent the clerk from hurrying past. 'Giles! Do you have a moment?'

'No,' said Abigny, trying without success to free himself. 'I must meet someone, and I am already late. You can talk to me later, in Stanmore's house where it is warm and dry.'

'Who are you meeting?' asked Michael.

Abigny stared at him in surprise, then laughed. 'All the power you have accrued from being the Bishop's spy and the Senior Proctor has made you insolent, Michael! It is none of your business who I am meeting, and you have no right to question me. I am no longer a scholar, and am therefore outside your jurisdiction.'

'I apologise,' acknowledged Michael, with a grin Bartholomew sensed was not genuine. 'I only wanted to ask you about Gosslinge, now that Philippa is not here to contradict you.'

Abigny gave a bleak smile. 'You have already heard all I have to say: Gosslinge was a puny little man who hid when there was hard work to be done; he was lazy and grasping; and he had an inflated opinion of his worth. He despised me because I am employed by the law courts – "priests' dirty work", he called it.'

'Did he indulge in criminal activities, then?' asked Michael, exchanging a meaningful glance with Bartholomew. Perhaps Gosslinge had been the Waits' accomplice after all.

'I doubt it,' replied Abigny. 'Walter was intolerant of any kind of wrongdoing by his servants, despite the fact that he used questionable practices himself to make his business a success. Gosslinge had a good life, and I do not think he would have risked losing it by breaking the law.'

'Walter engaged in criminal activities?' asked Michael, surprised. 'I thought he was a Prime Warden, and a fine, upstanding member of London society.'

'Oh, he was,' said Abigny wryly. 'At least, that is what he wanted people to believe. His good reputation meant a great deal to him. Why else would he go to the inconvenience and discomfort of a pilgrimage?'

'To atone for a mortal sin?' suggested Michael dryly.

Abigny laughed again. 'Do not be ridiculous! Walter had no fear of Heaven or Hell, and the pilgrimage was undertaken solely because he believed the murder of Fiscurtune – which he always claimed was perfectly justified, by the way – might damage his chances of being Lord Mayor.'

'His chances of becoming Lord Mayor look slim at the moment,' remarked Michael.

Abigny grinned. 'Perhaps that was the real reason for his death – he embarked on a pilgrimage without being properly contrite, and was struck down by God.'

'Why did Turke think he was justified in killing Fiscurtune?' asked Bartholomew. 'You said he stabbed an unarmed man during a guild meeting. That does not sound justified to me.'

'Walter was one of those men who believe they can do no wrong,' replied Abigny. 'How Fiscurtune's death appeared to me and a good many others was irrelevant to him. He believed he killed Fiscurtune honourably after many years of provocation.'

'You mentioned Turke was not wholly honest in business,' said Bartholomew. 'What criminal activities did he enjoy?'

'I did not say they were criminal,' corrected Abigny. 'I said they were questionable. He was ruthless, and destroyed more than one competitor as he made his way to the top. You will not find anything flagrantly illegal in his past, but there is a lot of unpleasantness and unkindness.'

'I am puzzled by Gosslinge's role in all this,' said Bartholomew. 'I do not understand why Turke employed someone lazy and indolent – even if he did remain on the right side of the law.'

Abigny hesitated. 'I could give you my views on the matter, but I have no evidence to back them, and there is no point in telling tales now that both are dead. It would hurt Philippa, and I do not want to do that. And anyway, I thought you had agreed to leave Walter in peace.'

'Turke, yes, but not Gosslinge,' said Michael craftily. 'I am not entirely satisfied that his death was natural.' He raised an eyebrow at Bartholomew, who stared at the ground, chagrined. 'I cannot allow him to be buried until I am sure there is nothing sinister about his demise.'

'Really?' asked Abigny, surprised. 'You think someone might have done away with him? I do not think it was Turke, so do not waste your time exploring that line of enquiry. He was too angry about Gosslinge's disappearance to have had a hand in it himself.'

Bartholomew rubbed his chin as he considered the clerk's claims. Was Abigny telling the truth about Turke's level of irritation over the servant's death, or was he just trying to dissuade them from including Turke in Gosslinge's murder investigation? Bartholomew realised with a shock that not only had Philippa changed to the point where he barely knew her, but so had her brother. Bartholomew and Abigny had shared a room for several years, and had been good friends, but Bartholomew now found himself questioning everything Abigny said.

'You still have not answered Matt's question,' said

Michael, as Abigny leaned against a wall and flexed one of his feet, wincing as he did so. 'Why did Turk employ a lazy scoundrel like Gosslinge?'

'I will tell you what I think,' said Abigny, repeating the operation with the other foot. 'But on condition that you leave Walter alone afterwards. I do not want Philippa distressed any more than she has been. Gosslinge's position in the household was more powerful than it should have been. He had some kind of hold over Walter.'

'Do you know what that hold might be?' asked Michael.

'Gosslinge lost a thumb when he was a boy – as an apprentice gutting fish for Walter, apparently. I have always wondered whether it was an accident, or whether Walter did it.' Abigny smiled ruefully when he saw the expression on their faces. 'I knew you would be sceptical. It does not make sense, does it?'

'Why would Turke sever Gosslinge's thumb?' asked Michael. 'And why would Gosslinge let him?'

'Gosslinge was puny,' said Bartholomew. 'Perhaps he could not stop it.'

'Or was it an accident?' mused Michael. 'But Turke felt responsible, so gave Gosslinge licence to live a lazy life. But, by all accounts, Walter was not a compassionate man, and so that seems unlikely, too.'

'It crossed my mind that St Zeno's finger was Gosslinge's thumb,' said Bartholomew. 'But Langelee sold it before I could look.'

Abigny made a disgusted face. 'I confess that possibility never occurred to me! I cannot envisage any situation that would lead Walter to revere other men's severed body parts. It is grotesque! You must be wrong.'

'We shall have to ask Philippa,' said Michael. 'She will know where the relic came from.'

'Do not,' pleaded Abigny. 'You will upset her if she thinks you are probing Walter's death after she asked you to leave him alone. She was fond of him, despite his shortcomings, and will grow fonder still once the bad memories have faded and only the pleasant ones remain. She will be a good widow, and will never say anything to harm his reputation – no matter what the truth.'

'And what about you?' asked Michael. 'What did you really think of Walter?'

Abigny smiled. 'I always said that Philippa made a mistake in her choice of husbands, which did not make me popular with Walter. You would have been a much better brother-in-law, Matt. We would have been friends.'

'Walter was not your friend?' asked Michael.

'Lord, no! He was too busy running the Worshipful Fraternity of Fishmongers and making everyone believe he was respectable and decent. Of course, the murder of Fiscurtune made people think again. Would you want the prestigious post of Lord Mayor filled by a man who had stabbed another in what basically amounted to a fit of pique? Fiscurtune *was* being abusive and he *had* brought the Fraternity into disrepute with his poor salting techniques, but honourable men do not resolve arguments by stabbing unarmed opponents. However, now you must excuse me . . .'

'Before you go, why are you here in Cambridge?' asked Michael. 'Is it really to protect Philippa?'

'Totally – and you can see I was right to have misgivings about the venture. I am glad I was here to help her when she needed me. But now I really must go.'

He gave them a jaunty wave as he entered the King's Head. Bartholomew waited a moment, then ploughed through the snow to the window. The shutters were drawn, to keep out the cold, but there were enough gaps in the wood to allow him to see through. He watched thoughtfully as Abigny doffed his hat in an amiable greeting to Harysone, then sat next to him and began to talk.

'The Chepe Waits. Abigny. Fish. Dympna,' said Michael, counting them off on his fingers late the following after-noon, as dusk was settling over the town. 'These are the strands that connect Turke and his lazy servant, the dancing

326

pardoner and the murder of Norbert. The only problem is that I cannot see how.'

Nor could Bartholomew, and he had been mulling over the information all day. The whole morning had been spent making enquiries about Harysone, but these yielded nothing they did not already know: the pardoner had arrived with his cartload of books, but no one knew anything about him other than that which he had chosen to divulge. No one could say how he had come by his curious fascination with fish. No one had seen him with Turke, but he had been noted in company with Gosslinge, although it seemed they had not spoken. No one could offer any plausible theories as to why someone should stab him, and the most likely explanation seemed to be Bartholomew's – that the pardoner's gyrations had driven him accidentally on to a knife worn in someone's belt.

Michael had listened to reports from his beadles about Dympna that morning, but was disappointed with their trawl of information. Several witnesses had heard of Dympna, but no one had actually met her. A man who had lost a foot in an accident with a cart claimed Dympna was a saint, but would say no more about her, despite Meadowman's best efforts and a large jug of ale. Later, Michael had gone to Ovyng. Ailred was preaching to his students – with apparent sincerity – about the virtues of honesty, but still insisted he had not left the hostel on the night the intruders had invaded St Michael's. Godric said nothing at all.

When he returned to Michaelhouse, the monk struck up a conversation with Makejoy. The woman said the Waits had been together five years, and had spent most of their time enjoying lucrative careers in Chepe. The journey to Cambridge was unusual for them, and was undertaken partly because business was currently poor in London, and partly because Frith had expressed a desire to see the Fen-edge town. For want of anything better to do, the troupe had agreed to travel.

'You would be better off without Frith,' Michael had advised. 'Not only is he surly and aggressive – and his rude tongue must lose you business – but he has no talent.'

Makejoy pulled a wry face. 'None of us are overly endowed in that area, Brother, but we get by. Frith is good at organising. It is he who secures us our customers, he who negotiates better pay, and he who invests our takings and turns pennies into shillings.'

Michael's interest quickened. 'And how does he do that?'

But Makejoy would say no more, and turned the conversation to how she had learned to tumble.

Meanwhile, Bartholomew had gone to Stanmore's house, to ask Abigny why he had met Harysone in the King's Head. Bartholomew did not imagine for a moment that Abigny would tell him, since he had already said his affairs were no one's business. But when he arrived he was told that both Philippa and Abigny were at St Michael's Church, talking to the man who was to embalm Turke's body for its journey to Chepe. Stanmore and Edith were at home, however, and both claimed that Abigny often went out on unspecified business, while Philippa refused to leave the house at all unless someone was with her. Stanmore remained convinced that something sinister was going on, and pressed Bartholomew again to discover why Turke had died.

When the physician looked into the church on his way home he found the embalmer working with his potions and knives, but Philippa and Abigny were not there. Bartholomew had not passed them, and he wondered where they could have gone. By the time he returned to Michaelhouse he was irritable, tired of being lied to and misled for reasons he could not understand, and there was a headache thumping behind his eyes.

He was just settling down for the evening, and was about to discuss the odd links between the Waits, fish, Dympna and the Turke household with Michael, when Cynric arrived to say they were invited to celebrate the passing of the old year at Milne Street. Bartholomew was surprised, because

Philippa had effectively turned Stanmore's home into a house of mourning, and a feast – even a small one – was an unexpected turn of events. He was sure Edith would not have made the suggestion, and so could only assume that it was Philippa's idea. Michael, usually more than willing to accept an invitation from the Stanmores – Edith's table was always well stocked – declared that he had some pressing documents to read, and Bartholomew saw that the monk no more wanted to pass an evening in the strained atmosphere at Milne Street than he did.

He considered declining the offer, too, pleading that he too was obliged to remain in Michaelhouse. But then Cynric mentioned a decree by Deynman that no one was allowed to speak English, Latin or French that evening; since few Michaelhouse scholars spoke any other languages, the occasion promised to be simultaneously silly and frustrating. Bartholomew knew Italian and some Spanish, and could converse with Michael in Greek, but the thought of trying to communicate with his other colleagues with hand gestures and gibberish was not at all appealing. Also, Edith was his sister, and he did not like to refuse her hospitality when he knew his absence would disappoint her.

Because his room was inaccessible under the snowdrift, he was obliged to share William's until it was cleared. The friar watched critically as he brushed mud from his clothes and pulled on his boots, still soggy from walking through the snow earlier that day.

'Are you going dressed like that?' William asked eventually, after a long silence punctuated by disapproving huffs and sighs.

'Why?' Bartholomew looked down at himself. 'What is wrong with me?'

William pulled a face indicating that while his lips uttered 'nothing', his mind was thinking something very different. 'Your woman will not be impressed,' he added, when Bartholomew appeared to take him at his word and prepared to leave. 'And she is newly a widow, so will be looking for a man. You will not ensnare her if you do not make yourself look attractive.'

'She is not looking for a man,' said Bartholomew. 'And I am not available, anyway.'

'So, you intend to continue with Matilde,' concluded William disapprovingly. 'I am not sure that is a good idea, Matthew. She may not want you, and it will be difficult to conduct a dalliance for long without it coming to the attention of the Chancellor. Still, I suppose if you are discreet it may work for a while, and you will eventually tire of the whole business of females.'

'I shall bear that in mind,' said Bartholomew stiffly, wishing his colleagues would mind their own business when it came to his love life. 'How is your leg?'

'This bad weather cannot last much longer, so I do not anticipate being an invalid for too many more days, which is just as well – the undergraduates will run riot if I am gone too long. I am sure there is already vice and debauchery wherever you look.'

'Not wherever *I* look,' said Bartholomew, thinking the season had been remarkably trouble free. The snow helped, keeping would-be revellers indoors and reducing the number of large street fights between gangs of townsmen and scholars. He glanced across at the friar and recognised the crude wooden covers of the book that lay open on his knees. 'Are you still reading that thing? What is taking you so long?'

'I have read it several times,' said William, the light of the fanatic gleaming in his eyes. 'I am unable to help myself. I have never encountered such bald heresy in all my days – and that includes among the Dominicans!'

'It must be the work of Satan himself, then,' said Bartholomew, amused. 'But the bits I read were just the ramblings of a misinformed and badly educated eccentric. I did not detect anything particularly heretical.'

'Oh, no?' hissed William, sensing a challenge as his large hands scrabbled roughly at the pages. He opened it to a section that, judging by the state of it, had been perused many times before. 'Then listen to this: "Godd has no Forme – this We all Nowe. However, Sometyms it Has been Nessessary for Him to Adopte a Shape in order to Appear to Man, and He has always Chose Attributes of a Fish to Manifeste Himselph." Do not tell me *that* is not heresy! If my leg were not broken, I would burn Harysone in the Market Square myself!'

'But it goes on to explain,' said Bartholomew, peering over William's shoulder to read the text for himself. 'It says those attributes include a silvery sheen, like the skin of a fish, and an ability to dominate the mighty ocean. Harysone is just using marine images to describe God's mystery.'

'He is saying God has scales and lives in the sea.' William hurled the book from him in revulsion, so it crashed into the wall and left a dent in the plaster.

'So it will not be going in the Michaelhouse library, then?' asked Bartholomew mildly.

'You had better go,' said William, not deigning to answer. 'Give my regards to Edith, and tell Abigny that the answer to his question is "no". I had forgotten him in all the fuss over my leg, but I can tell him what he wants to know now.'

'What was the question?' asked Bartholomew, flinging his cloak around his shoulders and trying to make his feet comfortable inside his damp boots.

'He asked me whether Pechem – the head of my Order here in Cambridge – had heard from Dympna recently,' said William. 'I told him I would ask, but Pechem said Dympna has been quiet, and has only acted once since the summer.'

Bartholomew stared at him. 'Dympna?'

'Dympna,' said William impatiently. 'You know.'

'I do not know. Who is she?'

William seemed confused and a little embarrassed. 'It seems I have already said too much. I thought you would know Dympna, being a friend of Abigny's. I see I was mistaken. Damn it all! I should have been more discreet. It is this wretched ice all around me. I cannot think straight with it lurking in every corner.'

In the interests of finding out what he wanted to know, Bartholomew refrained from pointing out that thinking and speaking had nothing to do with the fact that it was cold outside, and that the friar's apparent indiscretion had more to do with his gruff and loquacious personality.

The physician leaned against the windowsill. 'I think you had better tell me about Dympna, Father. Norbert received letters from her, asking him to meetings in St Michael's Church; Walter Turke muttered something that sounded like Dympna before he died; and even Harysone has some association with this mysterious woman. Believe me, Michael will not take kindly to his Junior Proctor withholding information that may help him solve this case.'

'But I cannot tell,' protested William in alarm. 'It is supposed to be a secret. I should not have assumed that Abigny had taken you into his confidence.'

'It is too late now,' said Bartholomew. 'And if you do not tell me what I want to know, I shall inform Langelee that your leg is not broken, and—'

'That will not be necessary,' said William hastily. 'But you cannot reveal to anyone it was I who told you about Dympna, or I shall have that Bradwardine book back. Dympna is not a woman. It is not a man, either. It is a group of people. A guild.'

'What kind of guild?' asked Bartholomew, startled. Here was something he had not anticipated. 'A trade association? A religious group?'

'Neither, although a religious fraternity would be the closer description. It is just a collection of folk who have sworn to do good works. It always works anonymously, and only it knows the identities of its members. It also—'

This was not the answer Bartholomew was expecting at all. He stared at the friar in astonishment. 'Good works? But this group is associated with at least two people who are dead – Norbert and Turke – not to mention sinister visitors like Harysone.'

William shrugged. 'Wicked and dead folk have breathed

the name of God, but that does not make Him responsible for their lives or their evil deeds. But to continue what I was saying, no one knows how to contact Dympna, so no one can solicit its help. However, Dympna often knows when folk are in trouble, and sometimes offers financial aid. It is not a gift – the money must be repaid in full at some point in the future – but there is no interest involved.'

'You mean it is a group of benevolent bankers? It offers loans to people in desperate situations, but it expects to be repaid?'

'Essentially, although there is no limit on the time, and Dympna asks for its money back only when the crisis is over. No threats are issued. It lent the Franciscan Friary twenty pounds to pay for a new roof three years ago, and was very understanding when the sum was returned only in small amounts. We still owe two pounds. It lent Mayor Horwood money when the Great Bridge threatened to collapse, a potter was helped when he lost his foot to an accident, and wood and food were sent to Dunstan when his brother died. That was unusual.'

'Beadle Meadowman mentioned the potter,' said Bartholomew, recalling being told about the man who had refused to give details about Dympna. 'But why was helping Dunstan unusual?'

'Because there was no expectation of repayment. Dunstan was ill and old, and the benefaction was a gift, not a loan. Dympna knew it would not be getting its money back there.'

'Dympna,' said Bartholomew thoughtfully. 'Kenyngham said she is a saint associated with the insane.'

'And the desperate,' added William. 'She was famous for charitable acts, especially to lunatics and people without hope. It is a clever name for the guild, is it not?'

'I suppose so,' said Bartholomew, who thought it was rather obscure. 'But why should Norbert receive letters from a charity?'

'I imagine because he had been lent money and Dympna wanted it back, so it could be passed to more deserving cases. Dympna is generous, but it will not be abused.'

'So, the messages were demands for repayment,' surmised Bartholomew. 'That makes sense. Would Dympna kill him, do you think, if he refused to give the money back?'

'Dympna is a benevolent institution. It is understanding about the time needed to repay loans, and does not issue unpleasant threats, like moneylenders do. I cannot see it harming Norbert.'

'What about Turke? Why would he die uttering that name? And why was Philippa so relieved once he had spoken?'

'You will have to ask her that,' said William, not liking the fact that Bartholomew was raising questions to which he had no answers, because it made him feel incompetent. 'Perhaps Turke was a member of Dympna, although he did not seem the benevolent type to me, and I was under the impression Dympna was a local charity. But I may be wrong.'

'Do you know the identities of anyone who definitely belongs to this guild?'

'I am aware of one, but, as I said, it is a secret organisation, and only they know all its members. I believe Giles Abigny is involved.'

Bartholomew was thoughtful as he struggled through the drifts between Michaelhouse and Milne Street. It was already night, and the darkness was made blacker and more intense by the great snow-filled clouds that slouched overhead. Bartholomew could barely see where he was putting his feet, and was grateful Stanmore had left an apprentice outside his gates with a lamp to guide him.

His conversation with William, and the fact that it had taken longer than he had anticipated to travel the snow-smothered streets, meant that he was late. Stanmore, Edith, Abigny and Philippa were already seated in the solar when he arrived. It was a comfortable room to be in on a cold winter night. The window shutters were barred against the wind, a huge fire flickered and roared in the hearth, and lamps with coloured glass sent pretty shadows up the walls.

Someone had added pine cones to the fire and the scent of them filled the room, along with the spiced wine that sat warming in a pot and the chestnuts that were roasting in a tray.

A cosy, happy scene greeted Bartholomew as he entered. Abigny, dressed in dark blue tunic and hose, was playing raffle with Edith. This involved three dice, and the objective was to throw an equal or higher number than a rival. Edith was laughing as she won a pile of sugar comfits, and Abigny was teasing her about her good fortune. For an instant, Bartholomew glimpsed the long-haired, foppish young man with whom he had shared a room, and Abigny seemed almost carefree. Then he happened to glance up at Philippa, and his expression became sombre again. Bartholomew wondered whether it was because laughing was something one did not do in the presence of a recent widow, or whether the sight of her reminded him of matters in which amusement had no place.

Philippa was sitting near the fire with some darning lying unheeded in her lap. She was watching the raffle with a fixed smile on her lips, as though she realised she had to make at least some pretence at good humour. Bartholomew sensed that her thoughts were a long way from the game and from Stanmore's solar. Stanmore himself sat apart from the others, a goblet of wine in his hand as he watched Philippa as intently as a hawk that was about to seize a rabbit. He rose to greet his brother-in-law, and Bartholomew could tell by the tense way he held his shoulders that the merchant was not happy.

'Have you learned anything new about Turke?' he asked in a low voice, pretending to help Bartholomew unfasten the clasp on his cloak so the others would not hear him. 'Edith will not allow me to tell Philippa and Giles to leave my house. She says it would be rude. But with each passing day, I grow more certain that Philippa had a hand in her husband's demise. I have encountered several murderers in my time – one of which was my own brother – but I have

335

never met one as calm and collected as Philippa.'

'Oswald,' said Bartholomew, half laughing as he pulled away from the merchant. 'We know Turke died from falling in the river. She may be involved in some plan involving the inheritance of his estate, but she did not kill him.'

'I am not so sure,' said Stanmore uneasily. 'Once, she told Edith she needed to rest and went to bed. Giles was bathing his feet, on your instructions. Later, Edith went to Philippa's room to make sure all was well and found it empty: she had gone out.' He regarded Bartholomew with pursed lips, as though that alone was sufficient to indict her of the most heinous of crimes.

'But slipping out does not mean she murdered her husband,' the physician pointed out.

'But when she goes out openly, even if it is only to St Michael's, she insists on having an escort. She says it would be improper for a recent widow to be seen on the streets alone. So what was she doing escaping my house all by herself? Answer me that!'

Bartholomew knew about Philippa's obsession with appearances, and agreed with Stanmore that it was odd that she insisted on an escort sometimes, but conveniently dispensed with one on other occasions. 'Do you know where she goes?' he asked.

Stanmore shook his head. 'Giles is worse – he disappears most days. These snows could isolate the town for months, and I may have this sinister pair in my house until February or March! It does not bear thinking about.'

'You are over-reacting,' said Bartholomew firmly. 'Even if Philippa or Giles did play some role in Turke's sudden desire for skating – and I doubt they did – there is no reason for either to set murderous eyes on anyone here. You have done them no wrong and, perhaps more importantly, they are not about to inherit your estates.'

He went to join Edith and Abigny at the fire. His sister glanced up at him, her dark eyes bright with laughter and happiness, and Bartholomew experienced a peculiar protective feeling. He hoped Stanmore's fears were unjustified, and the guests did not bring trouble to her house.

'I have just been told about a certain charity – a guild – that operates in the town,' he said, sitting opposite Abigny and watching him. Abigny did not glance up, but, like Edith, fixed his attention on the cup that held the small pieces of wood. He made his throw.

'A three, a five and a one,' he said. 'I am sure there are a good many guilds in Cambridge, Matt. Oswald is a member of two.'

'St Mary's and the Worshipful Guild of Drapers,' said Stanmore proudly. 'But which one are you talking about, Matt? Giles is right: there are dozens in Cambridge.'

'Dympna,' said Bartholomew, trying to watch Philippa and Abigny at the same time. 'It is a benevolent society that makes loans to desperate people.'

Neither Philippa nor Abigny responded in any way the physician could detect. Philippa still wore her fixed smile, and her eyes were full of distant thoughts. Bartholomew was not even sure she had noticed his arrival. Meanwhile, Abigny handed the dice to Edith and sat with his hands dangling between his knees to see what she would throw.

'I have never heard of it,' said Stanmore, the only person who seemed to be listening to the physician. 'What is it? A religious guild?'

'Two sixes and a four!' exclaimed Edith, clapping her hands in delight. 'I win! All three of my numbers are higher than yours.'

All three numbers, thought Bartholomew to himself. Was that the meaning of the triplet of figures he and Michael had seen on the vellum in Gosslinge's throat? But it could not be: most dice only went to four or six, and one of the numbers on the vellum had been eight.

'I know very little about Dympna,' he said, in reply to Stanmore's question. 'Other than the identity of one of its members.'

He fixed Abigny with a stare that was so intense that his

337

old room-mate was eventually obliged to look up. He appeared to be astonished. 'Do you mean me?' he exclaimed, with an expression of bemusement. 'You think *I* am a member of this institution with the odd name! Why?'

'Someone told me you asked for information about Dympna. His message to you is "no".'

'Father William!' said Abigny, with a smile. 'He approached me at the Christmas Day feast and started chattering about some mysterious society or other. You know how he is – subtle as a mallet in the groin. He was tapping his nose and winking and making all kinds of gestures that indicated he thought he and I shared a secret. Naturally, I was intrigued, so I let him believe I knew what he was talking about in the hope he would reveal more.'

'And did he?'

'Not enough to make sense. He seemed to think I was responsible for the loan of funds to the Franciscan Friary, and wanted me to know it was appreciated. I asked whether he had been offered any more money, to see whether the question would loosen his tongue further, but he merely offered to speak to Prior Pechem, and that was the end of the matter. I did not know what he was talking about then, and I do not now.'

'I ask because this society is becoming more aggressive about the return of its loans,' said Bartholomew, persisting with the discussion, even though he could see Abigny considered it over. 'Norbert received letters from Dympna and then was stabbed. I cannot help but wonder whether the two are connected.'

'Perhaps they are,' said Abigny with a shrug. 'But I do not know anything about it. What do you think, Philippa? Are you aware of this particular charity?'

Philippa dragged her thoughts to the present with obvious effort. 'The guild that paid for the repair of the Great Bridge when it started to collapse?' she asked, evidently struggling to recall what they had been talking about. 'Mayor Horwood talked of it at the feast – in tedious detail.'

338

'What did he say?' asked Bartholomew.

'Just that this charity had helped him with a problem, and that it is good there are still folk prepared to donate their wealth to help others.'

'Its name is Dympna,' said Bartholomew, watching her closely. When she did not react, he decided to adopt a more direct approach. 'That was the word your husband breathed with his dying breath.'

She stared at him, and some of the colour drained from her face. 'No one heard what he said,' she whispered at last. 'He spoke too softly.'

'I heard,' said Bartholomew. 'He said "Dympna".'

Stanmore disagreed. 'Actually, Matt, he said "temper". I told you: he was warning Philippa to be of a polite and gentle disposition.'

Philippa regarded him with as much disbelief as she had Bartholomew. 'Why would he do that? I do not warrant that kind of advice from a dying man.'

'Brother Michael believed the word was "Templar",' added Edith, looking from her husband to her brother. 'He thought you two had heard wrongly.'

Philippa gave a tired smile. 'And you have been speculating about the meaning of poor Walter's final words ever since? If it is so important to you, why did you not ask me? I would have told you.'

'You would?' asked Bartholomew uncertainly.

Philippa rubbed her eyes. 'You have all been kind since Walter died, and playing the role of a grieving widow has not been easy. Walter was a difficult man – rude, aggressive and demanding – and I cannot deny that life holds a certain charm without him in my future. But I did not want you to think me heartless; I wanted you to believe my grief was real.'

'Are you telling us it is not?' asked Edith in surprise.

'I married a man far older than me because I wanted a life of comfort and security. I sacrificed a good deal for it – my freedom and my spirit, not to mention a handsome lover who would have been a friend as well as a husband. Walter has sons who will inherit his fortune, and I saw that his premature death would end the life I had built at such cost. I will be a fat, middle-aged widow with nothing to offer any suitor.'

'You are not fat,' said Bartholomew gallantly. 'But there are dietary regimes that promote good health as well as a thinner figure. If you like, I can draw up—'

'Matt!' said Edith sharply. 'This is not the time.'

'I would have helped,' said Abigny, regarding his sister with gentle affection. 'I admit I have not amounted to much, with my token post at the law courts and my squandered fortune, but I would have looked after you.'

She gazed at him bleakly. 'You will wed this year. Do you think your salary can support me *and* your new wife? Will Janyne want her husband's sister living in her house? And you have missed my point: I do not want to struggle along on pennies. I would have married Matt if I had been content with that.'

Her face was haunted, and Abigny leaned across to take her hand in his. 'Your finances and your dreams are your business, Philippa. You do not have to share them with others.'

'It is better they know the truth,' she said tiredly, indicating Bartholomew and his family. 'I do not want them speculating, and coming up with answers that show me in a poorer light than even I deserve.' She took a deep breath and turned to Edith, apparently finding it easier to address her than the others. 'I did not know what to do with myself when I first heard the news about Walter. I could not imagine what would become of me – and Giles – just because Walter had elected to go skating.'

'You said he would never have done that,' prompted Bartholomew, when she fell silent.

'I still think he would not. He was too cautious to have ventured out on to weak ice. I suppose I shall never know why he did it. But then, when I heard he was still alive, I felt a sudden relief, as though I had been reprieved. He opened his eyes and looked at me, and I am sure he read the fear and apprehension for my future in my face. He said two words: "Temple" and "you".'

'Temple?' asked Edith, curiously. 'What does that mean?'

'It is the name of our home,' said Philippa. 'Temple House – because it has arches on the front like the Temple Church in Fleet. Those words told me that the house was mine, that he had made provision for me in his will. I am not penniless after all.'

Bartholomew gazed at her. So that was the reason for the change in her behaviour between when she first learned about Turke's accident and his death. She had gone from being a penniless widow with no future to the owner of a large and substantial home. He recalled their discussion at the Christmas feast, when she had mentioned the splendid house that bore resemblance to the Temple Church with its columns and round-headed windows.

'So that explains all this odd behaviour?' asked Stanmore, relieved. 'You were trying to maintain a grief that you do not genuinely feel?'

Philippa looked pained. 'Now you think me a hypocrite. I loved Walter in my own way, and I will miss him. And I shall respect his memory and do all a good widow should do. But I am not devastated by his death. However, I shall need to act my part until we have buried him and allowed his Fraternity friends to say their farewells.'

'You should have told us,' said Edith, sounding hurt. 'We can be trusted not to tell people that you are looking forward to a brighter future now Walter is gone.'

'You said you did not understand the meaning of Walter's final words,' said Bartholomew, trying not to sound accusing. 'But you did.'

Philippa gave a wry smile. 'Do you think I should have told you I had just received the happy news that I am the owner of the best house on Friday Street while my husband's corpse was still warm? That would not have been appropriate!'

'Neither was changing from debilitating grief to cool

efficiency in a matter of moments,' muttered Bartholomew. He spoke aloud, wishing she had chosen to be honest sooner. It would have saved a good deal of agitation for Stanmore. 'So, Walter did not mention Dympna, and my theories associating him with Norbert are wrong?'

'The only time I have ever heard that name was when Mayor Horwood mentioned it at the feast,' replied Philippa. 'He thought Dick Tulyet might be its leader.'

'Dick?' mused Bartholomew thoughtfully. Was that the link between Dympna and Norbert – that the beneficiary of one loan was Tulyet's cousin? But Tulyet would not have asked Michael to investigate if he had been responsible for Norbert's death, surely? 'Did Horwood say anything more about this guild?'

'Not that I recall,' replied Philippa. She shivered and edged closer to the fire. 'I had forgotten how cold it can be in this little town. I am not surprised Gosslinge succumbed to the weather.'

'When I was re-examining Gosslinge, I found something trapped in his throat,' said Bartholomew, watching as Edith fussed around Philippa with a woollen blanket. 'I think he choked, rather than died of the cold. Was he in the habit of putting things in his mouth?'

'Yes,' said Abigny immediately, nodding in surprise. 'His mouth was never empty, now that you mention it. There was always something poking out – a blade of grass or a sliver of wood for picking his teeth. He had restless jaws that always liked to be working on something.'

'He sounds like Brother Michael,' said Edith with a giggle. She prodded Abigny with her foot and indicated he was to roll the dice again. The conversation was at an end. Philippa huddled closer to the fire, and continued to stare into the flames, while Stanmore went to fetch more wood. Bartholomew watched her while he sipped his wine, thinking that for someone who had just been relieved of a tiresome husband and presented with a fine house, she still seemed preoccupied. He was certain there was something she had still not told them, and recalled Matilde's words – that there was something sad about Philippa. He wondered what it could be, and why she had not unburdened herself of that secret, too.

It was too late, too cold and too dark for Bartholomew to return to Michaelhouse once the evening was over – the traditional games of cross and pile, raffle, hasard and queek had been played, the seasonal food eaten and the spiced wine drunk – so he accepted a bed in Stanmore's attic. Once again, his dreams teemed with confused images and conversations, most of them featuring Philippa. He lay, half awake and half asleep, watching patterns made by the firelight move across the ceiling, and tried to make sense of the information he had gathered.

For the first time in several days, no snow fell during the night. A thick blanket of cloud served to insulate the Earth from the frigid night sky, and the temperature crept up until it was actually above freezing point. Compared to the conditions of the past several days, the little town was positively balmy, and Bartholomew felt overdressed and hot as he donned his various layers of tunics and jerkins the following morning. The warmer air weakened the icy hold of winter, and everything dripped. For the second day in a row, the streets were full of hissing, sloughing and cracking sounds as melting snow parted company with roofs, trees, walls and eaves. The ground no longer comprised hard-packed ice, but a lumpy brown slush that was knee deep in places.

Bartholomew left Stanmore's house before dawn, and prepared to wade through the thaw to St Michael's Church. He thought he was the only one awake, and was surprised to discover Philippa waiting for him, dressed in her black clothes. She wanted someone to walk with her when she went to say morning prayers for her husband's soul. She leaned heavily on Bartholomew's arm, her hood shielding her face in the manner expected of a woman who had been recently widowed. He noticed her shoes were thin and dainty

343

and did little to protect her feet from the icy muck of the High Street. The Philippa of his memories had been a practical woman, who would have worn boots. He wondered whether this Philippa had donned shoes because they looked better with her elegant fur cloak, or whether her mind was absorbed by other matters.

He stopped suddenly and turned to face her. They were near St Mary the Great, where hundreds of candles sent a flickering orange glow through the traceried windows to make intricate designs on the snow in its graveyard. People were gathering to celebrate the first Sunday after Christmas. She faced him with a wary expression, evidently anticipating what he was about to say.

'Those scars on Walter's legs,' he said. 'Why did you not want me to see them?'

Her face darkened. 'I have already told you. I do not know how he came by those marks, but he disliked them being seen by others. Of course I did him the service of keeping them from curious eyes when he lay dying. Why do you want to know, anyway?'

'Because there are questions about his death that remain unanswered,' said Bartholomew, standing his ground. 'You say he would not have gone skating on thin ice, and yet that is how he died. Why? And why did Gosslinge choke to death on a piece of vellum? Was he trying to eat it? Was he hiding it from someone? Was the vellum what the two intruders in our church were looking for?'

Philippa glared at him. 'Most of your questions pertain to Gosslinge's death, not Walter's. But why do you persist in meddling when I have asked you to leave us alone? I have already told you that Walter and I were not a happy couple. Is that not enough for you? Perhaps I should leave Edith and hire a bed in a friary or a convent until the roads clear and I can escape from this miserable little town.'

'All the friary guest halls are full, and I doubt you want to revisit St Radegund's Convent. The only place I know with spare rooms is the Gilbertine Friary, but their guest wing is close to the King's Head, which makes it noisy and sometimes dangerous.'

'Why do you mention the Gilbertine Friary, specifically?' she demanded coldly. 'What is it about that particular institution that makes you associate me with it?'

'It is the one with the vacant beds,' said Bartholomew, wishing he had never mentioned Walter's legs. 'Do not abandon Edith. She will be upset, and then she will be angry with me.'

'You would deserve it,' said Philippa, starting to walk again, this time without holding his arm. She skidded on slick ice, but stubbornly refused his help.

'I understand you hired the Chepe Waits last summer,' said Bartholomew, not wanting to walk in silence and so trying to make conversation. The words were only just out of his mouth when he realised this was not a topic entirely without contention either. It was something else he had suspected her of lying – or at least not being wholly truthful – about.

'Did I?' She sounded coolly uninterested as she negotiated her way around a sludge-filled morass that spanned most of the High Street. It was deep enough for a duck to swim on, and the bird poked under its lumpy surface in search of edibles with its tail in the air. 'Walter liked to provide music when colleagues from the Fraternity visited, so I suppose I may have employed them on his behalf.'

Since she sounded indifferent about the Waits, Bartholomew pressed on, grateful for any topic they could discuss without unpleasantness. 'Did they steal anything?' he asked. 'We have been told they remove things from the houses in which they work, and that they have amassed a fortune.'

She was surprised. 'Of course they stole nothing. Walter was very possessive of his property, and would not have tolerated any kind of theft by Frith and his cronies.'

'You know his name,' said Bartholomew, puzzled. 'A few moments ago, you barely recalled hiring them, and now you mention Frith's name.'

She gave a gusty sigh, to indicate she was unimpressed with the way he was reading so much into what was a casual discussion. 'It just came to me,' she snapped. 'Frith of Lincoln. And the woman with him is called Makejoy. I thought they seemed vaguely familiar at the feast, and you have just told me I had hired them. I suppose connections formed in my mind, and the names were suddenly there. Why are you interested in these Waits? Because they come from Chepe and may have known Gosslinge?'

'Did they know Gosslinge?'

'I have no idea,' she said, becoming exasperated. 'Chepe is more like a village than part of a large city, and residents do know each other. Gosslinge liked to go out and meet folk – Giles would say his motives were more commercial than friendly, but I do not know about that. All I can tell you is that Gosslinge knew a good many people.'

'What did Gosslinge think about Fiscurtune's death?' asked Bartholomew. 'Did he believe Walter was justified in stabbing him in Fishmongers' Hall?'

'Gosslinge was loyal,' she said simply. 'It would not matter what he thought, because he always supported what Walter did or said. But we are at St Michael's, and your friends are waiting for you. Goodbye, Matthew.'

CHAPTER 10

'YOU DO NOT SEEM TO BE WOOING YOUR WIDOW WITH MUCH skill,' said Clippesby critically, watching Philippa enter the Stanton Chapel to kneel by Turke's coffin. Suttone was with him, waiting for the morning mass to begin. It was peaceful in the church, which still smelled of the greenery that bedecked it. 'She is angry with you. If you want to attract her to your bed, you need to flatter and cajole her, not send her away like a swarm of angry bees.'

'I am not wooing her,' snapped Bartholomew, irritably. 'We do not even like each other.'

'That is a sign of love,' said Suttone knowledgeably. Bartholomew regarded him warily, and wondered why a pair of celibate friars thought they were in a position to advise him about romance.

'Antagonising her is a risky strategy, nonetheless,' Clippesby preached. 'Women are complex creatures, and sometimes do not grasp that bad temper is really an expression of love. I have seen more than one promising affair fail because of such misunderstandings, especially in the world of cats.'

'You should take her a lump of marchpane,' suggested Suttone. 'Women like sweet things, and marchpane should have her swooning in your arms.'

'He does not want her swooning,' said Clippesby practically. 'It is better she is conscious, so she can appreciate the full extent of his manly charms. I shall lend him my best shoes tonight. And my second-best cloak. Then he will look the part for lovemaking.'

'I have some scented oils he can douse himself with,' said Suttone, addressing Clippesby. 'And we can ask Cynric to buy him some tincture of borage in the Market Square.

Master Langelee tells me that borage encourages amorous feelings and gives a man plenty of strength for his exertions. She will soon be begging him to take her to the marriage bed.'

'Gentlemen, please!' begged Bartholomew, too appalled by their images of courtship to ask why the Master and the Carmelite friar should have had such a conversation in the first place. 'Why are you so intent that I marry? It is because you want me to resign my fellowship, so that Michaelhouse no longer offers a secular subject like medicine? Or are your jealous eyes on my room? I am not particularly attached to it. We can change, if you like.'

'That is not why we are trying to help,' said Suttone, offended. 'We are thinking of your happiness.' He slipped a fatherly arm around the physician's shoulders, and his voice became gentle. 'You see, Matthew, whatever Michael and Langelee tell you, there is no future in your affair with Matilde. She will never consent to marry you. She mentioned it to Yolande de Blaston. Yolande told Prior Pechem of the Franciscans at one of their sessions, and Pechem told William. So, you see, we are only trying to find you an alternative.'

'Lord!' muttered Bartholomew, horrified by the number of people who seemed to be intimately acquainted with his personal life. 'I had not thought about marrying anyone.'

'But you refuse to take final vows as a monk or a friar,' said Clippesby. 'So, you must be saving yourself for a woman. We just want you to find one who is not too old, has all her limbs and most of her teeth, and a little dowry to help you along.'

'I am quite happy as I am,' said Bartholomew, not sure whether to be touched or irritated by their meddling concern. 'I do not need your help in securing myself a woman, anyway. My sister is quite capable of doing that.'

It was meant to be a joke, but Suttone nodded gravely. 'That is true. Edith is a sensible woman who has your best interests at heart. Well, we shall say no more about it, then.

But let us know if you need advice on manly matters. I had a woman once – before I took the cowl – and Clippesby has had two.'

'One was a horse,' elaborated Clippesby confidentially. 'But perhaps you are right about Philippa. Her heart is already promised to another, and competition is always difficult. If you are the only one pursuing a woman, there is a good chance of a favourable outcome. But it would be undignified to fight over her.'

'I do not think Turke will be doing much pursuing,' said Bartholomew, looking to where Philippa knelt next to the coffin in the Stanton Chapel. Her posture was stiff, as though she was still angry, and she looked larger than usual, with her fur-lined cloak billowing around her.

'I imagine not,' said Clippesby. 'But I was referring to the other one.'

Bartholomew shot him a puzzled glance. 'What other one?'

'She will not remain a widow for long,' replied Clippesby airily. 'That is why Suttone and I thought you should try for the prize. But she has been spending a lot of time with this other man, so perhaps you are already too late, and we are wasting our time.'

'That is her brother,' said Suttone. 'He always escorts her, because she dislikes being unaccompanied. I heard her complaining about it when I was saying a mass for Turke. Abigny wanted to go on some errand of his own and she would not let him.'

'But she often walks alone,' said Clippesby, surprised. 'Ask any of the ducks or geese. They are not fooled by dark cloaks and plumed hats.'

'You mean she disguises herself?' asked Bartholomew, not sure what the Dominican was telling him. Clippesby was often extremely observant, and was frequently in possession of valuable information; Bartholomew knew from experience that just because Clippesby claimed an animal or a bird as his source did not necessarily mean that the snippet should be disregarded. It was part of Clippesby's insanity that he talked to – and received replies from – animals, spirits and even plants. Unfortunately, his interpretations of what he had seen or heard were often in error, and it took careful questioning to sort fact from supposition.

'She has a distinctive walk,' replied Clippesby. 'Her boots are too big, so she limps.'

'Limps?' asked Bartholomew. 'And wears a brown feathered hat? That sounds more like Giles to me.'

'Of course it is,' said Suttone in an undertone to Bartholomew.

'She goes to the stables behind the Gilbertine Friary at least once a day,' Clippesby went on, unperturbed by Bartholomew's scepticism. 'The horses are growing quite used to her now, and inform me that she always greets them politely.'

'The Gilbertine Friary?' asked Bartholomew, his thoughts whirling. Was that why she had snapped at him when he had inadvertently mentioned the friary to her in passing? 'She enters the stables, rather than the friary itself?'

'Of course,' said Clippesby, as though the physician were stupid. 'How could she greet the horses otherwise? They are not allowed in the friary: the Gilbertines do not want a mess on their floors. Philippa meets her lover – your rival – in the hay. There is never anyone there, because people cannot travel on horseback now that the snow has locked us all in the town together.'

'Who is he?' asked Bartholomew, wondering how Philippa had managed to secure herself a Cambridge beau so quickly. He rubbed a hand through his hair. Or was the man an outsider – perhaps one of the Waits whose names she had conveniently recalled a few moments before?

'The horses could not tell,' said Clippesby. 'But if you want to find out, you should visit the Gilbertine stables and lie in wait for them. Of course, it could be a member of Dympna. You know who I mean – the group that lends money for good causes?'

Bartholomew gaped at him. '*You* know about Dympna?

350

But we have only recently learned of its existence, and it has been a major question in this case from the beginning.'

'I do not know what it is,' said Suttone resentfully. 'No one told me.'

'I did not know it was important,' said Clippesby to Bartholomew. 'Michael does not discuss his investigations with me, so I never know what I can do to help. I have offered him my services in the past, but he has always declined.'

'That is probably because you are insane,' Suttone explained gravely.

'It should not make any difference,' objected Clippesby, hurt. 'But I know about Dympna, and have done for months. I learned about it from the King's Head horses. They hear a good deal, of course, residing in a place where there are so many travellers. They told me Robin of Grantchester is a member, but he is excluded when major decisions are made.'

Bartholomew regarded him with open scepticism. 'Robin of Grantchester? I do not think so! Why would a group of well-meaning men invite Robin to be a member? You know what he is like. He is not even honest.' But even as he spoke, he recalled that it had been Robin who had brought Dunstan his supplies – the supplies that William said had come from Dympna. Perhaps Clippesby was right after all.

'The horses do not know the answers to everything,' said Clippesby impatiently. 'You will have to ask Robin himself. But I should go. I promised the Sheriff's donkey I would drop by today.'

He left abruptly, without waiting for the office to begin, and Bartholomew and Suttone stared after him in silence. His habit swung around his ankles, and the hair around his tonsure stood up like a spiky, irregular crown. He was wearing a boot on one foot and a shoe on the other, and Bartholomew noticed a ferret poking from his scrip.

'He is a strange fellow,' said Suttone unnecessarily. 'He is quite serious about these conversations with beasts and birds, you know. He really believes they speak to him.'

'I know,' said Bartholomew. 'But the truly frightening

thing is that his discussions with animals sometimes make a lot more sense than the ones I have with people.'

Breakfast that day was not a relaxed occasion. Quenhyth had lost the leather scrip he used to carry his pens and ink, and was making it clear he thought the Waits were responsible. Langelee informed the student that even vagrants were unlikely to set their sights on such a meagre prize, and declined to bow to Quenhyth's demands that the jugglers' belongings should be searched immediately. Deynman quickly became bored with Quenhyth's complaints, and offered to buy him another scrip, but Quenhyth was implacable.

'The Senior Proctor must take action,' he announced, rising to his feet and pointing a bony finger at Michael. 'A crime has been committed.'

The monk, sitting in the body of the hall between Bartholomew and Suttone, was unmoved. 'I am eating, and you know I allow nothing to interfere with such an important task.'

'But this is a *crime*,' insisted Quenhyth, unrepentant. 'The Waits have broken the law, which means that you are a traitor to the King because you are refusing to uphold the laws he has made.'

The expression on Michael's face made the student sit again, very quickly, and Quenhyth saw he had gone too far. In the hall, no one spoke or moved, as every scholar and servant waited to see what Michael would do. The silence seemed to stretch for an eternity. Eventually, Michael started chewing again.

'I am eating,' he repeated. 'And, as I have already informed you, nothing interrupts that which I hold sacred. If you are so convinced of the Waits' guilt, then *you* can rummage through their possessions.'

Quenhyth gazed defiantly at him, then stalked out. Deynman gave a cheer, which was quickly taken up by the others in the hall, and Bartholomew was surprised at how

352

unpopular Quenhyth had become. He was not hated, as Norbert had been, but he was despised, and no opportunity was allowed to pass that enabled his fellow students to express that feeling.

'I am not sure that was good advice, Brother,' he said to Michael, walking to the window to watch Quenhyth stalk across the yard. 'No one wants his belongings pawed through, and your challenge may well see Quenhyth in more trouble than he can handle. Frith and Jestyn are rough men, while Makejoy and Yna can probably hold their own in a fight, too.'

Michael waved a knife dismissively. 'They will let Quenhyth nowhere near their things. And anyway, he knows I did not mean it literally. He is not entirely stupid.'

'He should have become a fishmonger, like his father,' said Suttone disapprovingly. 'He is much more suited to dealing with dead fish than with living people.'

'I had forgotten he hails from a fishy family,' said Michael, his mouth full of bread.

'His father knew Turke and Fiscurtune,' Bartholomew reminded him. 'They were in the Fraternity of Fishmongers together. Quenhyth knows Philippa, too, and has visited her once or twice at Edith's house.'

While they ate, and the Lord of Misrule entertained himself by ordering various students to stand on their heads and recite ribald ballads, Bartholomew told Michael all that had transpired the previous night concerning Philippa and Abigny, and mentioned Clippesby's claim that Robin the surgeon was a member of the altruistic money-lending group. The monk was thoughtful.

'You were always suspicious of the fact that Philippa declined to acknowledge her previous association with the Waits. Now you learn that not only does she remember them, but she knows their names. However, you must bear in mind that when she first saw them, it was at the Christmas feast, where they had that row with Langelee about whether they should be fed. I would not blame any respectable lady for declining to admit she had hired them under those circumstances.'

'We do not know that was the first time she saw them,' Bartholomew pointed out. 'In fact, it was almost certainly not. Philippa had a room in the King's Head before going to Edith's house – and that was where the Waits stayed while they looked for an employer.'

'True,' acknowledged Michael. 'However, she had planned to be gone from Cambridge quickly, and probably thought it would not matter whether she was truthful about them or not. Then the snow prevented her from leaving, and she was stuck with her lie for longer than she anticipated. What do you think? Should we follow her when she goes to her lover?'

'No,' said Bartholomew shortly.

'Why not? Are you not interested to learn who has captured her heart?' Michael snapped his fingers in sudden understanding. 'I know why you are reluctant! You think that if she is meeting a secret lover in a location like the Gilbertine Friary, then it is likely to be someone she met during her previous life here in Cambridge. That means it is someone she knew while she was courting you, and you do not want to learn you were jilted long before she went to London.'

'That is not the reason at all,' said Bartholomew irritably. 'I just do not think that sort of behaviour is courteous. It can have no bearing on our investigation, and we would merely be satisfying a salacious urge to pry.'

'You are wrong,' declared Michael immediately. 'Of course it has a bearing on the case! A woman with a lover is far more likely to rid herself of an unwanted husband than one without. Who could it be? A master from another College? It will not be a Michaelhouse man – there are only Kenyngham and William left from the old days, and I do not see her indulging in a clandestine affair with either of them. Although William has always been a dark horse . . .'

'You cannot believe everything Clippesby says, Brother. Philippa may well be meeting someone, but that does not necessarily imply an affair. That was an assumption on his part. Horses and rats are not reliable sources of information.'

'I was also busy last night, while you were enjoying your sister's hospitality,' said Michael, changing the subject as he reached for more bread. 'I have learned more about Fiscurtune, the man Turke murdered.'

'How?' Bartholomew was surprised. 'Did you meet someone who knew him?'

Michael nodded. 'And you and I are going to see him together, as soon as we have finished this excellent breakfast.'

Bartholomew wanted to know there and then what Michael had discovered, but the monk was annoyingly secretive, and refused to divulge anything. After Gray had concluded the meal with a clever imitation of one of Langelee's careless Latin graces, they drew on cloaks, Bartholomew looped his medicine bag over his shoulder, and he and Michael left the College to walk in the direction of the Great Bridge. At first, the physician could not imagine who they were going to see, and then it became clear. He smiled with pleasure.

'Matilde! She has her network of informants, and we are going to see what she knows.'

'No,' said Michael, grinning at his friend's disappointment. 'We are going to visit Dick Tulyet – for two reasons. First, he happened to mention to me last night that he once met Fiscurtune in Chepe. And second, Mayor Horwood seems to believe that Dick is a member of Dympna, so I thought we should ask him about it.'

'We did ask, Brother,' said Bartholomew, glancing resentfully up the lane where Matilde's cosy house was located. 'When we first learned Norbert received letters from Dympna, Dick told us, quite categorically, that a woman called Dympna could have nothing to do with Norbert's death and that we should look elsewhere for our answers.'

'I know,' said Michael. 'And so I am inclined to believe Horwood was right, and that Dick knows more about Dympna than he was prepared to tell. But luck is with you, my friend, because here comes Matilde. You will see her after all.'

Matilde was a shaft of bright light in a dowdy scene. The loose plaits of her hair shone with health, her clothes were clean, neat and colourful, and her face had the complexion of smooth cream. Bartholomew thought she made everything around her look shabby and soiled. When she saw the physician, her face lit with a smile of welcome.

'I have barely seen you since Dunstan died,' she said reproachfully. 'It would have been nice to share a cup of wine and exchange fond memories of him.'

'I have been busy,' said Michael, assuming that he was included in the comment. 'Although I have little to show for it. Norbert's killer still walks free, while there are all manner of questions surrounding the deaths of Turke and Gosslinge.'

Matilde nodded. 'Edith mentioned that Oswald believed at first that Philippa had hastened their ends. Then he learned that most of Philippa's curious behaviour relates to the fact that she wanted to celebrate her widowhood, but could not. However, there is more to it than that.'

'Meaning?' demanded Michael peremptorily.

'I mentioned days ago that I thought she carried a sad secret with her. She was sorrowful even before Turke died. I still think I am right: there is something in Philippa's life that is causing her considerable anguish. She is not good at hiding it.'

'A lover?' suggested Michael casually.

Matilde was thoughtful. 'Possibly. But not one who makes her happy. Her sour expressions and irritable temper are not signs of a woman riding on a whirlwind of glorious infatuation.'

'You do not like her, do you?' said Michael, regarding her closely.

'No,' said Matilde bluntly. 'I cannot imagine what made you fall for her, Matthew. She is everything you profess to dislike: obsessed with wealth and appearances, and difficult to draw into conversations that do not include hairstyles, jewellery or food prices.'

'She was not always like that,' objected Bartholomew. 'She

was lively and funny, and we talked for hours about many things – philosophy, foreign countries, music, medicine . . .'

'Who did the talking?' asked Matilde coolly. 'I cannot imagine *her* holding forth about Galen's theories pertaining to the colour of urine or the architecture of Italy. But your betrothals are none of my affair, although I am glad for both of you that that one failed.'

She walked away, leaving the two men staring after her. 'You should ask Matilde to marry you,' recommended Michael. 'She may accept, and she keeps a good cellar. I would not mind visiting you in *her* house.'

'Rumour has it she does not want to marry anyone,' said Bartholomew, thinking about the whispers that had reached him via the Mayor, the Franciscan Prior, Father William and finally Clippesby and Suttone.

Michael shook his head in amused contempt. 'You know nothing about women, Matt! Let me give you an analogy. Lombard slices are my favourite pastry. If I were to tell you that I would never touch one again, what would you do? You would buy me a dozen, to induce me to rethink my position. That is what Matilde is doing: she is saying she will not do something so that you will persuade her to do otherwise. Also, the poor woman has been waiting a long time for you. You cannot blame her for wanting folk to think it is her refusals that are preventing the match, rather than the fact that you have not bothered to ask.'

Bartholomew gazed at him. 'Do you think she would agree?'

Michael shrugged. 'Perhaps. But perhaps not. Who knows? You may have dithered too long, even for her. However, I can offer you one piece of advice: if you do become betrothed, do not allow another fiancée to disappear to London without you.'

Bartholomew was deep in thought as he walked with Michael towards Tulyet's house near the Great Bridge. When he happened to glance up from watching where he was placing his feet in the treacherous muck, he spotted a familiar figure making its way towards them. For a brief moment he thought it was Philippa, but it was Abigny.

Philippa and her brother were of a similar height, and both had abandoned the flowing locks of youth for the more conventional styles of middle age – Abigny's cropped short and Philippa's coiled in plaits. Both possessed cloaks with hoods, like most winter travellers, and neither was in the habit of walking fast. However, Abigny's plumed hat made him distinctive, whereas Philippa favoured a goffered veil – yellow when she had arrived, but dyed black since Turke's death. The goffered style comprised a half-circle of linen draped over the head with a broad frill along the straight edge framing the face. Philippa and Abigny wearing their preferred headgear could not be mistaken for each other, but Philippa and Abigny with their cloaks' hoods raised or their hats exchanged might.

The physician thought back to the time of the plague. Philippa and her brother had changed places then, too, fooling folk for several days. Could they be doing the same thing a second time? He recalled Stanmore commenting on the amount of time Abigny spent outside. Was it actually Philippa in disguise? No one would look too closely, because it was common knowledge that she declined to leave the house on Milne Street without an escort. Bartholomew saw that was probably just a ruse, designed to ensure no one would suspect her of going out at all.

All at once Bartholomew knew Clippesby was right: it was not Abigny who ran the errands around the town, but Philippa. He knew perfectly well Abigny was not exaggerating when he complained about the pain in his feet, and the physician realised with disgust that he should have guessed days ago that the clerk had not been traipsing endlessly around in the cold and the wet. His feet simply would not have allowed him to do it.

'Giles,' he called, attracting his old room-mate's attention. 'Where is Philippa?'

'In the church with Walter,' replied Abigny, wincing. 'These feet are no better, Matt. Do you have no stronger cure to offer me?'

'Only the recommendation that you stay in and keep them warm and dry.'

'I *have* been staying in,' snapped Abigny, pain making him irritable. He glanced at the physician furtively, realising he had just said something he should not have done.

'I know,' said Bartholomew softly. 'It is not you who has been seen all over the town. What has Philippa been doing?'

'I do not know what you are talking about.' Abigny tried to push his way past.

Bartholomew grabbed his arm. 'Who has Philippa been meeting? Why does she feel the need to sneak around in disguise, rather than going openly to meet her friend?'

Abigny sighed heavily, while Michael listened to the exchange in astonishment. 'I am no good at this kind of thing,' said the clerk tiredly. 'It is a pity, because I might be offered a better post at the law courts if I were more expert at lying and subterfuge. The King likes men with those skills.'

'So?' demanded Bartholomew, not to be side-tracked. 'What do you say to my questions?'

'I say you should ask Philippa. They are not my secrets to reveal. I have my failings, but breaking confidences is not among them.'

'Then you can reveal some secrets of your own,' said Michael. 'You met a man called Harysone in the King's Head. Why?'

Abigny gazed at him in astonishment. 'That is none of your business! What did you do? Follow me there, after I met you near the Trumpington Gate?'

'Yes,' replied Michael bluntly. 'And Harysone is a suspect in a murder enquiry, so it is not casual inquisitiveness that makes me ask you about him: my questions are official.'

'I went to buy his book,' replied Abigny, evidently alarmed by Michael's veiled threats. 'It is about fish, and I thought it would make a suitable gift for the Fraternity of Fishmongers in Walter's memory. It is packed in my saddle-bag at Edith's house. I can show you, if you like.'

'You bought Harysone's scribblings?' asked Michael in disgust. 'To commemorate Turke?'

'Why not?' flashed Abigny. 'There is a certain justice in purchasing a volume of dubious scholarship as a tribute to a dubious man. Walter would have hated the errors in it, and it will give me no small satisfaction to see the thing forever bearing his name in the Fishmongers' Hall.'

'What about Dympna?' asked Bartholomew, changing the subject. 'I do not believe you know nothing about that. Pechem and William would not have answered your questions if they thought you were asking out of idle curiosity.'

Abigny rubbed his hands over his face, then gave a rueful smile. 'I thought I had deceived you successfully about that. You seemed to believe me at the time.'

'We did not,' said Michael. 'It takes a far more accomplished liar than you to fool the University's Senior Proctor.'

'You were not there – it was a discussion between Matt and me,' Abigny pointed out coolly. He addressed Bartholomew. 'You were right to assume I knew more about Dympna than I revealed. However, my knowledge dates from the Death, when the charity was established. I was a founding member, but resigned when I left Cambridge and have heard nothing from it since. That was why I pestered William for information. It really was "idle curiosity", as you put it.'

'Why him?' asked Michael.

'I heard in the King's Head that Dympna had financed some repairs to the Franciscan Friary. I thought William might be able to tell me more about it. Of course, he could not, and neither could Pechem. It was never an open charity, but it has become much more secret since I left. I suppose it is to safeguard itself against too many claims for its funds.'

'Tell us what you do know,' ordered Michael. 'It may help.'

'I doubt it,' said Abigny. 'Dympna started during the Death, when men were healthy one moment and dead the next. Wealthy folk gave friars gold for the poor, hoping their charity would save them from infection. Dympna was founded using these benefactions, so the money could be fairly and properly distributed. You see, once or twice, mistakes were made, and unscrupulous folk made off with funds they should not have had. Including Michaelhouse, I might add.'

'Michaelhouse?' asked Michael, astonished. 'We never made a claim from Dympna.'

'Thomas Wilson did, though,' replied Abigny. 'You will recall he was Master during the Death and was greedy and corrupt. He inveigled funds from Dympna that he should not have been given, and they went directly into his own coffers. You must have heard the stories about how rich he was when he died.'

Bartholomew knew all about Wilson's ill-gotten wealth. He and Michael had recovered some of it a couple of years ago, but not before men had died over it.

'Is that all Dympna is?' pressed Michael. 'A charity?'

Abigny raised his hands, palms upward. 'It was a charity five years ago, but who knows what it is now? That was why I asked William about it, and why I have made several journeys around the town, even though my feet pain me. I am curious to know what it has become.'

'Why?' asked Bartholomew.

Abigny smiled. 'Because I feel honoured to be one of its original members. It is a worthy cause, and I hope it thrives for many years. But standing in the cold is agony for me. You must come to Milne Street, if you wish to talk further. Good morning.'

'Is he telling the truth now, do you think?' asked Michael of Bartholomew, as the clerk hobbled away.

'He is telling the truth about his sore feet. And as for the rest – I have no idea.'

Dick Tulyet was pleased to see Bartholomew and Michael, and invited them into the warm chaos of his house on Bridge Street. His energetic son was racing here and there with a

361

wooden sword, an item that Bartholomew thought was far too dangerous a thing to place in the destructive hands of the youngest Tulyet. The child was in constant trouble, much to the consternation of his sober and law-abiding parents.

Tulyet led Bartholomew and Michael to the room he used as an office, where he slipped a bar across the door, explaining that young Dickon would dash in and disturb them if it were left unlocked. The ear-splitting sounds of the boy's battle calls echoed from the solar, where his mother and a couple of servants tried to keep him quiet until his father's visitors left. The Tulyets would never have another child, and both treated the boy far more tenderly than was warranted for such a brutish little ruffian. Dickon was rapidly becoming a tyrant, and Bartholomew's heart always sank when he was summoned to tend the brat's various minor injuries – cuts and bruises usually acquired by doing something he had been told not to do.

'Dympna,' said Michael, pouring himself a cup of wine from the jug that stood on the windowsill before settling comfortably on a cushioned bench. 'What does that mean to you, Dick? Mayor Horwood intimated you know something about it.'

'Is this relevant to Norbert's death?' asked Tulyet warily. 'Only I would rather not discuss it, if there is a choice.'

'Dympna sent a number of notes to Norbert, summoning him to meetings in St Michael's Church,' said Michael. 'You already know this, because I told you. Then a note from Dympna was discovered inside the corpse of a man called Gosslinge. So, I think information about this strange group could well be relevant – if not to Norbert's murder, then to Gosslinge's death.'

'Very well,' said Tulyet reluctantly. 'We swore an oath that we would not speak about Dympna without due cause, but the murder of my cousin *is* due cause. I think no one would take issue with that. I shall tell you about Dympna, but please do not make anything I say public.'

'You claimed you knew nothing about it on Christmas

Day,' said Michael accusingly. 'You told me I would waste my time if I investigated Dympna.'

'The latter statement is true, but the former is not,' replied Tulyet evenly. 'I denied knowing a woman called Dympna – and that is correct – but I did not say I knew nothing about it. And I genuinely believed that enquiries into Dympna would bring you no closer to Norbert's killer, that it would lead you to waste time. It seems I was wrong.'

'You were,' affirmed Michael testily.

'But I do not see how! Norbert *did* petition Dympna for funds, but apart from a single message refusing his application, Dympna had no correspondence with him. I cannot imagine where these other missives came from.'

'Let us go over what we know,' said Michael. 'Dympna is a charitable group that helps people in need. We know it supplied funds to the Franciscan Friary, for example.'

Tulyet nodded. 'It was founded during the Death, but I was made a member later, when I became Sheriff. Originally, gifts of money were made to the needy, but it soon became clear that Dympna would run dry if that practice continued. It was decided to make loans instead, so that larger and more useful sums could be offered. By the time I joined, most of Dympna's transactions involved loans; there are very few gifts these days.'

'So, Dympna is just a money-lending fraternity,' said Michael dismissively.

'Not at all. Moneylenders make profits from interest. But Dympna does not charge interest, nor does it demand repayment by specific dates.'

'Then why do people repay you at all?'

'Because Dympna does not help just anyone. Each case is carefully considered, and the honesty and integrity of the applicant is assessed. We would not lend money to someone we could not trust to pay us back. So, for example, we made loans to pay irate builders at Bene't, when the College suddenly found itself without the funds to pay for work already completed; and we made one to allow the Carmelites to buy new habits when a fire robbed them of most of their clothes.'

'And the recipients always pay you back?' asked Michael doubtfully.

'Always, but never with interest – unless they choose to make a donation for our future work. The Carmelites were generous in that respect, although there was no pressure on them to do so.'

'Who are the other members of Dympna?' asked Michael.

Tulyet hesitated, but then seemed to reach a decision. 'There are four of us. But you must *never* reveal our identities. If that happens, and everyone learns who we are, we will be overwhelmed with demands for help, and our funds will dissipate like mist in the summer sun. Then Dympna will be dissolved, and the town will lose something good.'

'Who?' pressed Michael. 'You, and three others?'

'Master Kenyngham is one, and Robin of Grantchester is another.'

'Robin?' asked Bartholomew, astonished that Clippesby had been right, and even more astonished that a disreputable fellow like Robin should be chosen to serve an altruistic organisation.

'Kenyngham?' asked Michael at the same time. 'I suppose that should not surprise me. He is exactly the kind of man to engage in kindly acts and keep his beneficence a secret.'

'Robin is not, though,' said Bartholomew. 'Why did you select him to help?'

'Many of the people he treats die or become very ill,' explained Tulyet. 'They often need Dympna to pay for healing potions or to allow their families to bury them. Robin keeps us informed of who might require such assistance.'

'I should have guessed this ages ago,' said Bartholomew, putting together facts in his mind. 'All the evidence was there, but I did not make the connections. We were told that Robin has been associated with various acts of charity recently – by Ailred, among others. It was also Robin who brought food for Dunstan after Athelbald died.'

'That was not Dympna,' said Tulyet. 'Each transaction

must be agreed by all four members, but we have not met for several weeks now. Dympna did not help Dunstan. As I said, we seldom make gifts, only loans. We would not have lent money to Dunstan, because dying men are unlikely to pay us back. Robin must have arranged that out of the goodness of his heart.'

'I do not think so!' said Bartholomew, laughing at the notion.

'Kenyngham, then,' said Tulyet. 'He is generous and compassionate. So is Father Ailred of Ovyng. I am lucky to have two such honest and kindly souls to work with.'

'Ailred is the last member?' said Michael. 'Now, that *is* interesting! What was his reaction when Norbert's classmates said he had received messages from Dympna, Matt? Can you remember? Indignant? Thoughtful? Concerned?'

'He told us we should look elsewhere for answers,' said Bartholomew. 'Just like Dick.'

Tulyet winced. 'What else could I do? Dympna has done a great deal of good in the town. Ailred feels as I do – that we should do all we can to protect it, so it can continue to help the needy.'

'Robin lent Ailred a backgammon board and pieces,' recalled Bartholomew. 'I was surprised at the time that they knew each other well enough for borrowing and lending, but now I see exactly how that came about: they are colleagues.'

'Robin is hardly our colleague,' said Tulyet in distaste. 'But he serves his purpose, and we have no complaints about the way he discharges his responsibilities.'

'We shall speak to him and the other two members later,' vowed Michael. 'But where do you keep Dympna's money?' He looked around him, as though he expected a large chest filled with coins to manifest itself.

'I cannot tell you – not because I am refusing to co-operate, but because I do not know. It moves between members, so no outsider will guess where it is and steal it – a chest of coins is a tempting target for thieves. It is Kenyngham's turn to be keeper at the moment.'

'Kenyngham?' asked Michael doubtfully. 'You entrust all that gold to a man who cares so little for worldly possessions? What if he forgets where he has stored it?'

Tulyet laughed. 'He is not *that* absent-minded. But we know accidents happen – it would be unfortunate if the keeper died, and no one knew where the box was hidden. So, the keeper always tells one other member as a safeguard. He must have told Ailred, because I do not know, and we do not let Robin near the actual money. The temptation might prove too much.'

'How long has it been with Kenyngham?' asked Bartholomew.

'Three weeks, perhaps. Ailred had it before him. Why? Are you saying that Norbert's death has something to do with the chest being passed from Ailred to Kenyngham? That Ailred stored it somewhere in Ovyng, where Norbert lived?'

'It is possible,' said Michael. 'The timing certainly fits, because Norbert has been dead for twelve days now, and he started to receive letters from "Dympna" about a week before he died. That is roughly three weeks in total. Do you really have no idea where Kenyngham keeps it?'

Tulyet's face creased in a frown of concentration. 'I imagine it is with the Gilbertine friars. I expect you would have noticed a chest in Michaelhouse.'

'How big is it?' asked Bartholomew, trying to envisage potential hiding places.

'It is a walnut chest, perhaps the length of my forearm, and about two hand widths deep.'

'I know where it is,' said Bartholomew, smiling as he recalled various incidents that should have warned him sooner that something was amiss. 'The conclave.'

'It is not,' said Michael firmly. 'The conclave's contents comprise benches, a table, two chairs and some rugs. There are no walnut-wood boxes there, because we would have noticed.'

'About three weeks ago – the time the chest passed to Kenyngham – the floorboards in the conclave became

366

uneven,' said Bartholomew. 'We have all stumbled over them, and William hurt himself quite badly. I suspect that is where Kenyngham has stored Dympna.'

'I do not see Kenyngham prising up floorboards to make himself a secret hiding place,' said Michael scornfully. 'He is not sufficiently practical.'

'That is probably why the floor is now uneven,' said Bartholomew. 'However, he did tell Langelee that he worked with wood before he became a friar. Remember?'

Michael gnawed his lower lip. 'I do, now you mention it. And I recall his odd reaction when he learned the students planned to use the conclave for the duration of the Twelve Days. He was appalled, and that surprised me because he does not normally care about such things. He was not concerned about his personal comfort, as we all assumed: he was worried about access to his chest.'

'And once I saw him working on some documents,' said Bartholomew, remembering the first night he had been driven by cold to spend the night in the conclave. 'I asked him what he was doing, and he declined to tell me. Doubtless that was Dympna's business, too.'

'We shall look into it, and recommend the thing be moved to the Gilbertine Friary,' said Michael. 'I do not want our students unearthing it – especially this week, when we have a Lord of Misrule to make stupid suggestions about how it should be spent.'

'You say Dympna refused to lend Norbert money?' asked Bartholomew of Tulyet, wanting to bring the discussion back to the student's murder.

'He did not meet our two basic criteria – that the money is for a worthy cause and that it will be repaid. Where are these messages? May I see them? I may recognise the writing.'

'All destroyed,' said Michael. 'I have searched Norbert's possessions on at least three occasions, and found nothing.'

'Perhaps Godric was lying about them,' suggested Bartholomew. 'Ailred said he has peculiar ideas about love-letters and suchlike.'

'Norbert received them,' said Michael firmly. 'The other Ovyng lads saw them too, remember?' He turned to Tulyet. 'And you are sure Kenyngham, Ailred or Robin have not written to Norbert in Dympna's name?'

'I am sure Dympna gave nothing to Norbert. We discuss every loan made – no one person is allowed to act alone, because that would leave us open to charges of corruption.'

'Ailred,' said Bartholomew. 'He had the chest, and Norbert lived in his hostel. There is a connection here. Perhaps Norbert found the chest and stole from it, so Ailred sent messages demanding it back. Or perhaps Ailred made an exception for Norbert, because he was a member of his hostel.'

'Made an illegal loan, you mean?' asked Tulyet doubtfully. 'Ailred is an honest fellow. I do not see him breaking our rules – especially for Norbert, who would have spent the money on his own pleasures.'

'Well, we shall have to ask Ailred himself,' said Michael, draining the wine in Bartholomew's goblet as he prepared to leave. 'And we shall ask him about the murdered Chepe fishmonger John Fiscurtune, too, since I have reason to believe he and Ailred were related.'

Bartholomew and Tulyet gazed at him in astonishment, and Michael's face became smug when he saw he had startled them.

'Fiscurtune?' asked Tulyet. 'The man Turke killed, whom I told you last night that I had met many years ago?'

Bartholomew had forgotten Michael's mention of a previous association between Tulyet and the dead fishmonger. He raised his eyebrows questioningly, and Tulyet spread his hands to indicate he knew little of interest.

'I met Fiscurtune before the Death, in the market at Chepe. He sticks in my mind for two reasons: first, because he was unforgivably rude, and second, because he was totally devoid of teeth. Fortunately, an excess of gums rendered his speech indistinct, so most folk could not understand him. But I am not surprised someone tired of his offensive manners and murdered him.'

'We should see Ailred, Matt, and ask him about Fiscurtune. I think he has met the fangless fishmonger far more recently than Dick has done.'

'How do you know that?' asked Tulyet, surprised. 'Fiscurtune had no association with Cambridge as far as I know. He has certainly not been here recently, because I assure you I would have noticed him.'

'I came across the information last night, when Matt was visiting Edith,' said Michael, pleased with himself. 'I trawled through some University documents and discovered that Ailred hails from near Lincoln – not Lincoln itself, but a small village just outside it.'

'We know that,' said Bartholomew. 'It is no secret: he is very proud of the fact that he is a Lincolnshire man.'

'The name of his manor is Fiscurtune,' announced Michael momentously.

'It is a common name,' warned Tulyet. 'I imagine any village with some kind of fishing industry may have taken the Saxon word "fisc" for fish, and added "tun" for village or manor. You cannot connect Ailred with your dead fish-monger on that evidence alone.'

'I do not believe in coincidences,' said Michael pompously and untruthfully. 'Anyway, when I learned where Ailred spent his early years, I visited Sheriff Morice, who gave me permission – for a price – to refer to the taxation lists compiled in the days of the Conqueror. They are a good source of information about places in obscure parts of the kingdom.'

'Lincolnshire is not obscure,' said Bartholomew, amused by Michael's description.

'Morice asked for money before he let you see Domesday?' asked Tulyet, horrified. 'It is just as well he is not investigating Norbert's death, because I do not want to be presented with a bill for his labours, as well as with a killer!'

'It is your fault for resigning,' retorted Michael unsympathetically. 'But I learned from Domesday that Fiscurtune boasts three and a half fisheries.'

'Fisheries,' mused Bartholomew. 'Fiscurtune was a

fishmonger, and so was Turke. Now we learn that Ailred hails from a village with fisheries. Perhaps there *is* a connection here.'

'Fiscurtune village is small,' Michael went on. 'So, assuming I am right, and the murdered John Fiscurtune and Ailred hail from the same settlement, then it follows that they must have known each other. Indeed, I feel they knew each other rather well. Was there any physical resemblance between Fiscurtune and Ailred, Dick?'

'Fiscurtune had no teeth,' said Tulyet apologetically. 'It changed his face so much it is impossible to say.' His expression became thoughtful. 'However, now that I think about it, I do vaguely recall Fiscurtune mentioning a kinsman who was the head of a Cambridge hostel.'

'Ha!' exclaimed Michael with immense satisfaction.

Bartholomew walked briskly towards Ovyng Hostel, urging Michael to hurry. He sensed that Ailred had the answers to many questions, and wanted to speak to him as soon as possible. Michael puffed along behind him, growing more breathless and red-faced with every step. The thaw was continuing apace, and the town was a morass of sticky slush and sloppy, ice-spangled puddles. Snow was dropping from roofs in clots, and Bartholomew paused for a few moments to excavate a cat that was buried by a sudden fall. It clawed him when it was freed, and raced down one of the darker runnels, as if mortified by its sodden fur and bedraggled appearance.

'There is Robin of Grantchester,' said Bartholomew, pointing to a hunched figure that was making its way uncertainly down the High Street. 'Robin!'

The surgeon leapt in alarm and started to run. It was an instinctive reaction, and something he often did when someone hailed him. It usually meant he had lost a patient and was afraid the deceased's family were out for revenge.

'Oh, it is you,' said Robin, relieved when he saw it was Bartholomew who had caught his arm and arrested his desperate flight. 'I thought it was a relative of Dunstan and Athelbald.'

'Why would they chase you? You did not treat them – I did.'

'They are both dead, and people tend to associate me with deaths, even though I am not usually there when they happen.' Bartholomew knew that was true: Robin's patients died of fright, pain or poisoned blood days or hours after he had finished his grisly business with his rusty knives. 'Fifteen years ago I extracted a nail from Dunstan's hand. I thought his kinsmen might believe that brought about his demise.'

'Dympna,' said Michael, pronouncing the name with relish. 'Tell me about Dympna.'

Robin's small eyes narrowed. 'What are you talking about? I know no one of that name.'

'It is a money-lending charity,' said Bartholomew, watching Robin shift and turn uneasily, like a cornered rat. 'And you are one of its four members.'

'Clippesby,' said Robin in disgust. 'I had a feeling he was eavesdropping when I confided in Helena. She is my only true friend, and I often talk to her when I am lonely or have enjoyed a little wine and wish for a companion who will listen without interrupting.'

'She sounds like a saint,' said Michael. 'But I do not know her.'

'My pig,' said Robin. 'A man needs friendship, and there is none better than that offered by an animal. They are loyal and do not judge you. Clippesby feels the same way, and likes to spend time with the horses in the stables of the Gilbertine Friary, near my house. Doubtless he heard me confiding in Helena then.'

'And he assumed the disembodied voice came from the horses,' said Bartholomew, amused. 'I wondered why information from his animal friends is so often accurate. It is not because the animals speak to him, but because he overhears other people's conversations.'

'It is almost impossible to know he is there,' said Robin disapprovingly. 'He sits still and quiet for so long you think you are alone, and then he hears your innermost secrets.' A horrified expression twisted his face. 'He did not mention Mayor Horwood's goat, did he? I would not like *that* bandied about the town!'

'Fortunately not,' said Michael with a shudder. 'But what can you tell us about Dympna? Did it ever make a loan to Norbert?'

'Of course not,' said Robin scornfully. 'The money is used for pious and deserving cases, not for folk who will spend it on themselves. I have my own ideas about recipients, of course, but the other members seldom listen to me. They never lend money to the cases I bring before them.'

'Why not?' asked Michael.

Robin effected a careless shrug. 'I suppose they think the causes I support might benefit me personally, although I am an honest and compassionate man, and would never do such a thing.'

'I see,' said Michael, in a way that indicated he held his own views on the matter of Robin's honesty and compassion. 'Why have you never mentioned your involvement with this worthy charity before? You must realise that helping the sick and desperate is a thing to be proud of?'

'I would love people to know that I have been working for years to alleviate pain and suffering,' said Robin resentfully. 'But the others pay me a retainer on the understanding that I will lose it if I mention Dympna to anyone. Money is money, and not to be refused. So, I obey their rules, and the only person I tell is Helena. I suppose I will be deprived of that income now you know about Dympna.'

'Not necessarily,' said Michael. 'We can be discreet.' Bartholomew noticed he did not say he *would* be discreet.

Robin went on, in full flow now the secret he had kept so well was out. 'I am a member, but I do not know how much money Dympna owns. The other three tend to exclude me from the financial discussions, and I am only involved when they ask for a list of my current patients or when they want me to deliver something for them.'

'Like food and fuel to Dunstan?' asked Bartholomew.

Robin nodded. 'And gold for the Carmelites' new robes, or to help that potter through the inconvenience of a lost foot. I arranged for Bosel the beggar to borrow a cloak for the winter, and I did most of the organising when the Franciscans needed a new roof. It is me who tells folk they will only be lent money if they do not tell anyone how it came about.'

'You did not ask Dunstan not to mention Dympna,' Bartholomew pointed out. 'You left the food, fuel and Yolande de Blaston, then went home.'

'That was different,' replied Robin. 'Dunstan was the town's most active gossip when Athelbald was alive, but that changed the instant he died. I doubt Dunstan even knew I was there. There was no point mentioning the fact that the food and fuel came courtesy of Dympna.'

'Dick Tulyet said the funds for Dunstan did not come from Dympna,' said Bartholomew.

'Of course they did,' replied Robin waspishly. 'I have no money to throw away on dying men, while Kenyngham and Ailred are friars, who have little in the way of worldly goods. Perhaps the two of them acted quickly and did not have time to consult Tulyet.' His smile became malicious. 'Now *he* will know what it is like to belong to a group that does not bother to solicit his opinion!'

'Ailred was certainly aware of Dunstan's case,' said Bartholomew thoughtfully. 'We mentioned it when we were at Ovyng, and he knew all about it.'

'We have taken up enough of your time, Robin,' said Michael. 'Thank you for your help. And give our regards to Helena.'

Bartholomew and Michael continued towards Ovyng, where both scholars felt they would have better answers from Ailred than those they had squeezed from Robin. It was obvious that Robin was not involved in the more important decisions, and that Tulyet had been correct in saying he had been invited to join only as a way for the group to know which of the townsfolk had hired his services and so might be candidates for Dympna's charity. Robin received payment for his membership, indicating that the others knew he was the kind of man whose help and silence needed to be bought.

Bartholomew's feet were sodden by the time they reached Ovyng, and his toes ached from the icy water inside his boots. Michael's face was flushed and sweaty, and he removed his winter cloak and tossed it carelessly over one shoulder; part of it trailed in the muck of St Michael's Lane. He knocked loudly and officially on Ovyng's door. It was eventually opened by Godric.

'You took your time,' said the monk accusingly. 'We have come to speak to your principal.' He pushed past the friar, and Bartholomew followed, surprised to find the main room of the hostel empty. The hearth was devoid of even the most meagre of fires, and the room felt colder than the air outside. It smelled stale, too – rancid fat mixed with boiled vegetables and dirty feet. Godric had been given the tedious task of rewaxing the writing tablets the students used for their exercises. The size of the pile on the table suggested that Godric would be labouring for some hours to come.

'Father Ailred is not here,' said Godric sullenly, stating the obvious. 'He has gone out and taken the others with him. Except me. I am obliged to remain here.'

'Why?' asked Michael. 'What have you done to displease him? Gambling? Taverns?'

'Telling you he went out when he claims he stayed in,' said Godric resentfully. 'At least, I am sure that is the real reason. The official one is he thinks my humours are unbalanced, and that I should stay inside until they are restored.'

'Do you feel unwell?' asked Bartholomew. The friar looked healthy enough, despite his unshaven and pale cheeks. But most people in Cambridge had a seedy sort of appearance during winter, when days were short and chilly and shaving was an unpleasant experience involving icy water and hands made unsteady by shivering.

'I am cold and hungry, because we have no money for fuel and not much for food. But other than that I am well. I think Ailred is angry with me for telling you the truth about his evening out. I should never have allowed you to bully me into talking about it in the first place. He was furious.'

'Was he, indeed?' asked Michael, intrigued. 'And why would that be? What is he hiding?'

'I do not know; I was not with him,' replied Godric petulantly. 'And anyway, he says he was in, and I am mistaken about his absence.'

'Where is he now?' asked Michael. 'Or will he later say he was here all the time and you have been mistaken about that, too?'

This coaxed a rueful smile from Godric. 'He is skating on the river. Ice skating.'

Michael gazed at him in surprise. 'You mean fooling around, like children? That does not sound like a suitable activity for the principal of a hostel.'

'Ailred says ice is a gift from God,' said Godric. 'He does not like cold weather particularly, but he adores ice. He says it is Heaven's playground, and has all our students out at the First Day of the Year games near the Great Bridge.'

'I thought the ice there was breaking up,' said Bartholomew.

'Apparently not,' said Godric. He jerked a thumb at the window. 'Although it will not be long if this thaw continues.'

'Do you know where he was born?' asked Michael.

Godric seemed startled by the abrupt change of subject, but answered anyway. 'Lincoln. Surely you must have heard him waxing lyrical about the place?'

'He comes from a village *near* Lincoln,' corrected Michael. 'Not Lincoln itself, although our records say he had his education from the school in the city.'

'Oh, yes,' said Godric, frowning as he remembered. 'I think his home was called Fisheby or Fiscurtone or some such thing. Why do you ask?'

'Does he have family?' asked Michael. 'A brother or cousins? Male relatives of any kind?'

Godric shook his head. 'Not that I know. But we Franciscans are supposed to renounce earthly ties once we take final vows, so it is possible he has put his kinsmen behind him.'

'Damn,' swore Michael softly. 'I was hoping you would know whether he was related to a man named John Fiscurtune, who was murdered in London last year.'

'If he was, then he never mentioned it,' said Godric.

'Do you know whether he has any association with fishermen or fishmongers?' asked Bartholomew. 'I recall him gutting fish very expertly when we were here once.'

'Other than the name of his home manor?' asked Godric. 'He always catches more trout from the river than anyone else, and he prefers fish to meat. But that is all.'

'It may be enough,' said Michael, nudging Bartholomew in the ribs. 'But we should have this discussion with Ailred himself. Come, Matt. Let us see this Franciscan on his skates.'

Bartholomew and Michael took their leave of Godric, and struggled back through the melting drifts in the direction of the Great Bridge. At last they reached the river, which curved around the western side of the town and looked like another road, with its frozen surface and recent dusting of snow. However, all manner of filth lay strewn across its surface – sewage, animal manure, inedible items from the butchers' stalls, fish entrails, rotting vegetables, and some items Bartholomew dared not identify, although he suspected they had once belonged to a dog.

Because it was a winter Sunday, and a day when many folk enjoyed a day of rest, there was a large gathering of people near the Great Bridge and on the water meadows that lay to either side of it. The fields were prone to flooding in spring, and so were mostly devoid of houses – although a few desperate folk had erected shacks along the edges. The meadows were used for grazing cattle in the summer, but now they were blanketed in snow and were the venue for the town's traditional First Day of the Year games.

Sheriff Morice had seized control of the event, and was sitting astride his handsome grey stallion, watching the proceedings from the vantage point of the bridge itself. He was surrounded by his lieutenants, a gaudy and frivolous group who, like Morice, were more interested in making money than in promoting law and order. The townsfolk seemed to be enjoying the games, although there was none of the excited anticipation associated with the annual camp-ball.

A number of activities were in progress. Butts had been set up, and townsmen were showing off their skills with bows and arrows. Dangerously close to their line of fire was a game of ice bandy-ball, where strong men smacked a small wooden sphere with terrific force, so that anyone in its path could expect serious injury. Meanwhile, an impromptu session of ice-camping had started, using the same leather bag that Agatha had powered into the gargoyle's maw a few days earlier. It was more a case of 'snow-camping' than ice-camping, because the soft surface was slowing the speed of the game. Bartholomew thought this would mean fewer injuries for the participants, although he could not but help notice that it, too, ranged perilously close to the butts.

Nearby St Giles's was supplying church ale to the spectators, and women stood behind trestle tables, selling slices of the sausage-like hackin. A shrid pie was on display, too, decorated with its traditional pastry baby-in-a-basket. Bartholomew noticed that the women had cut their wedges carefully around the crib, with the result that the baby was left teetering atop a pastry precipice.

A crowd had gathered around a stall where hot spiced wine was being sold for wassailing. Some folk had already toasted the health of too many friends, and had passed out in the snow. Bartholomew hoped they would not be left to freeze to death after the games had finished, but was reassured by the watchful presence of the Austin Canons from the nearby Hospital of St John. He felt a tug on his cloak,

377

and turned to see Sergeant Orwelle, a grizzled veteran who usually manned the town's gates.

'Morice is demanding a penny from anyone who wants to play in the games,' he said with disapproval. 'That is why there are not as many folk as we expected. Morice says it is because I closed the river, but I think it is because he is charging for something that was free last year.'

'You closed the river?' asked Bartholomew. 'Because of the thaw?'

Orwelle nodded. 'I have lived near the water for fifty years, and I know its wiles. The ice stopped being safe this morning, so I gave orders that no games should be played on it today. Morice was furious, because he wanted to hire out skates for ice bandy-ball and ice-camping. He claims my actions have lost him a fortune.'

'He is not fit to be Sheriff,' said Michael in disgust, looking angrily at the arrogant man on the grey horse.

'Why are you here, Brother?' asked Orwelle. 'Have you come to try your hand at bittle-battle? I can lend you my club and a ball, so you will not have to pay to hire Morice's.'

'Not in the snow, thank you,' said Michael haughtily. 'It would ruin my stroke. I am good at bittle-battle; no one can use a long stick to knock a tiny ball into distant holes like me.'

'How about wrestling?' asked Orwelle, looking Michael up and down. 'You are probably good at that, too.'

'Tilting,' said Michael, picking the game where the object was to charge a horse at a pivoting bar and knock it hard before it swung back and dismounted the rider. 'I excel at tilting. But I am not here to win prizes today. Have you seen Ailred from Ovyng? We shall never find him among these crowds.'

'He left when I closed the river, because he wanted to skate. His students are here, though – in that snowball fight over there.'

Bartholomew looked to where he pointed, and could see Franciscan habits among the swirling crowd heaving icy missiles at anyone in the vicinity. Shrieks and howls filled the air, not all of them delighted ones. The physician could see blood on several faces, and suspected the Sheriff would need to police the event very carefully if he did not want it to turn into something darker and more dangerous. Already apprentices, fresh from the wassail stall, were reeling to join the throng, while scholars were massing on the sidelines, evidently planning some kind of retaliatory strategy.

'Where did Ailred go?' asked Michael. 'Home?'

'To find some quiet patch of river where he can skate without being warned of the dangers, I imagine,' said Orwelle disapprovingly. 'Although, I must say he *is* extremely good; I have watched him before.'

Bartholomew and Michael abandoned the simmering atmosphere of the Sheriff's winter games, with Michael passing orders to Beadle Meadowman to keep an eye on the snowball fight and Bartholomew promising the Austin Canons his services, should they be required later. They then made their way along the towpath that ran beside the river.

The river possessed several arms and drains that ran this way and that, comprising an interlacing system of waterways. The King's Ditch and the river met in the south near Small Bridges, where they formed the Mill Pool. The King's Mill, which stood nearby, used the power of the swift current to drive its sails and grind its corn, although this could not operate as long as the river was frozen. It stood still and silent, the massive wheel that drove the mill lifted out of the water to protect it from the ice. The Mill Pool itself was sluggish compared to the rest of the river, so it invariably froze first and thawed last in icy weather. It was here that Bartholomew and Michael found Ailred.

The Franciscan had attracted a small but appreciative audience as he demonstrated his skills. His bone skates were fastened to his feet with leather thongs, and the blades had been carefully sharpened, so they hissed and sizzled as they cut across the ice. Others had also been enjoying a little gentle recreation while the ice remained firm, but had ceased their efforts to watch the spectacle provided by the priest. Ailred seemed to soar, rather than skate. He jumped and skipped and danced and turned, and did not seem like the same man who had sat grim-faced gutting fish in Ovyng's dismal chamber a few days before.

'Lord!' muttered Michael, impressed. 'Where did he learn to do that?'

'He is good,' said Bartholomew in admiration. 'He makes the others look clumsy.'

'He is enjoying it, too. Look at his face; he is ecstatic.'

The friar was laughing, encouraging his audience to join him, and rocking with mirth when they attempted to emulate him and failed. He made skating look easy, which Bartholomew knew it was not. It was simple enough if the surface was smooth and the skates well made, but Bartholomew could see the ice was pitted and ridged, and marvelled that the friar did not trip himself. A crowd of admiring children gathered around him, and he began to instruct them. The sound of their delighted chatter rose to where Michael and Bartholomew stood watching, and they were loath to disturb him while the youngsters were enjoying his company.

Eventually, Ailred abandoned the ice, although he was clearly reluctant to do so. His departure was followed by disappointed cries from his new friends, who begged him to stay and 'play' with them. Amused to be invited to join a children's gang, Ailred patted one or two affectionately on the head, then sat on the bank to untie the leather straps that held his skates in place.

'Those are good blades, Father,' said Michael, making the Franciscan jump by coming up behind him and speaking loudly. 'But they look old. You must have had them for some time.'

'Years,' said Ailred, flushed and happy from his exertions. 'I love skating, and had these made specially for me before I became a friar. But what can I do for you? I am sure you did not brave this inclement weather just to watch my little display.'

'No,' agreed Michael. 'We came to ask more questions about Norbert – questions that we think might help us find his killer at last.'

'Really?' asked Ailred, bending a leg so he could inspect one of his feet. 'That is good news. You were taking so long I was beginning to fear it would never be solved. Damn! A broken thong!'

'We are very close to solving this mystery,' said Michael, although this was news to Bartholomew. 'We have uncovered a good deal of evidence since you and I last spoke – including the fact that you are a member of Dympna.'

Ailred glanced sharply at him. 'Who told you that? It is supposed to be a secret. Was it Kenyngham? He is at Michaelhouse, so I suppose he must have decided that loyalty to a member of his College was more important than Dympna.'

'It was not Kenyngham,' said Michael. 'And our source is irrelevant, anyway. The point is that we know. I am surprised you were among Dympna's members. Your hostel is not wealthy.'

'I do not provide the money myself,' said Ailred, a little testily. 'That came from people during the plague, who pledged their wealth to benefit others. Many friars were given quite large sums, with instructions to pass it to the poor. But Kenyngham and I decided handing out coins with gay abandon was a short-term solution, and we needed to think more carefully about what we could achieve. So, we established Dympna.'

'You were an original member?' asked Bartholomew.

'I was an early member,' corrected Ailred. 'The original ones were Kenyngham, Giles Abigny and three Dominicans. The Black Friars died, Abigny left the town, and Kenyngham was obliged to appoint new colleagues. He chose me. Currently, we also have Dick Tulyet, who is discreet, honest and absolutely trustworthy, and Robin, who is not.'

'Nearly all the Cambridge Dominicans died during the Death,' said Bartholomew soberly to Michael. 'Of all the Orders, they suffered the heaviest losses, because they continued to visit the sick and grant them absolution.'

'They were good men,' said Ailred sadly. 'I still remember them in my prayers, and so do those who have been helped by their legacy. Even the Franciscans and the Carmelites pray for them, because they have benefited from Dympna.'

'Let us return to Norbert,' said Michael, not much interested in Dympna's lofty history. 'You heard Godric say that Norbert had received messages from Dympna, and that he went to meet "her" in St Michael's. Why did you not tell us about Dympna then? It would have saved a lot of trouble.'

'I said – several times – that you should not waste your time with Dympna, but you did not listen, and preferred to consider Godric's interpretations. I tried to stop you from following a futile line of enquiry without betraying Dympna, but you ignored my efforts.'

'You were Dympna's "keeper" until recently,' said Michael, unmoved by the reprimand. 'Did you lend Norbert money?'

'No,' said Ailred shortly. 'Norbert was not a worthy cause.'

'Why did he receive messages from Dympna, then?' pressed Michael.

Ailred looked tired. 'I did not see these missives, so cannot tell you anything about them, other than to assure you that *my* Dympna did not send them. Perhaps Godric is right: there is a woman called Dympna who likes to send decadent young men messages begging secret meetings. It is an unusual name, but someone may have christened a daughter after the saint, I suppose.'

'There is another matter I would like to discuss,' said Michael. 'I understand you are from a village near Lincoln.'

'Yes. I often think about Lincoln, and how much better it is than Cambridge. Its cathedral is the most splendid—'

'You are from Fiscurtune,' interrupted Michael. 'And Fiscurtune is a village that has suffered the recent death of someone who was born there – a relative of yours. James Fiscurtune had the misfortune to be stabbed by a fishmonger named Walter Turke. I find it a curious coincidence that Turke happened to die while he was skating. He is obviously as clumsy as you are talented.'

'I do not know what you are talking about,' said Ailred, standing and testing the thong he had just repaired. 'I know neither Walter Turke nor John Fiscurtune.'

'Precisely!' said Michael in triumph. 'The murdered man's name was *John* Fiscurtune, not James. I knew you would hear the correct name and not the one I spoke. You *do* know him.'

'I do not,' said Ailred stiffly, although his denial was unconvincing.

'You lied to us,' Michael went on relentlessly. 'You claimed you were with your students the evening St Michael's Church was invaded, but you were not. Why did you feel the need for dishonesty? What are you trying to hide from us?'

'Who told you that?' asked Ailred, sounding panicky. 'If you are referring to Godric, then you should know he has not been well. I have ordered him not to join the winter games today, so the warmth of indoors will help him recover his damaged wits.'

'What is wrong with him, exactly?' asked Bartholomew, thinking that if Ailred had thought warmth would heal Godric, then he should have lit a fire. The hostel had been bitterly cold.

Ailred made an impatient gesture. 'I am not a physician! All I know is he sometimes imagines things. There are other Ovyng scholars besides Godric. Ask them whether I was out that night.'

'There would be no point,' said Michael. 'They have been instructed to say you were in.'

Ailred regarded him with dislike. 'You are accusing me of grave offences, and you are insulting my integrity. I will not stand here and listen to this.'

'Then tell the truth,' said Michael harshly. 'I know you are lying. Where did you go that night? Was it on Dympna's business? Or was it some errand of your own?'

'This is outrageous!' shouted Ailred, finally angry. 'I shall complain to the Chancellor about you. I am the principal of a University hostel, and I will not be questioned as though I were a common criminal or one of your secular students caught in some minor mischief.'

'We are not talking about minor mischief,' said Michael coldly. 'We are talking about murder and deceit on an enormous scale.'

Ailred glanced across the river, and bent down, as though to brush something from his gown. Then, before Bartholomew or Michael could do anything to stop him, he had pushed off and was scooting down the river at a furious pace.

'After him, Matt!' ordered Michael in a shriek. 'Do not just stand there!'

Bartholomew jumped on to the ice, but feet were no match for skates, and the physician's awkward slithering was no match for Ailred's speed and power. The Franciscan rounded a bend on the river, and was gone from sight.

CHAPTER 11

MICHAEL WAS STILL FURIOUS AT AILRED'S ESCAPE THE following day, claiming he would have had the answers to many questions if the physician had managed to seize the Franciscan before he could skate away. Bartholomew disagreed. He did not think Ailred had been in the mood for throwing light on Michael's mysteries, and believed the friar would simply have continued to lie. It came down to Godric's word against his principal's, and Bartholomew sensed Godric might not keep to his story anyway – he would capitulate, and declare that Ailred had been in after all. Loyalty was important in hostels and Colleges.

It was almost noon, and Bartholomew had spent the morning trailing around after Michael in a futile attempt to discover where Ailred might have gone. They had visited Ovyng Hostel twice and the Franciscan Friary once, but no one had any idea where a fleeing Grey Friar might go in an emergency. They all said much the same: Ailred was a quiet man, respected and liked by his contemporaries, whose life had revolved completely around his hostel and his students.

'Only another four days,' growled Suttone irritably. The bell had just chimed to announce the midday meal, and he was walking across the yard with Bartholomew and Michael, just back from their futile hunt. 'Then this ridiculous charade will be over.'

'You mean the season of misrule?' asked Michael. 'It has not been too bad this year. The cold weather spoiled some of the wilder schemes, and the fun is wearing too thin now for there to be many more surprises in store for us. Some students are already settling back to their studies.'

'Quenhyth never stopped his,' said the Carmelite in disgust. 'Smug little beggar.'

'I thought his obsession with learning would endear him to you,' said Bartholomew, surprised the dour Carmelite so disliked Quenhyth. The student was dull, pedantic and single-minded, which were traits Suttone usually approved in a scholar. 'He has not engaged in any of the antics surrounding the Lord of Misrule.'

'Yes and no,' replied Suttone. 'His character makes people want to tease him. Indeed, his very presence in Michaelhouse has been the cause of pranks that would not have taken place had he been gone. We must remember to send him away next year – especially if Deynman is re-elected.'

They walked into the hall and went to the servants' screen, where large pots of food were waiting to be distributed. The Fellows were still obliged to serve the others on occasion, and some students continued to occupy the high table, although many had reclaimed their own seats in the body of the hall. The novelty of eating with Deynman had completely worn off for Agatha, however, and she declined his invitations, claiming that she was bored with the prattle of silly boys. She had reverted to dining in the kitchen, along with the rest of the servants.

'Where is Langelee?' demanded Michael crossly, snatching up a dish of something that was coloured a brilliant emerald. 'It will take us ages to serve everyone without him. And what in God's name is this?' His attention had been caught by the contents of the bowl.

'Deynman said all food served today should be green,' said Bartholomew, laughing when he saw the mouldy bread that Agatha had piled into a basket and the platter of rancid pork that had been prepared. 'He should have chosen a different colour, because if anyone willingly eats this stuff he deserves to die of poisoning.'

'That will teach Deynman to make life difficult for Agatha,

with his ridiculous demands and orders,' said Wynewyk in delight. 'Decaying meat, mouldy bread, cabbage and pea soup with added colouring. It is all green, but Deynman did not specify it also had to be edible!'

'I shall be glad when this is over,' said Suttone vehemently, grabbing the bread and preparing to distribute it to hungry students who would be in for a disappointment. 'Because the servants are not allowed to work, the hall has not been cleaned for days, and it stinks.'

The odour of stale rushes and spilt food was indeed becoming noticeable, and Bartholomew was aware that fewer students used the hall for sleeping, preferring the fresher, if colder, air of their own rooms. The walls were splattered with wine and fat, where the Fellows' inexpert handling of heavy serving vessels had resulted in mishaps, and the floor was lumpy with discarded scraps. It had almost reached the point where Bartholomew felt obliged to scrape his feet clean before he left.

He escaped from the hall as soon as Deynman said the final grace. It was an unusually short meal, because so little was actually edible, and it was not long before the students were clamouring to leave, so they could find victuals elsewhere. Because his room was still encased in a cocoon of snow – although it was melting quickly and it would not be long before it would be accessible again – Bartholomew went to William's chamber.

The friar had not been obliged to consume green food. He sat replete and contented, with the remains of fish-giblet stew, and fine wheat-bread, which Bartholomew imagined had also been enjoyed by Agatha, lay in front of him. William informed Bartholomew that his meal had been excellent and that he was considering 'breaking' his other leg in order to be cosseted and excused from unpleasant duties.

'Do not let Agatha know you are only pretending to be infirm,' the physician advised. 'If she discovers her charity has been in vain your life will not be worth living.'

'The weather is changing,' said William ruefully. 'And the

ground underfoot is not nearly as slick as it was. You can remove the splint in a day or two, but I may bribe you with books again, if I feel the need for a period of respite.'

'Bribe away,' said Bartholomew, running his hand lovingly over the fine cover of his Bradwardine. 'Did you know that Michael spent all morning searching for one of your brethren? Ailred from Ovyng ran away when our questions became too uncomfortable.'

'I heard,' said William. 'And I am astonished. Ailred is a kindly, God-fearing man. I cannot imagine him fleeing from anything.'

'Has he ever spoken to you about kin from the village of Fiscurtune, near Lincoln? No one else seems to know much about his family.'

'He has kin,' replied William. 'Or should I say *had* kin, since we Franciscans often renounce family ties once we have taken our vows. I know a little about Ailred's, though, because we went on retreat to Chesterton together once. He talked about them then.'

'What did he say?' asked Bartholomew, feeling his excitement quicken.

'Very little,' came the disappointing reply. 'He has a brother. Or was it a sister? I cannot recall now. And there is a nephew he is fond of.'

'Do you know anything else about them?' asked Bartholomew.

William thought for a moment. 'They used to go fishing together.'

Bartholomew told Michael about his conversation with William as they sat in the Brazen George, eating roasted sheep with a sauce of beetroot and onions. There were parsnips and cabbage stems, too, baked slowly in butter in the bottom of the bread oven, so that the flavour of yeast could be tasted in them. The more he thought about it, the more likely it seemed to Bartholomew that Ailred was indeed associated with the dead John Fiscurtune. And he wondered whether there was some significance in the fact that Walter Turke had died while skating, when Ailred had shown himself to be a veteran on ice.

'Do you think Ailred did something to bring about Turke's death?' he asked.

'Possibly,' said Michael. 'There are too many connections between them to be ignored. So, Turke murdered Fiscurtune, then bribed the local Sheriff to ignore the crime. Fiscurtune's family must have been outraged. Then Turke embarked on a pilgrimage to "atone" for his sin, making it clear he was doing so only because he intended to be elected Lord Mayor and did not want an inconvenient matter like murder to stand in his way.'

'It would have added insult to injury,' agreed Bartholomew. 'And then this pilgrimage took him through Cambridge, where one of the wronged kinsmen lives. When the snows isolated the town and trapped Turke here, it must have seemed as though fate was screaming for vengeance.'

'God was screaming for vengeance,' corrected Michael. 'Ailred is a friar, remember? What did he do, do you think? Force Turke on to the ice somehow?'

'There were no obvious injuries on Turke's body, so I do not think violence was used.'

'Ailred could have threatened him with a crossbow,' suggested Michael.

'In broad daylight on the Mill Pool? Someone would have seen them.' Bartholomew rubbed a hand through his hair, and asked the question that had been gnawing at the back of his mind ever since he had first learned about the possible connection between Ailred and Turke. 'Do you think Philippa suspects her husband's death was not an accident, and she knows or has guessed that Ailred is involved?'

'I do not see how, unless she was there.' Michael studied his friend with sombre green eyes. 'And I do not think she was there, despite the fact that we know Giles regularly locked himself in her room, leaving her free to wander.'

'Then why do I feel as though she is not telling us the

truth? Even Matilde can see there is something strange about Philippa, and they do not even know each other.'

Michael patted his arm. 'Eat your parsnips, Matt. Then we shall search again for the elusive Ailred. He cannot be far – the roads are still closed, and he has nowhere else to go.'

Bartholomew and Michael left the Brazen George, and were about to turn down St Michael's Lane when they encountered Langelee striding towards them, gripping Quenhyth by the scruff of his neck. Langelee's face was impassive, but the student's expression revealed exactly how he felt: angry, maligned and humiliated. He was trying to explain something to Langelee, but Langelee was refusing to listen.

'I was on my way to your prison,' Langelee said, thrusting Quenhyth at Michael, so hard that the lad bounced into Michael's substantial girth and almost lost his balance. 'I want you to take charge of this miserable specimen.'

'What has he done this time?' asked Michael, fixing the hapless student with a stern eye. 'Another whore in his bed? Or has he hidden Father William's crutches again?'

Quenhyth bristled. 'I did neither of those things, and you know it. They were pranks designed specifically to land me in trouble.'

'I caught him searching the servants' belongings,' said Langelee to Michael with considerable anger. 'The steward came to me in a panic, saying there was a burglar in the stable loft, and when I investigated I found Quenhyth. I cannot imagine what he was thinking of.'

'I was not among the *servants'* possessions,' said Quenhyth. 'I was looking through baggage belonging to the Chepe Waits. Brother Michael himself gave me permission to search them, so I could prove they stole my scrip. I would have gone sooner, but I had to wait until they were out.'

'Your obsession with the Waits verges on the fanatical,' said Michael, shaking his head. 'Such an attitude will land you in hot water one day.'

'It has landed him in hot water today,' said Langelee sternly. 'I cannot condone students rifling through our servants' belongings. They will leave us, and then where will we be? Good retainers do not grow on trees, unlike bothersome students.'

'I was only doing what you told me to do,' cried Quenhyth, appealing to Michael. 'And I discovered something important, so it was worth my efforts.'

'You found your scrip?' asked Bartholomew.

'Something much more important than that,' said Quenhyth, a note of triumph entering his voice when he saw he had Michael's attention. 'I can prove the Waits knew Dympna – the woman who sent notes to Norbert and lured him to his death.'

Michael raised his eyebrows. 'And how can you do that?'

'Because I have a message written by her,' said Quenhyth smugly. He produced a piece of parchment with a flourish. 'I decided to take it, because Frith would have rid himself of it by the time I had alerted you. The message was in plain view, between two floorboards.'

Michael snatched the note from him, read it quickly, then handed it to Bartholomew. It contained nothing other than the name Dympna and a series of numbers, just like the ones they had seen on the parchment in Gosslinge's throat. These were one, thirteen and four, and the ink was pale enough to be all but invisible. The message still made no sense to the physician, although Quenhyth was right in that it indicated an association between the Waits and the benevolent moneylenders. Or perhaps they had gained possession of one of the messages sent to Norbert.

'Being between the floorboards is not in plain view,' said Bartholomew, passing it to Langelee.

'It was in plain view to anyone conducting a thorough and meticulous search,' said Quenhyth pedantically. 'Well, what do you think? It is damning evidence, is it not?'

Michael took Bartholomew's arm and pulled him away, so they could speak without being overheard by Quenhyth.

Langelee followed, raising an imperious finger at the student to tell him to stay where he was.

'It is possible that the Waits applied for a loan from Dympna, and this message is Dympna's response,' said Michael. 'It is obviously in some kind of code.'

'The one we found inside Gosslinge was written with onion ink or some such thing,' said Bartholomew. 'It only became visible when warmed. I wonder why this is not the same.'

'I was once fooled by that, too,' said Langelee, who knew a lot about codes and secret messages from his days as a spy for the Archbishop of York. 'I believed a message had been written invisibly, but it transpired some cheap inks just fade with extremes of temperature – as this has started to do. The recent weather has been very cold.'

'So Gosslinge's note was not written in secret ink?' asked Michael, shooting Bartholomew a look that indicated he felt the physician had misled him.

'Probably not,' said Langelee. 'Why write invisibly, if the message is meaningful only to the recipient? However, remember also that codes are only good if the recipient knows what they mean, otherwise there is no point in using them.'

Bartholomew took the parchment, and thought about Langelee's words: something that would be understood by each recipient. The fact that these possibly included Norbert, Gosslinge and the Waits meant it had to be something very simple. Suddenly, the whole thing was crystal clear.

'Of course!' he exclaimed. 'I understand! One, thirteen and four.'

'I can see that,' snapped Michael testily. 'The question is, what does it mean?'

'There are three numbers here, just as there were three on the note we discovered in Gosslinge. And those numbers represent pounds, shillings and pence.'

'Can it really be as basic as that?' asked Michael, inspecting the parchment with renewed interest. 'Someone makes an application, and Dympna responds by sending a note specifying the amount it is prepared to advance?'

'Why not?' asked Bartholomew. 'There is no reason to believe it is more complex. The Waits have asked for five nobles – one pound, thirteen shillings and fourpence. Or perhaps they have borrowed money, and this is the sum Dympna would like repaid.'

'Yes,' said Michael, nodding excited agreement. 'The latter. Such a scheme would explain why Norbert received messages from Dympna with such frequency: he had borrowed money, and Dympna was issuing demands for its repayment, either in full or in part.'

'But Norbert had not borrowed money,' Bartholomew pointed out. 'Tulyet, Robin and Ailred all said his was not the kind of case they sponsor.'

'Then perhaps Dympna's members have not been acting together,' suggested Michael. 'It seems to me that one has been making loans without the knowledge of the others. We know Robin is not involved in financial decisions. Meanwhile, Kenyngham's retirement has made him very absent-minded and Dick Tulyet is busy watching Sheriff Morice destroy everything he has worked to achieve. Neither of them will be watching Dympna very carefully at the moment.'

'That leaves Ailred,' said Bartholomew. 'Do not forget the chest was in his care until recently, so he was in a position to raid it without the others being any the wiser.'

'And then he wrote messages to Norbert demanding it back,' said Michael nodding. 'And as long as Norbert was crippled by repayment obligations, he would remain at Ovyng, where his uncle would pay for his education.'

'Did Norbert know the principal of his own hostel was a member of Dympna?' asked Bartholomew. He answered his own question. 'Of course he did not. Ailred would not have written notes if that were the case – he would just have asked Norbert for the money.'

'Ailred was in a perfect position to demand reimbursement from Norbert,' said Michael thoughtfully. 'He would have known exactly where and when to leave messages, and Norbert must have imagined Dympna had eyes everywhere. We know Norbert had debts – it was one of the first things I learned when I started to investigate his murder. He must have borrowed money from Dympna in an effort to repay some of them.'

'But Norbert would have recognised Ailred when they met in St Michael's,' said Langelee reasonably. 'Even if Ailred wore a disguise, there would be small traits to betray him – his gait or his voice. He must have recruited someone else to help him.'

'Who?' asked Bartholomew. 'I doubt Robin could be trusted with that sort of thing – and certainly not unless he was paid.'

'Not Robin,' determined Michael. 'He would have blurted it out when we spoke to him earlier. And not Kenyngham or Tulyet, either, because we think Ailred has been acting without their knowledge in this matter. It is someone else. But who?'

'Someone who lives here,' said Bartholomew. 'It cannot be a stranger, like Harysone, because Ailred will not have known him long enough to establish any kind of trust.'

'Perhaps,' said Michael, reluctant to admit that Harysone could be innocent of something. 'But we have to remember the changes that have taken place in Dympna recently. Everyone says Norbert would not have been granted a loan, and yet it appears he had one. Similarly, it looks as if the Waits and Gosslinge also had them – and neither of those are worthy cases.'

'The Waits,' said Bartholomew, closing his eyes as something else occurred to him. 'I *knew* their connections to so many aspects of this case were significant!'

'The Waits are not Ailred's accomplices,' said Michael dismissively. 'Why should a respectable principal throw in his lot with a band of jugglers?'

'Because of Lincoln,' said Bartholomew. 'Remember how Frith first introduced himself? Frith of *Lincoln*. It is not

394

unknown for folk to claim they come from large cities instead of small villages, thinking it increases their credibility, so Frith may well be a Fiscurtune man.'

Michael was unconvinced. 'That represents a huge leap in logic,' he warned.

'It would explain why Frith's music leaves so much to be desired,' said Langelee. 'He is not a real Wait at all, but joined them as a disguise, so he can help Ailred avenge Fiscurtune.'

'Makejoy said the group has been together five years,' said Bartholomew. 'But revenge may well be the reason why Frith and his friends are so far from Chepe, where they were said to be doing so well.'

'*Were* doing so well,' said Michael meaningfully. 'Makejoy *and* the singer we met in the Market Square told us the Waits' business had taken a downward turn recently. Makejoy also mentioned that it was Frith who suddenly expressed a desire to see Cambridge.' He scratched his chin, fingernails rasping on the whiskers. 'And there is something else. The Market Square singer also said the Waits had friends in "high places", who recommended them. Quenhyth told you that his father hired the Chepe Waits because *John Fiscurtune* said he should.'

'So, Fiscurtune was the Waits' "friend",' said Bartholomew. 'So if we think Ailred and Frith *may* be related, and we have surmised that Ailred and John Fiscurtune are kinsmen, then we can also assume there is a connection between Frith and Fiscurtune. Frith's "friend" – Fiscurtune – was his relative, which explains why a powerful merchant deigned to recommend a lowly juggler to his colleagues. Fiscurtune was the reason the Waits were doing well in Chepe. When Turke murdered him, he did more than merely kill a rival fishmonger; he destroyed the basis of the Waits' success. This is beginning to make sense. Loss of livelihood would be a powerful motive for murder – except that Turke was not murdered, of course.'

'Gosslinge and Norbert were, though,' said Michael. 'But

395

unfortunately, we shall have to wait until Ailred is apprehended before we can test our theories. We should certainly speak to him before we tackle Frith and his cronies, since we have scant evidence to convict them without his testimony. But there are other matters that require our attention first, and one of them is regarding us very balefully.'

Quenhyth,' said Langelee heavily, looking over at the student, who had given up trying to overhear their conversation. 'Damn the lad! I do not know why he has taken such an unnatural dislike to these Waits.'

'We have just shown he is right to be wary of them,' said Michael. 'Not only have we been told by several different people that they steal from their patrons, we now suspect they are here for a darker purpose.'

'I do not want them in my College any longer,' said Langelee decisively. 'Deynman's reign as Lord of Misrule is almost over, and even he has grown weary of their uninspired performances. I shall ask them to leave immediately – and damn their written contract.' He hailed Quenhyth, and asked whether the student knew where the Waits might be.

Quenhyth's face lit up at the mention of the subject so dear to him. 'They are in the conclave – which is why I knew it was safe to look through their things.'

'The conclave?' asked Langelee suspiciously. 'I said they were not allowed in the hall or the conclave unless accompanied by a member of the College. Why did you not stop them?'

Quenhyth glowered. 'They are accompanied by a College member: Kenyngham is with them.'

'What are they doing?' asked Bartholomew. He was aware of a sensation of unease developing in the pit of his stomach.

'They asked whether the conclave was empty, and when he said it was, they told him he and they should go there immediately,' explained Quenhyth.

'I do not like the sound of this at all,' said Bartholomew.

*   *   *

396

Bartholomew was not the only one uncomfortable with the notion of Kenyngham in company with a rough group of people like the Chepe Waits; Michael and Langelee were worried, too. Langelee led the way down the slippery lane at a cracking pace, dragging Quenhyth with him. Quenhyth looked pleased with himself, as though he imagined he had finally proved some point and was going to avoid a sojourn in the proctors' cells after all.

'It was something about prayers,' he said breathlessly, trying to be helpful. 'You know how Kenyngham is always praying? Well, Frith asked if he knew any prayers for musicians, or some such nonsense, and Kenyngham offered to teach him some. He said he knows one by St Cecilia.'

Michael stopped dead in his tracks, grateful for a respite from running through the sludgy snow. 'Kenyngham is praying with the Waits in the conclave? That sounds innocent enough. I thought they were doing something else.'

'The Waits do not pray!' said Quenhyth in a sneering voice. 'They would not know how.'

'Perhaps that is why they asked Kenyngham to teach them,' said Michael cautiously. 'We may be doing Frith an injustice here.'

'Then they will have no complaint when we burst into the conclave to see what is happening,' panted Langelee.

'Actually, I imagine the reason for escorting Kenyngham to the conclave is more closely related to the presence of the chest of gold under the floorboards than to devotions,' said Bartholomew quietly, taking Michael's arm and pulling him on.

'Chest of gold?' demanded Langelee. 'What are you talking about?'

'It is Kenyngham's turn to keep Dympna,' explained Michael. 'Matt thinks it is under the floorboards in the conclave, which is why they have been loose for the past three weeks. But there is a flaw in his reasoning: how could the Waits know where the chest is hidden? Its whereabouts is a closely guarded secret. Even Tulyet does not know where

Kenyngham has put it, and Kenyngham is a man who is stubborn about such things. He would never reveal where Dympna was kept, especially to a band of entertainers with a reputation for light fingers.'

'Ailred,' said Bartholomew heavily, as another piece of the mystery fell into place. 'Ailred knew where it was. Tulyet said the keepers tell one other person where they have hidden the chest, in case there is an accident. Kenyngham would not have told Robin, and we know it was not Tulyet, so he must have informed Ailred. And we believe the Waits are Ailred's accomplices!'

Michael skidded and almost fell in a particularly slick patch of snow. He slowed down, to try to think clearly. 'The Waits have been the common factor all along – just as you said. They associated with Gosslinge, Turke, Giles and Philippa in London; they were seen with Norbert on the night of his death; and they spoke to Harysone in the King's Head. It is obvious now we have the whole picture: Frith was the shadowy "Dympna" who met Norbert in St Michael's, and who was able to escape without being seen by Godric and his classmates.'

'The Waits probably killed Gosslinge, too,' said Bartholomew. 'Perhaps he went to repay a loan, and they thrust the note into his throat when he told them he did not have their money. That may have been why he wore beggarly clothes – to pretend he was poor.'

'It is possible,' said Michael. 'But we should catch these vagabonds before they make off with the gold and harm Kenyngham into the bargain.'

'Hurry, then,' said Bartholomew, breaking into a run again. He reached Michaelhouse and struggled with the gate, while the others fidgeted impatiently. As soon as it was open, he tore across the yard, heading for the hall. He almost collided with William, out in the milder weather for some much-needed exercise.

'I have been evicted,' said William peevishly. 'The Waits insisted on being alone with Kenyngham in the conclave, while he taught them some prayers. Why do they not want me there? I know as many prayers as he does.'

Bartholomew did not stop to answer, but pushed past the friar and made for the conclave, racing up the stairs and across the hall. The door was locked, and he kicked at it in frustration.

'They have him inside,' he shouted to Langelee, who was behind him.

'Calm down, Matt,' said Langelee, pulling him away. 'If the Waits have locked themselves in, then they have just sealed the door to their own prison. There is only one way in or out of the conclave, and that is through this door. We have them.'

'That is not the point!' said Bartholomew in agitation. 'Kenyngham is in there. He may be in danger. And they do balancing acts for a living, so do not imagine they cannot escape through the windows. Send Quenhyth to stand in the courtyard and sound the alarm if they try to leave that way. And fetch an axe.'

'An axe?' asked Langelee in horror. 'You are not taking an axe to one of my doors!'

'Kenyngham is alone with men who have killed,' hissed Bartholomew, grabbing the Master by the front of his gown. 'We will smash down the walls, if we have to.'

'There is no need to resort to that kind of measure,' said Michael calmly. He studied the door for a moment, took several steps back, and then powered towards it with his shoulder held like a battering ram. Bartholomew winced, anticipating broken bones. But just as Michael reached it, the door was opened and Kenyngham peered out, curious to know what had caused the sudden commotion in the hall. Michael shot past him, and there was a loud crash.

Bartholomew darted forward. The floorboards inside the door had been removed, and in the resulting recess sat a handsome walnut chest. Dympna. Bartholomew spotted it too late, and suffered the same fate as Michael. He caught his foot in the gaping hole, and slid the entire length of the conclave on his stomach.

He joined Michael in a mass of colourful arms and legs – the monk had evidently entered the room with such force he had collided with Yna and Makejoy and had bowled them from their feet. While the physician tried to disentangle himself and work out what was happening, the door was slammed shut and a heavy bench dragged across it.

'What are you doing, Frith?' asked Kenyngham in dismay. 'Now no one else can come in.'

'You do not want people wandering in and out while your gold is sitting in full view,' said Frith reasonably. 'It is better we keep the door closed until it is hidden again.'

'Very well,' said Kenyngham tiredly. 'Are you hurt, Michael? If not, you should stand up, because I think that poor lady underneath you is suffocating.' He turned to Frith. 'You said you would leave once you had the chest. There it is. Now take it and go.'

Michael gaped in astonishment, removing himself from Makejoy, who struggled to her knees and attempted to catch her breath. 'What are you doing, Father? This money has been used for good deeds. Why are you prepared to give it away?'

Frith smiled unpleasantly. 'Because I have just informed him that if he does not, I shall set light to his College and burn it to the ground with every Michaelhouse scholar inside it. The friar is an intelligent man, and knows when folk are speaking the truth.'

'They were just leaving when you crashed in,' said Kenyngham to Michael, sounding tearful. 'They promised they would take the chest and be gone by nightfall. It is only money. Ten Dympnas would not be worth a single life.'

'But lives may be lost once Dympna has gone,' Michael pointed out, ignoring Frith and addressing Kenyngham. He took Bartholomew's hand and allowed himself to be hauled to his feet. Makejoy and Yna stayed where they were, the former running tentative hands down her arms and legs as she tested for damage, while the other appeared to have been knocked all but insensible. 'It is not just a chest of coins: it is something that has helped a lot of people.'

'But, like all earthly wealth, it has become tainted,' said Kenyngham softly. 'I am not overly distressed to see it go.'

'Ailred,' said Bartholomew, watching him closely. 'You are referring to Ailred.'

Kenyngham nodded, and his saintly face was grey with sorrow. 'He was a good man, but the gold corrupted him. He started to make illegal loans from the chest, so I was obliged to demand custody of it three weeks ago. He was not pleased. He was even less pleased when I confronted him with the fact that a large amount was unaccounted for.'

'Did you tell Tulyet?' asked Bartholomew.

Kenyngham shook his head. 'There was no need for that. I simply gave Ailred notice that the missing gold had to be returned by the end of the Twelve Days – in four days' time now – because that is when we will lend a sizeable sum to Robert de Blaston to demolish the High Street hovels and replace them with decent dwellings. Ailred had almost a month to recover it all.'

'Ailred needed funds quickly, so he started calling in the loans he should never have granted,' said Bartholomew to Michael. 'The first note from Dympna to Norbert was about three weeks ago. We were right: Ailred did demand money from Norbert in Dympna's name.'

'Ailred gave funds to Norbert?' asked Kenyngham in horror. 'That young man made an official application, but it was refused on the grounds that he wanted it to squander on earthly pleasures. That is not the purpose of Dympna.'

'This is beginning to make sense,' said Michael, brushing himself down. 'The question that remains, however, is how did Ailred come to use the Waits as his accomplices? Did they travel to Cambridge for that purpose? Or was it just incidental to avenging the murdered Fiscurtune?'

He turned questioningly to the jugglers. Makejoy was flexing an arm in a way that suggested it was damaged, while

Yna held her head, still dazed. Frith had listened carefully to the exchange between the scholars, while Jestyn stood guard at the door, picking at a skinned elbow. Bartholomew understood exactly why Frith was prepared to let the scholars talk among themselves without interruption: he was giving the women time to recover, and then they were going to make their escape – with the chest.

'Langelee!' he shouted urgently, wondering whether the Master had gone for an axe, or whether he had decided to wait and see what happened before damaging his precious College. Considering the conclave door had been slammed in his face, Bartholomew sincerely hoped Langelee had the sense to do something practical.

'Quiet!' hissed Jestyn menacingly. 'Or I will silence you once and for all.'

Suddenly, both he and Frith had knives in their hands. Jestyn seemed uncertain and nervous, and Bartholomew saw that he was the kind of man who would use his weapon just because he could think of no other way out of the predicament in which he found himself. Bartholomew drew breath to shout again, to warn the Master the Waits were armed, but Jestyn was on him in an instant, and the physician found himself pressed hard against the wall with the blade of a knife held at his throat by a desperate and frightened man.

'I think Jestyn is suggesting we shall have no more shouting,' said Frith, when he saw his friend was fully prepared to slit the physician's throat if another sound was uttered. 'He is right: we do not want everyone in a frenzy over nothing. People might get hurt.'

Michael took a step forward, to go to Bartholomew's aid, but stopped dead when Frith grabbed Kenyngham's arm and waved his own weapon menacingly near the old man's face.

'Sit on the bench by the wall.' Makejoy's stern voice came from the other side of the room. She was kneeling next to Yna, who had apparently suffered the most from the monk's onslaught. 'All of you. And put your hands on your knees, where we can see them. If you do as you are told no one will be harmed.'

There was no option but to obey. Bartholomew eased past the agitated Jestyn and went to the bench, relieved to be away from the unsteady blade. Michael perched next to him, while Kenyngham sat on the monk's other side. They placed their hands on their knees and waited, watching while Frith had low and urgent words with Jestyn, obviously attempting to calm him. Bartholomew suspected he was lucky that Jestyn had not silenced him with a stab wound there and then; the fellow looked unsettled enough to commit a rash act.

He looked around, assessing his chances of reaching the door and removing the heavy bench before Jestyn could catch him. He decided they were slim. And what would happen to Michael and Kenyngham if he escaped, anyway? The Waits would still have hostages, and therefore the means to force Langelee to do what they wanted.

Frith hefted the box of coins from the hole in the floor and set it on the bench next to Bartholomew. The physician glanced at it, and saw it was about half full of gold nobles, along with some jewellery with precious stones. There were silver coins, too, and a neatly bound stack of parchments listing various transactions that had been made. Bartholomew looked at the top page, and saw Ailred had kept a careful list of his loans, despite the fact that they had been made without his colleagues' consent. Near the end was Norbert's name, with the numbers one, thirteen and four next to it. They were the same digits as on the note Quenhyth had found in the Waits' belongings. He wondered whether the parchment had been retrieved from Norbert when he had gone to meet 'Dympna' in the church, or if it had been written but never sent. Regardless, it was a strong indication that the Waits were Ailred's accomplices.

'When did you become involved in this?' asked Michael of Frith. 'And how?'

Frith smiled. 'Have you not worked that out yet? You

scholars think you are so clever, and yet you know nothing.'

'I know enough,' said Michael, unruffled by the jibe. 'I know you probably hail from a village called Fiscurtune, which is also Ailred's home. And I know you were keen to avenge the death of one John Fiscurtune, who was murdered by Walter Turke. It is no coincidence that you and Turke's household arrived in Cambridge on the same day.'

'Good,' said Frith, clapping his hands together in mocking congratulations. 'And how did you guess all this?'

'Because we know you helped Ailred regain his bad loans. Since he would not have told just anyone about them, it is reasonable to assume he told someone he trusted. A kinsman. You have been here since the fifteenth of December, which is about when Norbert had his first letter.'

'Ailred and John of Fiscurtune are my uncles,' said Frith. 'They were brothers to Isabella – my mother – who was Turke's first wife, God rest her poor soul.'

'Do you mean that you are Turke's son?' asked Kenyngham, bewildered.

Frith looked angry. 'Of course not! Turke was my mother's second husband, and my stepfather. He married her because she was a wealthy widow. When I learned he planned to embark on the pilgrimage he imagined would absolve him of Uncle John's murder, I decided a journey of my own was in order. Someone needed to prevent a killer from becoming Lord Mayor.'

'You make it sound altruistic,' said Michael scathingly. 'Be honest. You wanted to kill Turke because Fiscurtune's death meant there was no one to recommend you to wealthy merchants.'

'But Frith did not kill Turke,' Kenyngham pointed out. 'Turke fell through the ice while skating. The whole town knows his death was an accident.'

'Uncle John's son – my cousin – is not interested in avenging his father,' said Frith bitterly, ignoring the friar. 'He will spare a few pennies for a requiem mass, but that will be all.'

'I thought Fiscurtune's son had drowned himself,' said Bartholomew, recalling a story Quenhyth had spun.

'His rescuers should have let him die when he hurled himself into the Thames,' said Frith, turning angrily on him. 'Uncle John deserved better than that ungrateful wretch – he should have been disowned and I made heir in his place. I would have made Uncle John proud.'

'By playing the pipe and tabor?' asked Michael archly. 'However, although you may not have killed Turke, two other men have died in suspicious circumstances: Norbert and Gosslinge are connected to the chain of events that led you to help Ailred collect his lost pledges.'

'We had nothing to do with either of them,' said Jestyn furiously. He turned accusingly to Frith. 'You see? I told you they would blame us if we became involved in the mess your uncle created with his box of gold. Now they think we have committed murder!'

'Well, we did not,' said Frith shortly. Bartholomew found his denial unconvincing and, judging by the uncomfortable expressions on the faces of Jestyn and Makejoy, so did they. 'This is all Turke's fault. If he had kept control of his temper, Uncle John would still be alive and we would be enjoying a continuation of our success in Chepe.'

'We should not be here,' agreed Jestyn. He glanced around him disparagingly. 'I do not like these religious institutions. They are full of fanatics and lunatics. We are not safe.'

'We would have managed in Chepe without Fiscurtune, Frith,' said Makejoy, bitterly. 'But Jestyn is right: we should not have come and we should stay here no longer. I want to leave now.'

'In a moment,' said Frith, indicating Yna with a nod of his head and giving Makejoy a meaningful look. Yna was still unsteady on her feet, and Frith wanted to give her more time to recover before making what would probably be a dramatic escape.

'What was Fiscurtune like?' asked Bartholomew, taking advantage of the fact that the Waits were predisposed to talk. It occurred to him that the Fiscurtune described by Tulyet, Giles and Philippa did not seem the kind of character to inspire others to great loyalty. 'You were ready to avenge him, and yet others claim he was . . . less worthy.'

'I suppose you spoke to Abigny and Turke's wife,' said Frith with a sneer. 'Of course *they* would not like Uncle John. He could be rude, and the early loss of his teeth did not improve his looks. But, nevertheless, he was hurt when Philippa rejected him as a suitor.'

'Turke and Fiscurtune were both courting her,' said Bartholomew, recalling that Philippa had chosen Turke on the basis of his roofed latrine.

'My uncle was better off without her,' declared Frith vehemently. 'Later, he invented a new method for salting fish, but Turke would not give him permission to develop it, despite the fact that it would have made the finished product cheaper to buy. My uncle was an imaginative man.'

'So, you travelled to Cambridge after his murder, where you met Ailred and agreed to do two things,' surmised Bartholomew. 'First, you would ensure that Turke never finished his pilgrimage; and second, you offered to help Ailred extricate himself from the mess he had created with Dympna. Unfortunately – or perhaps fortunately, depending on your point of view – Turke died naturally before you could do anything about the first. But you have been very active as regards the second.'

Frith looked away. 'Ailred is not dishonest, just weak. I think he enjoyed the power to make people's wishes come true. He is just a man who cannot say no – even to someone like Norbert.'

'But he – with your help – intends to do something dishonest now,' Bartholomew pointed out. 'Once Dympna has gone, it will never help needy souls again.'

'Right,' agreed Frith. 'But its disappearance also means that the amount outstanding from Ailred's bad loans will be irrelevant, and he will be free from the whole nasty mess.'

Makejoy cleared her throat noisily, giving Frith the kind

of look that indicated she thought he was making a grave mistake by telling the scholars all their secrets. Bartholomew felt his hopes rise. Makejoy would not be concerned about such matters if she believed the encounter would end with their deaths. Meanwhile, Yna was recovering fast.

'Is that why you killed Norbert?' asked Michael. 'Because he did not pay what he owed?'

'We have killed no one!' shouted Jestyn, becoming distressed by the repeated accusations. 'We occasionally relieve folk of baubles, but we have *not* committed murder!'

'Baubles like our salt dish and Wynewyk's inkpot?' asked Michael. 'And Ulfrid's knife, which led me to wonder whether *he* had stabbed Harysone? And Quenhyth's scrip?'

'We would not touch anything of Quenhyth's,' said Makejoy in distaste. 'He hates us, because we made him look foolish over the "theft" of a chalice. He blamed us, but it later transpired that his father had sold the cup in order to pay for the wedding we were hired to perform at. He had not wanted anyone to know he was short of funds, and was furious when his son drew attention to his missing silver. It created a breach between them that has never healed.'

Bartholomew noted Makejoy had only denied stealing the scrip, and assumed they had indeed taken the other items. 'You took Gosslinge's clothes,' he said, thinking their light fingers probably explained other mysteries, too.

'He did not need them,' replied Frith. 'And I did not see why we should leave them for Turke to reclaim.' He spat into the rushes on the floor.

'If it was not you,' said Michael, 'then who killed Norbert?'

'Turke,' said Frith flatly. 'He was the sort of man who enjoyed taking the lives of the innocent – as poor Uncle John could tell you.'

'Can you prove that?' asked Bartholomew. He had suggested this particular solution earlier, but had discounted the possibility because he could not think of a plausible motive.

Frith sneered, in a way that suggested he could not.

'Gosslinge, then,' said Michael. 'Did you kill him by stuffing vellum into his throat?'

'We did not!' denied Jestyn hotly, the knife even more unsteady in his sweating hand. 'What kind of folk do you think we are? We have killed no one!'

'We have not,' agreed Frith. 'Indeed, I even tried to save Gosslinge when he started to choke, but the vellum was lodged too deeply inside him. It later occurred to me that his corpse was being kept above ground for an unnaturally long period of time, and I thought the physician here might be planning to dissect him for some anatomy lesson. I was afraid he might find the vellum, and associate Gosslinge with Uncle Ailred and Dympna . . .'

'Ha!' exclaimed Michael. 'So *you* were the intruders in St Michael's Church that night.'

'But we did not *do* anything,' said Jestyn in a voice that shook with tension. 'Those priests arrived before we could have a proper look for the thing, and as soon as they left we heard a commotion outside. We saw we were going to have no peace, so we escaped while we could.'

'I searched your room the night that blizzard raged,' said Frith to Bartholomew, gloating at the appalled expression on the physician's face when he realised that he had slept through the invasion. 'But when I saw what had become of the vellum after a week in a corpse, I could not bring myself to touch it. However, I was fairly certain that nothing would be legible, anyway.'

'But we killed no one,' said Jestyn, returning to a theme that was clearly important to him. He stepped forward and brandished his knife in a way that made Bartholomew think it would not be long before the juggler claimed his first victim. 'No one.'

'I shall make my own mind up about that,' said Michael, disdainfully watching the knife that quivered in the man's hand. Bartholomew nudged him, sensing Jestyn was near the end of his tether. As long as the Wait was brandishing a weapon, he did not think it was wise to aggravate him.

'Then let us return to Turke,' said Michael, the tone of his voice making it clear that he still had the entertainers marked as responsible for the death of both Norbert and Gosslinge. He looked at them one by one. 'Did you force him on to the ice against his will?'

'We were not there,' said Makejoy, casting another uneasy glance at Frith, as though she was not sure that was true of him.

'No one killed Turke,' said Frith firmly. 'I would have knifed him, as he killed my uncle, to let him see his life blood drain away and know that there was nothing he could do to save himself. And Ailred did not do it, either, before you think to abuse his good name.'

'If you divide Dympna between you – I assume you plan to share with Ailred – how will he explain his sudden riches?' asked Bartholomew. 'Surely it will raise questions, especially so soon after the mysterious disappearance of a large sum of money from his keeping?'

He saw Frith look at Makejoy, asking silently whether Yna was sufficiently recovered. He obviously wanted her alert and mobile, so they could leave and put an end to the uncomfortable inquisition. Makejoy examined Yna, then indicated that more time was needed.

'He can say it is a legacy from a kinsman,' said Frith. He grimaced. 'Perhaps even from his brother, John. That would be an ironic twist to the tale, would it not? Besides, no one will be looking at Ailred's finances when all attention is fixed on Michaelhouse. Fires are always breaking out in the winter, when the weather is cold and people are careless with their hearths. The one that starts here today will give people enough to talk about.'

'But you said if I gave you the chest you would leave with no violence,' objected Kenyngham.

'I never intended you to live,' said Frith coldly. 'I love my uncle, and I do not want you alive to denounce him as a thief. It would break his heart.'

'So will being an accessory to murder,' said Bartholomew.

'I do not know about this, Frith,' said Makejoy uneasily, exchanging an agitated glance with Jestyn. 'It is not what we agreed . . .'

'We cannot back down now, unless you want to hang,' said Frith, silencing her with a look. 'This is our only way out. If you leave these men alive they will set Sheriff Morice after us and we will all die.'

'That is not true,' said Bartholomew desperately. 'No one need—'

'I have made up my mind,' interrupted Frith. 'I will not leave you scholars in a position to harm us. Uncle Ailred will assume the fire started by accident, just like everyone else and will never know your deaths were a deliberate act.'

'But other people share our suspicions,' argued Michael untruthfully. 'We are not the only ones who know about Ailred's abuses of Dympna and your role in the affair.'

'Who?' demanded Frith, furiously. He approached Michael with menace in his eyes, fingering his knife. He drew back his arm, and with horror Bartholomew saw he intended to stab the monk there and then, perhaps in the hope of frightening the others into telling him what he wanted to know.

The physician cast around desperately, looking for something – anything – he could use as a weapon. Frith stood over Michael and assessed the monk coldly, as if deciding which part he should pierce first. With mounting panic, Bartholomew saw there was nothing available, that he would be obliged to watch while his friend was butchered. Then his frantic gaze fell on the open box of coins at his side. He dropped his hand and snatched up as many as he could hold, then flung them as hard as he could in Frith's face.

As the sharp edges cut into him, Frith howled in pain and Jestyn sprang forward with his dagger poised to strike. Jestyn was agitated, fearful that Frith's plan would see him hanged even if they did manage to escape with the gold, and Bartholomew saw again that he was irrational enough to kill all three scholars just because he did not know what

410

else to do. The physician braced himself as Jestyn lurched forward, ready to fight back if he could.

With cool aplomb, Kenyngham thrust out a foot and Jestyn stumbled into Michael. The monk gave the Wait a hefty shove that sent him sprawling into the two women. With shrieks of pain and outrage, Makejoy and Yna were bowled to the ground for a second time that day.

Bartholomew leapt to his feet and flung more coins at Frith, wondering how long he, Michael and the elderly friar could hold off strong, armed men like the Waits. He yelled for Langelee, shouting even more loudly when he saw the two women – Yna was now fully recovered – draw small, nasty-looking knives of their own. He lobbed more coins in their direction, then backed away in alarm as Frith uttered a howl of fury and advanced on the physician with his dagger stretched in front of him and his left hand raised to protect his bleeding face from further injury.

There was a loud thump at the door and everyone jumped in alarm. Even Frith stopped in his tracks. Then there was a crash, and the blade of an axe could be seen glinting through the wood before it was torn out again. Langelee was coming to rescue his colleagues.

Frith glanced at Jestyn, and Bartholomew saw them reach an unspoken understanding. Not wanting to find out what it entailed, he went on the offensive. He lunged for Jestyn but missed, and the burly Wait raced past and hurled himself at one of the tall windows. Glass flew in all directions as he hurtled through, leaving a jagged hole behind him. Frith followed, lumbering like an ox, while the women were more agile as they disappeared. Bartholomew darted forward, half expecting to see them lying with broken bones on the ground below. But all were up and running, and heading for the open gate.

'Catch them!' he yelled to Quenhyth, who was gaping stupidly at the spectacle. 'Do not let them escape!'

But even the Waits' mediocre skill in somersaults and tumbles made them adept at avoiding Quenhyth's clumsy

411

lunges. They jigged past him, and he only succeeded in snatching thin air. Bartholomew watched helplessly as they reached the gate and Frith turned to make a defiant and abusive gesture. Makejoy was fumbling with the latch, and Bartholomew saw she would have it open long before Quenhyth could stop them.

The Waits, however, had not taken Michaelhouse's stalwart Fellows into account. Alerted by Bartholomew's shouts and the sound of smashing glass, they emerged from the porters' lodge, where they had evidently been given gate duties by the Lord of Misrule. William was wielding a crutch like a madman, while Clippesby had grabbed a poker from the fire. Its end glowed red hot, and the Waits backed away in alarm. Wynewyk was waving the sword the porters kept for emergencies in a way that suggested that although he was not competent with it, he could still do a lot of damage. Suttone, while declining to go too near the affray lest he come to personal harm, lobbed logs at the escaping entertainers.

The Waits did not stand much chance once the Fellows had sprung into action. Makejoy dropped shrieking to the ground as a log caught her a nasty blow on one knee. Jestyn abandoned his knife in order to smother the flames that started to lick up his tunic, then surrendered to Clippesby when he saw the friar was prepared to set him alight again. Wynewyk had Yna backed up against a wall, and she was covering her head with her hands as the wavering blade threatened to scalp her. And, as for Frith, there was a sharp crack as a crutch met a head, and he crumpled into an insensible heap on the snowy ground.

The following morning, Bartholomew sat in William's room, explaining to the bemused Franciscan Thomas Bradwardine's theory about the relationship between moving power and resistance. It was a difficult text, full of mathematical statements and axioms, all leading to calculations showing the variations in velocity that occurred when the original ratios of moving force and resistance were less than, more than or equal to the *proportio dupla*, which was two-to-one. Despite its complexity, the physician regarded it as exciting scholarship, and tried hard to simplify it for William, so they could debate it together.

'Heresy,' muttered William darkly, before Bartholomew had reached the end of his analysis of the second of Bradwardine's twelve conclusions. 'You do not need to know ratios in order to apply force or resist something.'

'That is not the point,' said Bartholomew, frustrated. 'Bradwardine is explaining moving power and resistance in mathematical terms – to define them as universal laws.'

'Only God makes universal laws,' said William firmly. 'It is not for men from Oxford to try to do it.' So much contempt dripped from his voice when the name of the Other University was mentioned that Bartholomew decided he had better find someone else to debate with. His eyes lit up when there was a perfunctory knock at the door and Michael entered.

'Good,' he said, pleased. The monk had a sharp mind, and was easily the best Fellow to engage in a discussion about natural philosophy. The others tended to dismiss physics and mathematics as secular – and therefore inferior – subjects. 'Let me read you Bradwardine's refutation of Aristotle's theorem pertaining to the second opinion—'

'When will Matthew's own room be available?' interrupted William rudely. 'I do not think I can take much more of this velocity business. I should have offered him a copy of Thomas Sutton's *De pluralitate formarum* instead. That is a religious commentary, and would have kept him away from all this nonsense involving resistance.'

'You gave him a book?' asked Michael suspiciously. 'Why did you do that?'

William blanched, rubbing the still-splinted leg in agitation. He began to prevaricate, clearing his throat and coughing, while he tried to invent a reason for the gift that Michael would accept. He certainly did not want the Senior Proctor to know he had been malingering.

413

'It was payment for treating his leg,' replied Bartholomew truthfully, although he was aware that Michael knew perfectly well William's injury was not as serious as he claimed. 'And for keeping certain personal details confidential.'

'What kind of details?' demanded Michael immediately.

Bartholomew laughed. 'This is an excellent book, and I do not want to give it back by betraying William's medical history. Anyway, his injury is none of your affair. Leave him alone.'

'Thank you, Matthew,' said William, relieved. 'But I still mean what I said about Bradwardine. The next time I require your confidential services, you will be getting Sutton.'

'Look at this, Matt,' said Michael, proffering a piece of parchment.

'It is the list of loans made by Dympna since its origins during the plague,' said Bartholomew, glancing at it. His eyes strayed back to the much more tempting words of Bradwardine. 'I saw it yesterday, when Frith had us trapped in the conclave.'

'I have been going over it with Kenyngham,' said Michael. 'Ailred made loans totalling almost ten pounds over the last few weeks. Some money has been repaid, but most has not. Norbert was lent three pounds, eight shillings and fourpence, which was the amount mentioned on the note we found inside Gosslinge. Meanwhile one pound, thirteen shillings and fourpence, the amount on the note Quenhyth found in Frith's belongings, was demanded from him the day he died.'

'So, you were right about the "missing hour" in Norbert's last night,' said William. 'He left Ovyng and went to St Michael's to meet Dympna, who was actually Frith. It was only after that he went to the King's Head, where he stayed for the rest of the evening.'

'He left the tavern at midnight and was stabbed on the way home,' said Michael. 'By Frith, I imagine, because he failed to bring money for Dympna, yet promptly went to a tavern and bought ale and a woman. But Norbert's is not the only name next to an amount that is outstanding.'

Michael looked pleased with himself, and the physician knew why. 'Harysone's is there.'

Michael was crestfallen. 'How did you know that?'

'I noticed it yesterday. You must be happy: you have been looking for an opportunity like this ever since he arrived.'

'It is enough for me to expel him from the town if he refuses to pay. I am going to see him now, in the King's Head. Come with me.'

'No, thank you,' said Bartholomew. 'I do not want to help you victimise a man who has done nothing but borrow money. You had him marked down as involved in the deaths of Gosslinge, Norbert and Turke at various stages of the investigation, and you were wrong.'

'He borrowed two pounds, thirteen shillings and four-pence.' Michael grinned with delight. 'And that is what he must pay me today, or he can leave my town. I do not want debtors here: we have enough of our own.'

'But if you send him away, Dympna will never be repaid.'

Michael sat on the windowsill and folded his arms. 'You think I am unreasonable, but I do not trust that man. He has done nothing illegal – at least, nothing that I know about – but it is only a matter of time before he does. I want him gone. Trust me, Matt. I am not often wrong about these things.'

'Very well,' said Bartholomew, rising reluctantly and placing his new book on a shelf. He glared at William. 'Your splint can come off soon, and then *you* can trail around after the Senior Proctor like a performing bear.'

'Tomorrow,' said William. He cast a disparaging look at the Bradwardine. 'I would rather be evicting pardoners from taverns than listening to theories about things that push and pull, anyway.'

'Do not hurry on my account,' muttered Michael to Bartholomew as they started to walk to the High Street, Bartholomew still fastening the clasp on his cloak. 'It has been a pleasant relief to be rid of him for a while, although my fines chest is not what it was. You can let him malinger a little longer, so he has his money's worth for the book he gave you. You are as bad as Morice – prepared to sell your soul for material goods. But speak of the Devil and he will appear.'

Sheriff Morice was riding along the High Street on his handsome grey horse. His saddle gleamed expensively, and his fur-lined cloak was thick and heavy. His lieutenants flanked him, gaudy, fluttering hens around a strutting peacock. Morice was in the very centre of the road, where he was least likely to be deluged by the snow that still dropped from roofs. He rode carelessly, making no attempt to steer around other folk, and anyone who did not move was casually trampled.

'I have just seen some students in the King's Head,' he announced to Michael, reining in and gazing with brazen disdain at the monk. 'I ordered them out, but they informed me I had no jurisdiction over them. I want them imprisoned and fined for insolence.'

'What are their names?' asked Michael coolly.

'I did not bother to find out,' said Morice nastily. 'I have better things to do than engage in conversation with a group of ill-mannered louts who think a Franciscan habit gives them leave to insult the Sheriff.'

'I am on my way to the King's Head now,' said Michael, patting Morice's elegantly clad leg patronisingly. 'Do not worry; I will show them who is master. But what were you doing in such a disreputable institution? I hear there are some illegal gambling games scheduled in the King's Head this week. Were you planning to take part?'

'I do not gamble in taverns,' snapped Morice, leaving everyone who heard him with the impression that he gambled elsewhere. 'I was visiting a man named Harysone. Complaints have been filed against him for licentious dancing, so I was obliged to demand a fine of two shillings.'

'Really?' asked Michael, amused. 'I hope he paid, because I am about to order him to leave Cambridge. He has borrowed funds from a charitable chest, and if he does not

416

have the money to give me now, he will be escorted to the town gates tomorrow at dawn.'

'If he goes, he will never repay this charity,' said Morice, obviously regarding financial considerations first and foremost. 'But he may have sold enough books to make a respectable profit, so perhaps you will be in luck. Deal with those students, though, Brother, or I shall be obliged to teach them a lesson myself.'

He spurred his horse into a rapid trot, scattering people and animals as he went. His men cantered after him, following his cavalier example.

When Bartholomew and Michael reached the King's Head, a celebration was in progress. People were laughing and singing, and there was an atmosphere of gaiety. Michael looked around him in astonishment, while Bartholomew entered with a degree of unease, sensing something had happened that might mean scholars were unwelcome. But they were greeted with pleasure by Isnard the bargeman, who sang bass in Michael's choir. He clapped a large, calloused hand across Michael's shoulders and passed the monk his goblet. Michael accepted a drink cautiously.

The main room was full, and fires were burning in both hearths. All the shutters were firmly closed, but this was common practice in the King's Head, where the patrons did not want their activities observed by Sheriff's men or beadles peering through the windows. The air smelled of wood-smoke, spilled ale and unwashed bodies, and was close and humid. Bartholomew felt himself begin to sweat. A group of pardoners sat near one fire, Harysone among them, while Ovyng's Franciscans were standing around the hearth at the opposite end of the room. Godric seemed to be the centre of the general bonhomie.

'That Godric is a fine lad!' slurred Isnard, eyeing the friar fondly.

Bartholomew watched with amusement as he saw Godric glance in Michael's direction, look away, then back again with an expression of horror. He nudged his companions, who all hastily downed the remains of their ale and headed for the door, pursued by disappointed cries from their drinking companions.

'Godric,' said Michael pleasantly, stopping the young friar in his tracks. 'A word, please.'

'It was not my fault,' said Godric immediately. A chorus of support from his cronies told Michael that was true.

'Morice complained about you,' said Michael. 'He wants you arrested and fined.'

'Never!' declared Isnard warmly, removing his arm from Michael and draping it around Godric. 'This good priest told that leech where to go, and we will not see him fined for his courage. Will we, lads?' There were loud shouts of agreement. 'Morice prances in here and starts demanding money for all manner of imagined crimes. He ordered me to pay sixpence because my donkey fouled the Great Bridge, but look what *he* did!'

Bartholomew and Michael followed his accusing finger to a pile of fresh horse dung that sat in splendid isolation in the centre of the room.

'Morice rode his horse inside the tavern?' asked Michael in astonishment.

'Either that or he should lay off the hay,' muttered Bartholomew. He had not intended his comment to be overheard, but Isnard caught it, and repeated it in a braying voice to the delight of the other patrons. More back-slapping followed, and it was declared that scholars were splendid fellows, and worthy company for honest townsmen.

'He fined Harysone for dancing – two shillings!' added Isnard when the levity had died down. 'Mind you, Harysone's jigs do verge on the obscene, so I cannot blame the Sheriff for that. But when Morice tried to fine Godric for being in a tavern the lad pointed out the law regarding scholars, and sent him away with something to think about.'

'I was not abusive,' said Godric quickly. 'I just pointed out that clerics are under your authority, not his. I will pay *you* the four pennies he demanded. But we will not pay him.'

'That will not be necessary,' announced Michael to more cheers. He lowered his voice so the townsmen would not hear. 'But this tavern is no place for scholars, lad. Go home, and do not let me find you here again.' He caught Godric's arm as he made to leave. 'I do not suppose you have heard from your principal?'

Godric gave a rueful smile. 'Do you think we would be here if he was back? Anyway, I have already promised we will send you word if he returns. Ailred needs more help than we can give him, so you can rely on us to contact you.'

'But we do not believe him to be guilty,' added one of the students. 'We talked about it all last night. He may have made mistakes with this charity – Dympna – but we do not think he killed Norbert.'

'He is a desperate man,' said Bartholomew gently. 'And desperate men are often driven to do things they would never normally contemplate.'

'He may have been desperate, but he was not wicked,' insisted Godric loyally. 'I went through the hostel's finances last night, and do you know why we have been shivering in front of mean fires and eating bad fish all week? It is because Ailred gathered together all the funds he could find, and bought food and firewood to make Dunstan's last few days comfortable.'

'That was from Dympna,' said Michael. 'Robin of Grantchester organised its delivery, as he did with its other loans and gifts.'

Godric shook his head vehemently. 'I have the receipts for every item of food and every scrap of fuel that Dunstan received. They match outgoing sums from our own accounts – along with money Ailred had from selling a silver locket that belonged to a brother called John.'

Fiscurtune's locket, thought Bartholomew immediately. Since it was evident Ailred had loved his brother, selling something that had belonged to him would not have been easy.

'You said you did not know whether Ailred had any male kin,' he said to Godric.

'I did not,' replied Godric. He gestured to one of his colleagues. 'But he mentioned a brother called John to Nathan here. It was Nathan who sold the locket on Ailred's behalf the day Athelbald died.'

'He was fond of that trinket,' added Nathan. 'But he parted with it to help Dunstan. He is not a wicked man.'

Michael released Godric's arm, and watched the Franciscans troop out of the tavern, accepting the congratulations of delighted townsfolk as they went. They were a serious, sober group, and Bartholomew wondered why they did not prefer the quieter atmosphere of a tavern like the Brazen George or the Swan. He supposed it was because the King's Head was outside the town gates, so they were less likely to be caught there by other members of their Order.

Michael strolled nonchalantly towards Harysone, and Bartholomew was amused to see the pardoner's companions hastily slip away, reluctant to be with the man while he had yet another brush with town officials. The monk plumped himself down in a recently vacated chair and beamed alarmingly. Bartholomew sat next to him, while Isnard and the others went back to their ale.

'You owe Dympna a lot of money,' said Michael without preamble. 'When can you pay?'

'Never mind that,' said Harysone indignantly. 'I was stabbed in the back by the Franciscan friars you just spoke to. Why did you not arrest them?'

'There is no evidence those particular clerics harmed you,' said Michael. 'And I am far more interested in the fact that you owe Dympna three pounds. I repeat: when can you pay?'

'It was two pounds, thirteen shillings and fourpence,' said Harysone immediately. He did not seem surprised by Michael's demand, and Bartholomew wondered whether he had been anticipating it. 'I will pay you next week, since I will have sold enough books by then. However, I did not expect a request for repayment quite so soon. Loans are usually made for longer periods.'

'Your particular transaction was illegal,' said Michael. 'Father Ailred is ill, and made some poor decisions. When exactly did he make this loan to you?'

'He gave me the money last Wednesday evening,' replied Harysone. 'I was surprised by the speed at which he obliged me. It is the only good thing I have to say about your town: your moneylenders make rapid decisions. The interest was a little high, but I suppose haste costs.'

'Interest?' asked Michael. 'Dympna does not charge interest. That is its appeal.'

'Well, it charged me,' said Harysone firmly. 'I borrowed two pounds, but agreed to pay two pounds, thirteen shillings and fourpence by the end of next month. By loaning me six marks, Ailred was going to gain another two.'

'And you paid Langelee for the relic two days later, on the Friday,' said Bartholomew to Harysone, who nodded. The physician leaned close to Michael and spoke in a low voice. 'Ailred must have been trying to recoup his losses by charging interest. But although Harysone's tale answers one question, it raises another. It explains why Ailred lied about his whereabouts the night the intruders entered St Michael's: he was busy making an illegal loan. However, by last week, Kenyngham had already reclaimed Dympna and had stored it in Michaelhouse, so where did this two pounds come from?'

'That is something we shall have to ask Ailred,' said Michael. He eyed the pardoner coldly. 'Why did you need to borrow money, when you seem to be doing well with your book sales?'

Harysone smiled again, showing his unpleasant ivory teeth. He fingered the bag containing what Bartholomew believed was Gosslinge's thumb. 'This relic of St Zeno cost me five pounds – which was more than I could lay my hands on at short notice, so I was obliged to seek out Dympna and ask for funds. Langelee threatened to sell it to someone else unless I came up with the money quickly, you see.'

'How did you learn about Dympna?' asked Michael.

'I asked people,' replied Harysone. 'There was a fat laund-ress who let slip that Robin of Grantchester might help me. I was about to knock at Robin's door when I happened to hear him muttering to someone about Dympna and Father Ailred of Ovyng. A friar seemed a better class of person than that surgeon, so I approached Ailred and the transaction was agreed – very quickly, as I told you. I was to repay it by the end of the month, but you can have it next week, if you insist.'

Robin was talking to his pig again, Bartholomew surmised, probably railing bitterly that Ailred and the others did not consider him an equal member of Dympna. So, Clippesby was not the only one to overhear the man murmuring to himself, and Harysone had also benefited from the surgeon's dangerous and unwise habit.

'I want it today,' said Michael. 'And if you cannot pay, I shall ask you to leave. The road to London is now open, and we cannot afford debtors here. In my experience, they never raise the money they promise, but become entangled in a web of ever-increasing obligations.'

'Very well,' said Harysone stiffly. 'I would have paid you next week, but since you choose to be unpleasant I shall leave and you will never have it. I am weary of this sordid little town anyway. It is dirty and soulless, and I dislike the fact that you have harassed me continuously and your Sheriff has not stopped demanding money. I would not have had to borrow from Dympna if he had not fined me every time we met.'

'For jigging like a Turkish whore?' said Michael expres-sionlessly.

'For demonstrating my dancing skills,' replied Harysone huffily. 'And now, if you will excuse me, I shall set about packing my remaining books. Goodbye, Brother. I hope we never have the misfortune to meet each other again.'

'I quite agree,' said Michael, sitting back with a happy

smile. The pardoner was leaving, Dympna's remaining funds were secure with Kenyngham, and he had arrested the people who he believed had murdered Norbert and Gosslinge. Michael was a contented man.

'Just tell me again,' said Langelee, shaking his head in confusion. 'Simply this time, without all the details. How did you guess that Ailred and the Waits were planning to steal Dympna?'

Langelee and the other Michaelhouse Fellows were sitting in the conclave three mornings later. A fire burned brightly, but the shutters were closed because the Waits had smashed the largest of the three windows and it had not yet been repaired. In the hall next door, the students were sitting quietly, reading or playing innocent games like chess or backgammon. Deynman had tried to induce them to do something more daring on his last day of chaos, but Michaelhouse's students were not a seriously rebellious crowd, and most had already had enough of the season of misrule. They were keen to return to their lessons, and to settle back into the rules and regulations that governed their lives – where they would not be served green food.

'It is not difficult,' said Michael, holding out his cup to be refilled. Langelee stood to oblige him. 'First, a man named John Fiscurtune was murdered by Turke. Turke bought himself a pardon, and no more was said on the matter.'

'That is odd in itself,' said Langelee, frowning. 'Someone must have objected to a murder.'

'Someone did,' said Michael. 'Fiscurtune's kinsmen: his brother Ailred and his nephew Frith. Meanwhile, Turke knew he needed to atone publicly for the crime – which otherwise might prevent him from becoming Lord Mayor of London – by undertaking a pilgrimage.'

'Frith lived in Chepe, where his Uncle John Fiscurtune secured him plenty of business,' said Bartholomew. 'It must have been hard to watch Turke enjoy his freedom, while

Frith and his friends began to lose their custom. I imagine his hatred festered and he began to plot a murder of his own. But Turke was wealthy and it is not easy to attack such a man in a well-populated city. It was only when Turke announced his pilgrimage that Frith saw his opportunity.'

'The Waits are thieves,' said Suttone, holding out his goblet for Langelee to fill. He had listened carefully the first time Michael had told his story, and understood the twists and turns well enough to explain them to the slower-witted Langelee. 'They played in the homes of wealthy merchants in Chepe – thanks to Fiscurtune – and stole small things that would not be missed. These were passed to a third party to sell – Fiscurtune himself, I imagine. As time passed, wise investment and a steady trickle of pennies amassed them a fortune.'

'Never mind what they did in London,' said Langelee. 'I am interested in what they did here.'

'The same thing,' said Suttone, annoyed by Langelee's dismissal of his information. 'They stole things like inkpots, salt dishes and knives – along with gold from the King's Head.'

'The pilgrimage,' prompted Langelee, looking at Michael for an explanation. 'What happened when Turke decided to undertake the pilgrimage?'

'When Turke and his household arrived in Cambridge, Frith was hot on their heels. It must have been a shock for Turke to see him here.'

'He knew Frith was Fiscurtune's kinsman?' asked Langelee.

'Of course,' replied Michael, shooting the Master a glance that indicated he thought Langelee was being very slow on the uptake. 'Frith's mother was Fiscurtune's sister, Isabella. And Isabella was Turke's first wife. Turke did more than know Frith and Fiscurtune were kin: Turke was Frith's step-father, so of course they knew each other.'

'The fact that Turke and Frith were related by marriage explains the odd reactions of Turke, Philippa and Giles when the Waits performed at Michaelhouse on Christmas

Day,' said Bartholomew. 'Philippa refused to acknowledge them, and Giles immediately left the room – twice – when they appeared. Meanwhile, Frith jostled Turke – quite deliberately, I think – and made him spill his wine, but although Turke was furious at the insult, he did not make the sort of fuss I would have expected from a wealthy merchant doused in claret by an unrepentant juggler.'

Langelee still did not understand, so Bartholomew elaborated further. 'Frith had a hold over Turke. Meanwhile, Philippa was a loyal wife, and did not reveal Turke's nasty secrets even after his death, and Giles was just upset because he thought the Waits' presence would distress the sister he loves. They all had their own reasons for their individual reactions.'

'Gosslinge and Abigny were both seen talking to the Waits,' added Michael. 'Doubtless they were trying to find out what Frith had in mind. I think Frith intended to kill Turke, but Turke died before he could act.'

'Meanwhile, Ailred had been using his position as "keeper" of Dympna to make illegal loans,' said Bartholomew. 'Among others, he made one to Norbert about a month ago, and another to Harysone last week. Kenyngham noticed the losses, and demanded that Ailred should hand the chest to him. He set a time limit for the money to be replaced.'

'Next week,' said Kenyngham in a soft voice. 'We plan to use a large part of it to rebuild the hovels opposite St John's Hospital.'

'Ailred made the loan to Harysone last Wednesday,' said Michael. 'I know he did not lend his own money, because by then he had spent it all on supplies for Dunstan; and we know he did not use Dympna, because you had already taken it from him. So, we do not know how he came by two pounds to lend the pardoner.'

'I can explain that,' said Kenyngham tiredly. 'Ailred said he had devised a way of retrieving two nobles, but said he needed six to bring it about.'

'The loan to Harysone,' said Michael.

'I suspected that was the kind of thing he had in mind,' Kenyngham continued, 'and I was loath to give him the money. But he was so desperate to make amends for his earlier mistakes that I did not have the heart to refuse him.'

'You should have done,' said Michael. 'I doubt Harysone had any intention of giving Ailred two nobles in interest.'

'You cannot know that, Brother,' warned Bartholomew. 'Harysone was guilty of nothing except borrowing money. He was just a pardoner, who had the misfortune to arrive in Cambridge the same time as Turke and Frith, and who happened to have an interest in fish. He will talk to virtually anyone to sell a book, which explains why he was seen with Frith and Gosslinge, but it meant nothing significant. He was not the criminal you imagined.'

'Norbert was unable to repay Ailred, because he had already squandered his loan,' said Michael, electing to explain a different aspect of the tale, since he did not want to acknowledge he had been mistaken about the pardoner. 'Frith or Ailred – probably Frith – killed him after the several summons they issued failed to bring back the money.'

'But Frith said *Turke* killed Norbert,' said Kenyngham. 'I heard him myself.'

'He was lying, Father,' said Michael patiently. 'Turke had no reason to stab a student he did not know. Matt thought Turke was looking for the murder weapon when he went skating on the Mill Pool, but he is wrong, too.'

'I know that,' admitted Bartholomew. 'As you said, Turke had no reason to harm Norbert. It must have been Frith who killed him.'

'Quite,' said Michael, satisfied. 'But let me continue with my story. After Frith murdered Norbert, he devised a plan that would see Ailred relieved of the Dympna problem once and for all. It would also allow him to repay Michaelhouse for what he considered shabby treatment.'

'He planned to burn the College with Kenyngham in it,' said Bartholomew. 'That would protect Ailred – who was

doubtless unaware his nephew's plan extended to murder
– and would be a neat end to the adventure.'

'But we thwarted it,' said Langelee, pleased. 'The College
is still here, and Dympna is in the possession of a man who
will use it justly and wisely. I do not want the thing in
Michaelhouse, though, Father. When do you propose to
remove it?'

'It has already gone,' replied Kenyngham. 'I am shocked
by Ailred's role in this. We worked together for years, until
the sheen of gold seduced him. Gold is a curse, not a
blessing.'

'I hope you have not hidden it under any more floorboards,' said William accusingly, glancing at his leg, newly
relieved of its splint.

Kenyngham smiled. 'I have forgotten the skills I once had
with nails and wood, but I did not make a total mess of it.
You all looked at the boards, but none of you realised I had
created a storage hole below them. I did better than you
give me credit for.'

'So, Frith killed Norbert,' mused Langelee, still thinking
about the deaths that had occurred so close to his college.
'And Turke just had an accident while messing around on
the Mill Pool. What did you decide about Gosslinge?'

'He choked on a piece of vellum,' replied Michael. 'This
was marked with Dympna's name and a sum of money,
and was sent to Norbert the night he died. I think what
happened was this. Norbert went to the church and told
Frith he could not pay him. Meanwhile, Gosslinge had either
found the note or overheard the interchange between
Norbert and Frith. He was caught watching, and Frith – or
it could have been Ailred, I suppose – rammed the vellum
down his throat and suffocated him. Then Frith stole
Gosslinge's fine clothes and hid his body among the albs,
where it was found by us two days later.'

'But Frith denies killing anyone,' said Bartholomew,
thinking there were still questions unanswered about the
whole affair, such as why Philippa wandered around the

town wearing Abigny's cloak and why Turke carried Gosslinge's finger and claimed it was St Zeno's.

Michael waved a dismissive hand. 'Well, he would, wouldn't he? But do not cast shadows over our achievements, Matt. I want to bask in our success, and enjoy the fact that we have culprits for Dick Tulyet.'

'My God!' exclaimed William suddenly, stooping to retrieve something from the floor near the conclave door. With amusement, Bartholomew saw it was part of the marchpane Madonna Deynman had presented at his first feast as Lord of Misrule. Because the floors had not been cleaned, the piece had remained hidden among the rushes after Michael had flung it from him in disgust when he realised it was made from salt. 'What is this?'

No one liked to answer. The sculpted head had not fared well from its time in the rushes: it had been trampled and its face was distorted, and the hairs of the tonsure had slipped and were in a lopsided beard. However, Bartholomew thought it was still recognisable as William, and judging from the expressions of mirth on the other Fellows' faces, so did they.

'Marchpane,' replied Langelee nonchalantly, struggling not to laugh. 'It was one of Deynman's jests. Do not eat it: it is salty.'

'I am not in the habit of devouring scraps retrieved from the floor, Master,' said William indignantly. He turned it over in his hand. 'It seems familiar, although I do not know why. It is as if it is wearing a disguise, and the face is just beyond the reaches of my memory.'

'It is a good thing he does not spend much time in front of a mirror,' whispered Michael gleefully. 'Or his memory might be more reliable. It still looks like him, even though it is crushed.'

'It is the hair around the tonsure,' said Bartholomew. 'It is his most notable feature, and the thing I always imagine when his face appears in my mind.'

'I try to avoid that,' said Michael. 'I would rather dwell

on more pleasant images. Like Matilde. Or Yolande de Blaston. I tend not to contemplate the faces of men.'

'I did not say I was swooning over him,' said Bartholomew. 'And my point remains: most people have a distinctive feature that makes them unique. Take Suttone's big hands, Clippesby's mad eyes, Wynewyk's nose and William's hair as examples. This single feature can often be so distinctive that it masks all others. For example, do you know the colour of William's eyes?'

'Blue,' said Michael immediately. 'No, brown.' He sighed. 'I have no idea.'

'That is because you see the tonsure,' said Bartholomew, satisfied that he had proved his point. He was about to add more, but the door opened and Cynric entered.

'I think you had better come,' said the Welshman. 'Ailred has been found.'

CHAPTER 12

FROM THE TONE OF CYNRIC'S VOICE, BARTHOLOMEW ASSUMED that Ailred was dead. The book-bearer would say nothing more, and Bartholomew and Michael hurried after him as he led the way. Everywhere, Cambridge dripped. Snow still dropped from roofs, gables and trees, while melting icicles added a new peril as they plummeted like lethal daggers to the ground below. Bartholomew had already attended two nasty accidents that week, and hoped the thaw would soon be over. He wondered if Ailred had died because an icicle had fallen and pierced his skull. He sensed it was only a matter of time before someone did.

But Ailred was not dead. He had fallen through the sheet of ice that covered the Mill Pool near the Small Bridges, and a head and two clawing hands were all that could be seen of him. The ice was grey-white near the centre of the pond, indicating that it was rotten, and Bartholomew could not imagine what had induced the friar to venture out so far on to a surface that was patently unsafe. Ailred was making a valiant effort to stay afloat, but the ice was thin enough for Bartholomew to see the current running swift and strong underneath it, made more powerful by the melted snow that had flooded the river. He knew that the friar would be swept away if he relinquished his tenuous hold even for a moment.

'What happened?' asked Michael, horrified when he saw Ailred's predicament. A crowd of people had gathered, some to help and some to watch. Three of Stanmore's apprentices were tying together a number of planks, so that they could be used to crawl across the treacherous surface and reach the stricken man. Bartholomew sensed they did not have much time. Ailred's strength was being leached away by the cold water and the effort of clinging to the broken edges, and it would not be long before his frozen fingers failed him.

Godric was in the crowd, and hurried forward when he saw Michael. 'We cannot believe he is guilty of the crimes you have charged him with.' His eyes filled with tears. 'We know he is not a murderer, despite developing an uncharacteristic interest in riches over the last few weeks.'

'You are probably right,' said Michael kindly, squeezing his arm comfortingly, although Bartholomew was not so sure Ailred was the innocent Godric believed him to be. 'Has he become more interested in money recently?'

Godric nodded miserably. 'None of us understood it, because it was so unlike him. It was as if he had been seduced by something that had tainted him.'

Kenyngham had said the same thing, Bartholomew recalled. Access to large amounts of treasure brought a degree of power – the power to grant and refuse people things they craved. Perhaps it was that, rather than the gold itself, that had corrupted Ailred.

'What was he doing here?' asked Michael. 'Did he return to Ovyng first?'

'We have not seen him since he fled from you,' said Godric. 'But I was going to collect flour from the mill a short time ago, and I happened to glance over the bridge. Ailred was there, skating round and round in the centre of the pool. I shouted the ice was too thin, but he ignored me, or did not hear. Then there was a crack and he went down. He has been hanging there ever since.'

Bartholomew clambered over the bridge and slid down the river bank to join Stanmore's apprentices, who were still working feverishly on their makeshift ladder.

'It is almost finished,' said the freckle-faced youngster called Harold. He sat back to assess his handiwork, and exchanged a nervous grimace with his fellows, to indicate it was not all they could have hoped for. He glanced up at

431

Bartholomew. 'Are you ready? We will hold this end and haul it back again when the ice starts to crack.'

Bartholomew regarded him in alarm. 'You think I am going?'

Harold was surprised by the question. 'Cynric said you would; it was why he fetched you. He says the friar may need medical attention, and that it would be dangerous to tug him out of the water any old way. He thinks Turke died because inexperienced hands snatched him clear, and we should not let the same thing happen to Father Ailred.'

Bartholomew raised questioning eyebrows at his book-bearer.

Cynric was unabashed. 'Turke might have lived if a physician had been on hand sooner. You said so yourself. Do not fret, boy. I will tie a rope around you and will not let you sink.'

'This is very ironic,' said Harold, squinting across the bright ice towards the trapped scholar. 'Father Ailred was among the folk who rescued Turke from this very spot the day after Christmas.'

'What are you talking about?' asked Bartholomew in confusion. 'Ailred was not here when I came to examine Turke.'

'It was Ailred who ordered us to let Turke rest before summoning other help,' said Harold. 'Or was it his friend – that Chepe Wait? Anyway, they both agreed we should wait until the ice formed on Turke's clothes.'

'Are you sure about this?' asked Bartholomew, his thoughts whirling.

'Of course,' said Harold scornfully. 'Well, I am not certain exactly who said what, but I know they told us it is best to let a man freeze after a dip in cold water. They said it is something to do with slowing the blood and preventing the heart from exploding.'

'Who else was here, besides Ailred and Frith – the Wait?' asked Bartholomew, his own heart pounding as he considered the implications of the boy's statements. It sounded as though Turke had been deliberately allowed to freeze to

432

death, and a physician summoned only when it was certain that nothing could be done to save him.

'Just us,' said Harold, indicating himself and two other boys. 'When Frith and Ailred eventually decided that Turke might benefit from your services, they sent us to fetch Cynric.'

'And all this took time,' mused Bartholomew. 'When I arrived, Turke was beyond saving.'

Harold exchanged a frightened glance with his friends. 'You mean they were wrong, and we should have fetched you immediately? But I thought they were trying to help Turke.'

'They were not,' said Bartholomew grimly. 'Quite the reverse. By waiting until his wet clothes turned to ice, they ensured he died. He was murdered, after all.'

'They forced him to skate,' said Harold miserably. 'He said he did not want to, because the ice was too thin. But they promised him that if he could reach the other side of the Mill Pool, then he would be free of them for ever. We thought they were playing games, like we do – you know, daring each other to do dangerous things. Except that Turke was crying, because he said he was afraid.'

'Did Frith or Ailred see you watching them?' asked Bartholomew uneasily.

Harold gave the ghost of a smile. 'We were hiding under the bridge, because it is sheltered from the wind. They did not see us until we came to help – after Turke fell in.'

'Thank God,' muttered Bartholomew, aware that the apprentices might well have been forced to do some skating on thin ice themselves had Ailred and Frith known their murderous fun had been observed. He stared at the floundering figure in the distance, and thought about what Ailred had forced Turke to do. 'It looks as if he offered Turke a chance of life – saying that if he reached the other side, he would be free of their vengeance.'

'Turke did not have a hope wearing *those* skates,' determined Harold, the proud expert. 'They were not even tied properly.'

433

Michael had said that, Bartholomew recalled. But it had been decided that the inexpert tying of thongs was not significant, whereas in reality it had been a vital clue to the cruel game Frith and Ailred had played with Turke. They had offered him a chance, but had actually ensured he would never reach safety. And then they had deliberately let him freeze to death.

'Why did you not mention this before?' he asked.

Harold looked aggrieved. 'I tried! Twice! But no one would listen to me. I was sent off to warm myself by the fire like a small child. No one would even let me speak.'

That was true, Bartholomew remembered. Harold had tried to say something, but Stanmore had noticed the boy's blue hands, and had dispatched him home; his protectiveness had resulted in valuable information going untold. Another mistake had been made: Turke's murder had been deemed an accident, because there had been no marks of violence on the body. They had assumed – wrongly – that no coercion had taken place.

'Philippa was not here, too, was she?' he asked, wondering whether Stanmore's suspicions had been justified all along.

'No,' said the boy, regarding Bartholomew as though he was insane. He grabbed Bartholomew's arm in a sudden, painful pinch and pointed across the water. 'The friar is slipping! You had better see if you can save him, before it is too late.'

Cynric stepped forward and tied a rope around Bartholomew's waist, handing the other end to Michael, who wrapped it around his shoulders, like someone preparing to climb a mountain. The book-bearer gave Bartholomew a second length of twine, which he said he should throw to Ailred when he was close enough. The notion was that Ailred would either tie it around himself or hold it, and Michael would haul them both to safety. Bartholomew gazed at the ice with trepidation, not at all sure their plan would work.

* * *

Ailred had chosen the exact centre of the Mill Pool through which to crash, and was not easy to reach. Bartholomew had misgivings immediately, when he knelt on the planks and there was an ominous crack beneath him. He lay on his stomach, and began to inch his way along, trying to spread his weight over as wide an area as possible. Slowly, wincing at every groan and creak, he eased towards the friar.

'We have been looking for you,' he called, mostly to assess whether Ailred was still able to think rationally or whether the cold had deprived him of his wits.

'I have been staying with Robin,' replied Ailred softly. 'For two pennies a day, he offers a blanket near his fire, the company of a pig and no questions asked.'

'You lied to us,' said Bartholomew, as he crawled. 'And you made your students lie, too. Why did you say you were at Ovyng the night the church was broken into, when you were out?'

Ailred gave a gentle sigh. 'Because I went to make a loan to Harysone at the King's Head, and wanted to keep the matter quiet. After that I went to Dunstan the riverman. I waited until Matilde left, then slipped in to sit with him. He died in his sleep, quite peacefully, but I did not like to think of him waking to find himself alone in his last moments.'

'Why did you not tell us that?' asked Bartholomew, exasperated. 'It is not a crime to be kind to a dying man, and it would have saved us – and Godric – a good deal of worry.'

'I did not want anyone to know what I did for Dunstan,' said Ailred, 'partly because folk would assume I had continued to use Dympna illegally after Kenyngham told me not to, and partly because I believe charity should be practised quietly, so it does not become an act performed for the giver's sake. That was what Dympna was about – secret charity. I am sorry it entailed a lie, and I am sorry I distressed Godric by putting him in an awkward position.'

'This explains why you kept your vigil with Dunstan a secret,' said Bartholomew. 'But it does not explain why you refused to tell us about the business with Harysone.'

'Kenyngham forbade me to make any more loans.' Ailred grimaced in anguish. 'But it was the only way I could think of to recoup the losses before Tulyet learned what I had done. I was at my wits' end, and did not know what else to do.'

When Bartholomew was about two-thirds of the way across, he noticed that there was blood on the friar's hands, torn as he had scrabbled at the sharp ice in order to stop himself from sinking. The wounds were in a criss-cross pattern that was curiously familiar, and Bartholomew realised he had seen such cuts elsewhere. Turke's legs, he thought. The marks were identical, and must also have been caused by ice. He paused for a moment, thinking about other things he had learned. Harold had said Turke had wept when his killers had forced him to skate, saying he was terrified. The physician also recalled the extremes to which William had gone to avoid leaving the College while the worst storms raged, and realised the Franciscan was not the only one who had a morbid fear of ice: Turke had been afraid of it, too. The pilgrimage undertaken during the winter was more of an ordeal than anyone had realised.

'Turke was frightened of ice,' he said to himself. 'He did not like the scars on his legs to be seen, because answering curious questions about them forced him to remember how they were caused. And that memory was painful for him.'

'You have done well to reason that,' said Ailred, nodding approval. 'It was why I chose the river as a means to kill the man.'

'You killed Turke?' asked Bartholomew, startled. 'Godric maintains that you are innocent, and will be disappointed when he learns he is wrong. We all thought Turke's death was an accident.'

'Godric will understand when he learns my reasons,' said Ailred. 'So you must tell him. Turke murdered Isabella, you see, during the plague.'

'Isabella,' mused Bartholomew. 'Turke's first wife.' Clues suddenly slotted together in his mind. Turke had married

436

John Fiscurtune's – and therefore Ailred's – sister, and Philippa said she had died during the pestilence. Bartholomew had made the erroneous assumption that dying *during* the plague was the same as dying *from* the plague, which had apparently not been the case. 'Why did Turke kill her?'

'They both went skating on the Thames, to take their minds from the Death that raged in the city. The ice cracked.' Ailred gave a grim smile and indicated his own predicament. 'They were both left clinging to the edge of a hole.'

'And Turke saved himself, but could not rescue her?'

'He used her as a ladder to haul himself to safety,' corrected Ailred. 'John and I saw it all from a nearby bridge. Then he did nothing to help as she slowly lost her grip and was swept to a horrible death. That is how he came by his scarred legs. She gripped his feet in terror, but he kicked her off. As he did so, the ice cut into him. He was ashamed of those scars, and always avoided going near frozen water.'

'So, that was why Turke and Fiscurtune were such bitter enemies, and why they did all they could to harm each other's businesses. Turke did not kill Fiscurtune in a fit of sudden rage, but after years of seething resentment and guilt.'

'Turke paid us for saying nothing,' said Ailred bitterly. 'He bought our silence. All I can claim in my defence is that all my share went straight to Ovyng.'

And the loss of Ailred's 'share' after Turke's death was another reason why Ovyng was so suddenly plunged into poverty, Bartholomew thought. It was not just the fees the Tulyets paid for Norbert that were gone, but the money Turke provided, too. Meanwhile, all Ovyng's savings had been spent to help Dunstan.

'I suppose, when you heard Turke killed your brother as well as your sister, you decided you had remained mute for long enough, and it was time to dispense justice,' he said.

'I knew John could be difficult, and I wanted to hear Turke's side of the story. But Turke would only say the pilgrimage would wipe out all his debts – including the one owed to Isabella – and he would no longer pay to keep details of her death silent. I was angry that he felt he could murder my sister *and* my brother, and treat me so harshly, yet still expect to become Lord Mayor.'

'So, you killed him?'

Ailred coughed weakly. 'I had not intended to. Frith and I saw him hurrying towards the Mill Pool one day and we followed him. He was looking for the knife that killed Norbert – he was quite open about the fact that he had murdered my student – and even offered Frith a shilling if he would risk his own life to hunt for it. We did not plan to kill him, but once he was here, at the Mill Pool, it seemed the right thing to do. I suppose Stanmore's apprentice told you how Frith and I encouraged Turke to cross the river, and how we delayed taking him home when prompt action would have allowed him to live.'

'You knew Harold was watching?'

'I did; Frith did not. Frith dislikes loose ends, and I did not want the boy to come to harm.'

'Unlike Turke,' said Bartholomew. 'You gave him cheap skates and did not even let him tie them correctly.'

'It was more of a chance than he gave Isabella and John,' snapped Ailred, anger giving his voice a strength that had not been there before. 'Do not come any closer, Matthew. The ice is very thin near me. You will fall in and we shall both be swept to our deaths.'

'I will throw you a rope. Tie it around yourself and we will drag you out.' Bartholomew uncoiled the twine and hurled it as hard as he could, but it was short by the length of a man. He gathered it in, and began to inch forward again.

'No!' said Ailred, agitated. 'Stay where you are. I do not want your death on my conscience, too.'

'Why was Turke searching for the knife that killed Norbert?' asked Bartholomew, thinking that if Ailred talked, he might calm down. The friar's movements had caused more of the ice to crack, and it was becoming less safe with every passing moment.

438

'Because it was evidence against him,' said Ailred. 'It was a dagger he had borrowed from his servant, and it would have led you to him as Norbert's killer.'

'So, *Turke* killed Norbert after all,' said Bartholomew, recalling that he had dismissed the fishmonger as a suspect for the killing because there was no apparent motive for the wealthy merchant to slay the indolent student. 'I thought it was Frith.'

Ailred's voice was so soft it was difficult to hear. The physician inched forward a little more, and felt the ice begin to bend. He stopped in alarm.

'I sent Norbert several notes in Dympna's name,' Ailred was saying. 'I lied about that, too, I am afraid. Frith tried to force Norbert to pay me back, but it was Turke who murdered him. You should have known that; Turke was a natural killer. If you need evidence, look for bloodstains on his sleeve. His wife must have seen them, but perhaps she thought they were left from when he murdered John.'

'But *why* did Turke kill Norbert?' pressed Bartholomew, seeing the friar slip further into the water. He was weakening fast, and the physician saw he did not have much time left.

'Turke would not give us the details, but I was under the impression that Norbert overheard him making some insalubrious business arrangement and threatened to blackmail him. So, Turke stabbed Norbert, then hit him with a rock. Poor Norbert did not deserve to die in such a manner, even though he was dissolute and selfish. Now do you see why I so badly wanted you to catch Norbert's killer? The culprit was the one man in the world whom I truly despised.'

'Frith had no hand in Norbert's death?'

'None.'

'But it was Frith who pushed me and grabbed the salted fish?'

Ailred sighed. 'I think so. I cannot prove it, but I think my nephew met Turke here, in the middle of the night, and begged him to continue the payments for my hostel. I think he probably witnessed the murder, which is why he denied any knowledge of it to you. He does not want to be charged as an accessory to such a crime.'

'Did you really think you would get away with it?' Bartholomew felt the ice stabilise and began to move forward once more. 'Murdering Turke and Gosslinge?'

'No one killed Gosslinge. He managed to acquire one of the notes we sent to Norbert. Norbert was careless, so I imagine he threw the message in the street, where Gosslinge picked it up. Gosslinge must have asked Turke to it read it to him, then decided to hide in St Michael's Church to see what would happen. Those rotten albs are an excellent place to lurk unseen.'

'How do you know all this? Were you there?'

Ailred nodded feebly. 'Standing behind a pillar, so Norbert would not see *me*. But Frith and I discovered Gosslinge's presence long before Norbert arrived. Gosslinge was a noisy breather and we heard him. Frith demanded the note back. Gosslinge claimed this was not the first time he had watched, and said he had already told Turke about my muddle with Dympna. He maintained it was one of the reasons why Turke had decided not to pay me any more – because he knew something bad about me, just as I knew about the vile death of Isabella.'

'So, Gosslinge was spying for Turke,' mused Bartholomew. He recalled Harysone mentioning that Gosslinge had smelled of mould. The pardoner had been right: the servant had spent more than one evening hiding among the decaying robes in order to watch clandestine meetings in St Michael's.

'Turke used Gosslinge for underhand acts,' said Ailred. 'It was why Gosslinge held such a unique position in his household. Turke did not like the man, but he was useful.'

'Did Turke relieve him of his thumb?'

Ailred was surprised. 'I understood he lost it to the King's justices for stealing. But to go back to the church, Frith demanded the note from Gosslinge. Gosslinge looked him in the eye and ate it. Then he choked. We did our best, and Frith even broke one of the man's teeth trying to pull the thing from his throat, but it was all to no avail. It was a horrible thing to watch.' He closed his eyes.

Ailred's account tallied with Frith's, and explained why Gosslinge's mouth was damaged. Gosslinge's fingernail must have been torn in his death throes. Although bruised lips and broken teeth were usually indications that someone had been deliberately suffocated, in this case they had been the result of clumsy attempts to save him. Bartholomew was inclined to accept that Frith had been telling the truth after all – about this particular incident, at least. No one had killed Gosslinge.

'What else did Frith tell you?' Bartholomew could see that Ailred was beginning to lose consciousness, and sensed it would not be long before he relinquished his hold on the ice. And then there would be nothing anyone could do to save him. The friar had to be kept alert. 'Come on, Father! Speak to me!'

'Gosslinge was wearing his livery, but Frith said it was a pity to waste good clothes when such items are expensive. He took them, then replaced Gosslinge among the albs in exactly the same way in which we had found him. He hoped you would see what had really happened – that Gosslinge had choked on something he was trying to keep for himself, and that he had been spying. But you misunderstood and misdiagnosed everything.'

'The change of clothes did not help,' said Bartholomew defensively, hurling the rope. He did not want to hear again how he had failed everyone with his careless examination of Gosslinge. Ailred reached for the twine, but it was still too short. The ice under Bartholomew bowed more than ever, and he saw part of it disappear under the black water in front of him.

'Go back,' ordered Ailred. 'I do not want to be rescued.'

'You might have mentioned that before I started,' said Bartholomew, throwing the rope again. This time, it reached the hole where Ailred floated. The friar did not touch it.

'I want to die,' he said quietly. 'That was my intention

441

when I began to skate on ice that I knew was too thin. I have spent the past few days meditating on all that has happened, and it seems fitting that I should die in the same way as Turke and my sister. I have gone too far along a dark road, and all I want to do is atone for my mistakes. I was confused when I came to the surface again and allowed my fear to deter me from the course I had chosen. Go back. You have done all you can.'

'I can save you,' said Bartholomew urgently. 'Although I hate to admit it there is very little solid evidence against you, if you recant your confession to Turke's murder.'

The friar gave a grim smile. 'I know. And that is why you will allow my nephew and his friends to go free. But I do not want to live. I was a good man, but I do not like what I have become. So, go away, and leave me in peace.'

'But I can almost reach you,' objected Bartholomew, starting to move forward again.

The friar gave a smile that was unreadable, before lifting his arms above his head. The current immediately snatched him and his head disappeared from view. Bartholomew glimpsed his face, distorted with anguish, as it passed under the transparent ice below, and thumped the surface hard with his fists, trying to smash it and grab the man. But the current was too strong, and Ailred was gone.

Within moments, Bartholomew realised that striking the ice with such force had not been a wise thing to do. It started to crack, tiny zigzags spreading around him in all directions with a noise like close thunder. The planks on which he lay were suddenly on the move, and Bartholomew saw the black water of Ailred's hole rushing towards him. He was certain he was about to suffer the same fate as the friar, but the shocking cold never came. He felt hands hauling him to safety, and realised Cynric and Michael had tugged the wood free, with him on it. For a long time, he stared at the opaque surface of the Mill Pool, hoping that Ailred was not still struggling underneath it.

* * *

'You and Ailred had a lot to say to each other,' said Michael, rubbing his hands vigorously as he watched people disperse from the Mill Pool now that the excitement was over. The physician supposed he should feel satisfied – he finally had answers to the questions that had plagued him since Norbert had been murdered – but instead he felt tainted, as though he had uncovered secrets that should have been left undisturbed.

He gave Michael a terse summary of the friar's confession, adding that Turke had probably stabbed Norbert in a fit of outraged indignation. It was not the first time the fishmonger had vented his temper by using a knife on a man who had offended him. It also made sense that he had braved the ice he so feared in order to hunt for the weapon that would link his household to the crime – it was a desperate act of self-preservation.

'Why did he choose that particular day to conduct his search?' asked Michael doubtfully. 'Why not sooner? Or later?'

Bartholomew sighed. 'Think about what transpired when he identified Gosslinge's body. The matter of the missing knife was raised. Giles told us that Gosslinge had a dagger that was too large for him. We made the assumption that it was stolen with Gosslinge's clothes. Then Turke gave us the relic to pay for a requiem, and we discussed St Zeno and fishermen.'

'Giles said the relic would do Michaelhouse no good as long as the river was frozen,' recalled Michael, 'because anglers would not be able to break through the ice to reach the fish. Turke then mentioned a dislike of ice.'

'Exactly. Giles also said he had thrown a stone on the river, and it had skittered across the surface. I think Turke realised then that the knife he had used on Norbert might have suffered a similar fate – it was not in the water, but *on* it. He searched for it that very day, perhaps obliged to wait until the Mill Pool was suitably deserted, but knowing it would only be a matter of time before someone recovered the murder weapon. And, if you recall, he said we should not bother to look for Gosslinge's knife – only his valuable clothes.'

'Because he did not want us to find the thing at all,' concluded Michael, nodding. 'A cold killer indeed. Poor Ailred! How hard it must have been to meet the man who had murdered both his siblings, and see he felt no remorse. Turke's pilgrimage was not to atone for their deaths, but to make sure he was eligible to be elected Lord Mayor of London.'

'There is no evidence to convict Frith of killing Turke. Morice cannot charge him with the murder, because we only have Ailred's confession to go on, and Ailred is dead.'

'True, but Frith was about to incinerate Michaelhouse,' said Michael grimly. 'He and his accomplices will not go free.'

'They might,' said Bartholomew. 'How much do you think Morice demands from would-be arsonists for an early release?'

'More than Frith has,' determined Michael firmly. 'If Morice does release them, he will be in for a bitter dispute with the University. He will not want that.'

'Tulyet would not want that,' corrected Bartholomew. 'Morice does not care. And there is a lot you can do with the kind of bribe it would take to free four people from such serious charges.'

'Look, Matt,' said Michael suddenly, grabbing the physician's arm and pointing. 'It is Philippa, and she is heading in the direction of the Gilbertine Friary. She is going to meet her lover, just as Clippesby told us she would.'

'How do you know it is her?' asked Bartholomew, eyeing the huddled figure doubtfully. 'It is just someone wearing a cloak with the hood pulled up.'

'It is her – she is wearing those elegant but impractical shoes she always dons when the snow lies thick on the ground. Shall we follow her?'

'No,' said Bartholomew distastefully. 'I have just watched

a man die, and I am in no mood for chasing widows through the Gilbertines' stables. Besides, I am cold.'

'You are not cold,' determined Michael. 'And you must want to see the man Philippa loves?'

'I have had enough of Philippa, Turke, Gosslinge, Giles, Ailred and everyone else associated with this nasty case. We have solved your murders, Brother: Turke killed Norbert, Ailred and Frith killed Turke, and Gosslinge died because he tried to eat something he did not want someone else to have. That is all we need to know.'

'Well, *I* am going,' said Michael. He nudged the physician in the ribs and his voice became wheedling. 'Come on, Matt. It will be interesting.'

'No,' said Bartholomew firmly. 'Teaching starts tomorrow, and I have lectures to prepare. You go, if you must. I will see you in Michaelhouse later.'

They parted company at the end of Small Bridges Street. Bartholomew turned to walk along Milne Street towards the College, while Michael left the town through the Trumpington Gate, dodging this way and that as he dogged Philippa's footsteps along the road that led past the Hall of Valence Marie, Peterhouse and the King's Head. Bartholomew watched him zigzag back and forth like a huge black crow, and smiled. It was good that Philippa was concentrating on walking and did not glance behind her, or she would have spotted the monk's clumsy manoeuvres in an instant.

The physician walked slowly, thinking about Godric's tears of grief when he heard Ailred was dead. Although shocked by his principal's confessions, Godric insisted the recent changes in Ailred's behaviour were an aberration, and said there must have been a bad alignment of celestial bodies to induce him to act in such a manner. Bartholomew thought about Turke, too, and his careless attitude towards the people he had killed. However, the physician gained no satisfaction from the knowledge that he had been right about why Turke had ventured near the Mill Pool the day he had died. It was

445

not the kind of case where jubilation was in order.

The snow was still melting rapidly, and what had once been a pretty white carpet was now ugly brown sludge. Since the ice was thawing more slowly than the snow, the drains were still blocked, and filthy, slushy water stretched from one side of the High Street to the other in a foul lake. It was calf deep in places, and lumpy with pieces of rubbish, dead birds, straw, animal manure, fragments of ice and sewage. It was like walking through a cold porridge of filth and excrement.

Michaelhouse was alive with activity when Bartholomew returned. The snow had been dug away, so it was once again possible to enter the north wing. He went to his own room and threw open the window shutters, to fill the chamber with the milder air from outside and dispel the dank chill that pervaded it. He discovered a thin layer of ice coating the walls, where mildew and running damp had frozen solid, while there were slippery patches on the floor that reminded him of Ailred and Turke, and their diametric attitudes to ice. He begged some logs from Langelee and lit a fire, prodding it until it blazed furiously. Then he swept the last remnants of snow from the windowsill and shelves, while William shook the ice from the blankets on the bed. Eventually, the room began to look more homely.

Enjoying the luxury of a private fire, Bartholomew closed the shutters and sat at the table with a lamp. He worked on a lecture until the bell chimed for the midday meal, then strolled across the courtyard to join his colleagues in the hall. Michael was not there, but the monk often missed College meals when he was engaged on proctorial duties. Bartholomew was surprised, and a little disgusted, with himself when he realised he was disappointed, for there was a part of him that very much wanted to know the identity of Philippa's lover.

Since it was the last day of Deynman's rule, the student had gone to some pains to ensure it was pleasantly memorable. There was undiluted wine to drink, and several fine hams had been purchased, all glazed with honey and flavoured with winter herbs. The bread was made from expensive white flour, and there were pats of creamy butter to go with it. Bartholomew knew Michael would be chagrined to learn that spying on a lusty widow had deprived him of such a fine, if simple, meal.

After Deynman had struggled through what he considered to be an accurate rendition of the final grace and had dismissed his 'court', Bartholomew found Cynric waiting with a summons. Harold, Stanmore's apprentice, had been hit with a snowball that contained something sharp, and had a bleeding scalp wound. Bartholomew grabbed his bag and set off at a trot to Milne Street.

When he arrived, he saw that Edith had been overly hasty in demanding that her brother come at once. Harold's cut had clotted of its own accord, and the lad's initial fright at the sight of his own blood was being assuaged by piles of comfits and candied fruits. Bartholomew cleaned the gash, although it was obvious that Harold just wanted the physician to go away, so he could concentrate on the array of treats that were laid out in front of him on the kitchen table.

'They were throwing snowballs in the Market Square,' said Edith, smiling fondly as she left the boy to his feast and led Bartholomew to the solar. 'But the snow is not what it was yesterday, and it was apparently difficult to find a clean handful. In the excitement, missiles were thrown that contained more than snow.'

'Harold has had quite an eventful day,' said Bartholomew, following his sister up the stairs. 'First he helped with Ailred's rescue, and now he has himself a sliced head.'

'Oswald was proud of him for acting so promptly, and wanted to reward him. The best of the snow will be gone tomorrow, and he decided to give him a last chance to enjoy it. Who knows when we will see its like again?'

'Not too soon, I hope; I have only just retrieved my room. But this warmer weather must mean Philippa and Giles will be leaving soon?'

Edith nodded. 'Tomorrow morning, assuming there is not another blizzard tonight. I like company, as you know, but I confess I shall be glad to bid them farewell.'

'They have not been easy guests. Giles is no longer the carefree, amiable man he was before the Death, while Philippa is . . .' He gestured expansively, not quite sure how to put his thoughts into words.

'She is not the Philippa you were set to marry,' supplied Edith. 'Having a wealthy husband brought her luxury, but also disappointments. My heart broke when I saw what she had become.'

'Rumour has it that she fashioned her own remedy to Walter's inadequacies,' said Bartholomew, not wanting his sister to waste sympathies where they were not needed. 'Michael followed her this morning, when she went to meet a lover behind the Gilbertine Friary.'

Edith was startled. 'Philippa did not go to meet a lover this morning. She has been in her chamber, folding clothes and deciding which of her husband's possessions to donate to the poor. Did I mention that one of his sleeves was covered in blood? I suppose it must have happened when he murdered Fiscurtune in London, although the stain looks more recent to me.'

'She must have slipped past you,' said Bartholomew, more interested in Philippa than in the fact that the stained sleeve was evidence that Ailred had been right about Turke killing Norbert. 'I saw her myself, and we know she uses Giles's cloak and hat to go about business of her own. It was not him who wandered freely around the town – he is restricted by his chilblains – but her.'

'That may have been so in the past, but not today,' said Edith firmly. 'She is upstairs. Listen – you can hear her walking in the chamber above us. She has not left the house.'

'It must be Giles,' said Bartholomew. 'It is him you can hear.'

Edith cocked her head as footsteps sounded on the stairs. 'Here she comes. You can ask her.'

Philippa seemed tired and careworn. She smiled at Bartholomew as she entered the solar, although her expression was more wary than friendly. She was already wearing clothes for travelling, the others presumably packed away. Attached to the belt around her waist was a knife and a pomander for warding off the foul smells she was likely to encounter on her journey.

'Matt thinks he saw you out today,' said Edith bluntly. 'I have been telling him you have not left the house.'

'Edith is right,' replied Philippa, regarding Bartholomew with a face that was curiously devoid of expression. 'There is much to do if we are to go tomorrow. Giles has gone to check the horses, and I am obliged to pack our belongings, since Gosslinge is not here to do it.'

'Rachel is helping,' said Edith, indignant that her guest appeared to be complaining when assistance in the form of Cynric's competent wife had been provided. 'She has been with you all morning – and continued the work when you were receiving your various guests here in the solar.'

Philippa gave an absent smile. 'She has been very helpful, especially since visitors like young Quenhyth have interrupted me so often. But I shall be finished before dusk, and we will be on our way at first light tomorrow.'

'Quenhyth?' asked Bartholomew. 'Why did he come?'

'He visits me often,' replied Philippa. 'His father is a colleague of Walter's, and he feels obliged to see me on a fairly regular basis.' She gave a faint smile. 'London manners.'

Bartholomew glanced at her shoes as she left, half expecting to see the delicate leather sodden with muck from the High Street. But Philippa was not wearing her flimsy shoes, and he was not surprised she had been making such a noise on the wooden floor above when he observed the pair of heavy boots. He regarded them uneasily, wondering why she had donned such robust footwear when she had just claimed that she planned to spend the rest of the day packing.

* * *

Bartholomew was thoughtful as he strode the short distance between Milne Street and Michaelhouse. He asked Quenhyth, who had been assigned gate duty again, whether Michael had returned, and the student said that he had not. Quenhyth mentioned that Beadle Meadowman had asked the same question less than an hour ago, because the Chancellor had been demanding a report on Ailred's death and wanted Michael to provide him with one. A nagging concern gnawed at Bartholomew as he trotted up the stairs to Langelee's room to ask whether the Master knew where the monk might be. Langelee shook his head.

'Why do you ask? Is he in trouble? I heard there was a scuffle in the Market Square, when a snowball fight between scholars from Peterhouse and Stanmore's apprentices turned into something a little more dangerous. Perhaps he is still dealing with that.'

'You are probably right,' said Bartholomew, although his growing sense of unease would not be ignored. He went to his room, intending to spend the rest of the afternoon working on his lecture, but found he could not settle. He grabbed his cloak and set off again, heading for Michael's offices at St Mary the Great. On the way, he met Cynric, who also claimed he had not seen the monk since the incident at the Mill Pool. Without waiting for an invitation, the Welshman fell into step as the physician walked briskly towards the High Street.

Michael was not at St Mary the Great, and Meadowman claimed he had spent the last three hours trying to find him. The beadle's irritation with his master's disappearance turned to worry when he saw he was not the only one who had been trying to track Michael down. He mentioned the incident in the Market Square, and informed Bartholomew that it was unusual for the monk not to appear in person to ensure potentially explosive situations were properly diffused – especially since the incompetent Morice had become Sheriff.

'I am going to the Gilbertine Friary,' said Bartholomew,

looking both ways up the High Street, and half expecting to see the familiar figure sauntering towards them. 'That was where he was going when we last spoke. He wanted to follow Philippa, to see her lover – although she denies that she has left the house today.'

'I do not like this,' said Meadowman, his pleasant face creased with concern. 'Brother Michael does not usually wander off without telling a beadle where he might be found.'

'I am uneasy with him following this Philippa, who was not Philippa,' said Cynric. 'Edith is right: Philippa has not been out today, because my wife has been helping her pack. However, although Philippa may not have ventured out today, she certainly has done so on other occasions.'

'Clippesby said that,' said Bartholomew. 'I was sceptical at first, because I was under the impression that she always demanded a male escort when she went out – even when it was inconvenient for them.'

Cynric shrugged. 'She insisted on escorts so everyone would think she would never leave without one. But the reality is that she did. Often. I followed her once, just for something to do. She went to the Gilbertines' stables, where there are several derelict outhouses. Because there are not as many Gilbertines now as before the Death, most of these sheds have fallen into disuse.'

'We are wasting time,' said Bartholomew abruptly and, with Cynric and Meadowman at his heels, he ran along the High Street and through the Trumpington Gate. He pounded on the door to the friary, and fretted impatiently when the gatekeeper took his time to answer. But the lay-brother said there had been no visitors that day, and he had not seen Michael, Philippa or anyone else.

'I suppose he may have followed Philippa, then gone else-where,' said Meadowman, although he did not seem partic-ularly convinced by his own explanation.

'He did not follow Philippa at all,' Cynric pointed out. 'Or rather, it was not Philippa he thought he was following. She wears those silly shoes, but today she donned boots. It

451

is obvious she lent the shoes to another person, so people would think it was her hurrying to the friary.'

'I do not see why she would do that,' said Meadowman doubtfully. 'Especially since you just said she was at pains to make folk believe she never walks out unescorted.'

'I suppose the person wearing the thin shoes was actually Giles,' said Bartholomew, rubbing his head tiredly. 'There is not much difference in their size. He took her shoes with the intention of making people believe he was her.'

'We need to look in some of these deserted outbuildings,' said Meadowman, wanting to waste no more time in speculation.

Together they began a systematic search of the ramshackle sheds and storerooms that formed a separate little hamlet behind the main part of the friary. Most were lean-tos, which had been used to store firewood, peat, and hay and straw for horses in more prosperous times. There was also a disused brewery, a laundry and some substantial stables. But all were empty.

'I do not understand,' said Bartholomew uneasily. 'Where can he be?'

'Hopefully in the Brazen George, unaware of the worry he is causing,' said Meadowman. 'I shall go there now, then round up some of the lads to search his other favourite haunts.' He left without waiting for an answer.

'I will look in Peterhouse and the King's Head,' said Cynric. 'The food is good at Peterhouse, and he may have gone there for a meal and not realised how much time has passed.'

He slipped away, leaving Bartholomew alone in the overgrown yard. The physician supposed he should follow Cynric and Meadowman but he remained convinced that Michael's disappearance was somehow connected to Philippa, and was certain the monk was not far away. He walked through the outbuildings again, this time more carefully, searching for any clue that might tell him that Michael had been there.

The last place he explored was the stables, a low, thatched building with a sizeable loft. There were three horses in residence, none looking very wholesome. The place had not been cleaned since the snows, and the stink of manure and the sharp tang of urine was overpowering. But Michael was nowhere to be found. Bartholomew stood still and looked around slowly.

Clippesby said he had overheard Philippa talking to her lover from the stables, so her trysting place could not be far. The hayloft was derelict, so she had not scrambled up a ladder to frolic there among the straw. Hoping he was not wasting his time by placing so much faith in the word of a man who spoke to animals, Bartholomew continued his careful assessment of the building. If the upper storey was unavailable, and he could not see Philippa setting her pretty shoes in the uncleaned filth of the stalls, then her secret place must be in a downward direction. Many buildings contained basements for storage, and the friary had been built in an age where cellars were commonplace. Bartholomew began to walk back and forth, searching for a trapdoor.

It was not long before he found it – an iron-handled affair, which had been concealed under some straw. Bartholomew grasped the ring and began to pull, but stopped when he realised something was securing it. Initially, he assumed it was locked from the inside, but then reasoned that no one would be likely to lock himself in a cellar. He kicked away more straw, and saw that a bolt was keeping the trapdoor down.

He was completely unprepared for the attack when it came. He was off balance anyway, since he was bending, and fell heavily when the pitchfork slammed across his shoulders. He forced himself to roll, so he could use the momentum to scramble to his feet, and winced when two prongs stabbed violently into the floor where he would have been had he been less agile. The blow was sufficiently vigorous to cause the pitchfork tines to stick fast, and

Bartholomew used the delay to launch himself at his assailant. Both went tumbling to the ground.

The physician clawed wildly, using every scrap of his strength. His fingers encountered the hood that covered the man's face, and he snatched it away, expecting to see the soft, feminine features of Giles Abigny.

'You!' he exclaimed in astonishment.

Harysone used Bartholomew's momentary confusion to scramble to his feet and haul the pitchfork from the floor. Then he came at the physician in a series of smooth, fluid movements that suggested he had done this sort of thing before. Bartholomew backed away, flinging handfuls of muck and straw from the floor at Harysone's eyes. The pardoner's relentless advance did not falter. He stabbed again, and this time his tines became tangled in some rotting wood.

Taking advantage, Bartholomew darted towards the door, but a burly figure framed in the rectangle of light blocked his path. He knew he could not wrestle the fellow out of the way and escape before Harysone freed his fork and came after him again, so he snatched up a weapon of his own – a rusty hoe that was leaning against one wall, wondering how he would fare when Harysone's accomplice joined the affray, too.

Seeing that Bartholomew intended to do battle, Harysone gave a cold smile, so his large teeth gleamed in the dim light of the stable. Bartholomew was bigger and stronger, but Harysone possessed the better weapon. It was longer than the physician's, and less likely to break. It also boasted a pair of wicked spikes, each one polished and honed to a glittering sharpness.

'What are you doing here?' asked Bartholomew, edging away and aiming to keep as much distance between him and the pardoner as possible. He glanced at the figure in the doorway, but it made no attempt to move closer, for which Bartholomew was grateful. He focused his attention on Harysone, knowing the pardoner would take advantage of any lapses in concentration. 'Where is Michael?'

'Where you thought he was,' said Harysone, gesturing towards the trapdoor with his spare hand. 'I had decided to let you go free – it seemed you would not find my hiding place, and I would not have the bother of dispatching you. You should have left with your servants, and then you would have lived to see another day.'

'Is Michael dead?' asked Bartholomew. He was surprised to discover that neither the gloating pardoner nor his pitchfork frightened him, but the prospect of losing the monk's friendship did. His mind filled with a hot, red rage that threatened to overwhelm him. It was the kind of fury that induced rashness, and a cooler part of his consciousness warned him that throwing away his life in a futile attempt to harm the pardoner would be stupid.

'Not yet,' said Harysone evasively. 'But be assured you will see him in Paradise. Or Purgatory. Or even the other place, if that is where you are bound.'

'Why have you come back?' demanded Bartholomew. 'What do you want?'

'So many questions,' said Harysone, raising his eyebrows and parting his lips in a moist, toothy smile. 'I returned because I want my share of a certain treasure that Cambridge is known to possess. I shall have what is my due.'

'Your due?' asked Bartholomew, twisting away as one of the tines came slicing towards him. 'I do not understand.'

'No,' agreed Harysone. 'You do not, but I have no time to answer questions you should have been able to solve yourself.' His next lunge was in earnest, and Bartholomew felt one of the wicked spikes slice through the hem of his tabard. He grabbed the handle and tried to wrench the implement from Harysone's grasp, but the pardoner was ready for such a move and he twisted it viciously. Bartholomew was forced to let go or run the risk of being pulled from his feet.

'Was it you walking through the snow this morning?' asked Bartholomew. 'You took Philippa's shoes and enticed

Michael here because he wanted to know the identity of her lover.'

'At last,' said Harysone with mock encouragement. 'I do not take kindly to men who order me out of their towns for no good reason. I had done nothing wrong, and he had no right to evict me. I decided not to leave until I had exacted revenge. Now I have done that, I shall be on my way – as soon as I have collected my money and dealt with you.'

'In that case, I shall delay you for as long as possible,' said Bartholomew coldly. 'Then you will leave late, and the roads from Cambridge are dangerous after dark. You will attract the attention of robbers, and that will be the end of you.'

'I am an experienced traveller,' said Harysone, unmoved. 'It will take more than Cambridge roads to make an end of me.'

'We shall see about that,' said Bartholomew, making a series of hacking sweeps with his hoe that had Harysone backing away hurriedly. Then the pardoner darted forward, and a prong stabbed into Bartholomew's medical bag, so hard it came through the other side. Harysone wrenched hard to free it, almost pulling the physician from his feet. 'But you are not Philippa's lover. She has better taste than to choose you.'

'You do not know me,' said Harysone, angered by the insult. 'And anyway, I have better taste than to choose her!'

'You should know that, Matthew,' came a soft voice from behind him. Bartholomew whirled around to see Philippa. It had been her bulky form framed in the doorway while he fought. He backed away quickly, not wanting to be caught between the pair of them. 'Put up your weapons,' she added. 'Both of you. There has been enough killing, and I want an end to it.'

'Go away,' snapped Harysone. 'You should not have come. This is none of your business.'

'It *is* my business,' said Philippa sharply. 'You demanded to borrow my shoes and cloak, and Cynric has just told me

Michael is missing. I guessed immediately what you plan to do. Do you think I will stand by and allow you to murder University officials?'

'What is going on?' demanded Bartholomew, beginning to lose patience, although he suspected that displays of irritation were not appropriate just now. But he was angry – with Harysone for doing something to Michael, and with Philippa for being involved in something so clearly untoward. He appealed to her. 'How do you know this man?'

'We met in Chepe,' she replied, ignoring Harysone's furious sigh. She turned to the pardoner. 'Enough, John! I will do what you say, but you must put down your weapon.'

Harysone moved to one side and lowered the pitchfork, but made no effort to set it down. Bartholomew edged further away, keeping a firm grip on his hoe.

'You are not a pardoner at all, are you?' he said to Harysone, seeing a clue in something Philippa had said: they had met in Chepe. 'You are a fishmonger – or you have some connection to the Fraternity of Fishmongers. Your knowledge of fish is too great for you to be anything else.'

'I *was* a fishmonger,' said Harysone resentfully. 'But Turke destroyed my business – and then he almost destroyed me. Sorrow led me to throw myself into the Thames.'

'You are Fiscurtune's son?' asked Bartholomew uncertainly.

'He is John Fiscurtune,' said Philippa tiredly. 'The son, obviously, not the father.'

'Uncle Ailred and Cousin Frith always underestimated me,' said Harysone – whom Bartholomew could not think of as Fiscurtune the younger. 'Just because I did not scream for vengeance like a baying lunatic did not mean I was going to allow Turke to evade justice for my father's murder. I had a plan. I outlined it in a letter I sent with a professional messenger called Josse, but either Josse did not deliver it or they ignored it.'

'What plan?' demanded Bartholomew.

'A simple one,' said Harysone. 'It was I who forced Turke

457

to undertake this pilgrimage. I informed him that I would tell everyone the truth about Isabella's death if he did not. My father had given me all the details, you see, and during her life Isabella was much loved in Chepe. She was good and gentle, and folk would never have elected him Lord Mayor if they knew he had murdered that lovely soul, as well as my father.'

'And then what?' asked Bartholomew. 'Did you plan to kill Turke as he travelled to Walsingham?'

'Living in this violent town has given you a brutal perspective on life, Doctor. I was not going to kill anyone. My plan was that when Turke arrived at Walsingham, I would threaten to tell the priests about his crimes unless he paid me a lot of money.'

'Why wait until then? Why not demand it in London or here, and save yourself a dangerous winter journey?'

Harysone sighed at his ignorance. 'Because once Turke had arrived at the shrine I believe he would have done anything to get his absolution. So, it stands to reason that he would have offered me far more money to hold my tongue at that point.'

'Did you know about this?' asked Bartholomew of Philippa.

She nodded, white faced. 'Walter told me John was also travelling to Walsingham, and I suspected immediately that his sole purpose would be blackmail. I carried messages between them. That is why I have been obliged to go out so often.'

Harysone smirked. 'Turke was not even man enough to meet me and receive my instructions himself – the one time he did was when he stabbed Norbert. Usually, though, he sent his wife through the snow, while he sat by the fire, all safe and warm.'

Something in Bartholomew was relieved to learn that Philippa had not been meeting a lover, although he was not sure why. Perhaps the relief came from the fact that the lover was not the large-toothed Harysone, as he had feared when the man had first made his appearance.

'Surely Giles would have helped you?' he said to Philippa.

'Giles believes I was dallying with a suitor,' she said in a low voice. 'He lent me his hat, because he thinks meeting a man might bring me happiness. He would not have condoned me helping Walter to wriggle out of a charge of murder – and see himself elected Lord Mayor into the bargain. But I was Walter's wife, and it was my duty to do what my husband asked of me.'

'So, Frith and Ailred unwittingly spoiled your plans,' said Bartholomew to Harysone. 'Turke dead is not in a position to be blackmailed.'

'I made a mistake by not revealing myself to them when I first arrived,' said Harysone bitterly. 'I assumed Josse had delivered my message to Ailred, and that he knew what I intended to do, but now I see Josse failed me. I shall have words with that young man when I return to Chepe.'

'Did Ailred and Frith not see you?' asked Bartholomew, surprised. The town was not so large that three close relatives could spend days without meeting.

Harysone tapped his long teeth. 'My disguise as a pardoner was so good that even they did not recognise me.'

'But it was Frith – your cousin – who stole from you,' said Bartholomew. 'He took your gold at the King's Head. Morice returned it to you, but took a handsome finder's fee in the process.'

'That gold was money I had demanded from Turke when I met him by the Mill Pool, the night he murdered Norbert,' said Harysone. 'It was a pity to lose it, but it came easily, and I did not miss it too much. Frith is a natural thief, and I should have known he would see a pardoner as fair game. He burgled two other patrons, too, although they accepted the loss with stoicism and declined to involve the Sheriff. Anyway, you see why I agreed to Morice's vile arrangements. Obviously I did not want a Sheriff prying too deeply into where the money had come from.'

'It was also because you did not want to risk closer contact

459

with Frith, lest he recognised you,' said Bartholomew, disgusted. 'Your lenience was not because you wanted to protect your cousin, but to safeguard yourself.'

'I do not like Frith,' admitted Harysone. 'He was always trying to persuade my father to disown me and make him sole heir. However, it is Uncle Ailred's motives, not mine, that will provide you with your answers. Do you understand now why he was so keen for Brother Michael to solve Norbert's murder? It was because the hated Turke was the culprit. Turke admitted to Uncle Ailred that he had stabbed Norbert with Gosslinge's knife, and Uncle Ailred wanted him revealed as a killer, even after he was dead.'

'Does this mean *you* were with Turke that night?' asked Bartholomew in confusion. 'Ailred implied it was Frith.'

'Then he is wrong: it was me. I was demanding money from Turke to pay for my board at the King's Head.' He smirked again. 'I was the one who pushed you over after you heard Norbert scream. I grabbed my fish as I ran.'

'The tench was important after all,' mused Bartholomew. 'We should have known that only someone who was afraid of the association between the rotten fish and the murdered student would have bothered to snatch it up as he fled.'

'Quite, but you did not see that connection – luckily for me. But Norbert is irrelevant. It was Turke's death that really inconvenienced me. I did not imagine for a moment that my kindly uncle and my inept cousin would kill him and deprive me of my future fortunes.' He smiled nastily at Philippa. 'But fortunately Turke's wife is keen to protect her dead husband's reputation, so we have continued to meet, to see if we can reach an acceptable arrangement.'

Bartholomew shook his head, disgusted by Harysone's determination to wring money out of anyone unfortunate enough to cross his path. 'Was blackmailing Turke really worth a winter journey to Walsingham? Why not wait until the eve of his election or some other opportune time?'

'Because I need money now. You see, my father devised a new way of salting fish, and had invested all we owned in the venture. But Turke would not allow the method to be used and, after my father's murder, I learned I had no inheritance left. Nothing at all. Since I do not want to live in poverty I was obliged to act promptly.'

'I suppose the tench Norbert won was prepared using your father's method?' asked Bartholomew. 'That was why it was rotten.'

'The technique requires honing,' admitted Harysone. He fingered the relic that still hung around his neck, as if hoping to draw strength from it.

'And now you have St Zeno to help you do it,' said Bartholomew, not at all sure he did.

Harysone nodded. 'I know you think my relic is Gosslinge's thumb, but you are wrong. Langelee should have asked a good deal more than five pounds for this. I shall sell it to the Fraternity of Fishmongers for three times that amount.'

'I should have seen you were no pardoner when you showed your ignorance of theology,' said Bartholomew. He regarded Harysone closely. 'I should have noticed that your teeth are not real, too. They are too large, and you are unused to them, because I once heard them clang on the rim of your wine cup. A man comfortable with his teeth does not allow that to happen. Also, my students commented that your eating was a spectacle that caused them some entertainment.'

Harysone inclined his head. 'I would remove them for you, but they are not easily taken in and out. I cement them in with gum mastic each morning, and I do not want to slip them out without the aid of a mirror. I might lose some of my real ones in the process and I do not have many left. Like my father, I am sadly bereft of them.'

Bartholomew recalled what he himself had said to Michael, when William had discovered the remains of the marchpane figure: that people often have one distinguishing feature that outshines all others. Harysone's teeth were so prominent that they drew attention away from everything

461

else. Without them folk might have recognised his gait or the shape of his mouth.

Harysone scratched at his face until the beard came off on his fingers, and Bartholomew saw it had the same texture as the horsehair used to make false moustaches for the female Waits.

'My hair is dyed,' Harysone added, 'and I have also coloured my face, to make it swarthy. As I said – even my kin did not recognise me, and Frith and I spent time in the same tavern! We even exchanged one or two words, although not many. I did not want him too close.'

'That is partly because they did not anticipate meeting you here,' said Philippa. 'Poor Ailred!'

'Ailred did not recognise you when he arranged the loan from Dympna?' asked Bartholomew. 'Your disguise must have been excellent.'

'It is excellent,' said Philippa. 'Even Giles, who is very observant and has purchased one of John's books, has not guessed his true identity.'

'Uncle Ailred was a fool to loan me that money,' said Harysone, gloatingly. 'I had no intention of repaying it – not the original amount and certainly not the interest. That will teach him to destroy my hopes of a glittering future.'

'Frith and his friends will probably hang for Norbert's murder,' said Bartholomew, disgusted. 'Your testimony could save them but I am sure you have no intention of helping.'

'Frith has the funds to buy his freedom,' said Harysone carelessly. 'And I should know, for I am well acquainted with his financial situation.'

'You are the man to whom they passed their stolen goods?' asked Bartholomew.

'Certainly not,' said Harysone stiffly. 'My father was – but only in Chepe, obviously. They use other people when they travel. My father kept careful records, which I unearthed when I went through his possessions after his death. Perhaps I can blackmail Frith instead – threaten to tell the Chepe merchants about his activities. A percentage of his ill-gotten gains, along with Dympna, will suffice to compensate me for this horrible adventure and its unfortunate conclusions.'

'You cannot have Dympna,' said Bartholomew. 'Kenyngham has hidden it.'

'You are right,' said Harysone. 'He left it in that cellar you were so keen to explore. But I have retrieved it, as you can see.' He nodded to a corner, where Bartholomew could see the outline of the walnut-wood chest among the shadows.

'Kenyngham told you where he hid it?' asked Bartholomew uneasily, hoping Harysone had not harmed the old friar.

'Frith had the right idea when he said he would fire Michaelhouse unless the chest was handed over. I merely used the same tactic and offered to fire the Gilbertine Friary. Kenyngham claimed he was sick of the money and the evil it brought, and relinquished it almost willingly.' He nodded towards the trapdoor. 'He is down there, waiting until we leave. Join him, and see for yourself.'

'No, thank you,' said Bartholomew, knowing Harysone had no intention of allowing him to climb into the cellar or anywhere else. Harysone wanted him dead.

The 'pardoner' was becoming impatient and fingered his pitchfork. 'You have two choices, physician. We can dodge around like this and I will reduce you to small pieces slowly, or you can stand still and allow me to finish you in a single stroke. It will probably not even hurt – much as the knife did not hurt me when I was first stabbed in the back.'

'No!' cried Philippa, dismayed. 'Put up your weapons. Both of you!'

'Go to Hell, Harysone,' said Bartholomew between gritted teeth. 'It is a pity Philippa did not aim better, because then you and I would not be in this ridiculous situation.'

'Philippa?' asked Harysone, glancing at the agitated widow with an amused expression on his face. 'She would not harm me. She is too afraid I will tell the truth about Turke as I die.'

'Perhaps. But the knife with the broken point is in her possession, nevertheless. I can see the missing tip from here – I noticed it when she wore it in Edith's solar earlier today.'

Harysone looked at Philippa again, but this time he was not smiling. 'Tell me he is lying.'

Philippa did not reply, and Harysone's expression became murderous. He turned on Bartholomew and began to advance. He moved quickly, and the hoe was smashed in two in Bartholomew's hands. The physician saw that the man had done with playing and meant business. It was only a matter of time before one of the swiping tines hit its mark, the injury would weaken him and make him vulnerable to the next blow, and then it would be over.

'No!' Bravely, Philippa moved to stand between them. 'I will give you anything you want, John. You can have the house Walter left me. Just do not harm Matthew.'

'It is too late,' hissed Harysone furiously. 'He knows enough to hang me, and I do not want to settle into my new home only to be arrested for theft and blackmail.'

'You cannot kill him,' said Philippa, shoving the tines of the pitchfork down when Harysone raised them again. 'I will not let you.'

'What about Michael?' asked Bartholomew, taking the opportunity to dodge away from the deranged fishmonger's son and trying to drag Philippa with him. 'Where is he?'

'Locked in the cellar with Kenyngham,' said Harysone. 'Philippa can join them there, and I will send a message from London telling Stanmore where to find them.'

'But that might be days,' objected Bartholomew, knowing such a message would never be sent – just like the one that was supposed to have warned Ailred about his nephew's plan to blackmail Turke. If Philippa entered the cellar, she would die there.

'There is plenty of water, and a few days without food will do no one any harm,' said Harysone harshly. 'Move, Philippa or I will kill you, too.'

'Let Matthew go,' pleaded Philippa. 'And then we will

talk. Do not forget that I cannot give you Walter's house if I am locked in a cellar.'

Without warning, Harysone lunged towards Philippa with the pitchfork. She ducked, and Bartholomew darted forward to seize it, trying to wrench it from Harysone's grasp. They were locked solid, each straining to tear the implement from the other's hands. Harysone kicked out, but lost his balance and fell, dragging Bartholomew on top of him. He rolled, twisting the handle savagely so that it tore from Bartholomew's grip. The tines rose, then started to fall.

Bartholomew twisted hard to one side, thinking that the last thing he would ever see was Philippa's stricken face. He was startled when there was a loud thud and a sudden weight landed on his chest. Harysone was lying on top of him. He struggled furiously, not sure what was happening. Then he saw the unmistakable shape of Agatha holding the copy of Harysone's book that Deynman had bought for Michaelhouse. Bartholomew pushed the limp fishmonger away from him, and saw that Agatha had dealt him a serious blow to the head. Harysone was insensible.

Behind Agatha stood Abigny. He held out his arms to his sister, and she rushed towards them, then buried her face in his shoulder and sobbed. He held her gently, rubbing her hair as he whispered words of comfort.

'I hope he is dead,' he said, glancing up from his ministrations and meeting Bartholomew's eyes. 'I never liked Fiscurtune the younger – or Harysone, as he called himself here. It is a pity circumstances led you to deal with men like him and Turke, Philippa. You deserve better.'

'Matthew is decent,' she said in a low voice. 'I should never have chosen wealth over love.'

Agatha disagreed. 'Take the wealth,' she advised in a booming voice. 'You can always get love from other quarters. If you come to see me tonight, I shall tell you how it is done.'

'Someone should release Michael,' said Bartholomew,

kneeling next to the unconscious Harysone to see how badly he had been hurt. He saw he would recover. 'And Kenyngham.'

Agatha hauled open the trapdoor and Michael clambered inelegantly from the chilly hole, complaining bitterly about the rough treatment he had suffered. However, it transpired that the worst part was hearing the meal bells in Peterhouse and the Gilbertine Friary while his stomached growled with hunger. Bartholomew saw that no serious harm had been done. Kenyngham emerged more quietly, and slipped away to the Gilbertine chapel to give thanks for his deliverance.

Meanwhile, Abigny explained how he and Agatha had come to the rescue. 'I met Cynric, who said Michael was missing and last seen following Philippa. I knew immediately something was amiss. I noticed earlier she was wearing heavy boots that were not hers, and she had refused to answer my questions about them.'

'What could I say?' asked Philippa tearfully. 'If I said I had lent mine to John Fiscurtune, I would have been obliged to confess the whole miserable story to you.'

'You had no idea about any of this?' asked Michael of Abigny.

Abigny's face hardened. 'I did not. I came on this wretched pilgrimage because I sensed Philippa might need a friend. I had no idea Turke was being blackmailed by Fiscurtune's son, nor that Fiscurtune had kin in Cambridge – except Frith, of course. Seeing him juggling in Michaelhouse gave me a nasty turn, I can tell you!'

'So, you did know the Waits?' asked Michael, looking from Philippa to Abigny.

Philippa nodded. 'I recognised Frith immediately, and I was horrified that they might be in Cambridge to make trouble for Walter, to tell folk he was a murderer. That was why I told you the reason for the pilgrimage – in case Frith mentioned it first.'

'I assumed the same,' added Abigny. 'But I did not imagine for a moment they intended to kill Walter. I thought they were just going to embarrass the man. In case you have not guessed, Walter's violent past was the reason neither of us wanted you to look into his death. You knew he murdered Fiscurtune, but not that he had killed Isabella, too. What would Edith have thought if she had learned about that monstrous act?'

'Walter recognised the Waits, too,' said Philippa. 'And he was aware that when he murdered Fiscurtune he had also destroyed their friend in high places. That was why he was so keen to accept Edith's invitation – to escape from their company in the King's Head.'

'You lied about the scars on Turke's legs,' said Bartholomew to Philippa. 'You knew how he came by them.'

Philippa nodded. 'But it was not my secret to tell. It would not have been fair to mention it when Walter was not here to tell his own side of the story.'

'His own side was that he wanted to save himself,' muttered Abigny, 'and that he did not care how. I admire you for your loyalty, Philippa, but even you must see it is grossly misplaced. I know you take your oath of wifely obedience seriously, but I do not think it should include helping a husband evade justice as a murderer or acting as messenger between him and his blackmailer.'

'I swore a sacred oath when I married Walter,' said Philippa tearfully. 'In a church. How can I ask God to bless me with children when I break the vows I made in His house?'

'You met Harysone in the King's Head, Giles,' said Michael in the silence that followed. 'Did you not recognise him as Fiscurtune the younger?'

'Unfortunately not,' said Abigny bitterly. 'Or I might have been able to help Philippa sooner. As I told you, I bought the book for her to present to the Fraternity of Fishmongers in Walter's memory. Offering tokens to commemorate dead husbands is a tradition for widows in Chepe. That is what you saw me doing with "Harysone" in the King's Head – negotiating a price. I met him three times before a bargain

467

was struck. He was so sure I did not know who he was that he even danced for me.'

Bartholomew recalled the Waits mentioning someone in a cloak and a hat, who had continued to watch Harysone's dancing after the 'other' pardoners had left. His old room-mate was right: Harysone had been so confident of his disguise that he had been quite happy to meet all manner of people he knew – even his own kin.

'So, how did you know we were here, of all places?' asked Michael, gesturing around the stables.

'Cynric said Matt had stayed here, searching for clues to your whereabouts. Agatha offered to come with me, because she said I might need a mighty right arm. When we arrived, we heard you talking, and the rest you know.'

Agatha indicated the still figure on the ground with a jerk of her thumb. 'I did not hit him that hard. Why does he not stir? Is it because he has damaged the balance of his humours with all that vulgar jigging and writhing?' She shuddered in distaste at the memory of Harysone's dancing.

'Your right arm is mightier than you think,' replied Bartholomew. 'But he will recover.'

'Pity,' muttered Michael.

'I do not want to be here when he does,' said Philippa, clutching Abigny's arm. 'Our bags are packed and I want to leave this town.' She watched expressionlessly as Michael retrieved Dympna from the corner and prepared to take it to Kenyngham.

'That was well timed,' said Frith, entering the stable with a smile. Bartholomew's stomach lurched in horror. 'We have just purchased our freedom and have been given until night-fall to leave. Cambridge is an expensive town with Morice in charge, but at least justice can be bought.'

Jestyn, Makejoy and Yna were behind Frith, and all were armed with crossbows. As in the conclave, Frith's accom-plices were nervous and unhappy.

'And how did *you* know we were here?' Bartholomew asked them in a tired, hoarse voice.

'We followed Agatha,' said Frith, giving the laundress a nasty smile. 'She was bellowing to Abigny, so half the town knows her plans.' His fingers flexed, and Bartholomew saw he had neither forgotten nor forgiven the thump she had given him in the Market Square during the camp-ball. She glowered at him furiously, her eyes glittering with menace. Bartholomew thought Frith would be wise to dispatch her first if he did not want to risk another beating.

Rashly, the Wait turned his back on her. 'I do not intend to leave empty-handed, so we will have the chest, please. And then the rest of you can climb into that cellar, where I may light a fire to keep you warm.'

'Fire?' asked Abigny in alarm. 'But there are no windows. We would suffocate!'

'Quite,' agreed Frith coolly. 'But do not be frightened. It is not as unpleasant as death by a crossbow quarrel, which is the alternative for anyone declining to obey me. Now, move!' His voice was hard.

'No,' said Jestyn uneasily, dropping his weapon. 'I want no part of this. We have only just escaped with our necks unstretched, and we will not be so lucky next time, especially now we have no friends to shield us. Morice will not help us again, and Dunstan and Athelbald, who took care of the various items we accumulated here, are dead.'

Bartholomew gaped at them. 'It was the *rivermen* who helped you dispose of your stolen goods in Cambridge?' He suddenly recalled the inkpot that the dead Athelbald had clutched in his frozen fingers, and realised he should have questioned at the time why an illiterate man possessed an item usually owned by scholars and clerks.

Jestyn nodded. 'Father Ailred arranged it all. He said the money the old men earned from working for us would help them survive the winter. They were very good, too, because they knew so many people. It is a pity they both died so suddenly. Father Ailred was very upset.'

'Enough chatter,' said Frith sharply. 'We need to take the chest, set the fire and be gone.' He advanced on Agatha, but changed his mind when he saw her fists clench, and turned on Bartholomew instead. The physician felt a sharp jab as the tip of quarrel went through his clothes. 'What will it be, Michaelhouse man? Stabbing or choking?'

'Frith? Is that you?' Harysone's muffled voice came from the floor, and Bartholomew saw him ease himself up. Agatha's blow had knocked the false teeth from his mouth, and he had already pulled off his beard. He looked very different without his disguise – older, fatter-faced and more sinister.

Frith gasped in surprise when he recognised his cousin, and Bartholomew considered making a grab for the Wait's weapon while his attention was distracted, but Frith recovered himself quickly and moved out of reach.

'John? What are you doing here?'

'Turke,' said Harysone, clinging to his cousin as he clambered to his feet, wincing and holding his head. 'I was going to kill him myself, but you were there first.'

'Liar!' cried Philippa. 'You were—'

'Thrust these meddling souls into the cellar,' interrupted Harysone before she could reveal that killing Turke had played no part in his plans. 'Then set the fire and let us be gone. Hurry, Jestyn.'

'No,' said Jestyn again, exchanging a glance with the two women. 'We will lock no one in the cellar, and we want none of that tainted gold. We are leaving – alone.'

Frith's face was a mask of fury. 'You will do as we say, or you will join this motley crowd choking in the ground.'

Harysone ignored the quarrelling Waits and calmly reached for the chest. Then, before anyone could stop him, he had snatched it up and darted away. Frith abandoned his squabble with Jestyn and followed with a bellow of rage, leaving the others gazing after them in astonishment.

'I thought he was dazed,' said Makejoy stupidly. 'He could barely stand.'

'That is what he wanted you to think,' shouted Bartholomew. 'After him!'

The Waits had brought four horses when they had stopped at the friary stables, and Frith and Harysone were already mounted on two of them. They pushed and pulled at each other, as Frith tried to grab the chest from his cousin and Harysone fought to keep possession of it. They galloped across the main road, then down a lane that ran along the side of Peterhouse and towards the river. It was not the direction Bartholomew would have chosen to make a successful getaway, and he saw their attention was wholly focused on each other and Dympna. The people they had been threatening to kill were entirely forgotten.

Bartholomew raced after them, but had no idea what he would do if he caught them. Both were armed and dangerous, and he did not have so much as a surgical blade with him. But he ran, nevertheless, hearing the others pounding after him – the lighter footsteps of Abigny and Philippa, and the heavier ones of Agatha and Michael. The remaining Waits did not follow. They took the opportunity to escape, Jestyn on one pony and the two women on the other.

Bartholomew reached the river, and saw the two men still fighting and shoving each other as they fought to gain possession of the box. Their jerky movements were frightening the horses, which pranced and lurched, uncertain which direction they were supposed to take. In the end, Harysone's turned right, and started cantering towards the Small Bridges and the Mill Pool. Frith followed hard on its heels, and Bartholomew ran after them, doggedly trying to catch up.

The cousins reached the larger of the Small Bridges, where Frith managed to spur his mount ahead, so he and Harysone were riding neck and neck as they thundered forward. Fortunately, no one else was using the bridge at that point, or he would have been trampled.

Frith finally managed to secure a grip on Dympna, and ripped it from Harysone's hands. With a scream of fury, Harysone lunged after it, both hands reaching for the box.

His flying leap knocked Frith from his saddle, and both men went tumbling over the side of the bridge. There was a thump, followed by a series of cracking and popping sounds.

Bartholomew reached the bridge, gasping for breath, and peered over the edge just in time to see the two men sprawled on the ice, still struggling over the box. Then the ice opened into a great black hole, and men and chest disappeared from view. The water frothed for a moment, then became calm, until all that was left was a dark, jagged hole, a short distance from the one that had claimed Ailred. Bartholomew saw a hand break the surface, before slowly sinking out of sight amid a circle of gentle ripples.

EPILOGUE

THREE DAYS LATER, BARTHOLOMEW AND MICHAEL SAT SIDE by side on the trunk of an old apple tree that had fallen in the orchard. The day was unseasonably mild, and the blizzards of the previous weeks seemed a distant memory. The sun shone, albeit weakly, and Bartholomew could feel its gentle warmth through his winter cloak. Most of the snow had gone, although several of the larger and deeper drifts remained, like the vast mound outside Bene't College on the High Street.

A gentle breeze blew, rustling the dry grass and bringing the smell of the marshes that lay to the north. Bartholomew felt as though his life was finally returning to normal. The Lord of Misrule had been replaced with Master Langelee, Quenhyth's 'stolen' scrip had been found behind his bed, lectures were under way, and there were disputations to arrange and patients to see. He was sad that Dunstan and Athelbald were not among them, despite learning about their hitherto unknown penchant for peddling stolen goods for itinerant jugglers.

'Two bodies were found in the river near Chesterton village today,' said Michael, turning his flabby face to catch some of the sun's rays. 'I rode out to view them and they belonged to Frith and Harysone, as I expected. We found Ailred's corpse in much the same place the day before.'

'There was no sign of the chest?' asked Bartholomew.

Michael shook his head. 'I imagine that sank where it fell. The bottom of the Mill Pool is the best place for it. It is safe there.'

'Until the weather grows warmer. Then people will start to dive for it.'

'They will not find it,' said Michael. 'The pond is lined with deep mud, and the only way to retrieve the coins will be to drain the whole thing. That may happen one day, but I doubt it will happen in our lifetime.'

'Good,' said Bartholomew fervently. 'Kenyngham was right: Dympna may have been set up to do good, but it corrupted people. Thick and inaccessible mud will stop it from doing so again.'

'Speaking of corruption, Morice resigned today. People are angry that he never arranged another game of camp-ball, and claim he delayed just to keep the prize money for himself.'

'He did,' said Bartholomew, surprised that anyone should need to voice the obvious.

'Dick Tulyet has agreed to stand in until someone else can be appointed. I hope it takes a long time for a suitable replacement to be found. We cannot have a better man than Dick.'

They were silent for a while, watching the sun playing through the winter branches of the fruit trees and listening to the distant sounds of the town. A dog yapped in the High Street, and a cart lumbered slowly along the rutted mud of St Michael's Lane, which lay just over the wall. A man shouted something about a horse, and the gentle grunt of pigs could just be heard as they were driven towards the Market Square.

'Turke was a nasty man,' said Bartholomew at last. 'His failure to help Isabella escape from the frozen River Thames started all this. Fiscurtune and Ailred allowed him to buy their silence when they should have denounced him, and the hatred Turke felt towards the men who could damage him eventually led him to stab Fiscurtune in a brawl.'

'Do not forget Fiscurtune was not exactly an angel, either. He developed his salting method, but it did not work – as we saw with Norbert's tench – and Turke was probably right to prevent him from inflicting it on his customers. Also, Fiscurtune was quite happy to be paid for his silence over

474

Isabella, and so was Ailred. The records I examined with Godric yesterday indicate that Turke's money has kept Ovyng afloat for years.'

'I still do not understand why Turke was willing to dispense with his saintly finger,' said Bartholomew. 'Why did he not keep it for himself? He was a man who liked material wealth.'

'It was stolen property,' said Michael. 'I asked the Dominicans to investigate it, and they learned that St Zeno's finger was taken from a Carmelite chapel in London some years ago. A likely thief was caught and relieved of a thumb, but the relic itself was never recovered.'

'Gosslinge took it?' asked Bartholomew in astonishment.

'So it would seem. I imagine he stole it on Turke's instructions, and the resulting punishment put Turke under a certain obligation to him. But the net was closing, and the Carmelites were already on the relic's trail. By handing it to Michaelhouse, Turke paid Gosslinge's expenses with something he was going to lose anyway. I suppose if anyone had demanded to know how it came to be in his possession, he would have said it belonged to Gosslinge, and that he knew nothing about its origins.'

'What happened to it?'

'Godric found it among some reeds when he was looking for Ailred's body. The Carmelites paid him a princely sum for its safe return and Ovyng Hostel now has fuel and food aplenty.'

'I did not think for a moment it was a real relic. I always thought it was Gosslinge's thumb.'

Michael shuddered. 'That would have been perverted, Matt! Men do not adorn themselves with the severed digits of their servants. Even fishmongers from Chepe.' He chuckled suddenly. 'Speaking of perversions, Agatha claimed Norbert visited Robin's pig, to bestow affections on it. But, of course, Norbert was not visiting the pig at all. He was slipping into Robin's house by the back door, hoping to persuade him to extend the loan Dympna had made.'

475

'But Norbert could not have known Robin was a member of Dympna,' said Bartholomew. 'I know Robin was the man who dispensed agreed funds – and so was the person the successful applicants met – but Norbert had been turned down by the official Dympna. By the time Norbert had his loan, Ailred was being helped by Frith.'

'No. Ailred was making illegal loans before Frith arrived. Frith only became involved when Kenyngham discovered what had been happening, and set his ultimatum for Ailred to retrieve what had been lost.'

'So, Ailred used Robin to dispense the illicit loans?' asked Bartholomew. 'And Robin was blithely unaware of the fact that these were made without the consent of Dick and Kenyngham? I suppose that makes sense from the things they all told us.'

'Robin should have mentioned Norbert's visits,' said Michael resentfully. 'He has been apologetic ever since, but we would have solved his murder sooner had everyone been honest.'

'William persuaded his Prior to declare Harysone's book heretical,' said Bartholomew, after a pause. 'Anyone owning a copy is obliged to take it to the Franciscan Friary, where it will be burned. I do not approve of incinerating books, even ones like Harysone's.'

'I would normally concur, but Harysone's was worse than heretical: it was full of errors and insulting to its readers. The world will not suffer from the loss of that particular tome. Indeed, I imagine it will be a good deal better off: someone like Deynman might have read it and thought it was true. It would not do for him to live the rest of his life imagining God as a gigantic pike.'

Bartholomew laughed, then became serious. 'Harysone said he sent a message to Ailred, telling him he was coming to Cambridge. I think if Ailred had received that missive, the case would have ended very differently – especially for him. He and Frith would not have murdered Turke, but would have gone along with Harysone's plan to continue blackmailing him. Ailred would have used his share of the money to repay the bad loans he had made, and Kenyngham would have forgotten the whole mess.'

'Harysone *claimed* he sent a note,' said Michael. 'But there is nothing to say he was telling the truth. He was probably lying, as he lied about everything else.'

'You were right about him. He did come here intending mischief.'

'I knew it as soon as I clapped eyes on the fellow,' declared Michael. 'I have dealt with too many murderers and malcontents not to be able to identify a criminal when I see one. I should have told Sergeant Orwelle to deny him permission to enter the town. Then matters would have turned out differently.'

'But not much. Ailred and Frith would still have killed Turke, and Gosslinge would still have choked on vellum.'

'We were correct to be suspicious about the deaths of Turke and Gosslinge. I thought Turke's demise was odd, and you thought it strange that Turke and his servant should die in such quick succession. We were both right. You were also correct in believing Norbert's death was linked to Turke's: if Turke had not gone looking for the murder weapon, he might never have provided Frith and Ailred with a chance to force him on to thin ice.'

'And we were right to think fish was a strand that tied the whole thing together,' said Bartholomew. 'Norbert's tench, won from Harysone in a bet, was badly salted; bad salting was what initiated the final quarrel between Turke and Fiscurtune; and Harysone was a fishmonger, but his business – and his inheritance – were lost to Turke's Fraternity of Fishmongers' machinations. However, Quenhyth being the son of a fishmonger was merely coincidence.'

'Harysone wrote that dreadful treatise about fish, and the very name "Fiscurtune" should have alerted us to the connection much sooner. Also, we should have noticed that both Frith and Ailred professed to hail from the vicinity of Lincoln.'

'Lincoln is a large city, Brother. It might have been a spurious link. But, although we may have been right about many things, we made mistakes, too.'

'You mean like you telling me Gosslinge had died from the cold, when he had in fact choked to death? Or you assuming Turke's death was an accident when he had actually been murdered?'

Bartholomew winced. 'Actually, I was thinking about Harysone. You were convinced he played a role in Gosslinge's death, but he did not. Your feral belief was wrong.'

'Only in the details,' retorted Michael. 'I was wrong about which particular crime Harysone committed, but I was right in my assumption that he was guilty of something.'

'We made a mistake with Giles as well. We thought he was involved in something sinister, but he was not. The few times he did venture out on his painful feet were to buy a book on Philippa's behalf, to indulge an idle and harmless curiosity about Dympna, or to arrange for Turke's embalming. And when he was so clearly relieved to hear us say we would not investigate Turke's odd death, it was not because he had a hand in it, but because he did not want his sister distressed. He was being kind.'

'He was being a fool,' said Michael disparagingly. 'He allowed Philippa to borrow his cloak and that silly feathered hat without asking why. All this relates to your observation about distinguishing features – you said a really prominent characteristic will mask all else, and Philippa used Giles's hat to do just that. Harysone knew about distinguishing features, too, and adopted those teeth. His disguise fooled his kinsmen, as well as Giles. It was a pity Philippa was not more skilled in the use of her dagger. If she had stabbed Harysone properly, then he would not have dragged his cousin to a watery grave or locked me in a damp cellar for so many hours.'

'Matilde was right and wrong, too. She knew there was something sad about Philippa, which was correct, but it had nothing to do with love, as she surmised.'

'And we were definitely wrong about Dunstan and Athelbald,' said Michael, chuckling fondly. 'I still cannot believe they were so deeply involved in the case. The old devils! Still, it is good they had the last laugh. I shall miss them.'

'So shall I,' said Bartholomew quietly.

Michael nudged him in the ribs, wanting to dispel the sudden pall of gloom that had descended on them. 'There is another thing: I know the identity of the rogue who fashioned that wicked but very clever model of William out of marchpane.'

'You do?' asked Bartholomew uneasily.

'Oh, yes. There is only one man in the College who has a talent for drawing and other artistry, and a pair of skilled hands.'

'I see,' said Bartholomew, smiling. 'However, I did not know the thing was disguised under all those veils purporting to be the Virgin, nor that the marchpane was made from salt, so do not blame me for either of those.'

'You must have known about the salt,' said Michael in disbelief. 'Do not tell me you did not take a bite when you were labouring over those details!'

'I am not you, Brother. Gorging myself on the marchpane Gray provided for his prank did not cross my mind. Supposing there was not enough to finish it properly?'

Both scholars looked up when the latch on the orchard gate clanked, heralding the arrival of someone else. It was Philippa, leaning on her brother's arm and escorted by Cynric. Unfortunately, the sudden thaw had confounded the embalmer's calculations, and the resulting problems with Turke's body had kept her and Abigny in Cambridge longer than they had intended.

'We have come to say our farewells at last,' said Abigny, leaning against the wall. He was smiling, and Bartholomew saw again the carefree young man with whom he had once shared a room. A great weight had been lifted from Abigny. 'We are going to Walsingham, to complete our pilgrimage.

Personally, I would be just as happy to go home, but north-ward we shall venture.'

'What about Turke?' asked Michael baldly. 'Will you leave him here while he rots?'

Philippa winced. 'I wanted to take him with us. It was his pilgrimage, after all, and I think he needs to complete it. But the embalmer says he will not last, so we have compro-mised.' She held a small box in her hands, which she passed to Bartholomew.

'What is it?' It was heavily sealed, so he could not open it.

'Walter's heart. We will carry it to Walsingham and leave it there. Meanwhile, young Quenhyth is going home to make peace with his father over the misunderstanding with the Waits and the chalice he accused them of stealing. He has offered to accompany the rest of Walter to Chepe. It is very kind of him.'

'Very,' said Bartholomew, shoving the box back at her with some distaste. 'Quenhyth will take good care of Walter. The lad has his faults, but unreliability and carelessness are not among them.'

She turned to Michael. 'When I return home, I shall send funds from my inheritance that will help to establish a new Dympna.'

'All right,' said Michael warily. 'Although I am not sure we need another of those.'

'It will be safe in the hands of good men,' said Philippa.

'Ailred was a good man,' Bartholomew pointed out.

Abigny pointed to the sky, and took his sister's arm. 'We should go, or we shall have to delay our departure until tomorrow – and I am certain Edith and Oswald want us gone.'

'Edith has offered us her home when we return from Walsingham,' said Philippa shyly. She glanced at Bartholo-mew. 'When I come back, with all stains of these horrible events wiped from my conscience, perhaps I could stay a while in Cambridge, and you and I could resume our friendship. Perhaps where we left off, all those years ago?'

Bartholomew smiled. 'It is a tempting offer, but we have both changed over the years. Although I shall always remember you with affection, my heart belongs to another.'

'That is a shame,' said Philippa, disappointed. 'But I wish you happiness nonetheless. Do not spurn her because she is poor, and make the mistake I made.'

'I will not,' promised Bartholomew.

The huge drift of snow outside Bene't College did not thaw as quickly as was hoped, but attacking it with shovels proved to be hard and futile work, so the citizens of Cambridge were obliged to let it melt in its own time. It did so gradually, and people commented on its slowly diminishing size when they passed it on the High Street. Children played on it, using its slick sides for sliding, while some enterprising souls caused a good deal of delight by carving faces into it. Morice's was one that was prominently featured, and Agatha's was another.

Weeks passed, until eventually it dwindled to the point where people barely noticed it was there. Then, one morning, only the very base remained. It was Kenyngham who discovered its grisly secret. He was walking from Michaelhouse to his friary when he saw the hand of the long-dead Josse protruding from it. He knelt, sketching a benediction and muttering prayers for the soul of a man who had lain unmissed and undiscovered for so long. There was a piece of parchment clutched in Josse's hand. Kenyngham removed it from the dead, white fingers, and read the message.

It was from John Fiscurtune the younger to Ailred, and informed the friar of the imminent visit of his nephew and his 'plan' to relieve Turke of more money. Kenyngham recalled the events that had unfolded that Christmas with a shudder. He folded the parchment carefully, and put it in his scrip, intending to hand it to Michael later. But first, there was a man's soul to pray for, and Kenyngham lost

481

himself in the sacred words of a requiem for a man he had never met.

Sheriff Tulyet tried hard to discover the dead man's identity, but Josse had carried nothing to give him any clues, and a week later he was buried in an unmarked grave in a quiet corner of St Botolph's churchyard. Quenhyth, recently returned from delivering Turke's body to Chepe, heaved a sigh of relief. He had been afraid that someone clever, like Michael or Bartholomew, would tie the time of Josse's death to one of the days that Quenhyth had slipped out of Michaelhouse and had gone to the King's Head. Gray had told Quenhyth on two occasions that someone there had a note from his father, but both times the summons had transpired to be a cruel joke that had seen Quenhyth fined by William for being in a tavern. In normal circumstances, Quenhyth would have ignored Gray's message, but he had left home on bad terms with his family, and he had so desperately wanted them to write and tell him that all was forgiven.

Quenhyth recalled the day vividly. It had been after dusk, and the streets were deserted as he had struggled through the blizzard to the inn. When he had seen Josse, he had stopped dead in his tracks and stared in disbelief. It was the man who had stolen away his lovely Bess and broken his young heart: Josse was older and more handsome, and the fickle tavern wench had abandoned Quenhyth for the sturdy messenger without a backward glance. To soothe his hurt, Quenhyth had decided to give up his apprenticeship as a fishmonger and become a physician instead, wanting to change every aspect of his unhappy life.

When the snow had sloughed off Bene't College's roof to land on Josse, Quenhyth's first reaction had been to rush across and begin digging him out. But he had stopped himself. If Quenhyth could not have Bess, then Josse should not have her, either. He had stood for a long time, staring at the pile of snow and thinking about what would be happening underneath. And then he had gone to the tavern.

When he attended Josse's requiem – the only person to

do so – Quenhyth felt a grim satisfaction. Life was definitely looking better: he was reconciled with his father, Gray had left Michaelhouse to take up a new appointment in Suffolk, and no one had discovered his connection with the messenger he could have saved. Yes, he thought; things were turning out very well indeed.

Two weeks later, Kenyngham met Bosel the beggar, who made his customary plea for spare coins. The elderly friar emptied his scrip in search of pennies, and did not notice Josse's forgotten parchment flutter to the ground. Bosel noticed, however, and snatched it up as soon as Kenyngham had gone. He peered at it this way and that, but since he could not read, the obscure squiggles and lines meant nothing to him. He sold it to Robin of Grantchester for a penny.

Robin suffered from poor eyesight when the light was dim, and could not make out the words, either. He did not care what it said anyway, because parchment was parchment, and too valuable not to be reused. He scraped it clean with a knife, then rubbed it with chalk, and sold it for three pennies to Godric, the principal of Ovyng Hostel. Robin went to spend his windfall on a jug of spiced ale at the King's Head, where he listened, yet again, to Agatha relating the tale of the camp-ball and the gargoyle at St Mary the Great.

Later that night, Godric wrote a prayer on the parchment he had purchased from Robin. Then he folded it, and took it to the grassy mound in St Michael's churchyard, where Ailred had been laid to rest. He scraped a shallow hole and inserted the prayer inside, before bowing his head and walking away.

HISTORICAL NOTE

CHRISTMAS IS PAGAN IN ORIGIN, AND CELEBRATED MIDWINTER and the shortest day. The Church saw that people were unlikely to relinquish this popular glimmer of fun in the dark, fog-bound days of December, and incorporated it into its own religious calendar. Even today, some pagan motifs survive – the decking of homes and churches with green boughs, the eating of special foods, and the singing of particular songs.

Many of the traditions associated with Christmas today derive from the Victorians – the giving of gifts, the 'season of peace and goodwill', silver balls and glittery tinsel. In the fourteenth century, Christmas seems to have been a far more earthy and raucous occasion – an excuse for eating and drinking, and having a rollicking good time. Records from Benedictine abbeys list extra food and treats that were purchased for the festival, while contemporary chroniclers report kings putting on lavish entertainment and supplying astonishing amounts of food for lucky guests. But although the records of one or two Cambridge Colleges mention Christmas, it is not known exactly what happened there. Term was over, so it is possible some scholars went home. However, travelling in winter could be difficult, so it is likely that many remained.

Christmas marked the end of Advent, so the lifting of dietary restrictions meant feasts – and feasts meant meat. Richer folk had roast boar (flavoured with rosemary and bay, and often with an apple), although the poor made do with boar-shaped pastry.

Marchpanes (the medieval equivalent of marzipan) were a traditional favourite at Christmas. They were fashioned into models called 'subtleties'. Over the years, these became increasingly elaborate, with scale models of castles and cathedrals served by Cardinal Wolsey in 1527.

Other foods included hackin (a large sausage that went into boiling water at daybreak), shrid pie (a meaty, oblong affair that had a basket with a doll on the top – an early version of a crib), mutton, pork, cheese and souse (pickled pig feet and ears). To drink there was mead, church ale (strong beer that was sold in churches or churchyards) and 'lambswool' (hot ale mulled with apples). Wassailing, which survived the Victorianisation of Christmas, had its origin in toasting the success of fruit trees, and involved using stored fruit and plenty of alcohol.

Christmas entertainment took two forms. Experts could be hired in, or games could be organised for everyone to play. Records show that King's Hall hired people with the mysterious titles of 'buccinator', 'fistulator', 'ludens', 'ioculator', 'lusor', 'wayt' and 'pleyar'. It is probable these folk were professional entertainers, although whether they were hired in groups or did individual turns is difficult to say. In addition to these shadowy figures, there were also municipal entertainers – town 'waits', although these were not mentioned in Cambridge until 1394. In 1350–51, King's Hall spent two shillings and fourpence on minstrels. In 1306, a woman called Matilda Makejoy was paid as a minstrel, indicating that women, as well as men, were in the business.

Entertainment that could be joined by everyone included indoor and outdoor games. Gambling was frowned upon by Church and University alike, but restrictions were relaxed at Christmas, and small stakes on games of chance were permitted. Dicing with bones (the familiar cubes of today came later) could take several forms. Hasard was a straightforward throwing game, while raffle used three dice and you had to roll higher scores than your rival. Cross and pile was essentially heads and tails, while queek involved rolling pebbles across a chequered board, with bets being placed on whether they would land on light or dark squares. The more intellectual backgammon was being played in England in the eleventh century, and chess arrived with the Conquest. Merels was a board game akin to solitaire. Cards were a later invention, and did not become popular until the fifteenth century.

Outdoor games were often rough, particularly camp-ball. This was basically rugby, and involved a leather ball that had to be passed between fellow team members. There were two goals, which could be several miles apart, and hundreds of people joined in. It was often violent, and people were sometimes stabbed, usually when they fell against knives carried in belts. Mostly the ball was thrown, although 'kicking camp' used feet. 'Ice-camping' involved a lot of skidding and shoving on frozen rivers and lakes, while ice bandy-ball was a bat and ball game that also had few fules.

Boy bishops and lords of misrule are mentioned in fourteenth-century manuscripts. These were a paradox: they turned rank and social order upside-down, but at the same time they reinforced the rules by underlining what was normal for the rest of the year. It was a symbolic occasion, where seniors waited on their juniors, gambling was permitted and cross-dressing was a source of entertainment. Nevertheless, matters sometimes got out of hand, especially in a town like Cambridge, where the atmosphere was often volatile.

The climate of northern Europe has not remained unchanged over the last six hundred years. The 'Little Ice Age' of the sixteenth and early seventeenth centuries underlines the Earth's capacity for environmental change on a global scale. The fourteenth century experienced its own set of 'unprecedented' weather conditions, just as we are today. The climate after 1200 grew colder, and there was an increase in rainfall. Records tell us there was an exceptionally long and bitter winter in 1306–07, while there was a series of very wet summers between 1310 and 1317. In a country where weather is naturally unpredictable and variable – especially when the economy was strongly rural and poor harvests affected lives at every level – weather was a popular topic of conversation. Then, as now, folk would doubtless claim that things had been better in the past.

The Fraternity of Fishmongers became the Company of Fishmongers in the early 1370s. Several prominent names emerge during the middle of the fourteenth century, showing that this guild was powerful in the City of London, and that its members wielded considerable influence. Walter Turke was a fishmonger, who lived in Chepe in 1350. He had a house near the old fish market, and was buried in St James's Church on Garlicke Hythe. Friday Street was a popular location for fishmongers, since it was convenient for the river, but not too close to the noxious stenches of fish. Friday Street today is a noisy canyon of glass-sided buildings, and only its name suggests its ancient origins.

Finally, many of the characters in this book were real people. Ralph Langelee was Master of Michaelhouse until 1361. William (Gotham) and Michael (de Cawston) were also members of Michaelhouse in the middle of the fourteenth century, as were John Clippesby and Thomas Suttone. Thomas Kenyngham was a founding member, who resigned his Mastership before 1354. John Wynewyk was a Michaelhouse benefactor, mentioned in the Otringham Book (Otringham was Master of Michaelhouse in 1423, so Wynewyk's association was before this date).

Ovyng Hostel was owned by Michaelhouse. It was purchased in 1329 by John de Ilegh – the executor of Hervey de Stanton's will – and was a house with a long garden that stood at the junction of Milne Street and St Michael's Lane. Like other Cambridge halls of that time, it would have had a principal and a handful of students. Little is known about it, and we do not know who was its principal in the 1350s.

Cambridge in the fourteenth century was very different to the pretty, much-visited town we know today. It would have been indescribably dirty, and even the lives of rich merchants would have been bleak compared to our own. The Church dominated almost every aspect of life, and murders and accidental deaths were far more common than now. However, walk through Cambridge early one morning, before the streets are full of students on bicycles flocking to lectures and cars choke the narrow streets, and you will sense something of the past in the sturdy Colleges and ancient street patterns. You may even hear scruffy scholars called to meals when church bells chime the hour or imagine the noisy, boisterous crowds that once gathered in the Market Square to play Christmas camp-ball or to rail against weak or corrupt town officials. Visit, and see for yourself!

For more information on the Bartholomew novels and medieval Cambridge, visit the Matthew Bartholomew website at www.matthewbartholomew.co.uk.